DISCOVERING KATHARINE

Denise Faithfull

Content Warning:

Discovering Katharine contains content that may not be suitable for all readers. It delves into subject matter that references suicide (and a description of Hugo Throssell's suicide), sexual assault, emotional and mental abuse, animal cruelty, self-harm and infant and child death, as well as the inclusion of phrases and words authentic to the period but now recognised as inappropriate.

For Gabriella and Darcy

January 19th, 1966

'Vicki,' Gwenda said to me at morning tea, plopping herself onto the chair opposite and waving a book in the air with a triumphant little smile. 'You're a bit of a dreamer – always got your head in a book, like me. Well, I've just finished this novel. You'll love it. It's called *Coonardoo* by a writer named Katharine Susannah Prichard. She's still alive. Lives up in the hills, in Greenmount. Bet you've never read it!'

She's right. I haven't. But I have heard of Katharine Susannah Prichard. I've read bits and pieces about her, and I've heard Mum mention her. Mum says Katharine Prichard is known as the "Red Witch" because she's a Russian spy and a communist. She was married to a famous war hero, Hugo Throssell, V.C., and I read somewhere that she's been blamed for her husband's death, so she's a pretty controversial figure. I've never really taken much notice, but all of a sudden, I'm curious. If Gwenda likes *Coonardoo*, then I know it's worth reading. We love the same kinds of books, so I always trust her judgement.

January 24th, 1966

I'm halfway through *Coonardoo* and I'm bowled over. What a novel! I love the mesmerising descriptions of the landscape! Am shocked and disgusted by how Aboriginal people living in the North West are treated. I'm enthralled by the complex love story between Hugh Watt, a white landowner, and Coonardoo, an Aboriginal woman, who grew up together on a cattle station in the Kimberleys. As adults, where Coonardoo finds it perfectly natural to love 'Youie',

Hugh's deep prejudices outweigh his love for Coonardoo, and he brutally rejects her.

I've been keeping a diary since I was twelve and always promise at the beginning of every year that I'll record stuff happening in my life at least once a month. I've rarely managed more than a dozen or so entries a year – just little things about what books I was reading, how my typing class was going, meeting boys, parties, going to the pictures. About the arguments I had with my brother, Pete, over music. I love rock n' roll; he likes country and western. Yuk!

Well, things are about to change. I've decided I *have* to do something about my boring life. My routine is so bloody dull: get up, have breakfast, pack my lunch, catch the bus to work, type all day, catch the bus back home, have dinner with Mum, do the dishes, play some records, read, go to bed. Reading, going to the library, browsing in bookshops and having a yarn with Gwenda and Nora at morning tea are the most interesting things I do. But I have no real focus, nothing to think deeply about, nothing very important to do.

So, I'm going to keep a diary of discovery. I'm going to try to find out what makes Katharine Susannah Prichard tick. I'm going to read everything I can get my hands on by her and about her. I want to find out why she's so controversial. I want to find out about communism. I want to read and think about her ideas and see if I agree with them or not. Because anyone who can write a novel like *Coonardoo* is worth spending time with, I reckon!

Am thrilled to bits. I've found a project at last! I'm sure writing about Katharine will be a fantastic way to spend my time. I know I'm going to enjoy myself and learn a great deal.

January 25th, 1966

I'm glad Gwenda told me about *Coonardoo*. Gwenda, Nora and I always talk about what we're up to at morning tea. We get along because we like similar things. For instance, we've all read *Peyton Place* and *East of Eden* and love the films *Cat on a Hot Tin Roof* and *Dr Zhivago*. We all hate our boring jobs in the typing pool for Western Sunrise Insurance Company on St Georges Terrace. We all think Maggot, our boss, is a drongo. We all wish we'd been allowed to finish high school, but our mothers made us leave school early and learn to type at the local technical college so we could get a good job until we find husbands to support us.

Gwenda, Nora and I suspect that the most successful thing we'll ever do in life is marry and have kids, so looking for Mr Right is certainly a preoccupation. However, husbands are nowhere on the horizon at the moment! We go dancing, to milk bars, the beach, the pictures, and Nora's brothers' parties are okay, but I haven't met anyone I'd like to go steady with yet. In my book club, there is only one bloke, Larry, a retired English and History schoolteacher. He's nice and very intelligent but definitely not husband material.

At least Gwenda has goals. She goes to night school, reckons she knows a way to get into university, wants to travel overseas. Nora and I are a bit lazy – Nora's a beautiful blonde and spends a lot of time on her hair and make-up. I just seem to drift along, not caring about much at all.

I've got to try something different. Maybe Katharine will help me.

January 27ᵗʰ, 1966

At morning tea, I told Gwenda I'd finished reading *Coonardoo* and talked to her about my project. She told me that I should join a bigger library than my local one if I'm going to explore more about Katharine Susannah Prichard. I value Gwenda's advice, and so I headed straight for the State Library after work and joined!

I can't believe I'm now a member of the State Library of WA, a big, beautiful old library. I walked in and out of the front entrance twice, taking deep breaths before I got up the nerve to go up to the information desk.

As I was getting my library card, I told the librarian about my project. She sniffed and said she wasn't a fan of Katharine. 'But,' she told me, 'there's a librarian called Jill who has studied Katharine's work and does regular night shifts starting at five-thirty. She will be on duty tomorrow.'

I'm going back to the library tomorrow after work to check out Jill.

January 28ᵗʰ, 1966

Well, I checked Jill out. She has red hair, freckles and a cheeky grin. 'I've written a long essay on Katharine,' Jill laughed, 'and I like her work a lot. It took me ages to complete my thesis. Once I got stuck into the research, I couldn't stop!'

Oh, wow! I think I'm going to learn a lot from Jill! I'm also thinking about how much I'd love to write a long essay based on research about someone as interesting as Katharine.

Coonardoo, says Jill, won an equal share in the 1928 *Bulletin* prize. 'It was a very controversial story when it was published in serial form under Jim Ashburton. How many female writers over how many decades have had to use a male pseudonym to get their work published, I wonder?' Jill said with a sly smile.

Jill also told me that the editor of the *Bulletin* received hundreds of letters of protest from readers disgusted with Katharine's descriptions of the love affair between a white man of property and an Aboriginal woman. They also refused to believe that white men in the North West kept Aboriginal women and had children with them, accusing Katharine of telling lies.

Coonardoo reminds me of a book I read by an American writer called Lillian Smith. It was called *Strange Fruit*. I picked it up from a box of old books next to a rubbish bin in our street. The novel was about a beautiful Negro girl called Nonnie and a white bloke called Tracy Deen. They lived in the Deep South, USA and had loved each other since they were teenagers, although they always met secretly. I remember reading that Tracy often felt sick to his stomach and ashamed because he loved Nonnie. When Nonnie gets pregnant and won't have an abortion, Tracy asks his mother to give him $300, refusing to tell her why he wants the money. He gives $100 to a black man who promises to marry Nonnie and gives her the rest. I can't remember all the details, but Nonnie doesn't marry anyone and Tracy Deen is murdered by Nonnie's brother.

I don't think there are many stories published about black and white people loving each other. I'm not surprised many readers objected to *Coonardoo* or that *Strange Fruit* was banned.

January 30th, 1966

I've been thinking about Hugh's affair with Coonardoo. It's complicated. Hugh has always vowed to 'marry white and stick white' and lies about his connection to Coonardoo, assuring his suspicious wife, Mollie, that he's never had relations with an Aboriginal woman. Hugh believes what most believe: that a man could never love an Aboriginal woman – 'not a white man.'

Yet Katharine certainly doesn't make their relationship disgusting. Coonardoo is like Hugh's 'own soul…dark, passionate and deep inexplicable currents of his being flowed towards her.' The Aboriginal people on Wytaliba Station consider Coonardoo to be 'Hugh's woman', but Hugh is horrified that he could have had sex with an Aboriginal woman and abandons her.

When Coonardoo disappears, the Aboriginal station hands, Chitali and Winni, ask Hugh to help them search for Coonardoo. He refuses, telling them, 'It's beneath my dignity.' Coonardoo, who has always loved and looked after 'Youie' with 'unfathomable tenderness', dies wondering what she has done to make Hugh 'knock her about' and 'drive her away.'

Bastard!

The description of Coonardoo's return to Wytaliba, close to death, gave me goosebumps. The station is deserted. 'No breath of life went up from the homestead chimney, no white hens wandered about the verandas. Only fans of the big windmill moved slightly.' Coonardoo crouches over her fire of branches and sticks; she stretches out her arms that are 'brown and twisted like minnerichi.' (I had to look up that word – it's a small acacia found in arid Australia.) 'She crooned a moment, and lay back. Her arms and legs, falling apart, looked like those blackened and broken sticks beside the fire.'

Another real bastard in *Coonardoo* is that 'sullen and bad-tempered' Sam Geary. Owner of Nuniewarra, a nearby property, Sam is a bully and a drunk. He has Aboriginal women and a 'family of half-castes' swarming 'about his verandas' and lusts after Coonardoo. 'I might as well take Coonardoo,' he tells Mrs Bessie during one of his regular visits to Wytaliba. He explains his current favourite, Sarah, is 'getting a bit old and frowsy.'

I'm intrigued by Katharine's description of Coonardoo yielding to that scumbag. On the night Geary comes to stay at Wytaliba, she sees in his eyes 'what she had always seen.' And yet, as 'weak and fascinated as a bird before a snake,' Coonardoo 'swayed there for Geary whom she had loathed and feared beyond any human being. Yet male to her female, she could not resist him. Her need of him was a great as the dry earth's for rain.'

Wow!

I'm tucked up in bed with my diary and thinking about Hugh and Coonardoo. I'm wondering, could I love an Aboriginal man? The only Aboriginal person I've ever met is a girl I went to primary school with called Beryl. She didn't like me, and I didn't like her because she always beat me at the barefoot 100-yard dash. I've never met an Aboriginal boy or man.

Gwenda, Nora and I often discuss what kind of man we want to marry. Gwenda says her dreamboat is an Italian with blond hair and brown eyes. Nora wants to marry a tall, blond, blue-eyed dinky-di

Aussie. I'm not sure I even want to get married. Mum keeps nagging me about finding a nice young bloke to marry, but I reckon there has to be more to life than just getting married and having kids. Maybe one day I will, but I want to do something else first. I like writing, especially about people. I've written a few sketches about odd bods I've met, so that might be something worth trying. I'd love to travel. Perth is dull and always seems isolated and so far away from everywhere.

January 31st, 1966

This morning, I was telling Gwenda I think the scene where Coonardoo gives in to Sam Geary is very sexy and how, even though she hates him, she can't resist him. 'Gosh,' I said to Gwenda, 'I've never felt like that about any man. Have you?'

Gwenda looked puzzled, then said I was pretty naïve to think the scene was about sex. 'Coonardoo's submission is all about power,' said Gwenda. 'Think about it,' she said. 'Hasn't she been exploited by the whites, like all the Aboriginal people on Wytaliba? How can Coonardoo do anything else but give in to that sod of a man? Don't forget,' she added, 'Aboriginal people living on Wytaliba were paid with damper, sugar and tea. My friend, who lives in the Kimberleys, says they get bugger all for their jobs and are treated like slaves. Sam Geary wouldn't have thought twice about pouncing on Coonardoo.'

Gwenda often talks about explorers and settlers and land grants and exploitation and so on. I never really understand what she's on about, but I like listening to her arguments. She always has something interesting to say. I wish we'd learned about our real history at school instead of learning about all those dreary cities in England that bought our wool and blah, blah, blah.

February 3rd, 1966

The bus stank of ciggies tonight. Why are people allowed to smoke on the bus?

On the way home, I started thinking about how Katharine researches her stories. Jill told me she always goes to live for a while in the places she writes about and gets to know the people, the landscape, and their workaday world.

'In 1926', Jill said, 'Katharine travelled to Turee Station, up north in cattle country, with her four-year-old son, Ric. She lived there for nine months. Her husband, Hugo, always approved of her research trips.' Jill showed me a letter Katharine wrote to her friend, Hilda Esson, from Turee Station. 'Jim is really wonderful to me,' Katharine writes. 'To let me come on this journey for instance.'

'Katharine's husband was always called Jim,' said Jill, 'even as a kid growing up in Northam. Funny, isn't it, how some people don't fancy the name they were given at birth. My father's name was Paul but he always called himself Jack.

'Katharine also wrote to another close friend, Nettie Palmer, about how fascinated she was by the way of life on an outback station,' Jill told me thoughtfully, tapping her pencil. 'Nettie claimed Katharine has an interest in other people's jobs that is equalled only by her devotion to her own.'

Ah, ha! So that's why the descriptions of Wytaliba are so realistic! We learn all kinds of stuff about day-to-day life on an outback station, about mustering, droving, horse-breaking; about the housework and general maintenance around the homestead looking after sheds and windmills. There are descriptions of 'pink eye' and 'fire corroborees' and Aboriginal kinships and families.

I reckon Katharine's research strategy is a great idea. If I ever write something serious, I'll follow her approach so if anyone asks, I can say, 'I've been there. That's what I saw.' I'd enjoy that way of writing more than a piece based on research.

February 4th, 1966

I love the way Katharine describes the landscape of the North West. I can imagine myself being there with her, looking out across the plains where the 'smooth, polished stones, black and red' shine like metal; where the desert pea is 'the colour of blood newly spilt', and the air is 'fine and dry with that faint incense of paper-daisies and sandalwood.'

And the stillness – it is a 'breathless heaviness' that drowses the senses as if that 'mythological great snake the blacks believed in...were putting the opiate of his breath into the air, folding you round and round, squeezing the life out of you.'

I feel that strange, breathless stillness of this landscape on just about every page of *Coonardoo*.

February 6th, 1966

Coonardoo has forced me to think about certain things I've never thought about before – such as land and property – who owns what, and how they got it. For instance, Mrs Bessie grabs old Saul Hardy's lease of a million acres between the 'Nungarra hills on the west, To-morrow ranges on the east and tributaries of the coastal rivers north and south.' She gets all of this for 'a couple of hundred pounds.' She spends the rest of her life 'making the station for Hugh' and is known throughout the district as a 'regular skinflint' and as 'mean and hard as nails.'

Her 'white woman's prejudices' are frequently 'inflamed.' The Aboriginals are 'her blacks.' What a mistress she sounds like when she says to Meenie, 'We'll take Coonardoo into the house...and teach her to be a good house girl...teach her to cook and sew, be clean and tidy.' She resents Aboriginal rituals, especially initiation ceremonies, and has 'fits of loathing the blacks.'

Yet Mrs Bessie is portrayed sympathetically overall. We're told there was never any 'trouble' at Wytaliba because she was 'generous' and 'kindly' in her 'overlordship' of the station and 'the blacks recognised and accepted' her. They refer to her as 'Mumae' and she was 'proud of their name for her.' Father and mother to her son, Hugh, whom she adores, she does everything she can to make life easy for him and to increase his inheritance. People say she has her 'head screwed on the right way' because she's shrewd, hard-working and tough.

I don't really like Mrs Bessie as a character, though. I often found her irritating, but Mollie is unbearable. Once a 'maid-of-all-work in a boarding house' in Geraldton, she's thrilled to land Hugh as a husband. She takes one look at Wytaliba and decides, 'This is my home. These are my servants.' She is determined to show Hugh how a house should be run…This slow, lazy, go-as-you-please way of doing things would not suit her.'

Mollie never gets off her high horse. She's bossy and bad-tempered with the Aboriginal workers and insults Saul Hardy when he tries to stop her from beating her daughters. She wails and complains about every 'hardship and difficulty' and has furious rows with Hugh. She wants him to sell the station and buy a shop in Geraldton. After years of toil, Mollie's anger and frustrations boil over. Fed up with his wife, Hugh tells her she can leave if she wants. 'Give me the money and I'll go, all right!' she screams.

When Hugh chucks his cheque for £500 at Mollie and tells her, 'That's all the cash I've got in the world. Take it and go, for God's sake…you're like a maggot in my brain. You'll drive me mad, woman,' I laughed out loud.

Mollie's a real pain in the bum.

February 14th, 1966

Well, today, Australia officially uses dollars and cents instead of pounds, shillings and pence. Who can forget that jingle – it's everywhere! To the tune of 'Click Go the Shears' we've all heard a hundred times: 'In come the dollars/In come the cents/To replace the pounds, the shillings and the pence/Be prepared folks when the coins begin to mix/On the 14th of February 1966.'

My next pay will be in decimal currency! It will take me a while to get used to it. Everyone's been talking about royals, dollars, cents, crowns, emus, quids, and dinkums for months. Nora likes crowns; Gwenda and I prefer quids. I've always liked the expression my father used when he was really happy: 'Wouldn't be dead for quids,' he'd say, with a big grin.

February 20th, 1966

After work this arvo, I popped into the library to have a chat with Jill. She showed me the section in Miles Franklin's book, *Laughter, Not for a Cage*, where Franklin writes about *Coonardoo*. I copied this interesting quote into my notebook:

> 'The usual ending for most stories of dark women and white men was for the man to slough off the woman as naturally as a snake would an old skin, and leave her to pine away or commit suicide...KSP shows that Coonardoo was the real love of Hugh's life, his rightful mate, and he hers, but for the accident of pigmentation. The tragedy is as stark, as unrelieved as in the classical Greek...a terrible and beautiful story, irrefutable as a piece of sculpture.'

I think Miles Franklin is dead right.

February 25th, 1966

I told Larry at book group supper break tonight that I had finished reading *Coonardoo*. He was weighing up whether to have tea, whiskey or sherry, the three drinks offered at our meetings, and didn't respond. So I reached across him to grab a cup of tea and looked him straight in the eye. 'What's that, Vicki?' he asked.

'*Coonardoo*. I've finished *Coonardoo*!'

'Ah,' he said slowly. '*Coonardoo*, yes, well. You know, Vicki, Mary Gilmore thought *Coonardoo* was a dirty story. And so did an awful lot of other people!'

I gulped – I've read Mary Gilmore was sympathetic to the causes of Aboriginal people. 'Why on earth would she object to *Coonardoo*?' I asked Larry.

'Lots of people disagree with Mary Gilmore and so do I,' Larry replied. 'Personally, I think *Coonardoo* is Prichard's best novel, although I admit I haven't read everything she's written.'

Larry always speaks slowly and thoughtfully; sometimes, he puts his thumb and forefinger in his nostrils and pauses for ages before he finally speaks. I often wonder what he'd be like in front of a classroom. A bit boring, I reckon, but he's nice. He and his neighbour, Anne Barker, once the Head Mistress at a local high school where he worked, started the book group when they retired. We always call her 'Miss'. It's funny – they both speak slowly and deliberately.

We always meet at the same place – at Miss's house in the sunroom, a long, narrow room with a big window. On the window sill is a huge blue and white Chinese vase. It's really ugly.

Book club members come and go; I hardly know any of their names. When numbers get below five, Miss puts a notice on the community board in our local library seeking new members. That's how I came to join. I don't keep up with all their book choices but enjoy listening to the discussions. I'm happy to stay in the club because it's somewhere to go once a month on a Friday night. Gets me out of the house, which pleases both myself and Mum no end, although she often tells me I'd be better off going out dancing so I could meet my future husband.

February 28th, 1966

Jill said Larry is correct. She showed me the Mary Gilmore quote:

> 'What an appalling thing *Coonardoo* is. It is not merely a journalistic description of station life, it is vulgar and dirty. It has been a great blow to me as I thought it began so well. I am told A[ngus] and R[obertson] having read it said not if they were paid 10,000 pounds would they have the name of publishing it. And I have not heard one solitary person, man or woman, speak well of it. It has disgusted everyone.'

What rubbish, Mary Gilmore! Miles Franklin wasn't disgusted. I wasn't disgusted. And Larry and Jill both like it.

March 11th, 1966

Larry says Katharine was forty-three years old when she went up to Turee Station. She had just published her novel, *Working Bullocks* (must read!). Then off she trots, way up to the North West, to get set to write the next one. What an energetic woman she is!

Larry has travelled all over WA and told me that bits of the homestead at Turee Station are still standing. 'What a place to choose to write a novel! So isolated. But then, Prichard likes to go to the places she writes about. I suppose it's the journalist in her.'

'I think I'd like to be a journalist,' I said to Larry.

'Well, Vicki, I'm pleased to hear it. Have you written anything?'

'I'm writing a diary of discovery,' I said feebly. 'It's about Katharine, actually.'

'Oh, is it – actually?' he grinned. 'Well, good on you!'

I was a bit taken aback. Not sure if he was mocking me. I feel so uneducated around Larry.

March 14th, 1966

I went to the library after work this arvo and Jill showed me a quote by Katharine, which I copied into my notebook:

> 'I had models for Hugh and Coonardoo. When the book was published, I was always afraid that Geary would come some day and take to me. Hugh did: appalled that a man's inner conflict should have been so revealed…Coonardoo? She is an aboriginal woman I was close to (in all but the end which happened to another woman)…I'd rather *Coonardoo* was thrown on the scrap heap and forgotten than be regarded merely as background and poetic symbolism.'

Jill says Katharine defended her writing as realism because many critics didn't believe what she'd written about the Aboriginal people and how they live. 'She wrote in her foreword in *Coonardoo* "facts, characters, incidents, have been collected, related and interwoven. That is all." Above all, she did not want Coonardoo to be a symbolic figure. However,' said Jill firmly, 'while the portrait of Coonardoo is realistic, it is also symbolic. Her associations with water and fertility are everywhere in the novel. After Coonardoo disappears, Wytaliba misses the rains year after year when almost every other outback station gets it.'

I agree with Jill. There is a great deal of symbolism associated with Coonardoo. When she's driven off Wytaliba, storms break early, 'sun and hot winds' blast the earth, and the property becomes a wasteland.

Jill and I discussed the end of the novel, where we're told Coonardoo 'had loved Wytaliba and been bound up with the source of its life. Was she not the well in the shadow? Had she not some mysterious affinity with that ancestral female spirit which was responsible for fertility, generation, the growth of everything?"

'Katharine isn't a fan of symbolism, modernism or experimental writing,' said Jill thoughtfully, spinning her pencil. 'She insists her writing is realistic, based on personal experience and observation. But still, she can't control how readers respond to *Coonardoo*. I think it's a deeply psychological and symbolic novel.'

I thought about *Coonardoo* on the bus going home. I'm leaning towards Jill's interpretation, although I might change my mind after I've read more of Katharine's work.

March 17ᵗʰ, 1966

Yesterday, Jill gave me a copy of a 1949 article Katharine wrote for a newspaper called *The Northern Standard*. I read it on the bus going to work. It's about how badly WA treats Aboriginal people while claiming to protect them.

She writes that our treatment of Aboriginal people is a 'stain on the record of Australia' and that we must 'ensure practical measures for saving them from extermination.' I'm not sure exactly what she means, and 'extermination' is such a powerful word. It's something I've certainly never heard about, thought about, or cared about, but after reading this article, I'm on the lookout for more of the same, just to see what's what!

March 18th, 1966

I've been browsing through photos of Katharine in the library. There's a gorgeous photo of her in 1923 bathing her little boy on the veranda of their house in Greenmount. Jill told me that's where her husband would shoot himself ten years later. How sad.

In a lovely photo of her taken in 1928, her hair is swept back from her forehead and her eyes are penetrating and intelligent.

In 1933, home from a trip to the Soviet Union, she had her photo taken with a group of primary school children at Greenmount School. She's presenting a 'gift of seeds' to them from the 'children of Siberia.' How in the world did she get them past quarantine?

She looks elderly but determined in the photo of her receiving the World Council's medal for her services to peace in 1959. She's holding a huge bunch of flowers. 'They look like carnations,' Jill laughed, 'and Katharine probably would've preferred Australian wildflowers.'

In all these photos, she looks like a lady ready to get stuck into things.

Jill has collected some opinions from people who have met Katharine:

Eleanor Dark, whom Katharine visited in the Blue Mountains in 1943, said when she was with Katharine, she felt the presence of a powerful 'spirit' and thought she had a beautiful smile.

Jean Devanny, a communist colleague of Katharine, claimed Katharine's 'manner was quiet and serene, her expression deeply thoughtful, if not grave.'

Apparently, she has a way of 'listening intently' to people. One writer describes her eyes as 'dark...very soft and always perceptive, the eyes of a writer.'

I laughed at the quote by Katharine about herself. She says, 'there's steel underneath.'

Jill read out loud a funny little rhyme that Katharine's father wrote about his headstrong daughter:

'Her mandate admits no resistance,

She rules with imperious sway,

She sees but her right to insistence,

And deems it your place to obey.'

Sounds like she was a bit of a handful growing up! She may well be a bit of a handful now!

'In her autobiography, Katharine tells us how her father wanted her to become a domestic angel, but Katharine says that was something she'd never, ever be. She always wanted to be a writer,' Jill said thoughtfully.

A domestic angel? That's a funny expression. Bet it's one Mum would like. Bet she thinks she's one. She makes my bed and cooks my dinner. I eat it, although I can't say she's a great cook – the vegetables are always soggy and she makes too many dishes with mince.

March 21ˢᵗ, 1966

Another trip to the library this arvo. 'I'm enjoying my project, Jill!' I said as soon as I could get her attention. She laughed and said, 'Good on you!'

'So, what shall I read next?'

'Do you want to read Katharine's work in the order she wrote them or mix them up a bit?' she asked.

'Oh, scramble them up,' I said. 'Much more fun!'

So Jill chose *Black Opal* for me. 'It was published in 1921. Katharine was thirty-eight years old and hadn't yet written *Coonardoo*,' Jill said. 'I think you'll like it.'

March 22nd, 1966

In Dymphna Cusack's introduction to *Black Opal*, she writes that she thought the scene where Sophie drops Potch's black opal and sees all those coloured stars was 'improbable' and 'melodramatic' until she found 'the parallel of that story' in *The Lightning Ridge Book* by Steward Lloyd. 'The Empress of Australia...for which £650 was offered in 1914...was dropped by an inquisitive stranger and broke into three pieces...Katharine Susannah Prichard is truthful...in fact as well as to the imagination.'

Dymphna Cusack's idea that Katharine is 'truthful' to the world she is writing about is beginning to seem to me to be very important. Jill told me that Katharine wrote *Black Opal* based on her research when she went to live for a while in the White Cliffs opal fields in NSW and in Lightning Ridge. Apparently, she wanted to describe precisely the jobs and organizations involved in opal mining that existed back then.

Jill also told me that when Katharine was gathering material for *Black Opal*, she met a man called Michael, who showed her every stage of work on the opal fields. 'He was a worker, intelligent, well-read and interested in workers' rights,' said Jill. 'He was especially interested in how the opal miners could keep out the big corporations that wanted to take over the mines.'

This man is the model for Michael Brady, the hero of *Black Opal*.

On the bus coming home, I felt so excited because I've finally found a project that is interesting and educational. It gives me a sense of purpose and makes me feel much better about myself. It almost makes working at that stinky insurance company bearable.

March 24th, 1966

It's nearly midnight and I'm loving *Black Opal*.

Just finished reading Chapter Eight which has stunning descriptions of the landscape around Fallen Star Ridge. It is a 'country of wide plains stretching westwards for hundreds on hundreds of miles broken only by shingly ridges to the sea.' In summer the 'dry earth cracks'; huge coolabahs stand with 'their feet in the river ways...as if waiting with imperturbable faith the return of the waters.' During droughts, sheep and cattle lie rotting along the stock routes: their carcasses are disembowelled by crows, leaving an 'odour of putrefaction in the air.'

Ugh, I can almost smell it as I read.

But Katharine clearly enjoys springtime, giving us detailed descriptions of how the country is turned into a gorgeous 'flowering wilderness...and a tapestry of incomparable beauty...is wrought on the bare earth.'

In winter, cold winds 'blow in from the inland and there are nights of frost and sparkling stars.'

After reading Chapter Eight, I put down *Black Opal*, went outside and looked up at the night sky, wishing I didn't have to go to work tomorrow, wishing I could get away from dreary old Perth and go to a place like Fallen Star Ridge.

March 26th, 1966

Thinking about the characters in *Black Opal*. I like Sophie Rouminof, even though she falls for that snob Arthur Henty, the son of 'old Henty' from Warria Station, and a cut above Sophie who lives with her drunken father. Sophie and Arthur knew each other as children. When they meet as young adults, they stand 'smiling and staring at each other, under a spell of silence.' Arthur notices Sophie has 'strange, beautiful eyes, the green and blue of opal' and is 'bewildered and overcome.'

But Arthur's not going to get caught. He knows what strife there'd be in his family if he married a local nobody with a drunk for a father, despite her reputation as a very fine singer.

March 28th, 1966

I took *Black Opal* into morning tea and told Gwenda and Nora all about Sophie. How she's rejected by Arthur, is not interested in local boy Potch, who adores her, runs away to New York with an American businessman called John Armitage, dumps him and takes off with a rich playboy called Adler who introduces her to a world of 'beautiful places.' After partying hard, including an orgy on a yacht with what John jealously calls a 'rotten lot', Sophie becomes 'utterly demoralised...so sick with the shock and shame of it all' that she loses her voice.

'Brazen little hussy,' laughed Gwenda.

'So – what does she do next?' Nora asked.

'Well,' I replied, 'she scoots off to Chicago to work in a clothing factory where she has an "awakening". She remembers how Michael Brady, back home on the Ridge, always talked about greedy rich people exploiting others. Sophie realizes that Chicago workers in the factory are paid rock bottom wages and forced to live in slums "like bugs under a rotten log" so that stinking rich men like Adler can "live as they do".

Sophie goes home to the Ridge and ends up with Potch, who still adores her. They start the battle against old Dawe Armitage and son John, who want to take over the mines and exploit the miners.'

I read the passage where, on the night of the race night ball, Sophie runs into Arthur. They dance and both realize that the 'inalienable, unalterable attraction...was still there.' Arthur's will, 'working against hers, demanded the surrender.' They go outside and, 'as two waves meeting in mid-ocean fall to each other, they met, and were lost in the oblivion of a close embrace.'

A furious Potch bursts into the scene and bashes Arthur Henty until he's unconscious.

The girls and I discussed Potch. Sophie never loves him with the passion she has for Arthur. When Potch tells Sophie how ashamed he was for bashing Arthur, how he was ready to leave town in disgrace, Sophie admits she was partly to blame for what happened. She tells Potch she's always been afraid of 'the power' of her love for Arthur, that she wants to forget Arthur and marry Potch and 'have the sort of life that keeps a woman to man...mend your clothes, cook your meals...be your loving and faithful wife.' He can hardly believe his luck!

After their marriage, 'all the days were holy days' for Potch. When they're at home, he follows 'her every movement with a worshipful, reverent gaze.' For her part, Sophie gives up her desire to be happy and the 'restless turmoil of her soul and body' is soothed. Her days with Potch may be dull, but they are also 'long and peaceful.'

Much later, Arthur, a heavy drinker, shoots himself in the tank paddock. At his funeral, the Ridge gossips wonder what had gone wrong between Sophie and Arthur. They think they should have 'been true to that instinct of mate for mate.'

Nora said she feels sorry for Sophie, but we all agreed Potch is the type of man we'd like for a husband – we all want to be worshipped! 'Although...' Gwenda said thoughtfully.

'Although what?' I asked.

'Well, Potch is fine as a character in a novel, but in real life, I wouldn't want a boyfriend who'd go off his head like Potch and beat another bloke to a pulp out of jealousy.'

'Nor would I,' I said.

'I wouldn't mind!' giggled Nora.

Gwenda rolled her eyes. I shook my head in disgust.

April 4th, 1966

In *Coonardoo*, we get detailed descriptions of managing an outback cattle station; in *Black Opal*, we enter the world of opal mining.

We read about opal 'gougers' who leave at dawn and slog until late afternoon on their claims – sweating, digging, sinking holes, always hoping to strike it rich. We learn how opals are traded, hoarded, cut, shaped and polished.

I love Katharine's description of Sophie using the cutting-wheel. It's like looking at a painting:

'The wheel was in line with the window, and she sat on

the wooden chair before it, so that the light fell over her left shoulder. On the bench which ran out from the wheel were a spirit lamp and the trays of rough opal: on the other side of the bench the polishing buffers arranged one against the other. A hand-basin, the water in it raddled with rouge, stood on the table behind her, and a white china jug of fresh water beside it.'

Sophie sings as she works; the 'whirr of her wheel, the chirr of sandstone and potch sheared away, made a small, purry noise, like the drone of an insect.'

I'd love to learn to do something new – something more interesting than typing insurance documents. Maybe I should go up north and find work on a cattle station. I could learn to muster like Coonardoo. Maybe I should head off to Lightning Ridge and see if there's an apprenticeship in making opal jewellery.

Nah! I'd likely I'd end up cleaning a homestead or working in a shop near the opal fields. Doubt they'd spend too much time and energy teaching a city girl how to change her life.

I've been reading a bit about opals. There are 'nobbies', which are light grey and have colours shining through them, and there's colourless 'potch'. Black opals, which have a rainbow of bright colours and patterns, are rare and the most valuable opals in the world. They're found almost exclusively in Lightning Ridge, NSW.

I don't like opals much, nor do Gwenda and Nora. Gwenda likes diamonds, Nora loves sapphires. I don't like gems at all. 'I've heard that it's bad luck to buy yourself an opal,' I told Gwenda and she just laughed and said, 'That's just silly superstition.'

Jill told me a while ago that Katharine wears an opal ring. I hope she didn't buy it for herself!

April 18th, 1966

This arvo, Jill and I were discussing Katharine's descriptions in *Coonardoo* and *Black Opal* of people at work. Jill showed me a copy of a letter Katharine wrote to her old friend, Miles Franklin, in which she writes about her own work.

She says that sometimes, she's sure she works 'harder than any body in the world. And at so many different jobs – keeping house for my beautiful son...cooking, sweeping, washing, mending etc., organisational work and lectures, and somewhere in between I've got to find time to write and earn my living...and the terrible pressure of financial anxieties never growing less...It would be heavenly to work without fretting how bills are to be paid.'

Fancy being married to a famous war hero, being famous yourself, yet having so little money! Gee! Even my parents, who were never well off, always had enough to pay the bills. Even now that Dad's dead, Mum doesn't seem too worried about money, although we don't have a telephone. 'Can't afford one yet, Vicki,' Mum says when I ask. When I tell her I'll give her a bit more board so she can save up to get a phone, she shrugs and says, 'It's too complicated.' I reckon she doesn't want a telephone because she doesn't know anyone she could ring.

Anyway, I like the way Katharine describes workers. Obviously, she's a hard worker herself, although not well paid. She's the type who just puts up with things and gets on with the job. Overworked, underpaid, but sticks at it because she believes in what she's doing.

April 29ᵗʰ, 1966

I told Larry tonight at book club that I've finished reading *Black Opal* and he gave me a little punch on the shoulder and said, 'Congratulations, Vicki!'

'What do you think of Michael Brady?' I asked him.

'Well,' Larry replied thoughtfully, 'I can sympathize with Michael's point of view – he knows the miners want to be their own masters and the Armitage corporation will turn them into wage slaves. That would destroy their pride, dignity and independence.

'In a way, though,' Larry continued, 'I tend to agree with the Armitages that those Ridge men believe in a "Utopian dream." Even Prichard pointed out in her Author's Note that the novel was written in 1918 and based on the conditions that existed back then. She says that Michael Brady would be the first to admit that the miners were "behind scientific progress in industrial organisation."'

'But still,' I said, 'I'm glad Michael and his mob won in the end.'

'So am I,' Larry grinned.

May 2nd, 1966

Been thinking about Michael Brady. The so-called 'opal swap' is a big part of the story. I find it interesting that Michael, who's respected by all the workers on the Ridge, could steal from a mate. Katharine defends him by telling us Michael believes by swapping the opals, he will save Sophie from the sins of city life and that Paul, her father, has not really lost his stones because Michael always meant to return them.

But the point is, he doesn't return them, and he doesn't save Sophie from running away. Katharine describes Michael's obsession with black opals as holding a 'sinister witchery' over him; he trembles with 'instinctive eagerness, reverence, and delight' whenever he sees a 'piece of the beautiful stone.' It becomes impossible for him to return the opals he's swapped.

I like the way Katharine makes us think about choices and consequences. Makes me reflect on my own life and what I might do in similar circumstances. I doubt that I'd ever steal anything from a friend, but if I did, I like to think I'd return it and try to explain exactly why I stole it.

May 3rd, 1966

This arvo, I asked Jill what she thought about the opal swap. She said she reckons Katharine was much more interested in Michael Brady's idealism than his flaws. 'When you read more of Katharine's work, Vicki,' she said with a smile, 'you'll come to see that she is very forgiving of petty thieves and ordinary, honest people who do wrong for a reason they think is valid. They usually hurt one or just a few people as a consequence, compared with the major thieves, like banks and big companies, or sometimes even governments, who deliberately and thoughtlessly harm thousands. I suspect one of Katharine's favourite stories is "Robin Hood",' she laughed.

I laughed, too! Yep, I'll bet Katharine does like Robin Hood! I know I do!

May 17th, 1966

Dropped by the library this arvo to tell Jill I loved the ending of *Black Opal*: how it finishes on a note that soars: 'Hope and pride in the purpose of the Ridge' is restored; the principle of a 'life in common' is reaffirmed and the 'rhythm of everyday affairs' takes its course.

'I do not understand why Katharine is criticised for her views about life,' I said.

'Well, Vicki, it depends on your point of view, doesn't it? If you're like Armitage and believe that the old ways of the Ridge folk are simply not good enough anymore, that production and profit are all that count, then you might think Katharine is a bit of a dreamer.'

'I suppose lots of people think that about her,' I said sadly.

'They do,' replied Jill firmly. 'But I like dreamers!' she laughed.

So do I.

May 27ᵗʰ, 1966

Tonight at book club, Larry told me a funny little story about how Miles Franklin was wandering around Dymocks Bookshop in Sydney one day and saw *Black Opal* and her own novel, *Back to Bool Bool*, on the bargain table and how depressed she was when she saw them. Apparently, she told Katharine about it, who was very put out! I suppose authors need every penny of any royalties they get, and they'll earn hardly anything if their books are put out on the bargain table at Dymocks Bookshop in Sydney.

Larry also told me that Katharine wrote most of *Black Opal* in a small cottage in Emerald, Victoria. 'The cottage is still there, although it no longer belongs to her. She sold it in the early 1930s,' Larry said. 'I've been there and had a look at that cottage. In many ways, it's similar to the house in Greenmount where she now lives.'

One day, I'd like to go to Emerald to see that cottage. One day, I'd like to go anywhere away from here!

Before we left book club, Larry gave me his copy of Katharine's autobiography, *Child of the Hurricane*. He said he didn't like it. 'There's too much about her early life and it doesn't reveal enough about her as a writer or as someone so deeply involved in politics,' he said. He told me that Katharine was going to write a second volume covering her later years, but she decided she couldn't be bothered. 'I would've been much more interested in that volume,' he said with a grin.

He also told me Katharine wasn't happy with *Child of the Hurricane* because she doesn't like writing about herself. 'She wrote it,' he said, 'because she thought there were things about her life, work and ideas that needed clearing up. It was published in 1964, just a couple of years ago. She told her son, Ric, that she was going to write her memoirs to correct various interpretations of her life and work. It's a damned shame she stopped writing autobiography after the first volume.'

When I opened the book, I noticed Larry had scrawled a quote by Katharine: 'I do not want anything of mine to be published after I am dead that I have not approved of while I have my wits. I do not like to be seen in *deshabillé* even in manuscript.'

Sounds like she's a very private person; no wonder she didn't write volume two of her autobiography.

June 1st, 1966

I'm dipping into *Child of the Hurricane*, discovering more about Katharine. There are bits about her childhood, her married life, her son, a few explanations about her interest in socialism, communism and anti-war movements, about when she was writing what and how she went about her research, something that is obviously always very important to her.

She says she was born on 4th December 1883, in Fiji, during a hurricane and spent her childhood in Tasmania. She grew up in Melbourne. After working overseas, she returned to Melbourne, where, in 1919, she married Hugo Throssell, V.C. They moved to Greenmount and lived in a big old house called 'Wandu,' where, she tells us, 'on hot summer evenings' they 'disported' themselves like Adam and Eve.

Wow! I like the sound of that!

Later, they moved to a smaller house down the road. She still lives there. Mum told me this house is on Old York Road, and opposite her home is a memorial to Hugo. Must see if I can catch a bus up there one day and have a quick look around, although of course, she wouldn't want people like me gawking at her place, so I wouldn't linger.

When Larry gave me *Child of the Hurricane*, he told me that Katharine's father, a newspaper editor, hanged himself in 1907. He had been depressed and desperately worried about money. In *Child of the Hurricane*, she says that her father's death killed any interest she ever had in religion, which she calls 'superstition.' It is 'pitiful that people should surrender their common sense and intelligence to accept blindly the theories and dogmas of various religious organizations, based on suppositions, when scientific research has revealed so much about the creation of the world and the significance of men and women on this earth,' she writes.

Katharine's right: it is pathetic that some people blindly accept religious dogma. I reckon religion is superstitious nonsense.

June 2nd, 1966

I took *Child of the Hurricane* into work today. At morning tea, I read that passage about religion to Gwenda and Nora. Gwenda says when she was young, she was confirmed in the Anglican Church. But Gwenda isn't religious at all, never goes to church, never talks about religion. Nora is a Roman Catholic, goes to church occasionally and sometimes talks about God.

The only time I ever think about God is when our insurance

company manages to get out of paying a claim because of some so-called 'Act of God.'

June 3rd, 1966

In *Child of the Hurricane*, Katharine tells us that her brother, Alan, joined the Army during the First World War. She was devastated. She had visited the battlefields while working as a journalist in London and tried to talk Alan out of joining up, but he took no notice and willingly went off to fight.

However, in Alan's letters to her from the Front, he writes about the futility of the battles and how men are dying because 'someone had blundered'. He is beginning to agree with his sister: 'War is a rotten business. A way must be found to stop it ever happening again.'

Alan is killed, and his death and the deaths of so many young men makes Katharine's blood boil. What makes her furious are the 'reports of colossal profiteering in the war industries; the sacrifices demanded of working people in wage cuts; the persecution of conscientious objectors and trade unionists seeking to preserve rights won by working men and women in a century of struggle.'

Katharine comes to believe that there was a 'political purpose behind the movement for conscription' when she hears an 'influential politician' say 'we'll win the next referendum, and we'll know what to do with trade unionists then. It'll be the front line trenches for them.'

If that's true, that is astounding! I can't believe a man who was elected to office, perhaps even by a trade unionist or two, could be so vicious!

I've never thought much about trade unions. I'm not in a union. If there was a union at work, I might join it because we're paid next to nothing, though we work really hard all day bashing out those bloody insurance contracts till our wrists crack. If we dared to ask for more money, our boss would do his usual thing: glare, sneer and jerk his right thumb over his left shoulder, meaning 'shut up and get back to work.'

My father belonged to a union and once he went on strike. Mum was furious with him. When he tried to explain why he was striking, she wouldn't listen. Just told him that he was losing a day's pay and how that would affect her grocery shopping for the week.

June 4th, 1966

While I was reading about Katharine's Alan, I thought about my Allan. He's the only boy I've ever written a lot about in a diary. I was mad about him when I was fifteen. He had curly black hair, piercing blue eyes and always made me laugh. He liked reading, too, so we talked a lot about books. He left Perth for a job outback as a jackeroo. We wrote to each other for a while but his letters stopped after a couple of months. I kept writing to him but had no reply until one day I got a letter from the station owner telling me that Allan had drowned in their dam. Cried for months, then chucked that year's diary in the bin.

I sometimes think about Allan when Mum starts in on me to get cracking and find a nice young bloke to marry. 'If Allan were still alive, I would marry him,' I say to myself. He would've been a very nice bloke to have around. We would've had lots of fun together, and I reckon he would've been a good father too. He had a gentle way about him.

June 5th, 1966

Took the bus up to Greenmount this arvo to check out the memorial to Hugo. The memorial is a small shelter; I think it might be called a rotunda. I sat in it for a few minutes and thought about how devastated Katharine must've been after her husband died. I remember how utterly miserable I was when I found out Allan had drowned. I couldn't eat, couldn't sleep. I couldn't even read because I couldn't concentrate.

After a while in the rotunda, I felt really down in the dumps, so I got up and strolled across the road to look at Katharine's house. I felt a bit creepy, like I was being a nosy parker, and I was scared she'd come outside and catch me. I was glad to get on the bus and head for home.

June 8th, 1966

We find out in *Child of the Hurricane* that Hugo was pressured by the Army into promoting the pro-conscription campaign. The Army thought that his appearance at recruitment drives would encourage men to enlist because he had a Victoria Cross and looked good in uniform.

But expecting his support was a big mistake. Katharine tells us about how her husband was asked to speak at the 1919 Armistice Day celebrations in his hometown of Northam. Instead of supporting the war, he describes 'with deep feeling the horror and misery of war.' Being in a war could change your mind about anything!

I've never read a book about war, and I don't like war films. I saw 'The Longest Day' and 'The Great Escape' with Pete and some friends. I only went because they all wanted to go. Pete loved both pictures, I didn't like them. War must be horrifying to live through. I can't understand why Pete thinks going off to war would be an exciting adventure. I remember reading somewhere that Miles Franklin thought wars were 'looney' and 'the madness of men.' She believed the build-up of arms always leads to war. Sounds about right to me.

Bet Katharine would agree!

June 9th, 1966

'Does the library have a copy of Hugo Throssell's anti-war speech that he gave in Northam?' I asked Jill this arvo.

'I'll bet we do!' she said. 'I'll check. Come in tomorrow.'

June 10th, 1966

Left work on the dot and dashed off to the library. Sure enough, Jill kept her word, and I was able to read through Hugo's speech.

In his introduction, he said how pleased he was to receive such a warm welcome. But, he said, he had seen the horror of war and had decided he now wanted to work for peace. The war had made him 'think and inquire what are the causes of wars.' He concluded that wars happen because they occur 'under a system of production for profit...while it is possible for unscrupulous men, profiteers, and manufacturers of war materials to profit by war, we will always have wars.'

'If we do not want war,' he said, 'we must change the system of production for profit, and organise not for the benefit of a few people but for the community as a whole.' He asked his audience to 'think; talk to people who are opposing the system...study books on the subject and test what you read by the facts of everyday life.' He warned them not to 'bother about what the daily newspapers or the people interested in maintaining the system of production for profit may say...Go to the other side! Get their point of view...Work for the conditions which will make it impossible for any to make fortunes out of war.'

Wow! What fantastic advice from Hugo. My mum would have a fit if I showed her a copy of that speech! She'd tell me I should be ashamed of myself for reading such trash and rip the speech to bits.

Unfortunately for Hugo, his conservative family was in the audience, as well as their friends and many returned soldiers. They were all horrified.

June 13th, 1966

Jill told me that some people accused Katharine of manipulating her husband into making his speech. 'She admits she helped him write it and listened to him rehearse it,' Jill said, 'but I don't believe she manipulated her husband. I think he really believed what he said.

'The local newspapers were against Hugo, of course,' Jill continued. 'One journalist called the speech a bombshell and claimed the audience was dumbfounded and the soldiers in the audience felt betrayed.'

Jill said that after the Northam fiasco, Hugo and Katharine returned to Greenmount, and from then on, they were generally unpopular. About a year later, Katharine helped found the Western Australian branch of the Communist Party of Australia. Soon after that, she began to be called the "Red Witch."'

'Gee, some people are nasty,' I said. Jill laughed, then said, 'Nasty – and ignorant.'

Jill also showed me a copy of a letter Katharine wrote to Nettie Palmer shortly after Hugo gave his speech. 'You could have heard a pin drop,' she writes. 'Jim himself was ghastly, his face all torn with emotion. It was terrible – but magnificent.'

June 14th, 1966

At morning tea, I was telling Gwenda and Nora about Hugo's speech and how proud Katharine was. Nora said he shouldn't have done it, even if he believed what he said, because it was the wrong kind of speech to give in front of his family and returned soldiers.

'What rot, Nora!' Gwenda exclaimed. 'He had every right to say what he did. After all, he'd been to war and knew what it was really like and wanted to do his best to try to stop another war.'

Nora stuck out her tongue but didn't say anything. She knows when to shut up around Gwenda.

June 15th, 1966

Katharine doesn't write about her father's suicide in *Child of the Hurricane,* but she tells us a lot about her husband's. She admits to having had 'absolute faith in him' and doesn't know how she survived when she realized she would never see him again. 'The end of our lives together is still inexplicable to me,' she writes.

Hugo committed suicide after failing in one of the many get-rich-quick schemes he hoped would get them out of debt. He had a couple of jobs with the Government but lost them, probably because his wife was a communist, and he was sympathetic to her views.

She'd had trouble with Hugo for a few years before he killed himself. Katharine trusted him to handle their financial affairs. He mortgaged inherited land in Northam and invested the money in various escapades that never seemed to work. He sold off blocks of land they owned in Greenmount and, at one point, he and Katharine set off for the goldfields: he in search of gold, she in search of material for a book she hoped one day to write. He never struck it rich, no matter how hard he tried.

June 17th, 1966

This arvo, Jill showed me a letter Katharine wrote to Nettie Palmer in August 1931, in which she writes, 'I'm worn to frazzles...not sleeping and trying to work – as *deséspoir* about everything. Jim with no job and colossal debts, having to be sheered off and cheered off nervous breakdown all the time.'

In another letter to a friend, she writes that Hugo 'had dropped his bundle...and I just couldn't stand it; I saw it as a weakness and I didn't expect it of him.' She could, she claimed, carry her 'own and his bundle, but a lot will be lost in the doing. It always is – Damn! Damn! Damn! And again Damn! And I milk the blasted cow and feed the chooks – make the jam and kill and pluck the blasted brutes – and it seems a very good idea to sit on the veranda and drink beer. Only there isn't any beer!'

I felt sorry for Katharine all the way home on the bus.

June 20th, 1966

Jill tells me that Hugo was treated for depression and, like Katharine herself, had severe headaches. 'He'd suffered terribly from his war experiences — he had malaria and meningitis during the war and was probably suffering from shell shock as well,' said Jill. 'How many men must've endured years of hell because of that bloody war! How many men killed themselves because of it?' Jill said, biting her bottom lip and shaking her head.

'Anyway, it was a dude ranch that finished him off,' said Jill. 'It was his final attempt to make some money.

'He met an American who told him all about dude ranches in the USA where people dress up and pretend to be cowboys, and Hugo decided he'd give it a go. This was when Katharine was in Russia. Otherwise, she probably would've put her foot down. The whole thing was a complete disaster,' Jill said with a frown. 'He never made any money at all from the rodeo, and soon afterwards he killed himself. Poor bugger. What I think is very sad is that Hugo named some of the horses on the ranch after his wife's stories: they were called "Working Bullocks", "The Wild Oats of Han", "Windlestraws", and "Kiss on the Lips." Shows you how much he loved and admired her.'

I've written all those names in the 'Must Read' column in my notebook. Can't wait to read them!

'What's really awful about this whole story,' said Jill, 'is that Katharine read about Hugo's suicide in a newspaper in London as she was getting ready to board the ship to return to Australia.'

I felt sick when I heard this. 'How could that have happened? Couldn't someone have sent her a telegram? Or made a phone call to her hotel?' I asked Jill. She slowly shook her head.

On the bus going home, I recalled how, in *Child of the Hurricane*, Katharine tells us that she went to the Soviet Union in 1933, believing that Hugo would do nothing while she was away to make her regret leaving him. Instead, he 'embarked on a wild scheme which he thought would be a money-spinner', but it only pushed him further into debt and 'the depths of despair.' She says she 'could not have imagined that, as a result, he would take his own life.'

'Poor bugger is right,' I whispered. The man sitting next to me smiled and whispered, 'Talking to yourself, missy? Bit lonely, are ya?'

'Mind your own business,' I thought and moved seats. Unfortunately, I sat beside a schoolboy who was scoffing fish and chips – talk about a stink!

June 22nd, 1966

I was telling Nora and Gwenda at morning tea today about how Hugo killed himself and why. When I mentioned the dude ranch, Nora just about choked on her Granita. She said she's heard her grandmother talk about that event and she has seen an advertisement about the dude ranch in her mother's memory box. Nora promised to bring it in to work tomorrow.

June 23rd, 1966

Nora showed me a copy of the dude ranch advertisement! The ranch was called Lazy H1T. The opening was Sunday, 11 am, on 30th July 1933. Nora's mum told her that she and Nora's grandmother went up to the hills that Sunday with a family friend. The friend had just bought a brand new car and Nora's mum says she'll always remember that Sunday because it was her first car trip. She doesn't remember much about Hugo's dude ranch except that she had a horse ride.

Anyway, in the advertisement, the headline is 'To All Horse Lovers' and there's a list of attractions, including a buck jumping exhibition, a band, pony rides, lunch and afternoon tea. The entrance fee was 'One Charge, One Bob.' Nora said her mum told her she'd heard that, on the morning of the opening, the police came by to warn Hugo that, as the rodeo was on a Sunday, and Sunday entertainment was banned, he couldn't charge for admission. Hugo was allowed to collect a silver coin donation, but the money had to go to charity.

Nora also showed me a clipping from the *Swan Express* that was in the memory box. What I think is interesting is that this journalist writes that the Lazy H1T Ranch 'was opened to the public, for the purpose of assisting the funds of the RSL and Greenmount charities.' Poor Hugo! Here he is, desperately trying another get-rich-quick scheme to get out of debt and everything has to go to charity.

The report ends with the journalist pointing out that 'after an invigorating day on the hills, [people] returned home pleasantly weary, leaving the heights and valleys to again drowse in the creeping shadows of eventide.'

A poetic ending for a journalist writing for a local newspaper, one Katharine probably would've liked despite what she might have thought of her husband's dude ranch.

June 24th, 1966

Book group tonight.

Larry told me that before Hugo killed himself, he wrote a new will bequeathing everything to his wife. On the back of the will, he wrote, 'I have never recovered from my 1914-1918 experiences and with this in view, I appeal to the State to see that my wife and child get the usual war pension. No man could have a truer mate.'

So sad, but I like that he called her a 'mate.' My father would never have called my mother a 'mate.' His mates were male, and he was never a friend to my mother; in fact, he was often pretty aggressive towards her, especially after a few beers. When he started picking on her, she wouldn't fight back – just went outside and sat on the back steps and waited till he went to bed. A couple of times I caught her smoking but she denied it.

It's funny, Mum nags me to death about finding a nice bloke to marry, even though she knows she's annoying me, and she's had quite a few ding-dongs with Pete over money – he was always borrowing cash from her and would never pay it back, but she never fought with Dad. I think she might've been a bit scared of him. I reckon she just accepted that she'd be better off with him than without him. After all, she had no money of her own. Before she married, she was a salesgirl at Boans. She often tells me I'm lucky to be a typist and how making me leave school early was the right decision.

I suppose she's right. Typing is a good skill to have. Although, one day, I hope I'll be typing stories rather than insurance contracts.

June 27th, 1966

I saw Jill after work and asked her if she could find some information about Hugo's death.

'Just a tick,' said Jill, and checked the catalogue.

A few minutes later, she returned with some documents.

'This is Hugo's death notice,' Jill said.

The notice reads: 'On November 19, 1933, at Greenmount, Hugo Vivian Hope Throssell, the dearly beloved husband of Katharine and devoted father of Ric. Youngest son of the late Hon. George Throssell. Aged 49 years.'

Jill also showed me The Registrar General's official record, which states: 'Hugo Vivian Hope Throssell, Civil Servant, died by a bullet wound in the head self-inflicted while his mind was deranged due to war wounds.'

The third document was a *West Australian* newspaper clipping for November 20th, 1933, in which the journalist describes how Hugo Throssell was found 'seated in a chair...bleeding from a bullet wound in the right temple and resting on his right shoulder, but still retained in his right hand, was a revolver, from which one bullet had been discharged. He was in pyjamas and his feet were resting against some lattice work.'

I felt sick as I read that. I wonder if we need to know such gruesome details about his suicide. I'll bet Katharine would've been horrified to read that – hope she never did.

Hugo left a note, Jill told me, that read: 'I can't sleep and fear my old war head is going phut, and that's no good for anyone concerned.'

The final document was a clipping from the *West Australian* about Hugo's will and how he asks the government to give his wife a full pension. 'How irritated Katharine would've been to see her name spelt 'Katherine Pritchard' in the newspaper!' Jill said, biting her bottom lip.

Jill said that Hugo's plumed Light Horse hat and his sword were placed on his coffin, and he was buried with full military honours. His grave is Number 304 in the Anglican section of the Karrakatta Cemetery.

One day I'll catch a bus to Karrakatta and put flowers on his grave; I feel so sad for that man.

'After Hugo died,' Jill said, 'Katharine wrote to the government advising them that the war had affected her husband's physical health, but she resented claims that his mind was "deranged". She argued that when he had work, he was never depressed but whenever he lost his jobs, he became more and more desperate.' Jill frowned and slowly shook her head.

'Poor Katharine,' said Jill. 'She had to plead with the government for a war widow's pension.'

Bloody disgusting treatment of a war hero's wife! And how humiliating for Katharine – having to resort to begging for a pension.

When I got home tonight, Mum asked me where I'd been. I told her I'd been to the library and began to tell her about Katharine and Hugo. She listened for a few seconds, then got stuck into me. 'Never you mind talking about that Red Witch and her husband,' she growled. 'Just concentrate on getting your own self a hubby.'

July 8th, 1966

For some reason, I started thinking about Larry tonight. I won't see him until the end of the month but am already looking forward to giving him the latest on my project. He knows a lot about Katharine but always seems interested in what I have to say. He makes me feel like I'm doing something worthwhile. Sometimes I think, hmmm, perhaps Larry? But he's too old for me, although Katharine had a few boyfriends who were much older than she was, so…

In *Child of the Hurricane,* we find out that when Katharine was young, she attracted quite a few older men. She tells us about a sixty-year-old man called 'Dr Paul' who used to visit her when she was a governess in Gippsland. He came twice a week, they read Goethe together, and he helped her with her German. When this 'doctor' declared his love, she says she was 'cruel and uncompromising,' telling him he was too old and that she could never return his feelings. Much later, he tried to poison himself. Katharine writes she blamed herself and was anxious for days until she found out he hadn't died.

Then there was the Welsh sailor, John, an officer with 'sea-blue eyes' she met on a trip to New Zealand with her father. It was a trip she didn't want to take so soon after she arrived home from governessing in Gippsland, but her father needed the break. Katharine found John 'exhilarating' to talk to and was 'delighted and flattered' by his interest in her. He was amused by her determination not to fall in love or get married because she wanted to be a writer.

Speaking of older men, there's her *Preux Chevalier*, the gallant knight who squired her around Sydney after her New Zealand trip. She describes him as a 'man of the world, elegant and assured, accustomed to authority.' She spoke French with him, discussed 'politics, history and poetry', and he was always interested in her writing. He took her to the theatre, concerts, restaurants, the Art Gallery and the State Library. They took trips on the harbour and sat in the moonlight in Manly watching the ferries 'flit to and fro.' All in all, she was 'enchanted and flattered' and thought he was 'the most considerate and fascinating of cavaliers.'

Katharine never tells us who this man is, just that he was 'married, of course, and had a daughter my own age, which I thought was why he was so courteous to me.'

But I reckon she was naïve; he was definitely after her! Why else would a man spend so much time and money on a young woman? I love the bit in *Child of the Hurricane* where they meet an old lady in a park and she tells Katharine, 'Don't trust him, dearie. All men are gay deceivers.' When her *Preux Chevalier* later asks Katharine if she thinks he is a gay deceiver, she tells him that she wouldn't be deceived even if he were! But I think she *was* deceived. She thinks he is just being 'nice' to her and is taken aback when he asks her to make sure she tells no one they've 'been going about together.' He insists that 'people wouldn't understand...There would be no end to malicious gossip,' so Katharine agrees to keep their relationship 'a guilty secret.'

When she returns to Melbourne, she meets her *Preux Chevalier* often for coffee or walks, sometimes for dinner. She claims the 'intellectual companionship' she had with him was stimulating and that he was more 'interesting to talk to than any of the young men who were my friends. I was flattered, and thrilled too, at the thought of being his *chère amie*, but always aware that these meetings must remain secret.'

Oh dear, I thought when I read that.

What is she getting herself into?

Katharine may have preferred the company of older men, but there was one young man she was attracted to. While working as a governess on a property near White Cliffs opal fields, she met the 'red-bearded son of the station owner.' She writes in *Child of the Hurricane* that he was her ideal Australian male, 'tall, slender, reserved and sensible; walking with the graceful slouch of a man more accustomed to riding than walking.' She had promised herself that she would not fall in love but she says, 'for a while Red Beard and I looked at each other as if we were a little dazzled by something inexplicable between us.'

She also uses the word 'inexplicable' to describe the attraction between herself and Hugo. Hugo was thirty-one when they met in London at the hospital where he was being treated for war wounds. She was thirty-two, a journalist, and her first novel, *The Pioneers*, had recently been published. (Must read!) She describes him as a 'gay, irresistible soldier,' and he tells her much later that he'd fallen in love with her when he first saw her walking along the terrace towards him.

What an enormous tragedy that this brave, irresistible man drifted so badly after the war and shot himself after only fourteen years of marriage.

Thinking about the word 'inexplicable.' She uses it to describe the 'currents' between Hugh Watt and Coonardoo; she uses it to describe her feelings for Red Beard; she uses it to describe her feelings when she meets Hugo and again when she tries to understand Hugo's suicide.

Perhaps many things have been *inexplicable* to her throughout her life – but she seems to be the type to dig in and plough on.

I've had a few inexplicable things happen to me too. Allan's drowning, Dad's cancer, and I'm still wondering why we hardly ever hear from Pete. He writes rarely to Mum and never contacts me. I bet if we had a telephone, he'd ring us occasionally and let us know where he is and if he's coming home for Christmas.

July 9th, 1966

This morning, I took the bus to Karrakatta Cemetery and put a bunch of Geraldton Wax on Hugo's grave. I tried hard to imagine the battle he was in and how and why he earned a Victoria Cross but I have no idea what it would be like to be a soldier in a war. My brain just kept returning to how much Katharine loved Hugo and how devastated she was when he committed suicide. I felt heavy all over – the same heaviness I felt when I was reading *Coonardoo* – and was glad to get on the bus and go home.

Dad is buried at Karrakatta, but I wouldn't visit his grave without Mum! She'd be very upset. On the way home, I thought about Dad's funeral. There weren't many people there and I didn't know any of them except Aunty Sheila. I've never liked her – she's such a bloody snob – but I said hello to her towards the end of the ceremony.

July 10th, 1966

Hurray, Mum's gone out so I'm having a nice afternoon browsing *Child of the Hurricane* and reading about how Katharine didn't like painting lessons but at least her teacher, Mr Brookesmith, showed her a new way of looking at things.

He tells her to paint the landscape as she sees it, and she says she was 'surprised to find it was not all blue and green...I saw purple shadows thrown by the rocks, fading to amethyst; golden sands beneath translucent shallows; sapphire of the deep sea; indigo along the horizon. I was so excited to discover the colour and shape of rocks, waves and clouds.' She says that his was 'one of the most valuable lessons' she ever 'received as a writer.' She gained 'new eyes for the vagaries of light and shadow...and an understanding of the need for concentration on the deeper meaning of things and people.'

I like that she adds 'and people' because it seems to me, she isn't so interested in landscape for its own sake; she is interested in how a landscape influences the lives of people who live and work there.

I know I'll never be able to write about landscapes the way Katharine does – perhaps not at all – but she's teaching me how to look at and listen to people. Lately, I've been focusing on one person on my bus and trying to memorize small details like hair, eyes, nose, hands, shoes, bags, clothes, jewellery. If someone near me is chatting, I eavesdrop. At lunchtime, I try to write detailed descriptions of the people I've been watching or a short dialogue between the people I've listened to. I'm enjoying writing my sketches, but they're hard work!

July 18th, 1966

On Saturday night, Gwenda went out with a nice young bloke called Andy. She told us about him during morning tea; they went to the Ambassadors and he put his arm around her. When he was saying goodnight, he tried to kiss her but, for some reason, she ducked, and he missed. She fancies him but doesn't know if they'll see each other again. I'm betting he'll be in touch.

Pity girls have to sit around waiting for the boy to make the next move – so annoying. On the other hand, I would never have the guts to ask a boy out. What if he said 'No'! I'd be so embarrassed. Boys must feel awful when a girl refuses.

Gwenda's little adventure has got me thinking about how Katharine felt about Hugo when she first met him in London. She writes that there was an 'indefinable attraction' between them. Colonel Todd, the man who introduced them, later reckoned it was 'love at first sight.' However, when Katharine leaves London for Australia and Hugo comes to say goodbye, she says they parted 'shaking hands, sadly, without any acknowledgement of an emotional stir between us.'

When Hugo is 'invalided home, suffering from malaria,' and comes to visit her in Melbourne, she sees a 'tall, masterful figure in uniform – returned from the maelstrom of war' and her 'irresolution' about him vanishes: 'He held out his arms, and I walked down the stairs into them.' She tells him she thinks 'the passion' of their love is 'like the colour and wings of the butterflies.' His 'tempestuous love-making' makes her 'feel there was nothing more important than to be alive and in love.'

Katharine and Hugo celebrated their engagement with 'brilliant Queensland butterflies', and they were married in a registry office in Melbourne in January 1919. She was thirty-five and he was thirty-four.

In *Child of the Hurricane,* she says she had promised her *Preux Chevalier* never to marry. He had threatened her with 'dire consequences' if she did. Nothing happened, but he sounds incredibly manipulative, and she must've been worried for quite a while after her marriage that he might do something to hurt her or himself.

I felt uneasy reading these bits about Katharine's relationship with that man. I'd be horrified if an ex-boyfriend threatened me with 'dire consequences' if I ever married. What are 'dire consequences?' Would they include bashing me to a pulp? What if he committed suicide? I'd never forgive myself. I'm sure it would ruin my marriage. It would ruin my whole life.

July 29th, 1966

It's a shame Larry doesn't like *Child of the Hurricane*. I do. He told me tonight at book club to move onto another novel. 'Then we can chat about your Prichard project, Vicki,' he laughed, his brown eyes twinkling behind his glasses.

August 5ᵗʰ, 1966

Gwenda looked very pleased with herself at morning tea. 'What's up with you?' Nora asked her.

'I saw Andy on Saturday night,' she grinned. 'We went to the Ambassadors, then we had a stroll around town. We held hands and laughed and talked a lot. He's really good fun to be with.'

'I knew he'd be in touch,' I chuckled.

August 6ᵗʰ, 1966

Jill suggested I read *Haxby's Circus* next. 'Katharine creates a fascinating world – noisy, gaudy, full of challenges. There are loads of intriguing characters, especially Gina Haxby.'

Can't wait to read it.

August 13ᵗʰ, 1966

Finished *Haxby's Circus*! Loved it. Someone has scribbled in the margins on the first page that it's 'an allegory of the struggle for existence in the great circus of life.' Funny. I've never thought of life as a circus.

I like the way the novel came about. In *Child of the Hurricane*, Katharine describes how she 'kept house' for her brother, Nigel, a doctor. One night, she was alone in the house when a circus rider, about seventeen years old, was brought into the surgery with a broken back. She sat with her until Nigel returned from a house call, and 'the girl's agony and the spirit with which she endured it made a deep impression on my mind...She became the Gina of *Haxby's Circus.*'

So – like Hugh Watt, Coonardoo, Sam Geary and Michael Brady, Gina Haxby is based on a real person. I like that. It makes the story authentic.

Gina is a 'gypsy creature, bright eyed, rough haired, blood blooming under her swarthy skin.' Her circus trick is to somersault from one horse to another. One night she falls and breaks her back. She's 'laid up in plaster of Paris for three months' and while in hospital, she learns all the routines of the 'kitchens, laundries, and out patients departments...If an operation was being performed, she knew who was operating, and why; which nurses were in the theatre...She had sympathy for everyone, the rare irresistible smile of a sunny, exalted character.'

I love this description of Gina. I can imagine if Katherine were laid up in hospital, that's exactly what she would get up to!

As for Gina, she becomes 'a thing of ill omen' who, her family believes, will only be 'a drag on them.' Dan Haxby, dedicated to his 'Lightest, Brightest Little Show on Earth', is an abusive, ignorant bully. He gasps when he hears his daughter has to take it easy for at least two years: 'Gina on her back for another two years, in a wagon? My God, what did they think a circus was? A damned convalescent home?' Gina knows she'll never get to lie around after her accident. He won't even let his wife, Lotty, go to a hospital to give birth – why would he let his daughter slack off?

It's strange. Even though Gina constantly disagrees with Dan Haxby, she's always had a 'secret pride in her father.' She understands it has always been, and always will be, 'the show' that matters most to him. She doesn't blame him for her accident, although almost everybody else does. Gina has grown up 'within hail of the peaked one-poled tents' and she loves the circus world as much as her father does.

August 14th, 1966

Lazy Sunday. Cold and in bed, re-reading *Haxby's Circus*. The landscape descriptions aren't as poetic as in *Black Opal* or as powerful as in *Coonardoo*. They are much sparser and to the point. At the centre of most of them are the circus wagons, crawling like giant beetles across the land.

At one point, we see Gina and her mother passing 'through miles of country pale gold with ripening wheat.' Lotty, pregnant and miserable, has a face that is 'drawn and sallow' and her legs swell 'with the least exertion.' The last thing she wants to look at is wheat fields!

I couldn't help thinking while I was reading this about how much I wanted Lotty not to have another baby. She's already had five boys and two girls!

I feel sorry for Gina's mum, who is very much under the thumb – Dan Haxby's thumb. He controls his family, rarely letting anyone speak to his wife or kids. Gina tells her mother that Dan is 'selfish and careless, like most men.' Lotty's response is to complain. She grumbles and whines about her life, telling Gina her husband treats her like 'a machine for churnin' out acrobats and bare-back riders.' And yet, when Gina finally convinces her mother to run away so that Lotty can give birth to her baby in a hospital, all Lotty can think of is what Dan will say when he finds them. 'Won't he be mad?' she asks Gina. Lotty is not happy being apart from her husband: 'she grumbled and wailed...talked endlessly about Dan and the show.'

After six years – six years! – Dan finally catches up with them! He tells his wife, 'You stick to me, Lotty, and I'll stick to you.' Gina can't understand her mother's reply: 'I'll stick, Dan,' she says to her husband. Gina finally realizes that 'her mother would go through all the years of wandering, child bearing and hardship, again for him...What did she know of this husband-and-wife business which made you go through so much for a man?'

Gina, of course, will never know the answer to her own question because she never marries. I reckon her mum and dad's relationship would put her off marriage forever!

August 15th, 1966

Gwenda, Nora and I are wondering about this new pill girls can take to stop getting pregnant. We're all virgins (well, I think we all are, although sometimes I have my doubts about Gwenda). None of us knows much about birth control but we are curious about what it might be like to have sex. We joke about it occasionally, but in the back of our minds is always the scary thought, 'What if I get pregnant?' We'd have to marry the man, or if he refused, we'd have to give the baby up for adoption. We'd spend the rest of our lives wondering about that child. Then there's the other option – abortion – not something I want to think about.

August 19th, 1966

The routines of the circus are explored in detail in *Haxby's Circus*. As in *Coonardoo* and *Black Opal*, Katharine is very interested in different worlds of work.

Gina Haxby understands every circus routine and is 'shrewd and implacable in her dealing with business men.' She has a nest egg of £100 that she invests in the show. In return, her father agrees to let her 'look after things on the business side.' For a while, after her mother dies in childbirth, Gina's goal is to ruin Dan financially to pay him back for his selfishness. But eventually, having inherited Billy Rocca's estate, Gina relents, buys her father out, gives him the job of general manager and establishes a profit-sharing scheme. The circus makes money, the organisation works 'with a precision that would have done credit to a military camp' and things start to look up for the Lightest, Brightest Little Show on Earth.

I'm really enjoying reading all about the different jobs people have in Katharine's novels. Makes me think about my own job and dream about what I could be doing with my life instead of bashing a bloody great typewriter.

I've written a few sketches lately about interesting-looking people I've seen in town and on the bus, and I have my discovery diary, so at least I have something to do and think about.

August 20th, 1966

When Gina's father dies, she has a nervous breakdown, experiencing a 'deep dissatisfaction, unrest and discouragement with life.' The lion-tamer, Paul Bach, accuses her of standing 'aside from life.' When she asks him what else she can do, he tells her: 'If you give yourself to me, I will show you what else.'

I sniggered at Gina's answer. So formal, yet so eager. She says to Bach, 'I'd be glad to.' And so they become lovers.

I wonder if I'd ever have the courage to say that to a man putting the hard word on me!

After Paul Bach shoots himself. Gina gets drunk regularly and sleeps around with the various animal keepers and good-looking boys in the band. When trapeze artist Jack Dayne asks her 'What on earth's the matter with you, Gi, running amuck like this?' she replies, 'I want to know if there's anything in this business of living...What's the use of standing off from Life, watching it all go by. Three quarters of my life I lived that way. Then I wanted to feel something for myself. There's no reason why I shouldn't really.'

All up, Gina has quite a few lovers. She's a bit like Sophie in *Black Opal* in that respect, becoming a woman who has 'gone the pace' and is the subject of 'spicy gossip.' Not that Sophie or Gina could care less about what the gossips say.

But, unlike Sophie, there's no political 'awakening' for Gina Haxby; she becomes the circus clown and loves the job. How weird!

I hate people laughing at me. If someone laughs at something I say or do and I'm not trying to be funny, I always feel like a real idiot. Gwenda says I take things too personally. She reckons I'm too self-conscious.

When I think about Paul Bach's warning, I get a terrible sinking feeling. Am I just standing by, treading water, watching life go by?

Although I'm not going to do what Gina does to hop into it, I feel a bit anxious about where I'm headed.

Mum keeps nagging me to get married, but I haven't met anyone I want to marry since Allan. The chaps I've been out with were all boring. Maybe I should leave home and get a flat, but I can't afford the rent and I don't think Gwenda or Nora can afford to leave home either so they wouldn't be able to share with me.

I feel a bit trapped at the moment. I think I'd better just put *Haxby's Circus* away for a while.

August 24th, 1966

This morning, Gwenda was in a ferocious mood. She told us about a group of Aboriginal workers who yesterday walked off a station called Wave Hill as a protest against the way they've been treated. 'Lousy bastards,' Gwenda said, slurping her tea furiously.

Nora nodded and said, 'Yes, not fair. They should've talked to the station owners about the problem instead of just walking off like that.'

Gwenda jumped up and went to the sink to re-fill her cup, and her back was rigid. When she turned around, her face was full of thunder. 'I was talking about those lousy bastard owners of Wave Hill who give Aboriginal workers rotten pay or no pay at all and make them live in stinking conditions.'

'Oh,' said Nora. 'I thought you were referring to the Aboriginal workers.'

'Ah, give it a rest, Nora,' I sniffed.

Sometimes Nora gets on my pip.

August 25th, 1966

I spent my lunch hour writing three descriptions of people I've watched this week on the bus. So far this month, I've written twelve pieces. Once I've written them, I put them in a folder that I keep in a drawer on my work desk. Every now and then, I read a sketch or two at lunchtime and try to improve my writing.

Nora came into the tearoom, which was unusual. She usually eats her sandwich at her desk or goes out for lunch. Anyway, I read out one of my sketches. She listened carefully, twirling a strand of her long blond hair and pursing her lips. 'I quite like it, Vicki,' she said when I'd finished. 'But why are you interested in people on your bus?'

'I'm not especially. I'm just working on my observational and writing skills,' I replied.

'Oh, that's nice,' she nodded, taking out her lipstick and peering at herself in her compact mirror.

I could tell she wasn't interested, so I won't read any more of my sketches to Nora.

August 26th, 1966

Jill pointed out to me that Katharine dedicated *Haxby's Circus* to her 'good friends of Wirth's Circus in memory of our time together and their assistant lion tamer.' I hadn't noticed that, as I usually turn straight to page one when I'm reading a book and don't bother with things like dedications. That habit is going to change from now on.

Jill told me a funny story about what happened while Katharine was doing her research for *Haxby's Circus*. 'In 1927,' Jill chuckled, 'Hugo and Katharine watched Wirth's Circus putting up their tents near Midland Junction and Hugo asked George Wirth if Katharine could travel with the circus when they toured country districts of WA so she could see first-hand how circuses work.

'In return, Hugo agreed to take part in a dare-devil act involving his gold wedding ring. Hugo had to hold the ring between two fingers, and sharpshooter "Boris the Cossack" was supposed to shoot through the ring at a bottle in the background. The whole act went wrong because the Cossack missed the bottle. Gladys Wirth had to step in with a rifle, bust the bottle, and pretend everything was okay. It took a while to find Hugo's wedding ring! Sounds pretty dangerous to me. What wouldn't Hugo do for his wife!'

Jill and I had a good laugh, and she ruffled her copper hair. I hadn't noticed before but she's wearing an engagement ring! Don't know her well enough yet to make a comment.

I can't see the point of engagements – a waste of time and money, I reckon. Not that I'd ever say that to Jill.

August 31st, 1966

At the moment I'm extra busy at work. Pounding those bloody keys is wearing me out. Haven't got the energy to read at night, so I haven't done much on my project. Didn't even make it to book group this month. I've had to do Nora's work as well as my own because Nora is on sick leave; she'll be away for another week. I told my boss I didn't think it was fair that I had to do her job as well as my own and suggested he hire a temp. but he glared at me and snarled, 'Stop whining, Vicki. Just do as you're told.'

Actually, I'm finding morning tea lively without Nora. Sometimes Nora sulks and wants to argue. Gwenda thinks more like me than Nora does, as I've discovered since I started my project.

September 30th, 1966

Tonight, Larry and I talked about all the suicides and deaths in Katharine's personal life and in her work. Her father, her husband, Arthur Henty in *Black Opal*, Paul Bach in *Haxby's Circus* – they all commit suicide. Lotty and Dan Haxby die. Poor little Lin in *Haxby's Circus*, who is bullied by Dan into performing on the trapeze, meets a tragic end. Coonardoo has a miserable death. Alan, Katharine's brother, and Rick, Hugo's brother, are killed in the First World War.

This all leaves me feeling a bit numb. Must go to sleep.

October 3rd, 1966

Gwenda, Nora and I talked about suicide this morning. 'One of my uncles killed himself a few years ago,' Nora said. 'Mum was furious with him because he left her sister with three kids and no money. Aunty's never forgiven her husband, nor has Mum.'

'I reckon committing suicide is a cowardly way out,' said Gwenda.

'I do too,' I murmured, but I'm not quite sure about that. Perhaps life for some people really does become so unbearable the best way out is to end it.

I wonder what Katharine thinks about suicide in general. She's had her fair share of it, and she writes about it a lot, so she must have a definite opinion.

October 16th, 1966

A lovely, lazy Sunday. Went for a walk in King's Park with Nora. She doesn't seem very happy these days. She told me her favourite brother, Tom, has joined the Navy and now her oldest brother, Danny, wants to leave home. Her parents are having rows about it, and she's fed up listening to them. 'Mum doesn't want Danny to move out, nor do I,' she said mournfully. 'He's the one who organizes our parties. If he goes, we probably won't have any more. And I'll really miss Tom. We talk a lot about everything.'

'I always enjoy your parties, Nora,' I said, holding her hand. 'But maybe it's time to get a project.'

'Well, I know *you* have one,' she replied. 'And of course *Gwenda* has her night classes, and now she has Andy too. But *I* don't seem to have anything.'

I thought her tone was a touch sarcastic.

Could she be jealous? If so, she shouldn't be. She's very pretty; when we're out together, the boys always look at her first. She's good fun at parties, especially at her brothers' parties. She really lets her hair down! She can jive all night.

'Why don't you learn the piano?' I asked Nora later as we were slurping spearmint milkshakes. 'Or a language?'

'Nah, can't be bothered,' she replied, then sighed and looked sulky.

Sometimes I think Nora lacks imagination and likes to whinge.

October 29th, 1966

Larry wasn't at book club last night, so I had to talk to someone else for a change. Fortunately, I met a woman who has read *Haxby's Circus*. She told me that she'd read somewhere that *Haxby's Circus* was going to be turned into a film, but she doesn't think it was ever made.

Shame. I'd love to see a film of *Haxby's Circus*.

November 1st, 1966

Dropped by the library after work today, and Jill told me that Katharine wanted to call *Haxby's Circus* "*Fay's Circus*", but the Aussie publishers rejected the title. However, it was published in America under that name, and the Haxby family are called Fay.

There are sections in *Fay's Circus* that the Australian publishers cut out. Jill put paper clips on these pages for me to read.

In a nutshell, there's a fight over cards between two circus performers, strong-man Sailor and Jack. Later, they have a boxing match, which goes on for ages! According to Jill, Katharine based her description of the boxing match on one she had seen where Hugo had been the referee.

There's also a terrific description of a storm that the circus has to battle on its way to Wee Waa in NSW. The Aussie publishers shouldn't have cut that out. I love reading about storms. I like storms in real life, too, especially summer storms. I love the battle between thunder, lightning and galloping wind until they finally defeat the suffocating heat and then, at last – the deluge.

Jill also told me that *Haxby's Circus* sold lots of copies and made her some money at last.

November 2nd, 1966

Today, Gwenda, Nora and I decided to eat our sandwiches in the Supreme Court Gardens. We were chatting as usual about anything and everything. I told them about Dan and Lotty Haxby and how Lotty was willing to go back to her husband even though he was a bully. 'Did he bash her up?' asked Nora. When I told her he didn't, she said, 'Well, that's something I suppose. She probably thought she'd be better off with him than without him.' For some reason, I was really angry with Nora's response, but I just took a bite of my ham sandwich and changed the subject.

Gwenda didn't say anything at the time, but, on the way back to our desks, while Nora was in the toilet, she told me that one of her uncles used to get drunk and bash her aunty – twisted her arm, hit her in the face, swore at her, locked her out of the house once. 'Mum said Aunty Rosie put up with him until the day he dropped dead of a heart attack. She told my mother at the funeral his death was good riddance to bad rubbish.'

I can't understand how a man could bash his wife, and I can't understand why the wife wouldn't leave her husband if he bashed her. But I suppose husband-and-wife relationships are very complicated. Dad was verbally abusive but he never hit Mum. If he had, I reckon she would've wanted to leave him but where would she have gone? I wonder if she would've taken me and Pete with her. I think we would've had to go to a children's home or something because she never had any money of her own and would never have been able to afford to keep us and pay rent.

I've never thought about it before, but Mum's okay even though Dad has gone. The house is all hers, and she gets a pension and my board.

November 14th, 1966

This morning, Gwenda was telling us about her date on Saturday night with Andy. She says he tongue-kissed her goodnight. We all looked at each other, and Nora said, 'I wonder if it's the best kiss you'll ever get.' Gwenda giggled and said, 'I'll let you know.'

Nora glared at her and muttered, 'Don't rub it in.'

November 20th, 1966

Lately, I've been wondering why Katharine became a communist. Have to ask Larry. He'll know. I'm interested to find out why people seem to be so scared of communism, why communists are sneered at and called 'Reds', and why they always seem to be in the wrong in news stories.

November 25th, 1966

Tonight at book club, Larry told me a bit about a bloke called Guido Baracchi. 'He taught classes in Marxism in Melbourne, and Katharine was one of his students,' Larry said. 'And like her, he was a founding member of the Communist Party of Australia. He's still alive, and he has never given up on communism.

'I used to discuss him, among other anti-war activists, in my history classes. He's a good example of someone who completely disowned his wealthy, conservative background and committed to radical ideas his family would've hated. He's a bit like Katharine's Hugo in that respect. Baracchi joined various communist parties overseas, as well as the Communist Party of Australia, and was very active in the peace movement during the First World War. He was jailed in 1918 for discouraging recruitment for the War. He was seen by authorities as a troublemaker. Most of my students liked the sound of him!'

Larry laughed a lot when he was telling me about Baracchi's womanising. 'He's a bit of a ladies-man. Even Katharine fell for him. In an interview, she said she met him on board a ship in Ceylon headed to Australia and they discussed politics. He gave her a list of revolutionary books to read and she was so impressed with him and his political views that she read them all!

'Baracchi is a real larrikin. I'd love to meet that bloke,' he said with a big grin.

I can't sleep, so I'm browsing the bits in *Child of the Hurricane* where Katharine writes about the poverty and homelessness she saw everywhere in London: 'women...with their heads in paper bags and their feet wrapped up in newspaper...men of all ages...lined up in a queue...waiting until two o'clock in the morning when a soup-kitchen opened.' Katharine tells us that London became 'just the biggest, dirtiest, wickedest place I ever had room in my imagination for.' She writes that she could 'never forget the impression made on me by that night's experiences...The problem of how such poverty and suffering could be prevented, haunted my mind.'

Katharine finally decided the world needed a 'practical plan to prevent poverty, superstition and injustice wrecking so many lives.'

That practical plan, for Katharine, is communism. No wonder she was attracted to Guido Baracchi!

November 29th, 1966

I asked Jill this arvo if she knows anything about Guido Baracchi.

'I know he was a member of the Communist Party and I've heard he had an affair with Katharine,' she said. 'I read somewhere that Hugo had been jealous of Baracchi and once called him Katharine's "greasy, hand-kissing dago." When I was researching Katharine for my thesis, I noticed there seemed to be a lot of gossip about her. She's always been pretty controversial.' Jill scowled and banged a couple of books on the table. 'Anyway, I've got a headache,' she said, 'but I'll find something on Baracchi for you when I have time.'

I got the message she'd had enough of me for the moment, so I wandered over to a desk and sat quietly. I also noticed she wasn't wearing her engagement ring.

I've heard my mother use the word 'dago' when talking about the Italian migrants in East Perth. She also calls Catholics 'micks' and has some terrible names for Aboriginal people. My mother really gets on my pip when she calls people names, even more than when she nags me about getting married.

December 10th, 1966

Well, Jill found quite a few bits and pieces about this Guido Barrachi and gave me a bunch of notes.

One is about how Baracchi's great passion has always been communism and how he encouraged Katharine to learn as much as she could about it, which she has done.

A second note is a quote from a letter Katharine wrote to her friend Nettie Palmer in which she discloses that she'd recently spent 'two perfect blue days wandering about the hills' in Emerald with Guido. They stayed in her cottage and she wrote that she was 'better in mind and body than I have been for a very long time.'

In a third note, Jill has scribbled: 'Of all things Katharine liked most about him were his eyes. She says that he has "blue eyes, the colour of forget-me-nots...The blue in them is a finer flower and the pupils large and dark as his soul is. They have long lashes and even when I hate him I love his eyes.'"

Wow! A communist with a dark soul and blue eyes! I wonder what he's up to these days.

December 13th, 1966

'Tell me more about Guido Baracchi, Jill,' I said.

Jill laughed. 'Well, you seem interested in this chap, Vicki!'

'I certainly am!' I replied. I've never met or read about anyone like Guido Baracchi. I reckon he'd be the kind of man I'd go out with now. I'm dying to date someone completely different from some of the duds I've gone out with.

'Okay, well, I've read he's had lots of girlfriends, including a playwright called Betty Roland. You'd be interested in Betty Roland. She took off to the Soviet Union with Baracchi, and just before they left, they went to Greenmount to visit Katharine. In 1933, Katharine went to the Soviet Union and visited them in Moscow. I'm not sure Betty Roland thought much of Katharine, although she admired her as a writer.'

According to Jill, Betty Roland wondered why Katharine had married Hugo. She thought they had little in common and reckoned that Katharine wouldn't approve of the Victoria Cross.

Jill told me Betty Roland also claimed that when Hugo was alive, Katharine refused to call herself Mrs Hugo Throssell; she was always Katharine Susannah Prichard, the writer. 'But Betty Roland was wrong,' says Jill. 'She called herself Mrs Throssell in all kinds of situations when her husband was alive. These days she probably prefers Katharine Prichard. She's also Comrade Katharine.'

'Comrade Katharine.' That's nice. I wouldn't mind being called 'Comrade.' It has a nice ring to it and being a 'Comrade' would make me feel I belonged to a very big and important organisation. Maybe I'll breeze into morning tea one day and say, 'Hi Comrade Gwenda! Hello Comrade Nora!'

December 25th, 1966

Christmas tea was good this year. The ham was yummy and, for once, Mum didn't carry on because I refused to eat her trifle. Can't stand that muck!

We watched television for a while. Mum likes murder mysteries and funny shows. I like dramas and documentaries, but I don't watch TV much. I'd rather read.

I got bored and walked around the block. It's a hot night, and there are lots of kids playing in the street.

December 26th, 1966

Well, we did our usual thing for Boxing Day. Mrs Cook, our next-door neighbour, came around ten o'clock for drinks. She always brings beer and Sparkling Burgundy and guzzles almost the whole bottle! I'm allowed one glass. Mum hates wine. She drinks shandies.

I was proud of Mum this year because she served Christmas cake and walnuts, although they weren't shelled, and she didn't bring out the nutcracker, so we ended up not eating any. She usually doesn't offer food to neighbours. Mum's a bit mean where food and visitors are concerned; the best she'll do is a cup of tea.

By one o'clock, it was stinking hot, so Mum and I hopped on the bus and went to City Beach. Gorgeous day! The ocean sparkled turquoise, and there were lazy waves. Mum doesn't swim; she just splashes about in the shallows, but I love swimming out past the breakers at the end of the Groyne, floating on my back and looking at the sky. The rise and fall of the water always makes me feel completely relaxed. Unless there's a shark alarm, and then it's panic time trying to get to shore.

At sundown, we caught a bus back and, on the way home, Mum asked, 'Why don't you think about starting a Glory Box, Vicki? It could be your New Year's resolution!'

I was so angry that I didn't speak to her for the rest of the trip and went straight to my bedroom when we got home. Start a Glory Box! Will she ever stop nagging! If I ever have any money left over from my pay, it won't be going towards any bloody Glory Box. I'll stash it away with a detailed plan on how to leave home. Now there's something worth thinking about for a New Year's resolution!

December 30th, 1966

I am now so curious about Katharine's communist beliefs! Tonight at book group, Larry told me to read a copy of her essay, 'Why I Am a Communist.'

'Okay,' I said. 'I just want to find out how she thinks so I can better understand her work.' Larry nodded and said, 'That's right, Vicki. You have a project, so you should do it properly.'

He sounded just like a teacher talking to one of his students, and I couldn't help laughing. He frowned, then gave me a sly grin.

Anyway, we had our book club Christmas party tonight. As well as the usual sherry and whiskey – which I never drink, hate the smell of both – there was Sparkling Burgundy! I had a couple of glasses and was headed for a third when I spied that horrible Chinese vase at the end of the table, well away from its usual spot on the windowsill. I pretended to stumble and nearly managed to knock it off the table. Worse luck, the bloody thing stayed rock-solid.

January 8th, 1967

On the bus this morning going to work, I read Katharine's marvellous description in *Child of the Hurricane* of how she was walking across Prince's Bridge in Melbourne one night and saw the 'first posters proclaiming the revolution in Russia.' Suddenly, 'everything was suffused in golden light. In a daze of excitement and rejoicing, it seemed this was an omen for the future. That the revolution was an event of world-shaking importance I didn't doubt.'

She immediately begins to study books by Lenin, Trotsky, Marx and Engels and discusses them with her friends, including Baracchi, who confirms her 'impression that these theories provided the only logical basis...for the reorganization of our social system...It was the answer to what I had been seeking: a satisfactory explanation of the wealth and power which control our lives…and how in the processes of social evolution, they could be directed towards the well-being of a majority of the people, so that poverty, disease, prostitution, superstition and war would be eliminated.'

I read that passage to Gwenda and Nora at morning tea today. Gwenda sighed and said it was idealistic, but in her heart-of-hearts, she wishes everything Katharine believes in could happen one day. Nora snorted and said, 'What rubbish. How could anyone believe such rot?' I said to Nora it was like a religious experience for Katharine. Surely, she could understand that being a church-goer. Nora just glared at me.

Gwenda changed the subject. She's been out several times with Andy and is becoming keen on him. She says he's a great kisser!

January 15th, 1967

Our book group had an afternoon tea in King's Park today to celebrate the New Year. We talked about what we've been reading lately, apart from book club choices. I realised that the only books I've read since Gwenda told me about *Coonardoo* have all been by Katharine.

After afternoon tea, I told Larry how much Katharine occupies my time and he laughed. He seemed happy for me and said that although he hasn't read everything she has written, he likes what he has read. He doesn't agree with her communist ideas, but, he said, he can certainly see her point of view.

He didn't call Katharine's ideas 'rubbish' like Nora did.

As we were saying our goodbyes, he sang a little song that ended:

> With Lenin to guide them,

> And Stalin beside them,

> The workers' red flag was unfurled.

'Can't remember the rest,' he said with a grin as he waved goodbye, 'but that's the kind of song Prichard would like. Pity she feels that way about Stalin, though.'

January 16th, 1967

I went to the library today after work, and Jill found a copy of Katharine's article, 'Why I am a Communist.' She wrote it in 1956, and Jill told me that Katharine claims everything she believes to be important is in this pamphlet.

I've been reading 'Why I am a Communist' since I went to bed. Now it's past midnight and I must write something about it in my diary. I'll keep it short because it's late and I have to get up early to work for the capitalists. Here goes:

When she was a young journalist, she saw the 'poverty and injustices' people had to put up with 'in the slums of Melbourne' and she talked to girls from the Anti-Sweating League 'who were nervous wrecks as a result of working long hours on high-pressure machines for low wages.'

'What's changed?' I thought. Gwenda, Nora and I work long

hours for a pittance and I reckon those old typewriters are high-pressure machines. We all have sore fingers and stiff wrists from banging away at those bloody great monsters all day long. It's hell when you have to do two or three carbon copies!

Katharine goes on to say that she met women who told her that they were 'often expected to submit to the lust of unscrupulous employers' in exchange for extra work.' I giggled when I read that, and then I got angry. That is similar to what happened to Nora when she first started working in our typing pool. She wanted to make some extra money and asked if she could work on Saturday mornings. Our boss, Mr Bagot, said yes. Trouble is, he started leaning over her as she was typing and rubbing himself up against her as he was explaining complicated documents. One morning he kissed her smack on the mouth and put her hand on his crotch. Nora has told only Gwenda and me about it. She ended up working four Saturdays, then decided the extra money wasn't worth it. We both said, 'Good on you, Nora.'

Later, Gwenda suggested Nora should tell someone about what happened, but who was there to tell? Nora would've been too embarrassed and scared to report Mr Bagot to anyone. Besides, we all knew nothing would be done about it. Men rule the roost at work. We've never discussed it since, but from then on, we've called our boss Maggot.

Gwenda and I reckon Nora still feels anxious about the incident, especially when Maggot bangs on the tearoom window or gives us the thumb jerk. He always stares at Nora and, although she's never admitted it, we think she's a bit nervous around him.

In 'Why I am a Communist,' Katharine tells us that when she was about nine, she watched her family's furniture 'piled on carts driving along the road, and a red auctioneers flag over the gate.' Her father was 'ill and had no work' and they had to sell the furniture to pay the bills. She says that her parents were 'never well enough off to live without anxiety as to how they were going to provide for the needs of their growing children,' and that 'their struggle...made me naturally sympathetic to others struggling with the same problem.'

Katharine describes capitalism as an unfair and 'vicious system of every man for himself.' She believes capitalism promotes and rewards the competitive, the greedy and the already rich and powerful. It discriminates against the disadvantaged and neglects and abuses the weak. She urges workers to cooperate and unite to fight the capitalists who force them to work hard for low wages while making huge profits. She's convinced that communism would permit workers to control and administer their workplaces and reward them with a fairer share of the profits.

Katharine also believes that capitalism encourages the manufacture and testing of weapons and supports arms races and war, whereas communism's fundamental aim is to achieve peace via deterrence, dialogue and negotiation.

For Katharine, capitalism is overwhelmingly a selfish, unfair and unjust system operating under the guise of freedom and democracy. There can be 'no real democracy while wealth weighs the scales against the interests of the people,' she declares. After reading widely and thinking deeply, Katharine believes that communism is the fairest and best system to provide the material needs of people. This means life would no longer be a struggle to survive, giving workers more time to pursue personal interests. I love her conclusion: 'A plant grows to its most perfect flowering and finest fruit in good soil.'

I reckon it'll be an uphill slog for Aussie commies, but wouldn't it be fantastic if Katharine turns out to be right?

January 23ʳᵈ, 1967

Gwenda told us at morning tea that she remembers listening to a communist one Sunday arvo at the Esplanade. Gwenda stood on a chair, lifted her cup and imitated the speaker: 'Karl Marx tells us that "The proletarians have nothing to lose but their chains. They have a world to win. Working men of all countries, unite!"' Nora and I both laughed and clapped.

Nora snapped that she was clapping for Gwenda's performance, not for Karl Marx's ideas. I was clapping for both.

Gwenda told us that before her mum married her father, he used to go to political meetings at the Trades Hall. Gwenda's mother has always been interested in politics and Australian history and she's the one who told Gwenda to read *Coonardoo*. Gwenda's parents believe that working people will always have to battle hard to win better wages and conditions because employers will never forego profits to help their employees live better lives. Gwenda believes that too.

Gwenda knows so much and talks about serious things with her parents! My mum hardly ever talks about anything with me. If we do start a conversation that I think might interest her, it quickly ends up with the same old question: 'So when are you going to find a nice young bloke and get married, Vicki?' Nora says it's the same with her mother.

At lunchtime, Gwenda popped into the tearoom to eat her sandwich. 'What are you up to, Vicki?' she asked with interest. I gave her the sketch I was writing and asked her to read it. She liked it! 'Keep at it, Vicki,' she laughed. 'Maybe one day you'll be a writer.'

'I wouldn't mind having a go at journalism,' I replied.

'Good on you! You should check out how to go about it,' Gwenda smiled.

When she left the tearoom, I thought about how differently Nora responded to my sketches. It's nice to get some encouragement!

February 15th, 1967

This arvo, Jill showed me copies of some letters between Miles Franklin and Katharine where they discuss 'bloody revolution.' In one letter, Katharine tells Miles Franklin that communists 'want the transition to be without violence; but we refuse to deceive the people. We say the chances are that there will be resistance to a new order of society, from the money-grubbers & aristocrats of the old regime. But we must be prepared to defend the workers from their vengeance.'

In another letter, she tells Miles Franklin that she is 'so grateful to have understood Communism, which makes my mind clear & serene about what I should do. This, after long study & experience, keeps me fighting wrong & injustice. Communism is really a religion, a love & service to humanity – not sentimental & based on supernatural fantasies – but practical, courageously facing realities, & through education & organization, striving to bring people to a realisation of their own divinity & power.'

Interesting that she sees communism as a religion and that she believes people have 'divinity and power.' I like the idea that people have power, not so sure about divinity.

These letters are dated in the 1950s, and around that time, Jill told me, Katharine was nominated for the Nobel Prize. 'She never received it, but it shows what a great writer she is,' said Jill.

Jill suggested I read *The Real Russia*, Katharine's account of her trip to the Soviet Union in 1933, so I've borrowed it and can't wait to read it. Jill told me the Communist Party of Australia wanted Katharine to submit *The Real Russia* to them before it was published so they could check out what she said about the Soviet Union. Katharine refused.

She may be a communist but she's not going to be told what to write about by the Communist Party of Australia! Cheeky buggers!

February 28th, 1967

There are twenty-five short chapters in *The Real Russia*. In the first chapter, she tells us that she travelled 'something like thirty thousand miles. From the villages about Moscow and Leningrad to the Ukraine, the Kuban, the North Caucasus, through the Mordva, Baskir, Chuvash and Tartar Republics to Western Siberia and the Altai Mountains.'

I've never heard of most of those places. They all sound so exotic!

Katharine says she had 'yarns with Kazaks and Tartars: with old Bolsheviks who had never dreamed of watching their dreams come true. Yarns with gypsies, Cossacks, kulaks, aristocrats of the old regime' and many others, including collective farmers, women engineers, poets, dentists and musicians.

She tells us she 'did not want to be a tourist in Russia; to have it said that I had made a "conducted tour", saw only what the Soviet Government wanted me to see…Nobody suggested what I should do; where I should go. I just arrived, and proceeded, as I have done in London, Paris, New York, Melbourne or Sydney.'

Imagine being able to say you've walked the streets of London, Paris, New York, Melbourne and Sydney. Wow!

March 8ᵗʰ, 1967

This morning I told Gwenda and Nora about Katharine's trip to the Soviet Union. 'She travelled around the country meeting lots of locals. She loved meeting people and chatting about their lives. Everyone she met was friendly and happy.'

Nora looked sceptical, then declared she doesn't believe Katharine. 'Everyone knows,' she said, 'that the Soviet Union will say anything to persuade us that their way of living is the best.'

'But don't we do that too?' I asked Nora.

'No!' she sneered. 'We never pretend to be something we're not; we don't promote propaganda and lies like Russia does. We're free; they're not.'

I don't want to argue with Nora, but sometimes I think she's as inflexible and intolerant as my mum.

It's bedtime, but I'm still thinking about Nora's remarks: I don't feel free. I have to work hard all day at a boring job and get paid next to nothing. My wrists hurt from pounding those bloody keys. I can rarely afford to buy Christmas or birthday presents. I hardly ever buy new clothes. I've never had a holiday on my own or with a friend. If freedom means I have to marry a man who has a steady job so I can stay home and have kids, well, thanks very much, I don't want that kind of freedom.

March 13th, 1967

I love the chapter in *The Real Russia* covering everyday life – her descriptions of the open markets and co-op shops and what 'enormous eaters' the Russians are. She tells us about the workers' flats where tenants pay no more than 10 per cent of their income on rent.

If rents in Perth were no more than 10 per cent of a worker's income, I could move out of home! Sounds good to me!

I don't think I've ever read anything positive about the Soviet Union in the *West Australian* or *The Daily News*. We're bombarded with stories about 'Reds under the beds', about concentration camps in Siberia, how trade unions are full of communists and are always causing strikes, that communists want a bloody revolution, that they want to destroy our democracy and the Australian way of life. It is always 'The Free World' vs 'The Communist Bloc.' We're told we all enjoy free speech and the good life, whereas people living in communist countries, especially in the Soviet Union, are poor, oppressed and jailed for criticising their country.

Sometimes I put the newspaper down and think about a story I've just read about the communists and ask myself, 'Is that really true? Surely there must be something good about communism? After all, millions of people, including Katharine, believe in it.'

Anyway, I reckon there's a way to read newspapers: you can believe everything you read, as Mum and Nora do, and insist you're reading the truth. Or you can be sceptical about what you read, as Gwenda is. Gwenda questions almost everything she reads in the papers and often goes to the library to research what she has read. I lean more towards Gwenda's approach when it comes to newspapers.

I'd love to do what Katharine did – go to the Soviet Union and check things out for myself.

March 17th, 1967

Nora was off sick today with a cold, and Gwenda just wanted to talk about her boyfriend. Blah, blah, blah.

After work, I went to the library and asked Jill about *The Real Russia*. I was happy to wait until she found some information about it because it wasn't late, and I didn't want to go home and have tea with Mum.

All Jill could find was an article by a critic who said that Katharine 'eagerly swallowed everything…that was fed to her by the authorities.' According to this person, *The Real Russia* is 'pure propaganda' because she simply ignored anything that didn't fit in with her ideas about what the Soviet Union stood for.

Jill leaned across the counter towards me and said quietly, 'Katharine wasn't the only one who made the pilgrimage to the Soviet Union to see for themselves what it was like to live in a country trying to establish socialism. Lots of people did it, and most of them thoroughly approved of what they saw. Betty Roland even joined the Communist Party of Australia when she came back from Russia.'

'Oh,' I said. I couldn't think of anything else to say. Sometimes I'm a bit overwhelmed by how much Jill knows about the life of Katharine.

Jill also told me about a political stoush Katharine became involved in over the jailing in the Soviet Union of two Jewish writers called Sinavsky and Daniel. Apparently almost all Australian writers, including some members of the Communist Party of Australia, protested against the Soviet Union's treatment of these two writers but Katharine wouldn't support their petitions. 'Most of Katharine's friends who were members of the Communist Party of Australia left the Party in the 1950s, but Katharine has always remained loyal,' Jill said. 'Not necessarily to the Party itself, but to communism as an idea.

'Katharine once led a campaign in the 1950s against Prime Minister Robert Menzies when he wanted to ban the Communist Party of Australia, but she didn't get much support for her petition. Even her old friend Miles Franklin refused to sign it, saying, "No campaigns for me at the moment. I'm glad you still seem to have some strength left. I haven't. A plague on both sides.'"

Jill showed me Katharine's letter in reply: she writes 'Come what may, I'm content to serve my star, the well-being of humanity, in the only way which, as far as I can see, it may be served.' In another letter, she writes that she can serve, with her pen, 'the only cause on earth worth fighting for.'

Despite their differences, Jill told me that Miles Franklin and Katharine were great friends, although they rarely saw each other, given that Miles Franklin lived in Sydney. They wrote letters to each other often, right up until Miles Franklin died in 1954.

Jill showed me a letter Miles Franklin wrote to Katharine inviting her to visit and 'drink tea from the waratah cup,' a tea cup Miles Franklin offered all visitors, and to sign her visitor's book.

Katharine finally visited Miles Franklin in August 1947, and Jill showed me what she wrote in the visitor's book. It reads 'Exquisite and unique – as the psyche of Miles, herself – the waratah cup from which I have drunk and been refreshed. Katharine Susannah.'

Jill also showed me a photo of the teacup and saucer. It has a waratah design and looks beautiful and fragile.

Before I left the library, Jill said thoughtfully, 'Friends, even in similar political circles, often have different opinions. Miles Franklin was no communist but she was pretty left-wing, always supported workers' rights, and believed Katharine had every right to her promote views. According to Miles Franklin, Katharine is a writer "of tonnage."'

A writer of tonnage!

Love that description of Katharine!

March 31st, 1967

Larry told me Jill is right; lots of people from all over the world went to the Soviet Union in the 1930s and 40s to find out how their system was working.

He told me that Paul Robeson, the American Negro singer, and his wife, Essie, went to Russia in 1934. 'One day they were walking in Pushkin Square when a little girl ran up to Paul Robeson and hugged his knees,' Larry said. 'Paul Robeson was so thrilled with the little girl's action he laughed out loud and said to his wife that obviously kids have never been told to fear black men. Apparently, Robeson has been pro-communist ever since.'

According to Larry, Katharine met Paul Robeson when he came to WA in 1960. 'They shook hands, and he congratulated Katharine on receiving the Joliot Curie Peace Medal she had been awarded in 1959. There was a reception for him at the Palace Hotel and some guests told him the Collie miners were on strike. He said, "I don't know what they're striking about but I'm on their side."'

He sounds like a very nice bloke!

Larry also told me a bit about Betty Roland and Guido Baracchi's trip to the Soviet Union. 'They worked and lived in a small flat in Moscow,' he said. 'Sometime in August 1933, Prichard visited them. She was staying at the Lux Hotel, a fancy spot reserved for party members and overseas delegates. She was a persona grata in the Soviet Union compared with being a persona non grata as she is in Perth! Anyway, Prichard didn't like the Lux Hotel and Roland and Baracchi invited her to stay in their flat, which she did.

'Betty Roland later claimed that Prichard was disappointed with her trip to Siberia. When she returned to Moscow, she was disillusioned and fed up.'

'I didn't get the impression from reading *The Real Russia* that Katharine was disillusioned about anything she saw,' I said to Larry. He shrugged and replied, 'I haven't read the book. But I'd love to go to Russia one day. Of course, it wouldn't be like it was in 1933. I'd be interested in travelling around and having a good look at different cities and institutions, especially schools.'

As we were leaving, he said he'd read that Katharine was very disappointed with *The Real Russia* when it was published as a book in 1934. 'I gather there are loads of printer errors, and her name is misspelt on the inside.'

Come to think of it, I did notice that her name was spelt 'Katherine Suzanne Prichard' inside, although her name is spelled correctly on the cover. I'll bet that annoyed Katharine!

April 2nd, 1967

Mum's gone to Mrs Cook's to play cards. She reckons they don't play for money, but I know they do because Mrs Cook told me so.

Mum always seems to have a bit of money tucked away. When my dad was alive, she used to joke about how she hid a little bit each week from the housekeeping so she could layby for Christmas. Dad gave Mum what she called 'housekeeping' out of his wages, and he paid all the bills. I don't think he ever told my mum how much he earned. Mum would never have asked.

I've just read the chapter in *The Real Russia* where Katharine writes that there is a death penalty 'by shooting' in Russia but it is only ever authorised 'in the case of persons whose acts have been dangerous to the community in an extreme degree.'

It's not clear whether or not she approves of this practice. I certainly don't. I think the death penalty is out-and-out murder by the State. Even though Eric Cooke committed all those horrendous murders in Perth, and we were all terrified for months that he was prowling around looking for another chance to kill, he shouldn't have been hanged.

April 4th, 1967

We talked about Eric Cooke at morning tea today. Nora said she's glad he was hanged. 'He was a murderer and deserved what he got,' she growled. 'Mum put locks on all our windows and kept the front light on all night the whole time that monster was on the hunt.'

'We were all scared,' Gwenda nodded. 'I think that's when everyone in Perth started to lock their doors at night.'

Yes, we *were* scared. Something like that had never happened before in Perth. But still, that doesn't change the fact that I am against capital punishment. Hanging Eric Cook was not the right thing to do. Capital punishment is a primitive, eye-for-an-eye kind of justice. Gwenda agrees with me.

April 10th, 1967

In *The Real Russia,* Katharine tells us that in 1933, there were '548 universities in the Soviet Union', and she always found students she met 'self-reliant, fearless and friendly.' Five hundred and forty-eight universities! In 1933! How many are there in Australia right now? About ten? Places none of us will ever see the inside of, anyway, except perhaps Gwenda one day. If she's lucky, that is.

Gwenda told us the other day that she sat for the uni entrance exam but didn't get in. Not sure why. She didn't give us details. Her mother knows she hates working as a typist and suggested Gwenda try nursing. 'Can't see myself as a nurse,' she said glumly. 'I hate hospitals. I've decided to take a break, read lots of history books, see Andy more often. I'll go back to night school next year.'

'Getting serious with Andy, is it?' I asked Gwenda.

'Possibly,' she replied. 'I really do like him.'

'Well, aren't you the lucky one!' cried Nora, tossing her blond hair.

Gwenda said she had some urgent documents to type and left the tearoom. Nora asked me what I thought about Gwenda and Andy.

'I didn't think she'd be the first one of us to get a regular boyfriend,' she said quietly, opening her compact and pouting at the mirror.

'I always thought you'd be first,' I replied. She looked at me expectantly, so I added, 'Boys always notice you, and you know how to flirt.'

Nora put on lipstick, smacked her lips, smiled happily, and said, 'Let's go back to our desks before Maggot arrives to harass us.'

'Yep, let's,' I laughed. Arm-in-arm, we sauntered back to the typing pool.

April 21st, 1967

After finishing *The Real Russia*, I realized I'd never read a book about Russia by a person who has been there. That's one reason why I enjoyed *The Real Russia*. But I especially liked it because it's Katharine's personal account of what she did, saw and heard while she travelled all over that huge country.

One of my favourite passages is about how, one hot summer evening, she strolled along the canal in Gorki Park, 'brilliant with lights, and decorated with baskets of growing flowers.' Later, in the long twilight, she watched young men and women dive and swim far out into the river while 'older people' sat listening to an 'open air concert.' It sounds lovely.

April 25th, 1967

I thought about Hugo today and how sad Katharine must be on ANZAC Day.

And how sad lots of wives, sisters and mothers are today. I wonder how many of them are proud, how many are sad, and how many are angry at the waste of life?

May 14th, 1967

Nora gave me *The Pioneers* by Katharine. She said her mum gave it to her to give to me. 'She was cleaning out a cupboard and found it and remembered I'd told her about your project, Vicki,' said Nora.

I'm dying to read *The Pioneers*. It's the book that won Katharine a big prize in 1915 and made her famous.

May 15th, 1967

I read the first few pages of *The Pioneers* and I'm struck by how similar the opening of this novel is to the openings of *Haxby's Circus* and *Black Opal*. They all describe vehicles of some sort moving through a landscape.

In *The Pioneers*, a wagon comes 'to rest among the trees an hour or two before sunset. It was a covered-in dray, and had been brought to in a little clearing of the scrubby undergrowth. Two horses had drawn it all the way from the coast.'

In *Black Opal*, we see a 'string of vehicles' moving slowly 'out of the New Town, taking the road over the long, low slope of the Ridge to the plains. Nothing was moving on the wide stretch of the plains, or under the fine, clear blue sky of early spring, except this train of shabby, dust-covered vehicles.'

And in *Haxby's Circus*, a 'very dusty and jaded' bunch of 'circus wagons and horses' move 'slowly along the wide dusty street of the little up-country town, between scattered houses and weatherboard, sun-bleached shops with verandah posts over the footpaths.'

All of these openings are powerfully visual, just like the opening of a film. Katharine has such an imaginative approach to beginning a novel.

In *Child of the Hurricane,* she tells us an amusing story about how, when she visits Hugo in hospital in London, he tells her that he's been reading *The Pioneers*. She expected 'some complimentary remarks.' Instead, he says she has made 'a mistake in the first line.' She calls the wagon a 'covered-in dray' but Hugo tells her that a dray has 'only two wheels,' whereas a wagon has four.

I'll bet that impressed her no end!

May 16th, 1967

'Remember in *Child of the Hurricane,*' Jill said, tapping her pencil on the counter, 'Katharine tells us that when she was living in London, she took six months off work, put a notice on her front door saying "Gone to the Country" and sat down to write *The Pioneers*. As usual, she wanted her research to be accurate, so she rummaged through her notebooks, written when she was a governess in Gippsland, for background material on pioneers and convicts and got stuck into writing.

'She'd seen McCubbin's famous painting and probably had it in mind as she wrote,' said Jill. 'It's a triptych,' she murmured as she showed me a copy of the painting.

The three paintings are of bush clearings surrounded by enormous trees. The first panel shows two pioneers. The focus is on the wife, who looks tired and bored while, in the background, her husband is lighting a fire. In the centre panel, the wife is standing, holding a baby, talking to her husband, who is sitting on a felled tree. He looks exhausted! We can see their bush hut in the distance. In the final panel, a man leans on a bended knee before a grave. It could be the pioneer at the gravesite of his wife or child, or it could be a passerby.

I love this painting. I like paintings that tell a story.

May 17th, 1967

The Pioneers explores the lives of Donald and Mary Cameron, immigrants from 'the old country' who work hard to build a better life in Australia. Donald Cameron is greedy for land, land, and more land. 'This is mine...all this... a hundred acres...and more when I'm ready for it, more, and more, and more...' he says with delight. Mary, however, sees Australia as a 'strange lonely land' but goes along with her husband's dreams and schemes for their future, hoping there's something more to life than ownership of property.

Mary's 'sure instinct of protection' urges her to help two escaped convicts, even though they kill her dog. They're tough, these two men: they've 'felt the lash' at Port Arthur; they've cheated the 'bloodhounds'; evaded the sentry; crawled 'from one end of the Island to the other in the bush at night'; made their way in a 'cockle-shell of a boat in the open sea without any mariner's tools.'

Nearly mad with thirst, they head for McNab's shanty. Thad McNab is a murderous villain with a 'cunning brain', 'pale, shifty eyes' and an 'ugly, writhing smile.' Apart from other nefarious dealings, he helps convicts escape. When the convicts become well off, they pay him to keep his mouth shut about their origins. 'But there's a new game now,' says escaped convict Dan to Mary. 'A reward is out for the capture of escaped convicts,' and McNab has double-crossed them. Mary isn't the slightest bit interested in a reward, and because her husband is away on business, she knows she won't be in trouble with him, so she gives the escapees food and clothes and tells Dan, 'My heart is with you and all like you.'

When Donald Cameron discovers convicts have been at their hut while he was away, he turns on Mary. 'On the ship and in Melbourne it was the same. You were always doing such things, feeding, or giving your clothes to filthy, ailing gaol-birds and whiners...Show sympathy with lags, and what'll be said next? You're a lag yourself and that's why your sympathy's with them.'

Stubborn Mary has given her word: she will not tell her husband which way the convicts have gone. Later she admits that if she had been 'served' as the two convicts had been, she would have 'been a convict too.' She managed to get away with what she did by marrying Donald Cameron. We don't discover her crime until the very end, and boy, was I on her side!

May 19th, 1967

When I was telling Gwenda and Nora this morning about *The Pioneers*, Nora said she was told by her grandfather that they had convict blood in the family. He would never give any details, and she said she was relieved. 'I don't want to know about any convict blood in my family. If I ever find out, I'll never tell,' Nora growled.

May 20th, 1967

In *Child of the Hurricane*, Katharine writes about an 'elderly bachelor, thin and neglected looking', who says to her, 'You know...in England, we say, prick an Australian and you find the convict.' She tells us she was 'so astonished' she couldn't speak. When he informs her that the English 'regard Australia as the cesspool of England', Katharine is furious. 'We didn't make the convicts', she bursts out. 'You here in England, with your brutality and rotten conditions made the convicts, and dumped them wherever you could, overseas. Australia redeemed them.'

I told Gwenda that story this morning and she frowned, stuck out her chin, then said, 'Yes, well, Vicki, I suppose your Katharine Susannah Prichard forgets that white Australia redeemed the convicts at the expense of the Aboriginal people!'

I hadn't thought of it that way. I'm sure Gwenda's right.

May 21st, 1967

All of Katharine's main characters are bloody hard workers! To get their one-room hut ready to live in, Donald Cameron fells trees and clears the land. Mary rams 'clayey hill soil' into the crevices to keep the chill winds out. She makes a floor of 'beaten clay' and collects 'from the creek bed the grey and brown stones' that Donald builds into the hearth and chimney. She sweeps, sews, cooks, makes bread, carries water, gardens, feeds animals, collects eggs, and can 'leg-rope and bail' a cow as well as she can make butter.

Donald Cameron slogs for ten years, 'clearing land, breaking soil, raising crops and rearing cattle, doing battle with the wilderness...every line in his face was ploughed deep.' The harder he works, the wealthier he is, and the more silent he becomes, 'talking only when it was necessary and seldom for the sake of companionship...His mind was always busy with the movement of cattle, branding, mustering, breeding, buying and selling prices, possibilities of the market.' Where Mary always thinks about the well-being of other people, including her husband, Donald does everything to make himself rich and important and thinks of no one but himself: 'It gave him no end of satisfaction to realise that he was the master of Ayrmuir and...that he could do what he liked with...his property.'

He reminds me of Sam Geary in *Coonardoo* and Dan Haxby in *Haxby's Circus*. As much as I dislike Sam Geary, Dan Haxby and Donald Cameron, they are strong and unforgettable characters who leap off the page.

Can't say I'd like to know a man like that, and I certainly wouldn't want to marry one, but Katharine seems to know this type well. Perhaps she meets them on her research trips? I'm betting Katharine can size up people very quickly, and her first impressions would be pretty accurate.

May 22nd, 1967

Mary Cameron's relationship with her husband reminds me of Sophie and Potch in *Black Opal.* They have very practical marriages. Donald tells Mary that there's 'not what you might call much sentiment about our mating', to which she replies, 'May I be a true and faithful wife to you.'

Gee, could I put up with that kind of marriage, I wonder? I'd like to be more than just a 'true and faithful wife' who cooks, sweeps and sews.

May 23ʳᵈ, 1967

At morning tea, I read out the detailed descriptions of springtime in *The Pioneers* and Gwenda, Nora and I agree with Katharine: springtime is very special. We all love walking through the bush tracks in King's Park in spring – spider orchids, boronia, freesias, leschenaultia, kangaroo paws, Geraldton wax everywhere – all gorgeous to look at, lovely to smell.

When I was talking to Jill this arvo about Katharine and wildflowers, Jill told me that Katharine's own garden isn't native. 'She may have some natives,' said Jill, 'but I noticed when I went up to Greenmount to take a peek at her house before I started writing my thesis that her garden was full of lavender and climbing roses and blue wisteria, plumbago and morning-glory were all over the place. But she certainly knows her natives – all their names and where they grow. You just need to read her stories as proof of that!'

Mum plants the odd native, but mostly she goes in for daisies, marigolds and geraniums, and every year, for as long as I can remember, she has planted petunias in the spring. If I ever have my own garden, I want to plant only natives. I'd let them grow all over the place. It'd be like a little jungle.

May 24th, 1967

Jill showed me a 1920s edition of *The Pioneers*, which, she said firmly, 'cannot be borrowed.' Next to the image of a woman wearing a long skirt and boots, warming herself by a camp fire, we are informed that this book is 'Katharine Susannah Prichard's famous Prize Novel'. 'Look at what the *Daily Chronicle* says,' Jill chuckled. In the left-hand corner of the cover, we're told *The Pioneers* is 'One of the best written and the most entrancing stories we have read for many a day.'

'Just a tick,' said Jill, and returned with Katharine's *Child of the Hurricane*. She turned the pages until she came to the quote by Katharine that reads, '*The Pioneers* was finished and dispatched with acute consciousness of its many defects.'

It may have 'defects' but I like *The Pioneers*: the story moves along at a rollicking pace, there are some powerful descriptions of the landscape, and all the characters are interesting. I especially like its streak of Aussie larrikinism. Like Mary Cameron, I was always on the side of the escaped convicts.

May 26th, 1967

Tonight at book club, we were asked to share our thoughts about the book we most enjoyed in the last month.

When it was my turn, I said I'd been reading Katharine's novel, *The Pioneers*. The group had a bit of a giggle at my expense. They know by now I haven't been reading anything else lately but Katharine's work. I've only skimmed through our book club's choices and haven't had anything to say at discussion time.

Anyway, I said I think that *The Pioneers* is a good story about early Australia: convicts, violence, settlers, cattle duffing, bushfires, storms. I paused and waited for a comment but no one said a word, so I carried on with my summary. '*The Pioneers* isn't as interesting as *Coonardoo* or *Black Opal*.' Still no one said anything, so I decided to show off! 'Or *Haxby's Circus*.' Then I said, '*The Pioneers* – it's a bit predictable, but still, a terrific yarn.' I saw one woman roll her eyes. Tart! Larry nodded and grinned and gave me a sly look. I don't know whether he agreed with me or not, but he seemed satisfied with my summary.

As we were leaving, one of the members said I should read Katharine's semi-autobiographical novel about a girl called Han. 'My daughter loved it, and so did I,' she said, smiling. I felt relieved. I thought she was going to ask me to leave book club.

May 29th, 1967

Gwenda burst into the tearoom ten minutes late for morning tea. 'What's up with you?' Nora asked.

'Wish I could've voted on Saturday,' Gwenda replied. 'I would've voted Yes!'

'What are you talking about?' Nora frowned and stirred her tea noisily.

'The referendum! Now Aboriginal people can finally be counted in the census,' Gwenda practically shouted.

'Oh, that', sniffed Nora.

We're not yet old enough to vote but I've been listening to the news and am sure I would've voted Yes. I've been learning a lot about Aboriginal people from reading Katharine and her stories have convinced me that Aboriginal people must be treated a hell of a lot better. I think it's weird that they've never been counted. Including them in the Australian population numbers has to be important to them, I'm sure.

June 5th, 1967

Apart from spending yesterday arvo listening to Elvis and Beatles records in my bedroom, I did almost nothing over the weekend but read *The Wild Oats of Han*.

In the 'Author's Note' to *The Wild Oats of Han*, Katharine writes that the story is 'a truly, really story. Katharine Susannah would cross her breath on it…just here and there, a few details stray from the strict path.' So I'm reading it as if the characters are based on real people and assume Han is the young Katharine. I like this approach – I'm looking forward to reading what she got up to when she was a little girl.

The Wild Oats of Han was published in 1928 when Katharine was in her forties. It's dedicated to her brothers, Alan and Nigel, and full of stories about stuff kids do when they're out exploring the bush.

Despite her love of bush creatures, Han has a streak of violence in her. 'Cruelly, curiously,' Han likes to break old-man mushrooms in pieces just so she can 'watch the consternation of their infinitesimal inhabitants.' She's part of the gang who throw rocks and sticks at goannas until they 'spit fire,' leaving the goanna 'dead...his fat silver body...torn with stones.' This happens regularly until, one day, Han watches a goanna being smashed to bits by her brothers and decides that from now on, goannas will be enchanted princes who need her protection.

No protection is guaranteed, though, for the little boy Han attacks, leaving 'the mark of her fingernails in a long red scratch on his cheeks,' and she has no regrets whatsoever. In fact, she wishes she'd also smashed up his father's prize pumpkin!

Katharine won a World Council Peace medal and has supported anti-war movements all her life, yet, in her fiction, I notice that she doesn't shy away from cruelty and violence. Hugh Watt bashes Coonardoo and drags her through a fire. He smashes Sam Geary in the face. In *The Pioneers*, McNab is a murderer and Deirdre kills him. Potch brutally bashes Arthur Henty in *Black Opal* and would've killed him if he hadn't been dragged off. Paul Bach, in *Haxby's Circus*, murders his wife and then shoots himself.

Katharine's obviously not a violent person, but I bet she'd hop to and defend herself if provoked. Perhaps not physically, but I don't think she'd hold back the words!

June 7th, 1967

I was telling Gwenda and Nora this morning about how, in *The Wild Oats of Han*, Jack's father beats him with a leather strap. Nora said she had a friend called Jack in primary school who was beaten by his father. 'He came to school with bruises all over his arms and legs but never said a word about being hit by his dad,' she frowned. 'I found out much later, from a friend of a friend, about the beatings. Jack left the school when he was about ten, and I never saw him again.'

'Some people don't deserve to be parents,' Gwenda said.

I agree.

June 8th, 1967

In *The Wild Oats of Han*, Han has a special friend, a 'shingle splitter,' an 'unbeliever' called Mr Sam, who has 'strange revolutionary ideas about things as they are, and things as they should be.' I'm willing to bet he's someone Katharine once met. He tells Han stories about 'the black people' and how 'white people' have 'seized their land and become strong and wealthy on it; how they drove 'all wild people to a corner of the island where they died miserably within a few years.'

Little Han listens carefully to everything Sam says and is intrigued when he tells her that one day she will 'waken...that'll be the soul in you burstin' like a rose.' He convinces Han she'll never be like those who are 'afraid to think...afraid to feel. They carry themselves around like cracked mugs.'

Of course, Han's soul will be a wilful and rebellious one, and it bursts like a rose on the day that she and her brothers arrive home from playing in the bush, just in time to see the family's furniture being hauled away on carts and a red flag hanging over the fence. She doesn't understand why the family have to pack up the household, why Rosamund Mary's piano had to be sold at an auction, why her mother's face has lost its 'look of ease and contentment', why her father's face is 'worn and weary-looking.' Her mother's crying hurts Han 'like a bruise, with an aching soreness.' Han is only twelve, but from that day on, it seems that the 'weight of the world seemed suddenly to have descended upon her shoulders'.

It was sad to read this, knowing the things that I now know about Katharine and her mob. That, after moving to Melbourne, her family's fortunes never got any better. Her father commits suicide; her mother's illness means household chores and financial worries fall on Katharine's head, preventing her from going to university. One of her brothers is killed in the First World War.

June 9th, 1967

On the bus this morning going to work, I sat next to an old duck who said to me, 'I see you're reading *The Wild Oats of Han*. I bought that for my daughter for her birthday a long time ago. Do you like it?' I replied I like it very much. 'You know,' this woman snorted, 'the author of that book is a communist.'

'Yes,' I said, 'I know that.'

'Well,' she scoffed, 'when I found out she was a communist, I took that book away from my daughter, and I threw it in the bin. No good Christian mother would ever want her daughter to read a book written by a communist.'

I was so shocked I couldn't speak. First, that she could take back a birthday present, and secondly, that she could throw a book in a bin. Then I thought, those actions are not very Christian to my way of thinking.

Gwenda told us at morning tea that she's going out tonight with her 'steady.' Nora and I shared a sly smile. So Andy is now her steady boyfriend!

Gwenda sailed, head high, back to her desk. Nora and I dawdled. 'I'd like to have a steady,' Nora whispered.

'Me too,' I whispered back.

The trouble is, if I had one, my mother would expect me to marry him and explode like a bloody volcano if I didn't.

June 12th, 1967

On the way home from work, I popped into the library and asked Jill what she thought of *The Wild Oats of Han*. 'Haven't read it,' she shrugged. That was a surprise! I thought Jill had read everything by Katharine. I felt just a tiny bit superior, having finished *The Wild Oats of Han*, but then told myself to get off it. After all, Jill's the one with a university degree! And she's a librarian, and I'm just a typist.

Jill told me that Katharine has a granddaughter called Karen Han. 'I've read when she was born, she looked just like a little kewpie doll. She had bright black eyes and thick black hair,' laughed Jill. 'In Katharine's letters to Miles Franklin, she wrote how thrilled she was to be a grandmother, how much she adored the little girl and how pleased she was with the baby's name. She told Miles that "Han" is after that urchin in *The Wild Oats of Han* who was, Katharine claimed, "herself, as a matter of fact." I'm sure Miles Franklin chuckled when she read that!'

June 17th, 1967

I went dancing tonight with Gwenda. Her boyfriend is away for a couple of weeks and she suggested we go to the Embassy. We haven't been there for months so off we went.

'It's good to get out and about without Andy,' Gwenda laughed as we got on the bus. 'I love being with him but he can be a bit moody at times.

I had two dances with a tall bloke with crinkly brown hair. He was quite a bit older than me, held me too tight, and had bad breath, so I said to Gwenda, 'Let's go home soon.' She had four dances with a tall young man with a blond crew cut who laughed a lot about nothing in particular, I'm sure.

She told me at the bus stop that he'd asked her where she lived, which is the usual question they ask after the third dance. When she told him, he nodded but significantly didn't ask her for 'Moon River', which is always the last dance. Obviously, he doesn't have a car and probably lives a long way from Gwenda.

Mum barged out of her bedroom as soon as I got home. 'Meet anyone nice, Vicki?' I shook my head and told her my feet were sore and I was tired and going to bed. Her eyes narrowed but she didn't say anything about meeting my future husband.

June 27th, 1967

I was chatting to a woman on the bus this morning about my project, and she said that she has a copy of a play Katharine wrote called *Brumby Innes*. 'I was an actress once,' she laughed. 'And I tried out for May in the play. Didn't get the part, but.' She said she'll pop her copy of the play in her bag next Tuesday morning when she will be catching the bus at the same time to go into town to see her doctor, and she will give it to me.

June 30th, 1967

I told Larry tonight I'm going to read *Brumby Innes* next. He didn't seem very interested, though, and just said, 'Good to hear you're sticking to your project,' and took off to get a cup of tea.

I was a bit put out. I like talking to Larry, and he's always been so encouraging about my project.

July 4th, 1967

That woman on the bus is as good as her word! She gave me *Brumby Innes* this morning and doesn't want it back.

Some notes scribbled on the inside cover tell us that the play won the Triad Competition prize in 1927. It was considered immoral, and audiences would get the shock of their lives if they saw it on stage. In a quote by Nettie Palmer, she writes that 'Katharine's Brumby is surely as raw and ravening a figure as has ever been allowed on the boards…it will certainly send a cold shiver through the stalls.'

Wow! Am looking forward to reading it!

July 5th, 1967

Began reading *Brumby Innes* tonight.

I've only finished Act 1 so far, but I hate Brumby Innes already! He's a violent bully, a liar, he steals, drinks too much, threatens and insults everyone he meets.

Brumby believes he can kidnap Aboriginal women, shoot any Aboriginal man who comes to rescue them, and knows the police won't do a thing about it. In fact, attitudes by all the white men in the play towards Aboriginal men and women are brutal. Jack, the head stockman, thinks the 'natives is gettin' proper cheeky up here' and that 'you got to let'm have it now and again.' John Hallinan, owner of the neighbouring station, ignores Mickina, who's been shot and lies bleeding but still alive, out cold on a bunk.

It's strange, but Brumby Innes obviously has something some women like. An Aboriginal woman named Polly has lived with him 'weary booger years' and waits on him hand and foot, even though Brumby tells her to get out because he wants 'pretty young girl Wylba' to move in. Polly ambles about the house 'leisurely' and with dignity and sometimes with contempt, at one point admitting she's 'fed up' with Brumby. But she stays anyway, guarding her position in the household despite his spiteful tantrums and insults.

May, a white girl from the city, arrives and prowls around, 'posing for Brumby who is watching her.' Later she flirtatiously 'powders her face daintily and reddens her lips' in front of Brumby while he examines her 'intensely.' When he tells her she's 'like water on a dry stretch to a thirsty man,' she is 'frightened' at first until he throws his arm around her and holds her tight. 'I'll scream the place down,' she says. 'Scream away,' Brumby replies. May struggles a bit, then yields, and Brumby, 'laughing triumphantly and embracing her roughly as he pushes her towards the bunk', says, 'I like 'em thoroughbred and buckin' a bit at first.'

Yuk. I think I've had quite enough of *Brumby Innes* for tonight!

July 8th, 1967

Went to see *The Singing Nun* tonight with Nora. I wanted to see *Born Free* or *Alfie,* but she didn't want to see either. Gwenda is going out with her boyfriend. We were wondering if she's gone all the way yet and if she'd tell us if she has. Anyway, I didn't like *The Singing Nun.* Nora did.

It's midnight and I've just finished reading *Brumby Innes.* I didn't like it much. Too violent. I reckon Larry probably knew I wouldn't like this play. That's why he didn't want to say anything when I told him I was going to read it. He wants me to keep going with my project, even if I don't like something Katharine's written.

I can't stand Brumby, and I don't like John Hallinan, partly because he lies in court to protect Brumby but mostly because he insists that

May, his niece, marry Brumby to 'hush up any scandal', instead of protecting her from that pig of a man. When May begs her uncle to take her away, Brumby walks over, twists her shoulder and tells John to 'get out – and quick feller.' When Hallinan refuses, telling Brumby that May is going home with him, Brumby punches him in the face, telling May, 'You've asked for it' and 'pastes' her uncle 'unmercifully.'

How pathetic John is when he finally tells May to stay and 'make the best of it' because 'Brumby's generous in his own way.' As soon as John leaves, Brumby turns on May and sniggers, 'Think I'm shook on you, don't you? You damned silvertail. You poor, sickly, miserable-lookin' creature…What you've got to understand is, you're one of Brumby's mares. You gallop with the mob…You'll get feed and water…I won't bother you when y'r with foal. Like you are now.'

May's response is so weak. She tells Brumby, 'Oh, how I hate men.' He replies 'And I hate women. Hate their silly, wimperin' palaver about love…Dressin' themselves up…For why? To get men flutterin' round them…Do y'know what love is?…It's the smoke you blasted women put up to do men out of being plain, ordinary, decent male animals…My lust's not filthy. It's natural. Makes me feel good. Like the rain…and the rivers runnin' when everything's dead and dry, up here.'

Urgh! I think he's disgusting. I was hoping May would grab his gun and shoot him.

Worse luck, in the end, May is the loser, and Brumby dances around the room triumphantly with the 'little native girl', Wylba, who's next on his list for abuse.

July 10ᵗʰ, 1967

After work, I went to the library to talk to Jill about *Brumby Innes*. Jill said she'd read it a long time ago and all she remembers is that she hated the violence.

I asked Jill what she thought Katharine's mood was when she wrote *Coonardoo* and *Brumby Innes*. 'The endings are bleak compared to the rest of her books I've read so far, endings full of optimism, hope, work, duty, sacrifice.' Jill told me she thought Katharine decided that *Coonardoo* and *Brumby Innes* had to show how exploited and abused Aboriginal women are. 'He's a real pig, that Brumby Innes, isn't he?' I asked Jill. She nodded vigorously.

If *Brumby Innes* comes on stage, I probably wouldn't go to see it. Not that I'm an expert on theatre. I can count on one hand the number of times I've been to a play. They were all musicals except for a scary drama at the Playhouse called *The Desperate Hours*. I was frightened the whole time and wanted to leave, but I was with my mother's friend who had bought the tickets, and I didn't want to be rude.

Afterwards, I told my mum about the play. I was surprised when she said she'd been offered the ticket but didn't want to go. 'I only like comedies on stage,' she declared. Don't understand why because she doesn't have much of a sense of humour, in my opinion.

July 14ᵗʰ, 1967

Lately, Nora wants to argue about anything and everything I say about Katharine. Gwenda says she'd like to have morning tea without arguments, so can't we talk about something else. Which is a shame because I like talking to Gwenda about my project.

Jill has given me a collection of short stories by Katharine called *Kiss on the Lips*. 'There are two stories well worth reading,' Jill said. 'She wrote both around the same time she was working on *Coonardoo* and *Brumby Innes*. One is called 'The Cooboo', and the other is 'Happiness'.'

Jill had a few minutes to spare before closing time, so we had a general natter about Katharine and she told me about how, in the 1950s, Katharine had been slandered by a Liberal politician called Bill Wentworth, a fanatical anti-communist. 'He'd referred to her as "Mrs Thorsell" and suggested that she was trying to hide her real identity when applying for a grant from the Commonwealth Literary Fund, which, he claimed, was pro-communist.' Jill chuckled as she pointed out that Wentworth couldn't even get her married name right!

She laughed out loud as she told me that Miles Franklin wrote to Katharine telling her she hoped that Katharine's son, Ric, who was living in Canberra at the time, would confront Wentworth on the steps of Parliament House and punch him. 'Katharine tried to sue Bill Wentworth but nothing came of it. She couldn't be bothered pursuing the matter; it would've been too expensive and a waste of time,' said Jill. 'Probably a wise decision but what a good story it would've been if Ric Throssell had slugged Wentworth!'

I'm slowly beginning to understand that Katharine has always been criticized for her political opinions – by politicians, by most of the public, and sometimes even by friends. Jill told me that many of Katharine's colleagues believe that her political activities interfere with her writing. Some say she is so pro-Soviet Union that she won't accept any criticism of it. 'It's not so much that she's inspired by the Soviet Union,' Jill said. 'It's that she's inspired by communism. She says it's like a religion to her. And you don't turn your back on your religion because it doesn't live up to your expectations!' Jill had a big smile on her face. 'Katharine's an idealist, and I like idealists, even though I don't agree with them. Nothing like a bit of compromise here and there to get things done.'

Katharine is obviously an idealistic, tough woman. She can probably put up with any amount of criticism.

July 15th, 1967

Just finished 'The Cooboo.'

There's an Aboriginal stockman named Wongana in this story, and I'm wondering if he is modelled on someone she met in Turee Creek because there's a Wongana in *Brumby Innes* too. Anyway, in 'The Cooboo', Wongana has two women: 'Rose, tall, gaunt and masterful; Minni, younger, fat and jolly.' Rose has been a 'good stockman in her day: one of the best.' Minni isn't as good as Rose, but on this day, Minni has received high praise from station owner John Gray whereas he's called Rose a 'damn fool.' As Minni prattles on about how good she is, Rose's scowl 'deepened, darkened,' and she undoes the 'rag rope' which has been holding her wailing baby and gives him 'a sagging breast to suck.' She starts to blame her baby for all the 'wrong things' she has done all day, and she is furious with John Gray for yelling, 'Yienda, damn fool, Rosey. Finish!' Rose, 'irritated to madness', flings her cooboo to the ground and rides on, 'gazing ahead over the rosy garish plains, and wall of the hills, darkening from blue to purple to indigo.'

Back at the homestead, Mrs Gray sees Rose without her baby and asks her about her cooboo. Rose stalks off, Minni's 'scared eyes,' following her. No one says a word about what Rose has done. The story ends with Rose 'wailing for her cooboo in the dawn...cutting herself with stones until her body bled...screaming in a fury of unavailing grief.'

What a story! It is hard to imagine that John Gray had so much power that he could cause a mother to murder her own child. This story makes me sick to my stomach.

July 17th, 1967

I took 'The Cooboo' into work this morning and asked Gwenda and Nora if they'd like to read it. Gwenda read it at lunchtime. 'I'll never forget that story,' she said. 'Poor Rosey. I hated the way John Gray and Wongana ganged up on her. They bully and insult her while praising Minni to the skies. So unfair! No wonder Rosey goes crazy and tosses her cooboo on the ground. Rose's wailing and cutting herself with stones at the end of the story gave me chills.'

Gwenda has given 'The Cooboo' to Nora and I hope Nora reads it and has the same reaction.

July 18ᵗʰ, 1967

'I read "The Cooboo" last night,' Nora announced at morning tea. 'It's a shocking story, but I've read worse,' she said, taking out her compact and peering into the mirror.

'Is that right?' asked Gwenda, looking sceptical. 'In the Bible, perhaps?'

'I can't recall reading any other story where a mother is so furious with her baby she kills it,' I said.

Nora shrugged, turned to Gwenda and asked, 'What's the latest with Andy?'

'No latest. Just the same,' Gwenda replied.

While I was eating lunch, I tried to write a sketch about a mother who harms her baby because it won't stop crying. Couldn't do it.

'The Cooboo' is such a gruesome story. I can't imagine it's something Katharine witnessed. Is it possible she heard about it, or something like it, and felt compelled to write it down? Given her commitment to realism, it's difficult to believe she made the whole thing up. But if she did, perhaps it was because she wanted readers to know how powerful, manipulative white men behave towards Aboriginal women?

July 19ᵗʰ, 1967

Read 'Happiness' on the bus going to work this morning.

This story is told from an Aboriginal woman's point of view, which is unusual. She is called Nardadu, and, in the opening lines, she sits picking over the 'offal of a dead beast,' flies clinging to the 'sunken wells' of her eyes. She is preparing a meal for her son, and the 'stench of blood and filth' flows through the air.

We soon discover what she thinks of the three white property owners, John Gray, his wife, Margie, and his sister Megga. Nardadu can't understand how Megga manages to control the Station, why Megga's 'will should be stronger' than John's, or why John 'would hear no word of complaint' against his sister, who has always been 'mistress' of the house, and 'would always be.' To Nardadu, John is 'the all-powerful...giver of food and clothing, whose anger and boot you avoided; but who laughed and made fun with you...when all went well with him.' According to Nardadu, John is the one who should be the boss of Nyedee Station.

The battle between Megga and John's wife, Margie, is bitter and long-lasting. Nardadu realizes Megga's the winner when Margie and the children are driven out of the house. John becomes like a 'sulky old bull' wandering along the fences at night and, in the morning, his face turns towards the homestead where Megga reigns victorious as 'misery and bitterness crouch under the long, white house, with its back to the blue, wild hills.'

Nardadu doesn't understand much of what has gone on and doesn't really care. She knows her young son Munga will become a fine horseman, and she exults in the pleasure of always being able to feed him meat from her fire 'as though he were a man!' This, to her, poor woman, is happiness.

Thanks to Katharine, I'm discovering a lot about Aboriginal people in WA: how they live and how they're treated.

Won't discuss this with Mum – she'd sniff and say it's all lies, and even if it's true, there's nothing we can do about it.

July 26th, 1967

Had hoped to have a chat with Jill today when I dropped into the library after work but she was too busy to talk.

She handed me Katharine's *Working Bullocks* and said, 'You'll love this, Vicki! It's a beautifully written book!' before dashing off to the catalogue to find something.

July 28th, 1967

Larry told me tonight at book club that he taught *Working Bullocks* years ago in his English class, and out of the books he's read by Katharine, it is his favourite.

'*Working Bullocks* was published in 1926,' he told me. 'Not long after their marriage, Prichard and Hugo travelled through the forests of the South West where they visited timber mills and watched bullock teams at work. I remember my students loved the descriptions of those forests. One year, I took a trip down the South West during the Christmas holidays to check out the tall timbers. It's a fascinating place to go to.'

I almost groaned. How I'd love to go to the South West; how I'd love to go anywhere!

Anyway, Larry was on a roll, so I shut up and listened. 'I

remember reading a copy of a letter Prichard wrote to her friend Nettie Palmer about a talk Katharine gave in support of striking timber workers,' Larry laughed. 'You should know, Vicki, that she has addressed dozens of different workers on strike and she's always on their side.'

Wonder if Gwenda, Nora and I would ever dare to go on strike! Maggot would have a fit first, then sack us on the spot.

August 6th, 1967

Finished *Working Bullocks!* Must jot down a few thoughts before I go to sleep. First of all, I *love* this book.

This time, we're in WA's South West, red gum, karri and jarrah country. In the opening passages, bullockies are urging their great beasts forward on the heavy, soft earth 'between the bush and the track.' The bullocks are 'blowing hard...coughing, spewing froth...their backs steaming in the chill air and the pale sunshine.' Red Burke, 'one of the best bullockies in the south-west,' with his mate, Chris Colburn, are cracking lashes, yelling at the animals, trying to get them onto 'firmer ground in the centre of the track.'

In contrast to the brutal world of the bullocks, the forests are peaceful and beautiful; enormous trees stand 'breathless, steeped in haze, the sun at midday, an incandescence above the tree-tops, blazed on any patch of open ground.' In the early mornings 'light spilt through the trees, making luminous green of the saplings, glittering in shifting threads and patches of quick gold on the earth and old tree-trunks.'

Mary Ann Colburn is a familiar face. 'Vitality' flows 'beneath her skin, weathered and tough.' Mother of eighteen children, 'sixteen living and two dead,' Mary Ann Colburn is 'as hard and straight as nails.'

Mary Ann's eldest daughter, Deb, is young, eager, and keen on Red Burke. Red thinks Deb is a 'fine lump of a girl' and he never doubts that one day 'their life together would be like the flowering and fruiting of a tree.'

Throughout the novel, Deb is often compared to a tree. Deb understands, respects and believes in the 'power of the trees.' She is 'akin to them; and to the earth.' When she was a small child, she watched a 'king karri' being felled and has never forgotten the 'thunder of his pitching to earth.' Over the years, she watches these giant trees being 'felled, split, sawed and hauled away' and believes that the trees will never 'forgive what men had done to them.' She is 'aghast' at the way men treat the trees and believes in their 'vengeance.'

One afternoon, Red watches Deb sleeping in the forest, 'her limbs twisted over each other, brown legs and long brown arms bare', and he thinks of her as a 'young tree fallen there beside him.' He dreams of tearing her 'blue rags of dress from her young strong body.' He recalls the way his horse, Boss, had 'gone to his mate, and she had stood to him, tremulous, eyes dilated, squealing with delight as he bit her flanks' and decides that he wants to 'take his mate like that...no slobbering...none of this blather about love...sniggering and playing round...When he took a mate he would bite her flanks and she would spring to his passion...And she would be a woman like this girl, strong, with animal instincts, undaunted. Why not this one? Why not Deb?'

Wow! Shades of Brumby Innes!

Deb comes to believe there is something 'inviolable between herself and Red Burke. She could not utter it; she had no words. Perhaps it was no more than the mating instinct of animals.' When Red 'claims' her, she readily agrees to his claim.

Gosh, *Working Bullocks* is a very sexy novel! If I told Mum about it, she'd be embarrassed – or shocked. Or both. We've never *ever* discussed sex.

August 9th, 1967

In *Working Bullocks*, Deb is contrasted with Tessa, who has a 'baby face' and a 'fuzz of fair hair, wide-open brown eyes and heavy red mouth.' She carries on 'in the way of some of the moving-picture actresses she so much admired,' opening her eyes 'so that they would look pathetic and appealing.'

Although Red is fascinated by her, he thinks she's 'cheap' and that there are 'lots like her in Perth and other cities he had been in.' Red has slept with Tessa (and other women as well, including other men's wives and prostitutes, so he's very experienced in that particular area!) and at one point thinks it's possible he's the father of Tessa's baby. He can't stand her, and it turns out she's nothing but trouble for him. The pity he feels for Tessa when she goes into labour is simply the pity he'd feel for any 'creature in pain.'

What I think really odd is that, at the end of *Working Bullocks*, Red is full of a 'joyous, sensuous satisfaction' at having finally won Deb Colburn when suddenly he begins to think of Tessa, 'luscious as ripe fruit, a peach, one of those late golden peaches. She smelt like that! And ripe fruit is always good eating…'

I didn't get this bit. Does this mean he's going to marry Deb and have an affair with Tessa? Or is he just thinking about sex – the sex he's already had with Tessa and the regular sex he's going to have with Deb?

I don't understand men or sex, but I suspect Katharine might.

August 10th, 1967

At morning tea, Gwenda, Nora and I talked about how and when we first found out about sex. 'I found out about it from school friends,' said Gwenda. 'I must've been about ten.' Nora found out about it through a book a cousin gave her; she can't remember how old she was, but she thinks she was about eleven. I first found out about sex from a girlfriend who used to live up the street and seemed to know a lot about boys and periods. I think I was also about eleven years old.

We all wondered why our mothers never told us anything about making babies or periods. When I first got my period, I was really embarrassed and tried to hide it. But Mum did the washing and found out. She gave me a sanitary belt and said she'd give me the money to go to the chemist each month and ask for Modess.

That was so humiliating. I used to hover about the counter until no one was in the shop, and then I'd blurt out, 'A packet of Modess, please.' I always wished Mum had bought it for me.

August 11ᵗʰ, 1967

I'm always surprised at the fistfights in Katharine's work! There's a serious stoush in *Working Bullocks* when Red Burke, drunk and 'seein' blood,' attacks Leslie de Gaze, giving him a 'sledge-hammer blow over the heart,' pounding Gaze's stomach until his 'arms dropped to his side' and knocking him out with a 'crashing right.' To the crowd's delight, Red is still 'trembling with the rage and exertion of his fighting' and he feels 'good and strong...mad happy and exultant.'

I wonder if Katharine saw these kinds of fights in her travels. She seems to know quite a bit about them. She doesn't condemn drunken violence – sometimes it's almost as if she's amused by it.

August 14ᵗʰ, 1967

At morning tea, I was telling Gwenda and Nora about the fight between Red Burke and de Gaze. Gwenda told us that she grew up around fights between boys. 'At primary school, at high school, and even after school, boys would make arrangements to meet somewhere to fight, egged on by other boys,' Gwenda laughed. She thinks it's natural for boys to fight, and it doesn't worry her at all. In fact, she admitted she got into a couple of fights with girls in the playground at primary school. 'I always won!" she said with a big grin. 'The only fight that's ever bothered me was the one I saw between two old men one hot night outside a pub. One was knocked out, and the other was badly hurt. It really upset me.'

At that point, Nora sniffed and announced that she went to an all-girls school where the nuns forbade physical fighting. 'Most girls at school,' Nora said, 'paid back their enemies by spreading gossip and playing tricks on them, like hiding their hats so they'd get into trouble for being out of uniform or squirting tomato sauce on the back of their sports dresses so it looked as if they'd been caught out having a period.' Gwenda snorted, and I said that sounds like a pretty nasty thing to do. Nora just shrugged.

'The only fistfight I've ever seen was between my brother Pete when he was about ten years old and another boy about the same age,' I told them. 'They were strolling down the lane at the back of our house when all of a sudden Pete lashed out at the other boy, socking him in the face. They yelled and swore and thrashed about until they were both rolling on the ground. For some reason, they just stopped. Then they stood up and started laughing. I'll never understand the way the male brain works!'

'Kids fight a lot, but most fights between grown men happen because the men have been boozing,' said Nora.

'If more women could go to public bars, men might be more careful about how much they drink because they wouldn't want to look like bloody idiots in front of women,' Gwenda said with a frown.

'I'm not so sure about that,' I said. 'I reckon drunks will carry on regardless, and I bet there are loads of men who don't want women anywhere near their pubs.'

We talked about the story we'd read in the newspapers about how two women chained themselves to the rails in a pub in Queensland. Women aren't allowed in public bars, and they were protesting against the law. If they had been served alcohol, the publican would've been fined; if a man in the bar had bought them a beer, he would've been fined. When a policeman came to kick them out, they said they'd lost the padlocks. He pleaded with them to leave, but they refused, and he finally gave up!

'Mum thought those women were disgusting little trollops,' said Nora.

'Can't wait till we're twenty-one!' I laughed. 'We still might not be able to go to the saloon but we could legally go to a beer garden together and have some fun!'

It's not like we don't drink. There's always beer at Nora's parties (I hate beer, though, so I never drink at her parties). Gwenda drinks with Andy. I don't get into trouble at my book club for having a tipple. And Mum doesn't care when I have a glass of Sparkling Burgundy with Mrs Cook at Christmas.

August 15th, 1967

I told Gwenda and Nora about how, in *Working Bullocks*, when Red Burke was a child, he was 'thrashed' by his father until his 'limbs ached' and how Mary Ann Colburn wallops her kids. 'No one, not even the kids, thinks anything of it,' I said. 'Were you ever hit by your parents?'

'Mum often smacked me when I was growing up,' Nora replied. 'Dad whacked me once when I was about fourteen.' Gwenda and I were a bit shocked at that. 'Where did he hit you?' Gwenda asked Nora.

'Well, he didn't actually hit me. He pushed me hard and I slammed into a wall.' Nora said she couldn't remember why her father had a go at her, but she thought it was probably because she had been giving him cheek and she probably deserved it.

'My mother smacked me when I was little,' Gwenda said. 'I remember Mum whacking me a few times for being naughty, and once she hit me with a flyswatter, which really hurt. Mostly, she just threatened to hit me. My father never hit me, but he yelled at me a lot.'

'My mum never hit me,' I told them, 'but she threatened to. And she'd often hold up a bread knife and wave it around. That was when I knew it was time to run! I have no idea what happened to the knife, but I'm glad it's no longer in the kitchen drawer. Not that she would've ever cut me with it or anything like that – but it was scary and the best way to get me out of the house! My mother's favourite saying when I was growing up was "go outside and play."'

'That's what my mum used to say to all of us kids!' laughed Nora.

Gwenda and I agreed that if we ever have children, we will try hard to think of something besides smacking. Nora said she would thump her kids if she thought they deserved it.

August 21st, 1967

On the bus coming home from work, I started thinking about two extraordinarily strong women in Katharine's novels I've read so far: Mrs Bessie in *Coonardoo* and Mary Ann Colburn in *Working Bullocks*. I've been thinking about how similar they are in all kinds of ways.

Both women have married deadbeats. Mary Ann Colburn's husband, Tom, has one eye, likes beer, plays the accordion, and is almost irrelevant in her life. We find out that he's certainly not the love of her life! While checking out Red Burke's good looks and physique, she thinks, 'A girl might lose her head over the man quite easily...he was something like the man she nearly had lost her head over.'

As for Mrs Bessie, her husband is dead when *Coonardoo* opens – not that that seems to worry her. Everyone in the district wonders why she married Ted Watt, who was, according to Sam Geary, 'as rough as bags' and 'could neither read nor write.' When drunk, he 'went mad' and 'ran amuck.' He once shot an Aboriginal woman's dog and when she told him off, he 'kicked her off the veranda', and she died a few days later. A month later, Ted 'walked over the balcony of a hotel...and was killed.' No one mourned him, not even Mrs Bessie, and 'the blacks believed justice had been done.'

Both Mrs Bessie and Mary Ann Colburn have amazing amounts of energy. Mrs Bessie works 'with an energy and obstinacy which never flagged...her restless energy drove everything, everybody.' Mary Ann Colburn works 'like a bullock herself' and has 'taught her children to work like that too.'

Both women are not above exploiting others to profit themselves. Mrs Bessie 'snavelled' Wytaliba right under Saul Hardy's nose. Hardy is described as a 'shrewd hard-doer', but Mrs Bessie outsmarts him!' It's more out of guilt than generosity that Mrs Bessie lets Saul Hardy spend his days on the veranda or in the room she has given him. Mary Ann Colburn relies on her eighteen-year-old daughter, Deb, to look after her younger brothers and sisters and help out at the boarding house where her mother works – for no pay, of course. When Deb finally takes a job at the boarding house, her mother grabs Deb's wages every week, not even giving her enough money to buy 'a few pretty cotton dresses for herself.' Not that Deb complains. Her mum has taught her well!

Mrs Bessie and Mary Ann Colburn both love money. Mary Ann Colburn earns a living by selling milk, eggs, cabbages and cockerels, and washing and ironing. She saves as much as she can and admits she wants to 'lay a bit by for her old age and her old man's' but what she really wants is to 'accumulate.' She likes money and 'knowing she owned so much' gives her immense satisfaction. Her savings grow every year until she has 'quite a handsome hoard' tucked away in the State Savings Bank. Mrs Bessie, being a property owner, is much more successful than Mrs Colburn in accumulating wealth, and she's mean. She's 'earned the name of a regular skinflint...If a drover or prospector strayed into Wytaliba there was no whisky.' If people try to discuss her 'growing bank balance', she tells them she has a 'guts-ache' and forbids people to talk about it.

Mrs Bessie and Mary Ann Colburn are aggressive and, at times, quite nasty. Both have strong prejudices and like to get their own way. Before she dies of cancer, Mrs Bessie, knowing full well how superstitious Aboriginal people are, threatens to come back to haunt them as a 'white cockie...and give you bad dreams...guts-ache, and a pain, eating your inside out like I've got.' Mary Ann Colburn can be nasty too, especially towards Red Burke. She doesn't trust Red and she doesn't want Deb to marry him, at least not until 'he can go straight...keep off the drink and save a bit.' If he gets a team of bullocks, Deb might consider marriage. If he doesn't, she tells Deb, 'You ain't got to have him.'

Red Burke never does get his own bullock team, and Deb defies her mother and goes off with Red. When Red and Deb come out of the forest together to say goodbye, Mrs Colburn can't resist baiting

Red again for not having his own team. 'Nice team you got there, Red!' she screams, her 'derision' towards Red is as 'eerie as the cry of a bird.'

'Not me own,' Red flings back at her. 'Taking 'em into Marritown for Peter Moody!' Mrs Colburn is bitter in her 'defeat,' telling him, 'I'm too long in the tooth to make terms with you, Red Burke. You're no better than the beasts you're driving – the pair of you. You'll be driven...worked like them.' Red laughs his head off at that and yells back at her, 'But we'll breed...like you done!'

Bloody old cow, that Mary Ann, I thought when I read the ending. By then, I was on Red Burke's side. But later, I thought to myself, just a tick, so that's what poor old Deb has to look forward to: endless chores and sixteen children? Talk about working bullocks!

Although I think Katharine admires these two women because they're shrewd, tough, hard-working, and strong-minded, I'm sure she dislikes their main flaws: they take advantage of people who are weaker than they are, and they're greedy.

September 8th, 1967

Gwenda's going out tonight with her boyfriend. She hasn't told us yet about whether or not she's gone all the way with him. Nora and I think she probably won't tell us – we'll have to drag it out of her!

Not doing anything tonight. Nora and I considered going to the pictures, but we couldn't agree on a film.

Oh well, at least I have Katharine for company. I'm thinking about Mary Ann Colburn and how cold she is towards her kids. Deb has never kissed her mother, and she's never seen her mother kiss her children. Her mother, we are told, did not encourage 'mugging.' If one of her little ones wanted a cuddle, she would say, 'Oh go on, you great calf!' At the end of the novel, Deb goes to kiss her mother but changes her mind, instead simply saying, 'Good-bye mum' and off she goes with Red.

Makes me think of my own mother. She usually gives me a little hug on my birthday, but I can't remember her ever giving me a kiss. Mum's not the affectionate type, nor was my father.

September 29th, 1967

At book group, Larry asked me what I thought of *Working Bullocks* and I told him I liked it very much. He said that he'd read Katharine was happy with it but that it didn't make much money. 'In fact,' he said, 'I remember reading somewhere that her royalties didn't even cover the cost of having the manuscript typed.'

That really surprised me! Not the royalties bit, but the typing. What a shame she had to spend money on someone else to do her typing. I suppose it would've been a final draft, so it had to look perfect to submit to the publishers; perhaps she wasn't up to that standard or didn't have time. I wish I'd been the one who typed up that final manuscript of *Working Bullocks*: I'm a good typist, and I would've done it for nothing!

Larry told me the strike in *Working Bullocks* was based on a real event in karri country down south. 'When the novel was published,' he said, 'it was pretty controversial because Mark Smith, the leader of the strike, was a communist.'

I'm going home tonight to have a look at what Mark Smith says and does, especially during that strike, and see what I can make of it all. I will learn something new, I'm sure.

September 30th, 1967

Mum started in on me early this morning about how I should go out tonight. 'Go dancing or something,' she said. 'Make it clear to the world you're available. There are lots of nice young men in Perth looking for a wife. Marriage is your next step, Vicki. It may not be the best step but it's the one you have to take, otherwise you're in for a very difficult life. And you can't live at home forever.' Just to annoy her, I told her I've decided I don't want to get married and want to be an old maid. I didn't really mean it, but at least that shut her up.

I am sheltering in my room now and reading about Mark Smith and the strike.

Mark Smith works day and night trying to educate the workers, telling them that the reason why they earn low wages and live in 'shacks of bagging and waste timber as poor as any you saw in a slum' is because a 'few people had seized power and persisted in wielding it so that they and their kind might have a superabundance of food, clothing, houses to live in, ease and leisure.' He wants the workers to 'change all this. Insist on another deal of the cards.'

Red Burke, along with most of the men on the Six Mile, finally come to understand what Mark means when he talks about 'instruments of production and distribution, the proletariat, bourgeois ideology, economics of capitalism, socialization of industry, words which had flown about like birds making strange noises when they first heard him talking.' The men think Mark Smith is a 'likeable chap' whose 'brains and energy' are dedicated to 'this religion of his – "service to humanity", he called it, 'and "the fight for a better world."'

Next time I see Larry, I'll ask him to help me understand terms like instruments of production and distribution and the economics of capitalism. But really, when it comes down to it, I reckon it's not all those difficult phrases that interest the workers of the Six Mile. They're interested in wages, better housing, working hours, the risks of working under the big saws, the age of boys working in the mills. They hate having to buy goods at the company shop because there's nowhere else to buy from and they know the mill owners make huge profits from the high prices of sugar, flour, tea.

When Katharine spells out things like that, I understand why she believes the whole system needs to change.

Mark finally gets fed up when the men complain, telling them they've 'groused and growled' for months but do nothing about it. 'You look like men,' he says, 'but you're not. You're working bullocks. That's all you are. You'll go crawling back to work tomorrow when the whips are cracking. You'll let the boss do what he likes with you…You make me sick, the lot of you!'

Harsh words from Mark, but he's speaking from his heart: he cares deeply for the 'life of the place and its people,' and he can't understand why the workers accept 'whatever happened to them fatalistically, were static under disaster…he resented their apathy.' Have these men 'no spirit at all,' he asks himself, 'that they allowed themselves to be destroyed, their energy drawn off as if they were labouring cattle?'

I can understand Mark Smith's frustration, but I can also understand those poor workers. It's hard to stand up to bosses. Just ask Gwenda, Nora and me!

Mark wants the workers to unite and fight. And some are spoiling for a fight, including Mary Ann Colburn. Mary Ann tells the workers that Mark is right: they should strike 'while the iron is hot.' Up until now, she had always thought Mark a 'blatherskite,' and she'd never supported strikes, but she's 'right into this one, and no mistake.' She listens carefully to Mark Smith's 'crusade for a better world', as he tries to 'drag the best of them from their depths, their courage, hope, and that Promethean spark, the fighting spirit, which is the immortal of mankind.' Mrs Colburn may not have Mark's 'magnetism' or use fine phrases, but in her own way she tries hard to stir the workers into action, 'tongue-banging the bosses for all she was worth.'

I laughed out loud when I read that! That boss of ours could do with a bloody good telling-off; he's so full of himself.

The workers finally decide they'll strike for 'a rise to two bob a load' for piece-work.

Mark is 'brooding, bitter and hostile' when the strike fails. The timber workers, 'half ashamed' when they look at him, go back to work 'on the employer's terms, two pence a load rise on piece-work...and vague promises of improved conditions...pending further negotiations.' He doesn't really blame them, telling Mary Ann that it's 'all in the game...it's an old trick to let a strike drag out like this one, till the men get tired of it...will do anything...even go back to work...for a change.' He's pretty optimistic when he says, 'when the workers understand... pull together, we can drag ourselves out of this bog we've got into, and stampede the few that drive us so as they can keep all the good things of life to themselves.'

That makes a lot of sense to me, but putting his ideas into action would be very difficult. I can't imagine how we could get even a small pay rise out of Maggot. He would just say no. We'd have to accept that or look for another job.

October 2ⁿᵈ, 1967

I was telling Gwenda and Nora about Mark Smith and read a couple of passages over morning tea. Instead of listening, Nora yelled, 'Stop! Stop!' I asked her what in the world was wrong with her. She said she's never heard such rot in all her life. 'What's more,' she said, 'you wouldn't have a job if it weren't for these so-called capitalists. So stick that in your pipe and smoke it.' With that, she stormed off like the Queen Bee.

Gwenda looked me in the eye for a few seconds, then giggled. 'Watch out, Vicki,' she said to me, 'you're becoming a little red witch!'

October 9ᵗʰ, 1967

I've been thinking about ending to *Working Bullocks*: it's full of foreboding. Red, Deb and their bullocks disappear into the forest. It flows 'over them, with its silences, whisper of leaves, murmur of small birds.' Above the whispering and murmuring, which is eerie in itself, is the 'laughter of a butcher-bird, melodious and cruel.'

'What do you think of the ending, Jill?' I asked her when I dropped by the library this arvo. 'I was hoping it would be optimistic, like *Black Opal's* ending, but it's a bit bleak, don't you reckon?'

She held up her hand and said, 'Hold on,' and wrote something on a piece of paper and gave it to me. 'It's a quote by a writer called Flora Eldershaw about Katharine's writing. It's something I've never forgotten and I agree with her.'

The quote reads: 'The world of her books is harsh and hard, but it is not hopeless. Underneath lies faith in the courage and steadfastness of man.'

I really like it when Jill tells me something about Katharine's work she thinks I will understand and agree with.

October 11ᵗʰ, 1967

On the bus home from work, I read Katharine's short story, 'The Grey Horse.' Jill told me this story is based on a real horse that used to race around the stable yard near the Throssell's orchard. 'Apparently, Katharine loved watching him prance about and couldn't resist writing about him.

She is a fine rider, so she knows a good horse when she sees one.'

Jill also told me that 'The Grey Horse' has been listed as one of the world's greatest short stories, and Katharine herself thinks it's one of her best.

Grey Ganger is a beautiful stallion, a 'superb creature, broad and short of back, deep barrelled, with mighty quarters' who prances and tosses his head with 'kittenish grace.' Old Gourlay, his owner, a 'queer, fussy insect of an old man' is jealous of his horse's 'youth and virility', and refuses to lend Grey Ganger to his neighbour, young Bill Moriarty, vindictively depriving him of the means to plough his orchard and the stallion a chance to mate. Bill thinks the old man is a 'mean old blighter...Had two women himself, and won't give a handsome animal like that his dues.'

But Grey Ganger finally gets his way, and the passage where the mare Lizzie and Grey Ganger mate is very sexy! I'm going to read it to the girls and see what they think. We're told that the grey stallion comes down to the end of his yard and stares at Lizzie, 'snorting as she passes.' He prances up and down, 'throwing himself about to attract her attention,' trembling, his breath 'blowing in gusty blasts from his nostrils.' Lizzie swings her 'bland, white-splashed face towards him' and blinks at the stallion from behind her 'wide black winkers.' Her tail moves slowly, gently; she stretches her hind legs. A shower 'splashed, glittering in the sunshine.' Men working nearby smell its 'hot, herby aroma' and Moriarty runs up to stop the stallion from getting near the mare. It's too late: by the time he gets to the yard, Grey Ganger has broken through his fences and is whirling around the mare in a 'plunging fury.'

From then on, there is no 'keeping the Ganger from passing mares'; he is 'as flighty as a brumby on the rods.' Old Gourlay is disgusted at how his grey stallion is kicking 'over the traces...disgracing him in the district.' He sells Grey Ganger, his house and his land and moves to town.

Lizzie has a foal and Bill Moriarty marries his sweetheart, Rose. Their baby dies, Moriarty's dried fruit business fails and he ends up milking cows, feeding pigs and chooks and clearing the land for 'fodder crops.' His life with Rose becomes 'mostly a fitting-in of domestic jobs, talking about the cost of things, eating frugally, and sleeping without touching her.' Rose wants no more children.

When Bill sees Grey Ganger again, the stallion is 'imperious' and 'more beautiful than ever...his quarters moulded to perfection.' Bill experiences 'the anguish of his dissatisfaction with life' and groans, 'I wish it was me, old man...I wish it was me.'

I don't feel sorry for Bill Moriarty, and I'm not convinced Katharine wants us to. I reckon out of all the faults people may have, self-pity is, for Katharine, one of the worst. From all that I've read by her so far, she likes people with strong backbones who can stand up to things and not whinge.

October 12th, 1967

I read that sexy passage from 'The Grey Horse' to Gwenda and Nora at morning tea and did their eyes grow big! 'Plunging fury,' Gwenda said, stirring her tea at top speed. 'Oooh!' said Nora, tossing her blond hair. We all sat quietly for a minute, looking at each other.

Just as Gwenda was about to say something, Maggot poked his boofy head into the tearoom and gave us the thumb-jerk. Bugger that man.

October 16th, 1967

Popped into the library after work. Jill had put aside for me Katharine's *N'goola and Other Stories*. 'I'd forgotten what a good short story writer she is,' said Jill. 'You'll enjoy them. Read 'Yoirimba' first – I am sure you'll love it.'

'Yoirimba' means 'how beautiful' in an Aboriginal dialect. Katharine gives us a long list of Western Australian wildflowers that flourish in Miss Prissy's garden at 'Yoirimba': purple hovea, 'snowy blossom' grevilleas; 'prickly acacia and scrub wattle burst into golden bloom'. There are 'daviesia and dillwynia'; 'hakea bearing gaudy magenta plumes'; dampiera and leschenaultia, 'as blue as they sky'; wild myrtle, kangaroo paws, spider orchids and 'hundreds of other shy and lovely wildflowers' chase 'each other over that hillside.'

She doesn't mention freesias, my favourite spring flower, which Mum tells me isn't a native, just a weed. If that's true, it's my favourite weed.

Miss Prissy adores her garden but, while she's away teaching in the goldfields, her parents, who have sold their farm and have come to live with her, rip out her native flowers and plant vegetables, vines and fruit trees and build a chook house and a cow shed. They never understand why their daughter takes down 'Yoirimba', the nameplate she once tacked onto her front gate. Because she loves her parents, she never tells them.

I'm going to buy a copy of *N'goola and Other Stories* tomorrow at lunchtime so I can read all the stories in the collection whenever I feel like it.

I notice Katharine has dedicated the stories to 'leaders and members of the great Australian Trade Unions.' Yay to the unions of Australia! When I leave Western Sunrise, I'm going to make sure I work for a company that has a union and I'll join it.

October 27th, 1967

At book group, Larry and I were chatting about Katharine, as we usually do these days. He told me about the Modern Women's Club, a group Katharine and a few other women set up in Perth in 1938. It was active until the 1950s. They met in town on Fridays and listened to guest speakers over lunch. The women discussed peace and all kinds of social issues to do with women, including the ban on employing married women in public service and equal pay for men and women doing the same job.

I wouldn't mind belonging to a club like that. I'd love to talk about women and work. I have no idea what equal pay means, but it sounds good. I might even mention what Maggot did to Nora. I bet there'd be a few women who've had the same or similar experience, and I'd love to know what they did about it.

November 3rd, 1967

I've been driving Jill crazy lately – I want more general information about Katharine's life. Jill said she'd get something together for me when she had a bit of extra time but that I should give her a week or so. She gave a little sigh, and I asked if I was pestering her. She said no, but she'd been really busy all week and hadn't had any help.

She's a very nice person with a lovely smile; I wouldn't want to put her out in any way, so I'll leave her alone for a little while!

November 6th, 1967

Had a boring weekend; I didn't go anywhere except up to the King's Park tearooms with my mother for afternoon tea on Saturday. We didn't talk about much; we never do.

I did mention that I was really enjoying my reading project and told her a bit about *Coonardoo*. She just sniffed and asked whether I knew Katharine's son, Ric Throssell, was a communist spy.

'Oh, Mum,' I said.

'He was! I read about him in the *West*.'

'Oh, Mum,' I said again. It was all I could think of saying.

I'll ask Larry about Ric Throssell when I see him. He'll know what's what.

November 17th, 1967

What a feast Jill has come up with! She is so good at her job! She's given me copies of newspaper articles about Katharine and a list of activities Katharine is or has been, involved in.

Can't wait to read it all!

November 24ᵗʰ, 1967

I asked Larry about Ric Throssell being a spy, and he just laughed and shook his head. He told me that in the 1950s, a couple of spies from the Soviet Union called Petrov defected in Canberra and 'named' Katharine and her son. Apparently ASIO had already given them both code names: Katharine was called 'Academician' and Ric Throssell's code name was 'Ferro'.

'Ric was called before the Royal Commission on Espionage, but there was no evidence that he was ever a spy,' said Larry. 'He is always under suspicion, though. In fact, at one point, he and his wife were called traitors. I'm sure it affected his chances of promotion in the public service where he worked.'

Then Larry said, with a big grin, 'If you want to know about spies, look no further than ASIO – they're the real spies!' He took a huge bite of his sponge cake and swallowed it in one gulp.

Larry also told me a story about some signals that were reported by locals to have come from Katharine's Greenmount house during the Second World War. When ASIO investigated, they discovered the 'signals' came from a tin in the bush, glinting in the sun! 'What's more,' Larry said, 'no one had been in the house for ages – it was all locked up, and Prichard was in Sydney. But the authorities are always checking on her. They obviously think she's a real troublemaker.'

'I suppose that's why she's called a Red Witch,' I said.

'Yep,' he grinned. 'Though I doubt she's offended. I suspect she's proud of being known as the Red Witch,' Larry chuckled.

November 25th, 1967

Have been reading some of the material Jill gave me about Katharine. Gosh, she has always been, and probably still is, an incredibly busy woman! I'm amazed at the number of things she's done in life. So many public meetings, lectures, discussions, rallies. She's written and distributed political leaflets, including one called 'Ban the Bomb' that she wrote after the film *On the Beach* came to Perth. She's signed petitions, written dozens of letters to the editors of various newspapers, judged literary competitions, sub-edited a newspaper called the *Red Star*, led street demonstrations, supported communists who've been arrested, and been the guest of honour at countless gatherings. When she was seventy-eight years old, she rode on the Peace Council's float through the streets of Perth on Labour Day!

Wow!

There are dozens of general interest articles about her that have appeared over many years in different newspapers in their social pages, so she's obviously a bit of a celebrity.

I love this one:

The Kalgoorlie Miner on Monday, 24th February 1919, reports that 'Captain Hugo Throssell, V.C., and Miss Katharine Susannah Prichard, of Armadale, Victoria, were quietly married a few days ago...Captain and Mrs Throssell are spending their honeymoon at Emerald. They intend making their permanent home in West Australia.'

Good on Katharine for not making a big deal about her wedding. Weddings are noisy and boring. I've only been to three, but they were all awful. The men drank too much and, at one of them, a man tipped beer over his wife. If I ever get married, I want to marry 'quietly', just like Katharine did.

A sad story about Hugo Throssell's suicide appears in the *Sydney Morning Herald* on Monday, 20th November 1933. The headline is 'V.C. Winner Found Shot Dead. Revolver Nearby.' This article gives details of his bravery: how he held a trench 'practically by himself, killing six or seven Turks with a rifle.' How he was wounded in the shoulder and the neck but kept fighting for hours. How he was 'invalided to England' where he caught meningitis and nearly died. How he returned to Australia a war hero, 'receiving splendid receptions wherever he went.'

Katharine would've liked most of the article because she was very proud of her 'Jim,' but I reckon she would've been horrified by the headline. The report ends with this sentence: 'In 1919, he married Katharine Susannah Prichard, the well-known novelist, who is at present touring Russia.'

She must've been heartbroken to read the newspaper reports of her husband's suicide and worried sick about being so far away from home and her son.

A visit to Sydney by Katharine in support of the Russian Aid Appeal was reported in the social and personal section of the *Sydney Morning Herald* on Thursday, 4th December 1941.

So she obviously has long been a person worthy of the social pages in newspapers, even in the eastern states!

Perth's *Daily News* on Saturday, 9th April 1949, has a story about how a 'near-riot' was 'narrowly averted' in Midland Junction at a political rally. The rally was held outdoors because the Communist

Party's candidate had been refused permission to hire the local town hall.

Katharine was one of the speakers. Not long after the meeting began, anti-communists in the audience began singing 'Waltzing Matilda' and other 'patriotic songs.' There were arguments that 'looked like developing into brawls', so the cops stepped in.

What interests me about this story is that the journalist assumed 'Waltzing Matilda' upset Katharine. From all that I've read so far, Katharine is nothing but patriotic. I can't imagine her objecting to an audience singing 'Waltzing Matilda.' Her works are full of love for Australia, its people and its future. It's just that the future she imagines for Australia isn't what many people believe it should be!

On Wednesday, 15th March 1950, *The Daily News* reports that Katharine has been nominated for the Nobel Prize in Literature. She must've been thrilled to bits. Proves she's a writer of tonnage!

There's a letter to the editor of Melbourne's *The Age* on Saturday, 22nd August 1953, in which Katharine writes that now that an armistice has been signed in Korea, 'hope stirs again that the peoples of the world can solve international differences by negotiation and not war.' She asks, 'Who wants war?…Not those who have suffered the loss of sons and brothers, husbands and friends. Not those who know the misery and devastation war brings.'

Her hatred of war scorches every line in this letter.

November 26ᵗʰ, 1967

Everyone I know reads, or has read at some time or another, the *West Australian*. I reckon almost everyone believes every word they read in that paper. My mother certainly does. '*The Daily News* is a bit sensational, I'll give you that, and there are too many advertisements, but,' she insists, 'the *West* is the truth.'

Anyway, Jill has given me copies of a few items to do with Katharine that have been published in the *West Australian* and I've been browsing them this arvo. It's a stinking hot day, but the little park nearby has lots of shade and it's good to get out of the house and read in peace.

On October 5ᵗʰ, 1942, the *West Australian* reported that Katharine took part in a meeting urging the ban on the Communist Party of Australia be lifted. 'Mrs H. Throssell said that she has been a communist for 20 years, and that "the only people who wanted the ban maintained were those blinded by ignorance or prejudice."'

There's a series of letters to the editor of the *West Australian* between Katharine and a woman called Mrs Cardell-Oliver. This woman visited the Soviet Union in 1936 and she disagrees with Katharine about everyday life in Russia. One of the main points Mrs Cardell-Oliver makes is that, when she went to Russia in 1934, she noticed few children had many toys, and that of the children who did, their toys had to do 'with the military.'

Katharine's letter in reply says that she's 'interested to know precisely when and where Mrs Cardell-Oliver saw children in the Soviet Union playing with toys of a military character' because, she writes, 'never at any time, in shops, schools, homes, or in the hands of a child, did I see a toy with any military significance – unless aeroplanes and gliders, which the boys were fond of making and trying-out, can be so regarded.'

Instead of listing the towns or places where she saw children playing with military toys (because, she says, even if she did, Mrs Throssell would 'still be sceptical'), Mrs Cardell-Oliver, in her second letter, lists what she calls 'truthful reports' about the existence of poverty, corruption and food shortages in Russia and points out the hypocrisy of the Soviet Union's policy of preaching peace while arming for war.

Katharine's reply is that Mrs Cardell-Oliver's facts are out of date or inaccurate.

As I was reading their arguments, I thought about how people's views about places they visit can be completely different, even though they went to the same place at the same time. When Nora and I went to Fremantle last year, for instance, I thought it was a very interesting place, full of history, whereas Nora called it a dump and told me she'd never go back. When we were kids, Pete used to love going to Rottnest for Christmas holidays, but I hated the place. Too bloody hot for me! I always wanted to stay home alone, but Mum and Dad wouldn't let me.

November 28th, 1967

Tonight, Jill gave me copies of articles published in a communist newspaper called *Tribune*. I had no idea there was a communist newspaper in Australia! I won't mention this to Mum; she won't like the sound of it.

A *Tribune* article published on 15th December 1954 records the 'hundreds of greetings' that 'poured into Perth last week from all over Australia' to celebrate Katharine's seventieth birthday. There was a party for her organised by the Modern Women's Club where she told her guests that her 'belief in communism is not something apart from my writing but the very foundation of it.' Professor Alan Edwards of the University of WA called her the 'greatest living Australian writer'. Professor Walter Murdoch said that in the 'parliament of world literature, she is the Member for Australia; and we are proud of our representative.'

I'll bet she really enjoyed her seventieth birthday.

One article, dated 16th August 1945, reports that Katharine has been elected to the Central Committee of the Communist Party. Not sure what that means but it sounds important.

On Tuesday, 20th November 1945, Katharine was in Sydney and launched the Communist Party Chess Club. She played a game with a staff member of the *Tribune* that evening.

I wonder if she won. Gosh, imagine being able to play chess! I've never won a game of draughts!

An article written by Katharine with the title 'Australian Culture Must be Fought For' was published in *Tribune* on her birthday, 4th

December 1948. She writes that she agrees with Stalin that all workers should be 'cultured and educated' and, like the Soviet Union, Australia will 'achieve this in time.'

I was proud to discover in this article, my opinion that Katharine wouldn't have been annoyed with the audience for singing 'Waltzing Matilda' at that near-riot in Midland Junction is correct. She writes that she'd love to hear Australian songs being sung at the political meetings she attends. She suggests they sing 'Waltzing Matilda' because it has the 'real Australian spirit and would be a success at any party.' So there, boo to you, *Daily News!*

In March 1945, according to another article in *Tribune,* she was involved in International Women's Day celebrations 'in an atmosphere of hope that this terrible war will soon end.' Most of all, she wants Australian women to do everything possible to 'ensure that another generation is not swept into the barbarous holocaust of war.'

How could any woman in Australia not agree with that?

She also wrote a similar article for the *Tribune,* eight years later, in 1953, again celebrating International Women's Day, where she stressed the 'need for women to work strenuously in defence of their democratic rights as citizens, so that as wives and mothers they will be able to protect their children from the horrors of war, and their menfolk from the suffering and misery that war entails.'

I went into the kitchen around nine-thirty tonight to make a cup of tea after reading the *Tribune* articles. Mum happened to pop in to check something in the fridge. I asked her what kinds of things we could do, as Australian women, to stop Australia from getting involved in another war. She stared at me, and said, 'Well, I suppose we could pressure our men not to fight. Other than that, I have no idea.'

I quite liked Mum's suggestion about urging men not to fight. Wouldn't it be fantastic if men worldwide refused to sign up for any kind of war, and then we'd see what happens next.

December 4th, 1967

I asked Gwenda this morning what she thought of my mother's idea about trying to convince men not to go to war. 'A bit of a fantasy, I reckon,' she scoffed. 'Because if we managed to persuade our men never to go to war, eventually we'd be invaded.'

'Well,' I said, 'if we were invaded, then everyone would fight back in any way we could.'

I realized we were talking about two different things – a war defending Australia in Australia versus fighting in a war overseas. For instance, I've often wondered why Australian soldiers are fighting in Vietnam. Mum raves on about how we have to defeat 'the Commies.' On the radio and in the newspapers, we hear and read about the 'domino theory' which claims if communists win a revolution in one country other neighbouring countries will 'fall' too.

Not sure I believe that. I reckon Australia wouldn't just 'fall' to communism if the communists won in Vietnam. I doubt that New

Zealand would either! The domino theory sounds like scare-mongering to me.

Anyway, Gwenda said she's scared Andy might eventually be sent off to Vietnam. 'We haven't talked much about it,' she said, stirring her tea nervously. 'But it's possible he could go into the ballot.'

December 5th, 1967

Dropped into the library tonight and had a chat to Jill about war and invasion. Jill told me a story about a wealthy man who, during the Second World War, told Katharine that he was telling his friends it would be useless to try to stop a Japanese invasion. 'Well,' Jill laughed, 'Katharine told *him* that *she* would advise *her* friends and everyone else she could reach to resist to the utmost with anything they had – if it was only boiling water!'

'Good on her!' I exclaimed. Jill gave one of her dazzling smiles and saluted the air with her fist.

Going home on the bus I thought about a character in one of Eleanor Dark's novels. She says she's fed up with men fighting in wars and that women should simply say, 'No. I bear no more children into a world not fit to receive them.' Now that sounds like a great idea!

December 6th, 1967

Just finished the last of the *Tribune* articles Jill gave me. A very interesting one, too!

'The nobility of the two who have died stands in shining contrast to the brutality of their judges,' writes Katharine. She was condemning the electrocution of Ethel and Julius Rosenberg in the United States in 1953 and says that 'the rulers of the USA' have 'earned the horrified disgust of humane and decent men and women throughout the world.'

I remember hearing about that case when I was a kid. I was shocked to learn that people can be spies, but even more shocked to hear that spies can be electrocuted! What a horrific way to die.

In her article, Katharine argues that the 'evidence against Julius and Ethel Rosenberg was faulty and corrupt.' Jill has scribbled this note in the margin:

In 1951, David Greenglass, Ethel's brother, lied under oath, telling the court that he saw his sister typing information she intended to give to the Soviet Union.

What's horrifying is that the Rosenbergs had children. Mum says they had two little boys. How could children begin to understand that their parents died in an electric chair?

December 7th, 1967

At morning tea, I asked Gwenda if she'd heard of the Rosenbergs and she said she remembers her mother and father discussing them with some friends who'd come for lunch. 'The only thing I remember is that Dad didn't seem to care very much about their electrocution but Mum did,' said Gwenda. 'Mum thinks they were electrocuted because they were communists and Jewish, not because they were spies.'

'I'm with your mum, Gwenda,' I said. 'What about you, Nora? What do you think about the Rosenbergs?'

Nora shrugged, said she'd never thought about them, then asked Gwenda, 'How's your boyfriend?'

Gwenda tossed her head and said she had a lot of typing to do before five o'clock and had to return to her desk or she'd be in trouble with the Maggot.

Something's up with Gwenda…

December 18th, 1967

Nora called in sick today.

'That's the second time this month,' I said. 'What's going on with her, do you know?'

'Nora is looking for another job. She might have an interview,' replied Gwenda.

I wouldn't mind looking for another job, but what would change, really? I'm a very good typist, so I would probably end up with another job so similar to this one I'd hardly notice the difference. On the other hand, I might find a job that pays more, and then I could give Mum extra board to get a telephone!

I wish we all had telephones – I'd ring Nora and see what she's up to, then I'd ring Gwenda and tell her. The only person I know with a telephone is our neighbour two doors up. She brags about it to Mum, but Mum just sniffs, 'What's the point of bragging about having a phone when she probably doesn't know anyone who has one anyway, so who can she ring?'

But I often drop hints to Mum about getting a telephone, saying it would be good in an emergency; we wouldn't have to run up to the public phone box.

December 22nd, 1967

After work this arvo, I dropped in to the library to wish Jill a Merry Christmas and to chat about the Rosenbergs. She agrees with Katharine that it was a monstrous thing the US government did to them. 'I think you said you'd bought *N'goola and Other Stories*?' Jill said. 'You'll find a story about the Rosenbergs in that collection. It's called "The Long Shadow".' Read it when you can.'

'The Long Shadow' is about a twelve-year-old girl called Fran who, on her way to a ballet class, runs into a demonstration against the execution of the Rosenbergs. Her ballet teacher, Madame Nina Galin, is a Russian communist. During the class, the students express various views about the demonstration. A 'ginger-haired girl' calls the demonstration 'silly'; Marie Fuller, a student with a 'perky nose' calls it 'stupid.' She tells Madame that her 'daddy says the Rosenbergs are spies, and they should be executed.' Madame replies that perhaps her 'daddy' doesn't know 'all the facts' and that 'many people believe Ethel and Julius Rosenberg are innocent.'

Marie Fuller's parents immediately try to convince all the parents to withdraw their children from Madame's ballet school. Fran's mother refuses, pointing out to Mrs Fuller that everyone 'ought to be tolerant of each other's different opinions.' Fran's parents and Fran decide to join the demonstrations, believing that while it may not be much help for the Rosenbergs, it will be 'good…to have the courage to join in this protest.'

I really like this story – it's told in a simple way, mainly from the point of view of a child, and we see how people with different views respond to a shocking event.

December 25th, 1967

Boring Christmas Day except that this year, instead of Boxing Day, Mrs Cook barged through the back door this afternoon and handed Mum two bottles of beer and a bottle of Sparkling Burgundy. Mum told her to go home. I told Mum she should've at least given her a ham sandwich because food may have stopped her getting drunk, but Mum said Mrs Cook was already drunk and needed a good lie down.

December 31st, 1967

New Year's Eve.

Nora and I went into town and wandered around. We saw a couple of nice-looking blokes hanging around the Ambassadors, and Nora gave them a big smile and tossed her blond curls. One looked interested, but then two girls turned up and they all went into the pictures together.

Sniff, sniff. I wish Nora and I could meet someone.

Maybe 1968 will be a good year for boyfriends? It's a leap year. Maybe Gwenda will pop the question to that boyfriend of hers.

January 5th, 1968

This morning, we were joking with Gwenda about leap years, telling her she now has the right to ask her boyfriend to marry her.

'What's the latest with Andy?' I asked.

'I'm still keen on him, and we've been spending a lot of time together,' Gwenda replied. 'But I'm certainly not planning to ask him to marry me, leap year or no leap year. I'm going back to night school this year anyway, so I won't be seeing him as often.'

January 21st, 1968

Gwenda, Nora and I had afternoon tea yesterday at the King's Park tearooms and had a nice chat about nothing in particular. We wandered down Fraser Avenue, and I was thrilled to stop and stare at the Lighthorse monument and Hugo Throssell's tree. I've walked by that tree so many times, ever since I was a child, but never had any idea who Hugo Throssell was. Of course, now I have my project, I'm in the know.

January 26th, 1968

First book club of the year! And it's Australia Day. Not that I give two hoots. I don't like our flag and can't stand our national anthem.

Larry asked me how I was going with my project. I gulped, then muttered something about being busy. His eyes behind his glasses were brown and kind as he touched my elbow and said softly, 'Keep at it, Vicki.'

I haven't read much at all lately – must keep on track with my project – must focus on Katharine, no cheating. This is a diary of discovery. Will go back to the library next week.

January 31st, 1968

This arvo, Jill told me I should read something about Egon Kisch because Katharine was very involved in his trip to Australia. 'I'll get something together for you, Vicki,' she said.

I've heard of Egon Kisch. I read Frank Hardy's *Power Without Glory* some time ago and Kisch is a minor character. In the book, Mary West goes to an anti-war demonstration and joins the mob that boarded the ship Kisch was on. He was heading for Sydney, but the ship had docked in Melbourne for several days. Mary is fascinated by Egon Kisch's face; I can't remember all the details, but I recall he is described as having glinting eyes.

I'm thrilled that Jill will continue to help me with my project! Couldn't wish for anyone better to give me top-notch info!

February 14th, 1968

I've been reading the material Jill gave me about Egon Kisch.

In the 1930s, Katharine belonged to the Movement Against War and Fascism. This group believed that fascists hated trade unions, all working-class organizations, and 'Jews, Roman Catholics, communists and independent intellectuals.' Fascism, the Movement claimed, promotes war, suppresses free speech, and insists that 'private enterprise must remain the guiding spirit of industry.'

Kisch was a Jewish communist. He was born in Czechoslovakia, was a journalist, a writer of travel books and a political activist. In 1934, he was invited by the Movement to address one of its anti-war rallies in Melbourne. He arrived in Fremantle on a ship called the 'Strathaird' in November but was told by authorities he had been classified by the Federal government as an 'undesirable' and was refused permission to land.

When the ship arrived in Melbourne, supporters, including Katharine, demonstrated against the government's decision. Katharine was appointed his unofficial bodyguard and was told not to let Kisch out of her sight. The authorities insisted he would not be able to leave the ship, so a few days later, Kisch took a flying leap from the ship onto the pier and broke his leg. The police picked him up, carried him back to the 'Strathaird' (without first aid) and the ship set off for Sydney, where he finally received medical treatment.

On arrival in Sydney, he was given the 'dictation test.' Jill has written a one-page explanation of this test, which I read just a while ago in bed. It was part of the Immigration Restriction Act, and reads, 'Any person who when asked to do so by an officer fails to write out at dictation and sign in the presence of the officer a passage of fifty words in length in a European language directed by the officer' will be refused admission to Australia.

I was amazed to read that Egon Kisch was asked to write the Lord's Prayer in Scottish Gaelic rather than in one of the many languages he spoke. When he refused, because he obviously couldn't do it, he was told he'd failed the dictation test.

I had no idea about the Immigration Restriction Act, the dictation test, or being an undesirable! After reading this stuff, I don't know what to think. Won't ask Mum about it; she'll snort and say Australia has every right to choose how to let people come into our country.

February 23rd, 1968

At book club tonight, I chatted with Larry about Egon Kisch. 'Kisch had thousands of supporters all over Australia', Larry told me. 'They used the slogan "Kisch Must Land!" and he became a symbol for democratic rights and resistance to war. They dragged him from the ship to prison, from prison to hospital. He was in and out of the courts and in trouble with all kinds of authorities. Still, he insisted on speaking at rallies and going to anti-fascist meetings.

'The government finally gave in, and he was allowed to address rallies in Queensland, NSW, and Victoria. When he left for Europe, the ship stopped in Fremantle and Prichard was there to farewell him. Apparently, he spent an afternoon with her and some friends at her home in Greenmount before he sailed.'

Larry started laughing as he told me he'd read somewhere that

Egon Kisch had a feather and snake tattoo on his right shoulder and a bird on his left shoulder. 'He also had a dagger tattooed on the left side of his chest, a wild man with snake-hair and a dagger through his head on his left inner forearm, and a tattoo of a woman disappearing below his belt. He was a bit of a show off,' Larry said with a big grin.

I think Egon Kisch's story is interesting. It tells us a lot about Australia's immigration laws. But even more interesting to me is the man himself. I reckon Katharine has known so many intriguing men throughout her life – this tattooed Egon Kisch, dashing Guido Baracchi, her suave *Preux Chevalier*, magnetic Red Beard of Gippsland, and, of course, her famous, handsome war hero husband.

Are there any men like that living right now in Perth, I wonder? If there are, I'd like to meet one!

February 27th, 1968

Have a bad cold. Took today off work. Stayed in my room almost the whole time reading Katharine's short stories and sleeping. Mum has been very good to me, bringing me cups of tea, vegetable soup, aspros and Irish Moss. She's been asking me if I'd like her to turn up the radio in the kitchen really loud so I can listen to the programs, but I said no because I want to read.

Mum's always been good to people who are sick, except for Dad. She got a bit nasty with him towards the end.

February 29th, 1968

This morning, we told Gwenda today's the day she can ask her boyfriend to marry her!

'Nosy tarts!' Gwenda replied, vigorously washing her cup.

'Just checking!' Nora giggled.

At lunch, I wrote a dialogue in which a girl asks her boyfriend to marry her. I'll show it to Gwenda one day, just for fun!

March 9th, 1968

I've been going through the file Jill gave me about the Movement Against War and Fascism. Jill included a note about how Hugo always supported Katharine when she gave speeches against fascism. Here's what Jill wrote:

Katharine claims that 'Jim' accompanied her to all the meetings where she spoke against fascism, especially during the Spanish Civil War. If someone interrupted her, he'd glare at the offender. If they continued heckling, he'd stride down the aisle and stand beside the hecklers. Katharine told him that the opposition should have its say, but he said that if she was talking, they had to listen to her.

Hugo, however, thought Katharine would never be a good speaker because she was always nervous and never told funny stories.

March 14th, 1968

Had a fright earlier tonight on my way home from the library. I was waiting for my bus on St Georges Terrace; no one else was at the bus stop. A man approached me and whispered, 'Do you want to go up to King's Park and have a naughty?' He stank of alcohol and had a horrible smile, more of a leer. I took off – heading for the next bus stop, hoping there'd be someone waiting for a bus. That bastard chased me! I lost a shoe, but there was no way I was going to turn back to look for it. Fortunately, I ran into a couple walking in the opposite direction and I burst out that a man was after me. We looked around but he'd disappeared. 'Report him to the police as soon as possible,' the woman said. 'In the meantime, we'll walk you to the next bus stop and wait until your bus comes.'

When I got home, I told Mum what had happened and she went straight over to Mrs McIntyre, the neighbour with the phone, and called the police. Mum said the cops told her I should go to the local police station first thing in the morning and make a statement.

'See, Mum,' I said when she came back. 'If we had a phone, you wouldn't have to go to Mrs McIntyre's!'

'Don't sulk, Vicki,' she replied. 'Just talk to the police in the morning.'

March 15th, 1968

Well, I'm absolutely disgusted with the cops! When I arrived at the station, I said to the policeman behind the counter that I was the girl who'd been chased by a man yesterday evening along St Georges

Terrace, had lost my shoe while I was running away from him, and that I had been told to come in and make a statement. This cop didn't look interested; in fact, he looked a bit amused. 'Well, little miss, did you find your shoe?' he asked, swallowing a chuckle. I filled in a form and left.

On the bus going to work, I thought, *There goes my second pair of work shoes. Now I only have the pair I'm wearing and one pair of going-out shoes. I'll have to ask Mum if I can skip board for a couple of weeks to buy another pair to wear to work.*

On top of that, I got into trouble with Maggot for being late. I was too embarrassed to explain why, so I just said Mum was sick and I had to look after her for a little while before a neighbour came in and I could leave.

March 18th, 1968

At morning tea, I told Gwenda and Nora what happened to me on Thursday night and they both said I did the right thing by running away as fast as I could. We talked about why a man would do that kind of thing to a girl waiting at a bus stop.

'Some blokes are real predators,' said Gwenda. 'They see women as fair game.'

'I'm always nervous if I'm out alone at night,' Nora admitted.

'I'll be on the alert at the bus stop from now on,' I said.

None of us can understand why the cops weren't interested!

As we were talking, I began thinking about Katharine's *Preux*

Chevalier and that old 'Dr Paul' in Gippsland who fell for her. *Katharine's had her fair share of predators,* I thought. *She may have been flattered by their attention for a while but surely, she must've been a bit suspicious about what they wanted from her!*

'How's your boyfriend?' asked Nora, changing the subject.

Gwenda looked grumpy. 'Andy's been getting aggressive lately,' she growled. 'He's really pushing me to have sex with him, especially when he's had a few drinks. The problem is, when he's been drinking, he starts sucking on peppermint Lifesavers. I can't resist the smell of peppermint and I love the way he kisses me after he's had those mints. I'm scared I'll give in soon, but I'm even more terrified of getting pregnant! And then what? Bugger him!'

'Don't get carried away,' said Nora sympathetically.

'Watch yourself, Gwenda,' I said, nodding at Nora.

At the moment, I'm right off men, what with that creep chasing me the other night and Andy putting the hard word on Gwenda. I'm glad I don't have a boyfriend.

March 29th, 1968

Tonight, Jill gave me carbon copies of two plays by Katharine – *Bid Me to Love* and *Forward One*. 'I'm not sure how we got hold of these. Probably through the various writing competitions we hear from now and then. I thought of you when I found them; you might like them.

'She wrote *Bid Me to Love* at about the same time she wrote *Brumby Innes* and entered it in the same competition. She won for

Brumby Innes. *Bid Me to Love* won no prizes. I've heard it's a semi-autobiographical play. As far as I know, it's never been produced on stage, but I've read that *Forward One* was performed by the Workers' Theatre in Perth in the 1930s.

'I concentrated on her novels and stories in my thesis, so can't remember much about her plays. I do recall after *Bid Me to Love*, I read *Intimate Strangers*,' Jill said. 'They're similar stories, both very upsetting in my opinion.'

As she was talking, she was twisting her wedding ring. I hadn't even noticed it. I must have a blank spot when it comes to wedding rings!

March 30th, 1968

Read *Forward One* this morning. It's a short, powerful play about three young shop assistants, Elsie, Vera and Phyllis, and their awful manager, Miss Drew, who work in a frock shop in Perth. It's a stinking hot summer afternoon and the heat is just about killing the girls who are bullied and ridiculed by Miss Drew. Her cry, 'Forward one!' is her warning that a customer is coming into the shop and the nearest shop assistant has to hop to and serve her.

Despite the Shop Assistants Union rules, which Elsie and Vera both know, Miss Drew refuses to let the girls sit down when there are no customers in the shop: 'You can lean against the wall, or sit on the arm of a chair for not more than two minutes at a time – if there are no customers in the showroom.'

Elsie has been working 'at the game' for ten years and has a bad back: 'I can't sleep at night for the pain.' Vera goes home each day 'too dead tired to move and aching all over,' and is losing her boyfriend because he says she's *always* tired.

Phyllis, the youngest shop assistant, who has just started working and desperately needs the job, spends most of this boiling hot afternoon climbing up and down ladders, handing down boxes and being called 'stupid' by Miss Drew. She finally falls off the ladder and faints. When Miss Drew tells Vera and Elsie to 'take her into the packing room. I can't have the shop littered up like this. Supposing a customer should come in,' Vera rebels. 'I won't take her away until she's able to go. Not for you – or fifty customers.'

At the end of the play, the three girls walk out on Miss Drew, leaving the showroom 'with an air of defiant resolution.'

Oh boy, did I cheer for those three girls when they walked out!

I thought about how similar Maggot is to Miss Drew – bully bosses must be all the same.

April 1ˢᵗ, 1968

Gwenda told us this morning that she's thinking of breaking up with Andy because he gets so cranky with her for not giving in. 'I'm sick of him. I mean, I let him feel me up and we do some other stuff but why should I go any further until...' and then she stopped.

'Until what?' we both asked simultaneously, but she shook her head. Later, on our way back to our desks, Nora whispered to me, 'She means until he asks her to marry him.'

April 2ⁿᵈ, 1968

Tonight, I went to bed early and read *Bid Me to Love*. I did the dishes before I went into my room so Mum won't bang on my door and yell at me that it's time to clean up, as she usually does if I go to bed early.

There are some scribbled notes attached that read:

'The setting is probably Katharine's home in Greenmount.

Greg speaks a lot like Hugo, e.g., 'Cripes' and 'I say'.

Louise is very like what I imagine Katharine could be: flirtatious, passionate, unconventional, teasing; also very domestic; adores her children; worries about the house and money.

The Throssells had a young Italian who worked in the orchard and who sang opera songs to Katharine, possibly named Tony.

Hugo liked women and they liked him. Katharine told him that physical relations with other people weren't so important; true comradeship between husband and wife is what counts.

The Throssell family had a cat called Phoebus Apollo; the Reed family in the play have a cat with same name.

Based on fact or fantasy or a bit of both?'

The subtitle of *Bid Me to Love* is *The Caught Bus* and that's what Greg thinks his wife, Louise, is – a 'caught bus'; someone he no longer has to catch. He compares her to his thoroughbred horse, Joybells, telling Louise that she's the 'dead ring of her...plays up, prances around – all spirit, sweats herself silly over nothing at all. But there's not a spot of vice in her.'

He's won her; now she's just a trophy. 'Of all the trophies I ever won...I'm proudest of you, darling. Did it in record time too...' Greg says to his wife over breakfast on the morning of their sixth wedding anniversary, which is the play's opening. Although they 'kiss happily,' in the background is the 'ka ka' of crows – birds Louise hates and seems to fear.

Those crows gave me the same uneasy feeling I had when I read the ending of *Working Bullocks* when the butcher-birds screech through the forest.

When Greg goes off to play tennis, Louise has an interesting conversation with her old flame, Woodbridge, who's staying with them. She says that, after her marriage, she told Greg that if she doesn't like married life, 'Don't expect me to stick it...And if you don't like it, I won't expect you to stick it, either.' She believes that the success of their marriage 'has been due to...a sense of impermanence.' She also believes that 'physical fidelity doesn't mean as much...as psychological fidelity.'

And yet, Louise is furious when she discovers Greg has been writing to a woman in Brisbane, calling her Joybells, and arranging to meet her in Sydney when he goes there on business. 'Another of your little thoroughbreds?' she asks. 'That crow seems to have known what he was talking about!'

In the Second Act, Louise hates that she's jealous, even while Greg keeps pledging his love to her: 'I've told you I love you. You're the only woman in the world for me,' he tells her over and over. In return, Louise tells him not to forget that he is to be 'as free as air in Sydney' and refuses to tell him she loves him. 'You've got to say you care,' Greg says desperately, 'or I'll blow me light out. See. Say it. Say it!' But she won't. As he races off to catch the train to Sydney, she says to herself, 'I won't forgive you till you've got something to forgive me.'

Louise decides, 'Every woman of forty needs a lover to keep her self-respect...and her husband's.' There's no way she will be 'a caught bus'; she'll 'make love to a blind man on a dark road to get even with Greg for saying that.' When Woodbridge starts to flirt with Louise, she refuses him, telling him, 'You don't count, Woody.' (Poor ol' Woody!) Instead, she tells Woody she plans to ride out into the bush the next day with young Don, the handsome 'dago' who works for them, and seduce him. He's been bringing her little gifts like gorgeous moths and freshly-picked apples and singing 'Bid Me to Love' from afar. 'I adore his vigour and youthful beauty,' Louise tells Woody, declaring that she is '*passionée f*or this young Dago.'

After she has enjoyed 'bushfire love' with Don, Woody tells Louise if Greg finds out, he'll take the children away from her. Louise quickly decides to end her relationship with her 'young Dago.'

In a little twist, Greg is led to believe that Louise has slept with Woodbridge, who is promptly kicked out of the house. Gallant Woody tells Greg that he must forgive Louise and think about running after his bus again.

Towards the end of the play, Greg repeats the line about blowing his light out. He tells Louise how miserable he had been in Sydney: 'Miserable as a bandicoot. It's no good to me being without you, dearest,' he tells her. 'I could just blow my damned light out.'

Katharine wrote this play before Hugo killed himself. I wonder if she's ever thought about those lines as the years have passed.

Katharine had been married for about eight years when she wrote *Bid Me to Love*, so maybe she'd reached the point of being a bit bored, or perhaps not very happy, with her husband?

April 3ʳᵈ, 1968

Jill told me that Hugo didn't like *Bid Me to Love*, and he didn't like *Brumby Innes* either. He thought *Brumby Innes* was 'too brutal' and didn't think *Bid Me to Love* was funny, even though Katharine called it an 'honest-to-God' attempt at writing comedy.

I agree with him – I don't think *Bid Me to Love* is funny. It's sad that this couple needed to play silly little games and have affairs. On the other hand, what do I know about the games married people play with or against each other? I might play games myself if I ever get married.

I can't imagine Mum ever having had an affair. She isn't very attractive. She dresses well, but I don't think men would look twice at her. I've seen a couple of photos of her in her twenties, and she looked quite nice back then but not what you'd call a beauty.

When I got home from the library, I asked Mum casually if she and Dad had ever flirted or mucked around with anyone else. She looked embarrassed at first, then laughed. 'I remember one night before you were born, we went to a dance,' she said. 'I flirted and danced with a good-looking man who held me tight during the fox trot. He was a real charmer and a great dancer! Your dad was furious with me and threatened to knock the man down if he'd step outside.

'We argued about it on the tram all the way home,' she continued, looking a bit dreamy. 'It started to rain, and we got wet through. By then, I was so tired and fed up with your father that I ran into the house and started crying. I was scared he could hit me, but instead he slammed the front door behind him and told me to grow up.'

I can remember quite a few rows between Mum and Dad, especially towards the end of his life when he wasn't feeling well and was bad-tempered. She once said to me over the washing-up, 'I'm so browned off with your father. If he dies tomorrow, I won't care. It'll be a relief.'

At the time, I thought it was a terrible thing to say. Now I'm thinking that perhaps, after so many years of being together, they were sick of each other and could say things like that, although probably not to each other.

April 8th, 1968

Tonight began *Intimate Strangers*. She dedicated the novel to Hilda Esson.

I remember reading about Hilda in *Child of the Hurricane*. She tells us that as children, they lived in Melbourne next door to each other. They broke a paling in the back fence to talk to each other about school, the books they were reading, and what they wanted to be when they grew up. They shared their 'most intimate thoughts...their hopes and dreams in a friendship that grew stronger with the years.'

Hilda went to a private school, went to university and became a doctor. Katharine writes in *Child of the Hurricane* how 'deeply…disappointed' she was at not being able to go to uni, but her parents couldn't afford the fees. Katharine kept up with her friend's studies by reading the books on Hilda's lists at a public library in Melbourne.

April 11th, 1968

Dropped by the library this arvo and was chatting to Jill about Hilda Esson. 'Hilda believed that "Kattie" was an artistic personality who threw her life away by getting involved with the communists,' Jill said. 'They knew each other for fifty-odd years and Hilda never changed her views about Katharine's political activities. She always thought Katharine should stick to writing stories like *Coonardoo* and not try to solve the world's problems.'

I puzzled over this remark on the bus going home and came to the conclusion that I think *Coonardoo* does both: it's a terrific story – and it also tries to solve a world problem. Wonder why her friend didn't realize this?

April 15th, 1968

Easter Monday! Get paid for a day off! Hurray!

Mum's gone to Mrs Cook's, so I can spend the day with Katharine and eat my chocolate Easter egg!

Intimate Strangers opens with scenes of the Blackwood family on their summer holidays at a beach called Calatta, which, Jill told me, is probably Rockingham. 'The Throssells used to spend their summer holidays in the Rockingham area and she began writing *Intimate Strangers* there,' Jill said.

Greg and Elodie Blackwood have been married for fifteen years and the 'gilt was off the gingerbread, although they cohabited.' That phrase – the gilt was off the gingerbread – is also used in *Bid Me to Love*. And I'm struck by how similar the characters in this novel are to those in *Bid Me to Love*.

Greg and Elodie are a lot like Greg and Louise. Although Greg and Louise have been married for only six years, the two couples have the same kind of marriage: they're bored with each other and their suburban lives, they bicker, they look for other people to satisfy them, they try to find ways to pay each other back.

Elodie refers to her marriage as a 'mirage.' Everything about their marriage 'irks and infuriates' Greg. They have spent years 'quarrelling, tearing each other to pieces, worn to shreds by wakeful nights, fractious youngsters.' Elodie carries 'the house like a shell on her back' and tells Greg that there's been nothing for her in their marriage 'for a long time' and that he hasn't 'cared whether there was or not,' something Greg admits is true, although he 'wished it were not.'

Elodie's friend, Rachel, tells her that 'every woman over forty needs a lover.' Louise says exactly the same thing to Woody, her old flame. Louise makes 'bush fire' love with Don, and Elodie has a tempestuous affair with Jerome and dreams of running off with him.

There are other similarities: the children in *Intimate Strangers* and *Bid Me to Love* are called Peg and Bill. Molly, Greg's tennis partner in *Bid Me to Love*, is similar to Greg Blackwood's tennis partner, Dirk, in *Intimate Strangers*. Both young women are confident, physically strong and independent. Tony, the Italian 'fish-o,' has a fine voice and sings love songs, just as Don does in *Bid Me to Love*. Both men are completely at ease with nature – in Tony's case, it's the sea, whereas Don loves the bush.

On the dark side, both Greg Blackwood and Greg Reed threaten to commit suicide.

And then there are drains! Louise and Elodie are obsessed with dirty drains! Louise tells Woodbridge, 'The worst of being married is, you get so involved in the business of living together – meals, drains, mending, and bills.' Elodie complains to Greg that their drains are 'choked with rubbish and leaves' and need cleaning. She later reflects on the 'low comedy' of domestic tragedies where people are 'preoccupied with all the sordid and ugly details of a small house and smaller income. Dirty drains, black grease, mosquitos, flies, socks that have to be darned...dish washings and peelings of potatoes, scouring of dirty floors and emptying of slops...The great lovers of history and fiction never seemed to be bothered by such considerations.'

Drains seem to have interested Katharine since childhood: I remember her references to drains in *The Wild Oats of Han* and how proud Granny Sarahy was of Peter Barry when he rented the house in Launceston 'without reference to its drains, spouts, stoves, or washtubs.'

Katharine makes me laugh out loud with her observations about weird things like drains! I'm starting to notice her mischievous sense of humour.

April 20th, 1968

I really wish we had a telephone; I felt like a natter after dinner, although I'm not sure who I would ring. Gwenda doesn't have a phone, nor does Nora. I wonder if Larry does. I wonder if he did, would I dare ring him? I would like to talk to him about *Intimate Strangers*; he's much older than I am and I think he would understand it better. I suspect he's been married, although he's never said anything about that.

In the novels by Katharine I've read so far, many characters gaze at the stars. In *Intimate Strangers,* Elodie likes to lie on the 'dilapidated lounge on the veranda, content to rest and let her thoughts go wandering among the stars.' Watching the dark sky gives her a sense of 'bewildering delight' and she wonders why she is happier watching the moon over the sea amidst 'the glittering shells of stars' than she is being with people.

Star-gazing and Jerome Hartog are Elodie's two main distractions. She admits to herself that it's as if, in Jerome, she has found 'something of the sea and the stars… through which she could reach to freedom of thought and expression, an identity of conscious and unconscious being. Was it so? Or was she making another wild swan for herself? Had she been dreaming of an intimate ideal companionship so long, that she was ready to imagine the casual passionate impulse of a stranger might have that quality?'

When I read that, I thought, hmm…this fairy-tale romance isn't going anywhere, and, in her heart-of-hearts, Elodie knows it.

Jill told me that Jerome Hartog is based on a man called Captain Gregory. 'According to local gossip,' Jill explained, 'during the

Second World War, he was not allowed to sail past Geraldton because he was too friendly with the Japanese pearl divers in Broome. Isn't that just like Katharine!' she exclaimed. 'Picking someone exotic like him to put in a novel.' I nodded furiously.

April 21ˢᵗ, 1968

As Elodie muddles along in her affair with Hartog, she begins to distrust her feelings towards him. 'What was the meaning of it?' she asks herself. 'What was she up to? Was she a dissolute female to be so flayed alive by the kisses of a fascinating blackguard like Jerome Hartog?'

Even as she plots to run off with Hartog, Elodie constantly thinks of Greg and their children. It will be 'such a shock' to Greg if she leaves him; she couldn't 'endure all the prying of a divorce.' She reminds herself that she 'must leave everything in order. It would be indefensible not to. The children's clothes would have to be mended. Greg's pyjamas and socks overhauled.' After all,' she tells herself, 'a deserted husband' must have his 'clothes pressed and his buttons sewed on' as usual. As she patches one of Greg's blue shirts, she's sad to see 'how faded and worn Greg's shirts were. He liked wearing blue shirts. They matched his eyes.'

Going over the details of her escape, she tells herself that things should be 'quite simple and practicable.' There shouldn't be any ill feelings, she thinks. After all, the 'spirit had gone out of their relationship as husband and wife...Their life together was bankrupt of happiness.'

As Elodie sorts through the cupboards, getting ready to pack her bags, she reflects on how lovers in fiction live on an 'unearthly plane.' In the books she's read, an 'erring wife did what she could do to adjust the affairs of her family' then simply disappeared with her lover. As she sorts, Elodie puts aside the things that have sentimental value. She has an 'inexplicable reluctance' to give up a piece of lace and, as the 'stack of oddments she was loath to part with grew amazingly,' she eyes it 'with dismay.'

That little stack of goodies she won't part with convinced me that Elodie would never leave her husband and children.

Katharine uses the word 'inexplicable' again shortly afterwards. Jerome, who's responsible for Chrissie's pregnancy, refuses to feel guilty about Chrissie's death after her backyard abortion and begs Elodie not to let what's happened to Chrissie 'wreck' their plans. He tells her the incident is 'as inexplicable to me as it is to you.'

I don't like Jerome Hartog. The description of him coming out of the sea looking like a 'grotesque and terrifying' sea monster sums him up. Elodie looks at his wide open mouth and decides he looks 'rapacious and cruel.' Shortly afterwards, he threatens to drive the car with them in it over a cliff if she doesn't run away with him and, on top of that, he tells her that he'll wring her neck if she lets him down. Definitely wouldn't want to run off with a man like him! Definitely wouldn't want to marry a man like him, either.

I'm glad Elodie eventually rejects her 'fantasy of a gay, carefree existence' with Jerome, not because 'her desire for [him] had abated: not because her vision of their companionship was less alluring: but because in her devotion to Greg there remained something incalculable, intransigent—over and beyond all personal happiness. Elodie herself did not understand it. She could not argue about it. It was there. She had been subjugated by it.'

I keep wondering if Katharine's own marriage was a bit like this. Suppose we'll never know unless she tells us.

April 25th, 1968

I've spent most of the day walking in King's Park with Gwenda; we don't like the parades in town. We walked down Fraser Avenue towards Subiaco, looking at the trees dedicated to dead soldiers. We didn't talk much. I thought a lot about Katharine.

At Gwenda's bus stop, she told me she hadn't seen Andy for two weeks. She thinks he's getting fed up with her because she won't give in. 'He's been talking about going up north to work in the mines,' she grumbled. 'We've chatted about it a bit; he reckons it'd only be for a year, and he could make a lot of money. He just might decide to go!'

'In that case,' I said, 'you could finish night school and you might even be at uni by the time he gets back.'

She didn't look happy about my suggestion. I think she's dead keen on this Andy. I couldn't think of anything to say, so I grabbed her hand as she hopped on the bus and yelled, 'See you tomorrow!'

April 26th, 1968

Going to work this morning, I was thinking about how, in *Intimate Strangers*, Jerome Hartog's Aunt Lilla calls her nephew a 'gay deceiver' and, much later, Jerome jokingly asks Elodie if she thinks he's a 'gay deceiver.' That expression is exactly the same one the old lady used in *Child of the Hurricane* when Katharine sat in the park with her *Preux Chevalier*.

I wonder if Katharine thinks most men are 'gay deceivers'?

April 29th, 1968

At one point in *Intimate Strangers*, Hartog tells Elodie that it's 'ridiculous for a grown man and woman to play hide and seek like this about things that matter.' He's always 'gone after' the things he wants, he says, and this time he wants Elodie! 'Come and live with me in China,' he pleads.

Her reply is the side of Elodie I like best: she says she'd 'like to,' but she's 'too afraid of hurting others.' She doesn't want to leave her children and admits she doesn't want to hurt Greg. Although they are no longer 'husband and wife,' she wants them to be 'friends.' After all, she points out, there are 'all sorts of considerations, health, habit, the children and livelihood of the family.' Jerome accuses her of having an 'untidy mind,' insisting that 'marriage is a business contract...based on the property relation...not sentimental dust.'

May 10th, 1968

I took *Intimate Strangers* to work today, and we discussed Jerome's opinion that marriage is a business contract. Then I read out his overall view of marriage:

'In the days when a man began to acquire possessions, exclusive right to a female was his only means of insuring inheritance for his seed. What happens under the marriage laws of most so-called civilized communities? A woman sells out all sexual rights in herself for maintenance, and a man insures to himself a vicarious immortality through his progeny, and the possessions he can pass on to them.'

Gwenda says to some extent she agrees with Jerome, except she can't accept the idea that a woman 'sells out all sexual rights in herself for maintenance.' Nora nodded and said, 'That would make wives prostitutes, wouldn't it?' I reckon Nora is dead right!

I also read the bit where Elodie tells Jerome that she believes women 'think they marry for love.' Jerome agrees, then asks her, 'But do they stay married for love – or because they can't provide for themselves and their children?'

We talked about how tricky it is for a married woman with children to survive without a man's income. 'Mum often says she and us kids would've been on the poverty line without Dad,' I said. Gwenda and Nora agreed.

Gwenda said that's why she's determined to get a better education to get a good job. 'And if I do get married and have children,' she declared, 'I'll make sure I can at least support myself and them, so I don't have to rely on my husband for everything. And if the marriage is no good, then he can go to buggery.'

Nora sighed, 'Good luck, Gwenda.'

I took Gwenda's side immediately. 'If anyone can do it, you can, Gwenda,' I told her, looking hard at Nora.

May 11th, 1968

I've just been re-reading the scene in *Intimate Strangers* where Greg rapes Elodie. I'm even angrier than I was when I first read it.

Greg comes into her bedroom as she's lying down and having a rest. He says he's come to apologize for a nasty remark at lunch and asks to be forgiven. Elodie realizes that he's after more than forgiveness. She is 'alert and apprehensive to the thickened blue of his eyes, the slackening of his features, a crouch and cunning in his approach.' Greg's eyes are 'sly and rapacious' as his head falls against her neck and he starts kissing her. Elodie impatiently tells him to let her rest; she's tired and it's hot. Instead, he clings to her 'heavily, overpowering and crushing her. Elodie pleads with him, 'Don't, don't! I'll never forgive you.' But Greg laughs 'ruthlessly...undeterred, overwhelming and destroying her resistance.'

When Elodie lies back, 'weakened and vanquished...perspiration beading in tears all over her body,' he tries to make it up to her. She lies 'limp and unresponsive' and her 'air of suffering troubled him.' He tells her he loves her but his voice is 'lame and unconvincing.' Elodie gets up and stalks out of the room and he calls after her, 'All right, sulk if you like.'

Bloody sod!

Elodie stumbles as she leaves the bedroom, as though 'she were giddy, or blind.' Meanwhile, Greg stretches out on the bed, cursing the 'frenzy which had betrayed him to demonstrate to Elodie that she could not escape him.' He has always wanted to dominate her; now he's done it. 'She was his legitimate spouse,' Greg reasons and decides he has every right to his 'lust for her when he felt so disposed.

What was a man to do? If she had no inclination at the moment, chose to feel outraged, was he to blame?'

What *unbelievable* rubbish!

What's even more unbelievable is Greg's response the morning after the rape. Elodie is 'uncannily quiet' whereas Greg is chatty, trying to make it up to her and wanting her 'to know that he had decided to forgive her.'

To forgive *her*? Forgive her for what? For not being available whenever he wants sex? What a selfish, bloody bastard! When Elodie heads for the beach after lunch, Greg begins to 'feel incensed at her obstinacy'. He tells himself that 'after all, some women would have been proud of their husband's desire.'

Later at the beach, Greg resentfully watches his wife and children enjoy Jerome Hartog's yarns, thinking that if Elodie decides to 'amuse herself' with Hartog, it would be a 'rough spin,' but it would do her 'good to be taken down a peg: teach her to appreciate a decent husband when she'd got one.' He's always believed that he 'reigned...in her eyes' and cannot 'endure the idea of her fancy migrating to another man. Not likely that Elodie would go farther. She was not that sort: fundamentally his, fornication not her line.'

Elodie's friend, Rachel, who has known Greg since childhood, tells Elodie that Greg's 'rather a darling, of course. Fascinating when he likes. So long as everything's going his way, all's well...But he's predatory.'

Possessive, dominating, predatory – that's Greg Blackwood.

Elodie is such a forgiving woman, though. The afternoon after she has been raped, she comes back from the beach and sees Greg lying on the old lounge on the veranda of the cottage at Calatta, and her 'sympathy vibrated. He looked so conscious of bad behaviour.' But, as he also looks 'sullen and unrepentant,' she decides to 'remain cool and apart from him,' which she knows will increase his 'fury of remorse and resentment' because she won't forgive him – 'just yet.'

What a complicated relationship they have. I feel miserable sometimes as I read this novel. I hope if I ever do get married, my marriage will never be like theirs.

May 12th, 1968

At morning tea, I told Gwenda and Nora about the rape. Gwenda shrugged.

'I'm pretty sure married men can't be charged for raping their wives,' she said. 'But anyway, if they can be, there's no way they'd be convicted.'

'Then the law has to change!' I hissed.

Nora put her head down and said very quietly that she doesn't like to admit it, but she's often imagined what it would be like to be raped. 'I always wonder what I would do,' she said. 'I don't know whether I would just give in or start screaming for help.'

Gwenda stared at her. I could hardly believe what I was hearing.

'If anyone tried to rape me,' said Gwenda, 'I'd fight like hell.'

Nora sniffed and said, 'But it might not be a good idea to fight back because the man would hurt you, perhaps even kill you.'

I'm on Gwenda's side; I'm sure I'd fight back. I thought about the man who chased me in St Georges Terrace that night. What if he'd hit me? Or worse, had stabbed me? What if he'd dragged me into an alley and raped me? I just know I'd fight him with everything I had.

On the bus going home, I thought about Katharine's story in *Child in the Hurricane* about the man who tried to rape her in London and how she threatened to throw herself out of the window if he came near her. I remember shuddering at her description: he had 'pale shark's eyes.' Brrrrr!

May 16th, 1968

I've been thinking about how little tenderness there is between Elodie and Greg. There are only a few moments where they seem to care for each other – Greg worries that Elodie works too hard. 'All I've let you in for,' he tells her. 'I loathe to see you, looking worn out.' For her part, Elodie looks after him as she would a child, giving him hot milk and tucking him into bed when he gets 'wrought-up.' But most of the time they couldn't care less about each other.

I am trying to remember if I ever saw Mum and Dad looking after each other. I recall one incident when my mother had just come out of hospital after having a hysterectomy. Against the doctor's orders, she was vacuuming. As she was trying to move the couch in the lounge-room to vacuum behind it, my father walked in. He told her off, told her to stop it immediately, said she should be resting in bed. She turned the vacuum off, then said something like, 'Someone has to do the housework. Do you want to vacuum?' My father just glared at her and told her not to be stupid.

May 20th, 1968

Suicide comes up again in *Intimate Strangers*. So many people kill themselves, or threaten to, in Katharine's life and work!

At one point in *Intimate Strangers,* Greg tells Elodie, 'The best thing I can do...is get out of your way.' Elodie's father shot himself after being caught for embezzlement, so she knows exactly what her husband means.

Jill told me tonight that shooting himself was going to be the way out for Greg too. 'In the first draft of the novel, Greg shoots himself after making a mess of their finances and gambling away their house,' Jill said. 'But after Hugo shot himself, Katharine was terrified that he had found and read the first draft of *Intimate Strangers.* She thought he could have been influenced by the ending, so she changed it.'

Jill bit the top of her pencil. 'I've always wondered if that could be true,' she said with a frown. 'In the version we've read, remember how Elodie finds Greg slumped over his carpenter's bench, sound asleep in his pyjamas and dressing gown, a revolver and a suicide note beside him? '

'Yes, that's right,' I said. 'Greg wakes up when Elodie comes into the room and when she accuses him of trying to kill himself, he says, "I couldn't...Don't seem to have guts even for that."'

Jill showed me a letter Katharine wrote to her friend, Jack Lindsay, where she confesses that she thinks the novel failed because it 'didn't remain true to its conception...In it the husband shot himself and Elodie, disillusioned in her *affaire* with Jerome, seeks to identify herself with the universal flow of life towards that better earth...when I returned home my husband had died like hers. It was too painful then to write of what had happened to me. I changed the end. My literary conscience failed the test, I suppose.'

Jill told me that the title, *Intimate Strangers*, comes from a story Hugo told Katharine. Apparently, he was a fan of an English actress called Henrietta Watson and he wrote her a letter, promising that he would come to England and call on her. She replied, telling him that they might meet one day. They did! They met often during his convalescence at the Wandsworth Hospital in England and went to the theatre together. Hugo described their relationship as 'intimate strangers.'

'It's possible that Katharine thinks most married couples are merely "intimate strangers,"' said Jill. 'Hugo and Katharine obviously had their ups and downs and I'd be surprised if she didn't include some details about their marriage in the novel. But for all the worry he caused her – and she probably caused him a few problems too – she loved him deeply. I love her poem, "To Jim", which begins, "To you, all these wild weeds/and windflowers of my life/I bring, my lord/and lay them at your feet."' Jill was staring into the distance as she was reciting – she seemed to be in another world, so I didn't say anything.

'Anyway,' Jill said, coming back to the present, 'Katharine claims that *Intimate Strangers* is a simple story of two friends who recognized themselves when they read the novel. You know, Vicki, I'm not sure I agree with her that the story is simple; it's the most upsetting story I've ever read about marriage. I think *Anna Karenina* and *Madame Bovary* are pretty tough, but *Intimate Strangers* is tougher.'

I nodded furiously and made a mental note to read *Anna Karenina* and *Madame Bovary*.

As I was leaving the library, Jill told me that Katharine has never wanted to leave her house in Greenmount, even though she must have had horrible thoughts about how her husband shot himself right there on the verandah while she was away in Russia. 'Why?' I asked Jill.

'She thinks there's still something there of Hugo,' Jill replied. 'She says they were "great lovers". She must have many good memories.'

Jill and I both giggled, but I'm sure neither of us understands the in's and out's of Katharine's marriage – but then, why should we? It's none of our business!

May 29th, 1968

Called into the library after work today, and Jill showed me a monograph written by Henrietta Drake-Brockman, who, apparently, is a friend of Katharine, although they disagree politically 'In a nutshell,' said Jill, thoughtfully turning a page, 'Drake-Brockman believes that Katharine's *Intimate Strangers* is way ahead of its time because it's such a bold exploration of a disillusioned married woman's sexual desires. I certainly agree with that!'

Jill also showed me a letter Katharine wrote to Nettie Palmer during a family holiday in Rockingham. 'This holiday is a sham,' she wrote. I asked Jill what Katharine meant by that. She just shrugged and replied, 'The Throssells were probably having a few marital problems and she may have thought about them when she was writing *Intimate Strangers*.'

Jill told me Katharine didn't write a novel after *Intimate Strangers* until *Moon of Desire*, published in 1941 when she was fifty-eight. After Hugo's death in 1933, she threw herself into political work for the Communist Party and worked hard for peace in the Movement Against War and Fascism.

Jill suggested I read a short story in *N'goola and Other Stories* called 'The Happy Farmer.' 'It has echoes of *Intimate Strangers*,' said Jill. 'And it's very Katharine.'

May 31ˢᵗ, 1968

Missed book club tonight. Just don't feel like going. I don't want to talk to Larry about *Intimate Strangers*, although he may not have even read it.

Sometimes I wonder if Larry is, or has been, married, but I'm not sure I want to find out. I'm not experienced enough to talk about marriage, happy or otherwise. I like him a lot, but I'm not sure how much I want to know about his personal life. I like things the way they are at the moment.

Anyway, I spent the night writing a dialogue between an elderly couple I saw on the bus this morning. I eavesdropped; they were having an argument about a neighbour. I also tried to write a description of their marriage but I gave up.

June 16th, 1968

Cold day. Rain and thunder. Mum's still in bed; I think she's got the flu.

I just finished reading 'The Happy Farmer' and thought I recognized the title. It's a little tune Mum often hums. I remember asking her when I was about nine what was that song she was always humming and she tossed her head and said it was called 'The Happy Farmer' by Schumann. She learned to play it on the piano when she was a little girl and said she'd always loved it. I asked her if I could learn to play the piano, but she said she couldn't afford the lessons. Anyway, to this day, if Mum is humming 'The Happy Farmer' I know she's in a good mood. If she's singing 'Some Enchanted Evening' I know she's grumpy.

Nothing happy about this story, though. Like Elodie in *Intimate Strangers*, Molly Miller plays the piano, although Molly's piano is an old relic. It's out of tune, rattles and squeaks. She hates listening to little Bob practising 'The Happy Farmer'. Like Elodie, she's having trouble with her marriage and is anxious about Tom, her wheat farmer husband, who is 'one-armed and nervy' and in the process of losing the farm to the banks. Like Elodie Blackwood, Molly uses the word 'mirage' to describe her marriage.

When Tom tells Molly she'd be 'better off' without him, her heart 'cracked at the thought of his misery.' Minutes later, she hears a shot ring out, then a 'shrill scream.' Young Bob, who's been helping his father with the horses, rushes into the kitchen, 'blue eyes round and scared.' When he tells her that 'daddy' is 'covered with blood,' she knows in an instant what's happened.

So many suicides in Katharine's work! So depressing.

June 28th, 1968

Tonight, Larry gave me his copy of Katharine's latest novel, *Subtle Flame*. 'I read it in a couple of days – her discussion of the Korean War is fascinating. It's a war that's always interested me.' Larry looked so earnest I started to giggle, then put my hand over my mouth and coughed instead. 'Although,' he continued, and I immediately stopped coughing, 'the Korean War always makes me think of what Henry Lawson once wrote about the Boer War. He thought it was pointless for Aussie soldiers to trot off to South Africa to shoot men they'd never met and didn't understand. When you apply that to the war in Korea, I tend to agree with him.' He spoke slowly and deliberately, as he does when he's dead serious about something. I didn't know what to say so I said nothing.

Larry told me that *Subtle Flame* is dedicated to a woman called Annette. 'She's a leftie, of course, and an old and reliable friend,' said Larry. 'I heard she used to look after Prichard's correspondence and typed her work.' He also told me that the Evans family in *Subtle Flame* is based upon her memories and conversations with her own family as well as other people she knew.

'After you've read it,' Larry said, 'if you like, we could meet for a chat about the book.'

It's the first time he's ever suggested meeting me outside the book group, so I was flabbergasted but finally managed a bit of a grin and gulped, 'Okay.'

July 6th, 1968

At the beginning of *Subtle Flame*, David Evans goes bush to his daughter's cottage in the Dandenong hills outside Melbourne (Emerald?) where he reads and thinks about the next stage of his life. He's just lost his son in the Korean War and has resigned from his job as editor-in-chief of *The Dispatch* newspaper. Devastated over the loss of his son, he feels he's to blame for having 'shirked investigating and exposing the truth about this war in Korea.'

David asks himself the same question that is the first epigraph to *Intimate Strangers*: 'But do you think it possible rightly to understand the nature of the soul, without understanding the nature of the universe?'

Throughout *Subtle Flame*, David Evans struggles to do just that: he tries to understand his soul, and the universe.

I'm very interested in reading about someone like David Evans – it makes me wonder and think about my own muddles.

July 8th, 1968

Tonight, I'm thinking about the intriguing way Katharine writes about workplaces. I'll bet if she ever wrote a book about an insurance company like ours, she could even make our workplace interesting!

Katharine's description of the world of newspaper production in *Subtle Flame* is fascinating. There are 'teletypes clicking, rattle of typewriters, yapping on telephones, buzzers and messages flying: the great presses vibrating, disgorging hundreds of thousands of neatly folded copies of *The Dispatch*, still damp and smelling of printer's ink, to be grabbed and distributed far and wide through the city by hordes of newsboys.' If there's a late news story, there has to be 'recasting of make-up, headlines, telephone interviews, the writing of special articles, at racing speed…hands and brains worked at high pressure' so that the paper can be published 'according to schedule.'

Sounds like an exciting place to work! I think I'd like to work for a newspaper.

We're also told something I've never thought about – who owns newspapers and what journalists are allowed to write about, depending upon the newspaper's Board of Directors and their editorial policies. Despite *The Dispatch's* declaration that it publishes 'All the news fit to print,' David finally realizes that it publishes only the news that the directors 'permitted him to print.' His 'finest qualities' as a journalist have been 'sacrificed' to 'enhance the power and prestige' of the owners of the newspaper. He feels 'as guilty as others for lives lost' in the 'damnable Korean war', so he suggests to the Board that *The Dispatch* should start printing 'frank and accurate' facts about the war. They immediately reject the suggestion, believing he's 'going socialist in his ideas – or needed a holiday.'

'How could a man have any respect for himself if he failed to obey the imperative of his own mind and spirit?' David asks himself. *His* imperative, he suddenly realizes, is 'to reach the people: to know them better so that he could reach their common sense and instinct for action…Surely, there was no greater idea than the idea of peace, a world without the barbarous insanity of war. After all, at the end of every "ruinous carnage", the war-makers were forced to resort to negotiation. Why not before, rather than after, the murderous assault on men, women and children in modern warfare?'

Although I've never thought about it, it makes a huge amount of sense to me.

Myff, David's daughter, listens carefully to her father blaming himself for 'distorting' the truth about 'this dirty war' he has 'boosted' because it was 'the policy of the paper.' He admits he's always tried to make 'those lads think they were doing something fine and heroic by volunteering for active service' while his son's letters have been telling him the real truth about the 'blood and muck' of the 'whole rotten business.' David tells Myff that the newspapers have been 'slanting the news...pretending to uphold democratic ideas of a free press.... A free press!' he exclaims. 'There is no such thing as an independent press. We are the tools and vassals of rich men behind the scenes. We are jumping jacks; they pull the strings and we dance.'

Newspapers, he tells her, need a 'tremendous outlay of capital, forests to supply paper, ships to transport it, huge rotary machines to reduce time and labour, electrical and rivers of ink to feed them, a fleet of vehicles for distribution, advertising contracts. Only rich men can afford to own and control modern newspapers...The policy of every daily newspaper in this country is based not only on the profits of an individual publication, but on defence of the widespread financial interests of its backers.'

Katharine should know – the world of newspapers and magazines is familiar to her – after all, she was once a journalist, as was her father. She didn't need to research that world to write *Subtle Flame*.

I think I like to be a journalist, although perhaps not for a newspaper like *The Dispatch*. Surely there must be some newspapers around that offer a range of views on the world?

I'm enjoying writing about people I watch and listen to on the bus and have started giving myself a deadline – complete one dialogue and one portrait by the end of my lunch hour.

I wouldn't mind talking to Mum about my future goals, but she'd just tell me my goal should be to find a nice bloke and marry him – that way I wouldn't have to worry about my future. 'Just get married, Vicki!' she'd say. 'Then you won't have to work at all.' I don't like the idea of being dependent on a man.

July 10th, 1968

Katharine uses the word 'fornications' in *Subtle Flame*, a word she used in *Intimate Strangers*. I like that word! I've never used it myself, but one day I might.

David Evans has indulged in a few 'quite delightful' fornications, including a 'casual liaison' with a young widow called Isabel and a torrid affair with a promiscuous 'bitch' called Jan Murphy. None of these 'fornications' have involved 'any overwhelming passion,' including those with his wife, Claire, who has been brought up with a 'religious abhorrence' for the 'filthy lusts of the flesh,' and has 'never overcome her distaste for intercourse.'

Gosh, I thought, when I read that – I wonder if I'd like intercourse?

July 11ᵗʰ, 1968

At morning tea, I asked Gwenda and Nora what they thought of the word 'fornication.' Gwenda said, 'I know what it means, and that's exactly what Andy wants to do with me – fornicate. Bloody twit.'

Nora said she'd never use the word herself. 'I'd use sexual intercourse,' she said.

'Sounds better.' Gwenda said. 'But there's an even better word that starts with 'F,' and we all laughed.

They were a bit taken aback, however, when I asked them what they thought of the expression 'cock-teasing.' 'Bit rude,' said Nora.

'Bit off,' said Gwenda.

They wanted to know why I'd asked them, and I said it's an expression used by a character called Gwen in *Subtle Flame*. 'What kind of a girl is she?' Nora asked.

I was just about to tell them about Gwen when Maggot walked past and banged on the window, so we jumped up and drifted back to our typewriters.

July 12ᵗʰ, 1968

'What kind of a girl is Gwen?' I asked myself at the bus stop this afternoon.

I've been reading *Subtle Flame* slowly because I'm finding the novel a bit hard going. There's so much information in it – complicated political stuff – and I'm going to have to sort all that out with Jill and Larry because I'm not sure I understand it, really, although I get the main point – that the world would be a far better place if there were no wars.

Who could possibly argue with that?

Anyway, back to Gwen. David Evans has two daughters, Myff, whom he gets along with, and Gwen – his 'will-o'-the-wisp,' who baffles him although he loves her and is frequently 'stirred by an instinct to defend and protect her.' He also has two sons: Neil, a pathologist, and Rob, who was killed in the Korean War.

Gwen, or 'Gwennie,' as her father calls her, has an affair with a married man, gets pregnant, and, with Neil's help, manages to get an abortion. Fortunately, unlike Chrissie in *Intimate Strangers*, Gwen's abortion is successful, and she gets on with life.

Her abortion reminds me of what Dymphna Cusack says in a couple of her novels: that an abortion is just like having a tooth out!

Gwen goes overseas, has an affair on the boat coming back to Australia with a newspaperman called Claude Moyle and finally ends up marrying Brian McNamara, a farmer from Gippsland. Gwen is quite the modern miss and shows off in front of her father by using language like 'nympho' and 'cock-teasing' just to let him know how 'an uninhibited young thing talks, these days.'

July 15th, 1968

'What about the word "nympho"?' I asked the girls this morning.

Nora and Gwenda both laughed. 'What in the world are you reading?' Gwenda asked. 'Cock-teaser, fornication, and now nympho.'

'What about "orgasm"?' I giggled, interrupting Gwenda, who was about to say something else.

'What about it?' she asked sulkily. *Hmm*, I thought, *why did she change moods so suddenly? One minute she's laughing at nympho, and the next she's looking like she's ready to bawl.*

I'm enjoying saying these words from *Subtle Flame* out loud with Nora and Gwenda. Can't imagine saying them in front of my mother! I once used 'tits' when I was telling Mum about a fat old duck at the corner shop who was wearing a bikini top and a pair of shorts. She bent down to pick up the newspaper, and her breasts burst out of her top – big, floppy things, all wobbly. I thought 'tits' was an accurate description of them when I was telling Mum about it, but Mum told me off for being 'common.'

She often uses that word 'common': 'Don't be common, Vicki,' she'll say, or 'Oh, her, she's so common!' Sometimes Mum thinks she's the bloody Queen of Sheba.

July 18th, 1968

I like the way Katharine describes how characters heading into a relationship eye off each other.

In *Subtle Flame*, David is fascinated by Sharn's eyes: they are 'deep, mysterious eyes...which welled from the depths of an intense and sensitive mind...They were her only beauty, revealing a sensitive, passionate nature.' Her 'dreamy...gaze' makes David want to kiss her, but he tells himself that 'it would be unpardonable...to indulge in any sentimental philandering with Sharn' because he's old enough to be her father. He knows she isn't interested in 'a mere exchange of physical sensations' – oh, no – she expects marriage.

What I think is amusing, but also a bit odd, is the end of the novel when he's with Sharn at the cottage in the hills. They've been there almost a month; David is recuperating after a stroke and Sharn is looking after him. They're both happy, not because they're together, but because The Test Ban Treaty has been signed in Moscow. David by now is in his fifties (he is forty-nine at the start of the novel) and Sharn is years younger. Sharn has a simple proposal for David: 'Two people can work better than one,' she tells him. 'I can tend your "subtle flame": keep it burning brightly: help you in lots of ways: be your secretary and housekeeper: see that you get decent meals…Would do anything in the world for you.'

Now Sharn's plan doesn't exactly make David Evans sit up and take notice; he's always been a bit put off by her lack of 'coquetry' and her determination to 'draw him into the web of her political connections.' Nope – he wants all that she's offering and sex as well! So he tells her that these arrangements wouldn't be 'fair' to her and throws himself onto a rug in the sunshine, closes his eyes, and lets the 'silence of the forest' flow over him. Poor ol' Sharn thinks she's 'lost this chance of persuading David to let her live with him', but suddenly, he opens his eyes, smiles, and asks her to kiss him. As they kiss, Sharn (at last!) gives way to the 'sensuous delight flooding her.' David murmurs, 'That's the answer I've been waiting for.' His 'little laugh' is 'tantalising yet triumphant.'

That triumphant little laugh bothered me. He's not going to marry Sharn if sex isn't involved and he seems to be very pleased with himself that, at his age, he can conquer Sharn through 'lust.' I didn't like David Evans much at the end of the book.

Makes me think of Andy and Gwenda. I reckon he'll keep lusting after her until she finally gives in.

To be fair, though, David Evans is romantic. He gathers 'scattered violets,' weaves them into a bouquet, and swears 'by all the trees in the forest, the birds, bees and wildflowers – and all the life forces which make for peace and beauty on earth – to love and cherish you, Sharn, as long as we both shall live.'

July 19th, 1968

At morning tea, I read out the passage where David Evans swears 'by all the trees in the forest.' Nora twirled a strand of blond hair around her finger and said dreamily, 'Mmmm...that is nice, isn't it?' Gwenda laughed and said, 'Sounds like something out of *True Romance.*'

'I used to love reading that magazine when I was fourteen,' Nora confessed.

Gwenda rolled her eyes.

July 22nd, 1968

On the bus this morning I thought about how David Evans wants to write an article that will be like an 'intellectual bomb.' It will 'blast the apathy of readers, stir them to seek further information.' His quest will be to 'look squarely at his own life, and the lives of men and women who...had become like a mob of sheep rounded up by the press, the churches and big business, which doped and betrayed them to the shambles of war.' He will give his readers 'simple facts to...stimulate their courage, so that they won't allow themselves to be driven like sheep to the slaughter.'

July 23rd, 1968

I've been thinking a lot about the word 'apathy.' Katharine uses it often in her books. She uses it several times in *Subtle Flame* and in *Working Bullocks* when Mark Smith condemns the workers for not supporting the strike. She also uses it in *Intimate Strangers* when the crowd at the Esplanade takes no notice of the speakers calling for action on unemployment.

I don't believe that Katharine thinks people, in general, are apathetic, or 'cracked mugs', as old Sam the shingle splitter in *Wild Oats* calls them. She writes about the 'Promethean spark' too often to believe that. Even when David Evans argues that the 'human family had split in the struggle of the Mighty Few to keep power in their own hands and the Many in subservience,' he still believes in the 'kindness' and 'common sense' of 'most ordinary men and women...The great kindly heart of humanity was a reservoir from which could be drawn all manner of noble deeds...of compassion and courage.'

Myff, the 'starry-eyed idealist,' is the only one in David's family who agrees with him. Like her father, she believes 'the basic stuff of humans is good.' The 'rough and tumble of making enough money to get what we want' is responsible for the 'evil tendencies, greed, cruelty, indifference to the suffering of others. It's a sort of self-defence against the fear of being trampled on,' she tells David.

'Perhaps I can't help idealising, although I like to think I'm a realist.'

Out of all the characters in *Subtle Flame*, I like Myff best. I reckon Katharine might be a bit like Myff.

July 26th, 1968

Tonight, Larry and I were chatting about 'apathy' when suddenly he stopped talking, stood up tall, pulled his shoulders back, pushed out his chin and started reciting: 'The apathetic throng, the cowed and meek/Who see the world's great anguish and its wrong/Yet dare not speak.' That, my friend, is what Prichard writes about in *Subtle Flame*.'

My mouth dropped open, unfortunately, because I probably looked like a dill. I was so impressed that he could spout lines of poetry on the spot.

As book club was closing, Larry grabbed my elbow and asked if I wanted to meet at King's Park on Sunday. 'We can talk about *Subtle Flame*,' he said. 'And I'll tell you a bit about Bernard O'Dowd, a poet Prichard admires.'

I didn't know what to say, so I just nodded like crazy.

'Meet you at the café around one o'clock?' he grinned.

I was too flustered to say anything but 'Okay!'

July 28th, 1968

Met Larry in King's Park today!

I really enjoyed talking to him. Am so surprised how easy it was just to chat about *Subtle Flame* and not think too much about what I was saying.

I asked Larry's opinion of Myff. Larry chuckled and said, like Myff, Katharine thinks of herself as a realist. 'But I've always thought she's an idealist, and that's not to criticize her!' he laughed.

'Have you ever been to places like the Yarra Bank where David Evans goes to listen to the speakers?' I asked Larry. He grinned and said I should go down to the Esplanade one day and listen to people carry on about everything from Jesus Christ to communism. 'Even your precious Katharine has been on the stump at the Esplanade. I've read that she gave a terrific speech for the 1938 May Day rally in support of the Spanish Republicans. As usual, the Special Branch stood at the back, taking notes. They probably thought she was a spy.'

He told me how, when she returned from the Soviet Union, weak, ill, devastated over the suicide of her husband, the cops were there to meet her. 'Her luggage was searched, and Russian novels and letters were confiscated. The authorities never trusted her, and, after Hugo's Northam speech, they probably never trusted him either,' Larry said with a frown.

'Prichard's been under surveillance for years,' he told me. 'Her house in Greenmount has been raided a few times. Her son visited her during the Menzies crack-down on communists and they suspected a raid would happen any day. They packed an old tin trunk with all the illegal communist stuff they could find in her house – books, Soviet magazines, pamphlets, the *Workers Star*, which had been banned. They stuffed the trunk into her plumbago hedge. When the cops arrived at the house the next morning, they didn't find much – they took a red notebook containing thirty-odd years' worth of Prichard's collections of quotations, and cuttings they never returned. They also took her copy of O'Dowd's *Poetry Militant*, which she tried to get back, but they wouldn't return it.'

'I wouldn't want to be a communist in Australia,' I said, and he laughed. But I wasn't joking.

'You know,' he continued, 'she was always ready to go to jail for her beliefs. She reckoned that the experience of being in jail would give her interesting material to write about! During the crack-down, she believed her letters were being intercepted so she wrote to all her friends telling them she would keep speaking out in support of communism. But she also told her friends that the "nervous tension" she was suffering was "exhausting" and she kept wondering whether the pen *was* mightier than the sword. The government must have a file on her as thick as a brick. They probably think she's a "dyed-in-the-wool communist". Of course she'd never deny that, but she's so famous they wouldn't dare touch her. Instead, they take it out on her son, Ric. They watch her – and give him hell.'

Makes me wonder why my mother always insists that Australia is a free country.

I asked Larry about an Australian war correspondent called Wilfred Burchett, who's mentioned in *Subtle Flame*. Larry was enthusiastic at the mention of his name and told me that Wilfred Burchett is famous for his report on Hiroshima. 'He was the first Western journalist to go there after the atomic bomb had been dropped by the Americans,' said Larry. '"I write this as a warning to the world" was Burchett's opening line. The article was published in the *Daily Express* in London in September 1945, and he wrote about how thousands died instantly and those who survived began suffering from the atomic plague.'

'You know,' I said to Larry, 'I think that's exactly what *Subtle Flame* is: it's a warning to the world, don't you think? Katharine's not only interested in the Korean War, she's interested in the next war, which could be a nuclear war. That's what David Evans, Sharn and the others go on and on about, don't they?'

'Very good, Vicki,' Larry smiled. I felt like a school girl again.

Apart from *Subtle Flame*, we talked about all kinds of things, and he even listened to my complaints about my job and living with Mum.

I didn't want to be a whinger, so I changed the subject back to Katharine and asked him about Bernard O'Dowd. 'Oh yes,' he said, and his eyes lit up behind his glasses. 'You read *Child of the Hurricane*, didn't you, Vicki?' I nodded, and we chatted about Katharine's description of O'Dowd as a 'tall thin young man, very pale and ginger-haired' and how much she 'adored' him as a poet because his poems were 'so neat and orthodox...in form, and so revolutionary in sentiment.'

'Prichard adored a few male poets,' Larry chuckled, 'but I think she admired O'Dowd most because he believed poetry must have a purpose.'

He stared at me, his thumb and forefinger in his nostrils, and waited for me to speak. As usual, I couldn't think of anything. He thought for a bit then, using his classroom voice, he said, 'I remember when O'Dowd died, John Curtin wrote that O'Dowd's poetry was the voice of a man who thought deeply and passionately about the destiny of Australia. Like Prichard, O'Dowd believed in the power of literature to change the world.'

I sat up straight and thought, *Well, literature might not change the world, but it certainly changes how I think about the world.* But I didn't say anything because he seemed determined to keep talking.

As he took a deep breath and started to speak even more loudly about poetry and purpose, I thought about how my father would make a fist when he was rattling on about something he cared about and talk over everyone, not caring at all if anyone was listening, and I recall almost nobody ever was!

Anyway, Larry was looking into the distance at the Swan River and his voice dropped, thank goodness, as people were starting to stare. He told me that O'Dowd worshipped Walt Whitman, who believed a real poet must be an Answerer. 'According to Whitman, a real poet should write about things people are interested in,' Larry explained. 'Poetry should explore subjects people wonder about, like politics, religion, science, sex, social reform.'

'Like Katharine does,' I replied, but I couldn't think of anything else, so I gulped my tea, which he had just poured from a fresh pot, and burnt my tongue.

As I waited for the bus to go home, Larry looked me in the eye for what seemed like ages and then said, 'Let's do this again sometime, my friend. What do you think?'

'I think that would be terrific,' I replied, pretending to be more confident than I felt. We didn't have time to say anything else as my bus rolled up, and I hopped into it as fast as I could.

All the way home I couldn't make up my mind about how I feel about Larry. He's nice, he's too old, he's scary to be with because he knows so much, he must think I'm boring because I'm not educated, I like his eyes, I don't like it when he talks to me like a schoolteacher, I'm really glad he's always encouraged me to continue with my project. Is he interested in me, or am I someone he can show off to because he misses his students?

July 29th, 1968

Jill tells me that David Evans has views about writing very similar to Katharine's. Like her, he believes that writing is his most 'forcible means of expression' and, like Katharine, he also believes that telling the truth about the causes of war will 'energise the mass.' He reasons once they know the truth, people will use their 'will and intelligence to save the earth they love and the human race from immeasurable catastrophe.'

Jill had a bit of time tonight, so she showed me a speech Katharine delivered in 1919 called 'The New Order'. One of the things she said is people must realize they are being kept in the dark by daily newspapers in Australia because these newspapers aim to 'safeguard the interests of the Capitalist system.' If people understood this, they would never 'consent to support the injustices and tragedies wrought on humanity' by that system.

'And here we are, Vicki,' Jill chuckled. 'It's 1968, and Katharine has never changed her mind. And probably never will! And that's surely one of the reasons why she wrote *Subtle Flame* – to reinforce what she's always believed.'

Just before I left the library, Jill told me Katharine thinks *Subtle*

Flame will be her last novel. 'She's eighty-four years old, and I've heard she's having problems with her heart. Apparently, she asked herself, before beginning to write the novel, "What is most important in our lives at present?" and came up with one answer – "the struggle for peace."'

Good on you, Katharine, I thought as I waited for my bus. All the way home, I wondered how many wars there have been and how many men have died in them. And how many men have wanted to go to war to fight, I wonder? And I wonder why?

August 3rd, 1968

Had lunch with Nora and Gwenda in the tearooms in King's Park.

'How's it going with Andy?' Nora asked.

'We have fun and I really do like him but I wish he'd stop nagging me about sex,' Gwenda grumbled.

Nora and I had a quick look at each other but didn't say anything.

'How about your night classes?' I asked Gwenda. She shrugged and said she'd missed a few lectures and was trying to catch up.

August 5th, 1968

Jill told me that *Subtle Flame* was the hardest of all Katharine's novels to get published. 'Various publishers told her that it was too long and too controversial. When it was finally accepted by the

Australasian Book Society,' said Jill, 'they told her she had to cut it by 30,000 words, and she did, probably reluctantly.'

According to Jill, Katharine was disappointed with the reactions to *Subtle Flame*. Here's a quote by Katharine that Jill read out loud:

> 'All my Welsh guile, literary expertise and passionate faith in the grail of world peace, went into this book to make the story interesting, contemporary and convincing. But I'm afraid it had no effect on the people I had hoped to reach...The Promethean spark which lies dormant in everybody, and has triumphed over so many savage instincts and customs, in the past, had not been fanned by this book to the subtle flame which ultimately, I am sure, will burn out from human affairs the corrupt and cruel business of war.'

'There's that Promethean spark again,' I laughed. It was all I could think of at the time. Jill looked up from the article, gave me a dazzling smile, and said, 'Yep.'

Anyway, Jill had time to find some reviews of *Subtle Flame*, and, as she wasn't busy, we poured over them together.

One reviewer wrote that *Subtle Flame* is important and 'courageous', but she should have added some satire or humour because the novel is far too serious.

Jill was frowning as she read this review, then said, 'It's pointless to say that Katharine should've added humour to *Subtle Flame*. That might've been the way the critic would've written the novel, but it isn't how Katharine wrote it, and that, my friend, is that.'

I nodded furiously in agreement, mostly because she called me 'my friend.'

According to Jill, even Katharine thought that she'd tackled 'too big a subject' in *Subtle Flame*. David Evans, she wrote, is 'a sort of modern Don Quixote in the struggle for peace. But my touch isn't light enough – I'm too much in earnest to make him a figure of fun. Knight of the "rueful countenance" he may be, and after all he's not tilting at windmills which don't exist. However, I can't let my bloke go until I've done my damndest by him.'

I asked Jill if she thought Katharine would really care what her critics think about *Subtle Flame*. Jill shook her head slightly and said she thought Katharine has probably given up caring much, if at all, about what reviewers and critics write about her work. 'She's been around too long to take things like that too seriously,' she said. 'I think she wanted to write a book that explored ideas she's believed in for decades – and that's what she did.'

I felt better going home on the bus thinking about what Jill said. I have to admit that I've found *Subtle Flame* a challenge and I can't honestly say I've enjoyed it, although I have learned an awful lot from reading it. And I, for one, am glad she wrote it.

I also feel quite proud of myself because Jill called me 'my friend'. Now I have two people I admire who have called me 'my friend' – I am so lucky!

August 16ᵗʰ, 1968

I've been reading an essay by Katharine that Jill recommended. It's called 'On Purpose and Propaganda.' She wrote it a long time ago, in 1938, and according to Jill, it 'contains the core of Katharine's personal views about the role of literature in society.'

Katharine believes that all 'great works of literature are propagandist in essence' because 'there is no doubt that in choosing the persons and theme of a novel, a writer selects those for which he has some predilection and that they move in accordance with his own interpretation of the realities of their environment.' She admits that she is propagandist, as are all 'serious writers…whether they are conscious of it or not,' because they believe in 'the spreading of a certain set of ideas or principles,' through literature. Literature for 'self-expression' isn't a 'sufficient motive for writing.' Instead, she says that she prefers to 'live among the people and places' she writes about to 'draw' them as she sees, and overall, she feels 'impelled to interpret the life and ways' of people 'in their essential aspects: the struggle for existence and organization for a social system which will enable them to grow in beauty and strength of mind and body, in knowledge and reason, with all the spiritual blossoming that involves.'

If I read that passage to Mum or Nora, they'd snort. I think if I read it to Gwenda, she might nod.

I just shook my head when I read it and wondered again at Katharine's idealism and faith in humanity.

In 'On Purpose and Propaganda', she uses the phrases 'Promethean spirit' and 'spark of the Promethean fire.' I remember she referred to Mark Smith in *Working Bullocks* as having 'that Promethean spark', and she calls David Evans a 'lone Prometheus.'

I suspect Katharine's a bit of a Promethean herself. I'd never thought about it before I read 'On Purpose and Propaganda' but I agree with Katharine. All writers try to persuade us that *this* character is good because of what he or she believes and how he or she acts, whereas *that* character is bad because of his or her beliefs and actions. Serious writers always urge us to believe that *this* way of life is the best and the right way, *that* way of life is not.

August 29ᵗʰ, 1968

Tonight Jill showed me two magazines – one called 'The Realist Writer' and the other, 'The Realist', both published by the Realist Writers Groups of Australia.

'Katharine wrote for both magazines at one time or another,' said Jill. 'The Realists Groups were an interesting bunch. They started in Melbourne towards the end of the Second World War and by the early 1950s began publishing works by a range of Australian realist writers. They had two main goals: the first was to provide an outlet for progressive writers, and the second was how best to represent the workers of Australia.'

Jill told me there were lots of writers besides Katharine who contributed to these magazines and none of them liked Patrick White because his work isn't realistic.

Shame about Patrick White. *The Tree of Man* is one of my favourite novels.

August 30ᵗʰ, 1968

Tonight at book club, I told Larry I'd read Katharine's 'On Purpose and Propaganda' and he laughed and squeezed my arm. He said he always asked his students in his English classes to summarize it as an exercise then discuss the ideas. 'I think it's a very clear statement of Katharine's beliefs,' he said seriously, 'and it got my students thinking about the purpose of literature.'

After book club, Larry beckoned me and said, 'Got some photos to show you, Vicki.'

He looked very pleased with himself as he showed me a photo of a wooden box. 'It's called the Whitman Cabinet and it's in the State Library of Victoria,' he said with a grin. 'It was made by Jethro Fryer, a carpenter and a relative of Bernard O'Dowd's wife. Inside the cabinet are some books and magazines by Walt Whitman and bits and pieces about Whitman that O'Dowd treasured,' Larry chuckled. 'I took these pictures when I went to look at the cabinet on my last trip to Melbourne. It's a beautiful piece of work, isn't it?'

I nodded furiously.

'And now for the next one,' he laughed, handing me a photo. 'This, dear girl, is inside that tin trunk I was telling you about. The one Prichard and her son packed up and hid in the plumbago.' The photo is of an overseas calendar for 1965 and some magazines. There's one from the Soviet Union, another from Czechoslovakia and a couple of others that could be from China. They look interesting. I've never read a magazine from a communist country. I'll add that to my 'Must Read' list.

While I was looking at the photo, I put two hands over my mouth, pretending it was a big surprise. But really, all I was thinking was that he had called me 'dear girl.' What in the world does that mean? Or was he just being all la-di-da?

Larry said I could keep the photos.

I wanted to say something special to him but couldn't get it out, so I just said, 'Thanks, Larry. Terrific photos, very interesting.'

All the way home on the bus, I thought about Larry. I'm lucky to know him. I wish I could feel something more than admiration for him but he's just too old for me and far too well educated. Anyway, I'm sure he's not interested in me; I'm like a student to him. He obviously loves teaching and seems to enjoy telling me stuff.

August 31st, 1968

Nora and I went to see *Guess Who's Coming to Dinner* this arvo at the Ambassadors. We both loved it. Even though we were surprised to see a film about a love affair between a black man and a white woman, Sidney Poitier is just so gorgeous, we believed in their affair.

Nora always stands up for 'God Save the Queen' at the pictures, I never do. A few times I've been told to a by a member of the audience, and once an usher hissed at me. Nora just shakes her head. I don't care what people think. I can't *stand* monarchies.

Going home on the bus, I thought about *Coonardoo* and *Strange Fruit* and how marriage was out of the question in these two novels, whereas in the Poitier film, getting married was exactly what the couple wanted and got it in the end – although it was touch and go for a while because, at first, all four parents were against it.

September 3rd, 1968

Jill was busy tonight but suggested I read a collection of short stories by Katharine called *Happiness*. 'Keep at it, Vicki,' she smiled and took off to check something in the catalogue.

Mum was in the kitchen doing the dishes and singing 'Some Enchanted Evening'. I headed straight into my bedroom and slammed the door.

September 4th, 1968

I read 'The Curse' on the bus going to work. It's a short story in *Happiness* whose title refers to a 'noxious weed' called 'Patterson's Curse' that is 'sucking all the life blood' from the soil.

It begins with some men riding towards a clearing in the bush. The first line sets out what they see: 'Azure, magenta, tetratheca, mauve and turquoise: the hut, a wrecked ship in halcyon seas.' We hear the 'chinkle-chinkle' of reins; a man picks a blue flower, his 'clutched fingers and jutty knuckles' crouch over it.

They've come to visit a man called Alf. They're told he's gone to jail for stealing, but the way the story is told is so different from the dialogue she usually writes; it's more like poetry.

'Come to see Alf!'

'Alf?'

'He's in jail.'

'In jail?'

'Ayeh!'

'Harness, a rifle and bridle.'

These are what Alf has stolen, and we learn that Alf, as well as being a petty thief, is 'gutless' and 'lazy.' He's never even tried to beat the Patterson's Curse swirling over his old hut, 'lapping the doorstep' and 'ravening' the earth. Alf doesn't like work; he's given up; he prefers reading, going 'kangarooin'' with his dogs, and stealing. They all try to figure out what's wrong with poor old Alf:

'Daft?'

'Not a bit...'

'Touched, they said.'

'To let a place go, like this.'

'No.'

'Only done for.'

The story opens and closes with images of chattering leaves: 'Clatter and chatter of leaves, husky, frail...tongues, lisping and clicking together, twisting over and licking each other, whispering, gossiping.'

There's something menacing about these leaves. Reminds me of how Deb in *Working Bullocks* believes in the 'vengeance' of trees and how, in the end, she and Red seem to be swallowed up by the 'whisper of leaves' and that cruel laughter of the butcher-bird.

September 5th, 1968

Katharine notes in her Foreword to *Happiness* that Henrietta Drake-Brockman called 'The Curse' 'avant-garde-ish,' which seems to have upset her. She says she has 'no desire to be associated' with avant-garde's 'present developments.' Katharine wants to be known first and foremost as a realist writer.

However, I love 'The Curse'. Read it to the girls at morning tea. Gwenda liked it; Nora didn't.' Gwenda likes poetry; Nora doesn't, although she likes songs from musicals. She sometimes sings 'I'm Just a Girl Who Can't Say No' from *Oklahoma* while making the tea.

Lately, she's been giving Gwenda a sly smile as she's singing.

I didn't write any sketches at lunchtime today because I remembered I had a bit left over from my last pay. Dashed out to the bookshop and bought *Happiness*! Felt so good to spend my money on something valuable. When I got back to work and told Nora where I'd been, she just shrugged.

September 8th, 1968

Gwenda, Nora and I went up to King's Park this morning and, after our spearmint milkshakes, went for a bush walk. Afterwards, we sat on a bench near a playground and were having a gossip, glad to be out and about and away from work, when a man carrying a newspaper sat down against a tree directly opposite us, put his knees up, spread his newspaper across them and sat back to enjoy a good read – or at least that's what we thought he was going to do.

A couple of minutes later, Nora sucked in her breath and whispered to us, 'What's this bloke up to?'

We looked over, and the man's fly was wide open, penis erect.

'Why do we have to put up with these pigs,' growled Gwenda.

'No use reporting him,' I said, thinking myself to be an authority on the subject, given what happened to me that night in St Georges Terrace. 'Nothing would be done about it.'

We left King's Park right away and didn't talk much on our way home.

September 10th, 1968

Another story I like in *Happiness* is 'The Cow.' This cow, Katharine tells us in her Foreword, was their 'own beautiful Jersey, Cynthia' who had 'horns like the crescent moon.'

In the story, Lucia, married for three years but childless, watches Sloe-Eyes swagger about with yet another new calf and decides the cow is an 'insult to her...she was jealous of the cow.' One night, during a storm, Lucia takes off her clothes, flings out her arms and gives herself to the rain. She runs from tree to tree in the 'thin moonlight'; everything she can see around her is 'light, frail and shining as the rain'; she is 'prostituted to it all.' When she stumbles back into bed beside George, covering him with her body, he murmurs, 'Cripes,' then 'Hell!' as his hands find her.

Lucia's first child is born during the summer; a second child soon after the cow's next calf, and a third not long after. But where the cow accepts her lot, happily feeding and breeding, Lucia feels her 'creativeness' has been exhausted; there is 'no room...for pleasure' in the new baby; she has 'neither health nor strength' to give to the child. When she sees George driving the cow along the track, the cow's 'heavy sides and swollen udder' swaying, Lucia calls to her husband, 'She can have it on her own, George...I'm scratched.'

'Scratched' – that word got me thinking about motherhood and birth control; how did women back then avoid getting pregnant? How do they now?

September 11th, 1968

On the bus going to work this morning, I thought about asking Mum about how she managed to have only two kids. Then I decided against bringing up that subject with her – she'd be too embarrassed to discuss it with me, and so would I!

So, at morning tea, I asked Gwenda and Nora what they knew about birth control. Nora shrugged and said, 'Not much. I know about French Letters and douches.' Gwenda's eyes flashed, and she said the most common way to stop getting pregnant was for the man to pull out. 'That's why I won't go all the way with Andy,' she announced. 'Because I don't trust him to pull out, and he hates French Letters.'

September 13th, 1968

Gwenda and Nora were both in a bad mood at morning tea.

Gwenda says Andy is cranky with her, is talking more and more about going north and has cancelled their date for Saturday night.

Nora reckons she's fed up with her job and everyone and everything in her life is boring. She wants to go to Sydney to see her eldest brother, who just got a job there.

I'm feeling a little bit guilty because I'm having such an interesting time working on my project, and along with my sketches, I hardly seem to have time to think of anything else!

September 14th, 1968

Have just finished reading three short stories in the *Happiness* collection about three Aboriginal women: Marlene, N'goola and Esmeralda.

I've done a quick tally. So far, I've read seven short stories by Katharine about the lives of Aboriginal people, as well as *Coonardoo*. Katharine is clearly interested in showing us how Aboriginal people, especially the women, live and how they've have been shoved around by white folk.

I'm reading stuff I've never heard of and sometimes I can hardly believe what I'm reading.

'The Elopement' is an amusing story, but also violent and sad. Sixteen-year-old Esmeralda lives with her grandmother, Maria, in a squalid native camp just outside a township in the South West. Maria has promised Esmeralda to old Jindaba, but clever young Esmeralda has been able to 'keep her virginity by giving old Jindaba shillings for tobacco and wine' and bribes her grandmother with 'money for food, tobacco and plonk' to keep Jindaba away from her for as long as possible.

Esmeralda is keen on Rudy Redshirt, 'a handsome young half-caste.' Not only is he good-looking but he, like her, has nothing but 'contempt for the whites, their greed and hypocrisy pretending to be kind and generous when they gave a native some stale food or worn-out clothes, while all the time they were responsible for robbing the tribes of their hunting grounds, their pride and dignity.'

Rudy has been pestering Esmeralda to run away with him, but she knows they're 'forbidden to each other', both by white man's law, because he's married, and by 'the law of the Aborigines which required a girl to give herself to a man of the tribe selected for her.'

Esmeralda finally gives in and elopes with Rudy. She's hunted down by a small group of 'avengers' led by Maria and old Jindaba. They bash Rudy 'to pulp' and tie him to his horse. Esmeralda has her skirt pulled up and is held down while Maria inspects her: 'Too late,' Maria reports 'grimly.' The women knock Esmeralda's head from side to side until her nose bleeds; she's 'jeered at and scolded by the women, whacked with their waddies' all the way back to town.

When the mob try to get Constable Flannigan to support their efforts to 'uphold white man's law as well as their own', they're told to 'clear out' or he'll arrest them for 'assault and battery.' Pearl, Rudy's wife, 'can take action if she wants to.' Off they go to Pearl, who listens, 'unmoved.' 'Rudy, can he help it if the girls like him?' Pearl asks as Rudy meekly obeys her instructions to come inside so she can 'tie up' his head. Turning to look at Esmeralda, he sees a 'sullen and broken-spirited' girl. Love, we're told, 'no longer burned like a fire between them'.'

I did laugh at this story, and Rudy Redshirt's an interesting character, but I hated all the violence and was furious with Pearl for defending Rudy. I wanted her to kick him out!

N'goola is only six years old when a mounted trooper comes into the camp, ties her hands together, puts a handkerchief over her mouth, and rides off with her. She's put on a boat with other little 'half-castes' and sent south to Perth. Gwelnit, N'goola's father, goes to Perth to look for his daughter in all the Roman Catholic, Salvation Army and Methodist homes that are paid by the Government to house half-caste children.

After years of searching, Gwelnit arrives at a local native settlement and asks a woman named Mary if she knows someone called 'N'goola.' Mary is surprised to hear him asking about a woman by her native name. 'No one would know that,' Mary thinks. No woman in the settlement would remember they'd ever had a native name; they were all 'Jeans and Janeys, Kittys and Dulcies, these days.' Yet Mary is 'disturbed by something vaguely familiar' in the name 'N'goola.' Gradually, she comes to realize that *she* is N'goola. But if she admits she's N'goola and accepts the old man as her father, she will never get permission to build a house on her block, something she has always dreamed about.

I was dying to skip to the last few sentences to see what N'goola would do, but I managed not to cheat. The ending is a bit melodramatic but I liked it: Gwelnit's voice casts a spell on N'goola, forcing her to choose between her desire to live like a white woman or a return to her Aboriginal roots. After a long silence, she chooses loyalty to her Aboriginal ancestry.

A familiar beginning to the story 'Marlene': two women are riding along a bush track towards a 'native camp.' It's been raining 'steady for two months.' Everyone is wet through. There's 'not a dry blanket in the camp' and everyone is fed up.

When local white landowner Mrs Boyd suggests they 'shift camp for the winter', Aboriginal Albert tells her, 'This is the only place we're allowed to camp in the district...You know that, Mrs Boyd.'

'It's a disgrace you should have to live like this,' says Mrs Boyd.

Albert reminds Mrs Boyd that all the surrounding land is now 'private property.' They're not allowed to work in the mines. They're not allowed to sell the fish they catch. They're not allowed to shoot or trap. The white farmers won't give them work. They're not allowed to work on the roads. 'All we're allowed to do is draw rations and rot,' he says. When Mrs Boyd protests that she's always given the 'half-caste' men work on her farm when she could, he agrees with a 'wry smile' and points out that she's always paid them less than half of what she has to pay white workers. That really upsets Mrs Boyd, who accuses Albert of 'talking like one of those crazy agitators' and threatens him: 'If you're not careful you'll find yourself being moved on.'

And that is precisely what happens. The Aboriginal people are moved on less than a month later when Mrs Boyd discovers that sixteen-year-old Mollie has returned to the camp with her baby, Marlene, who, according to Mrs Boyd, is the 'ugliest scrap of humanity she had ever seen.' She believes 'these half-castes' are 'an immoral lot' and the 'sooner they're cleaned out of the district the better.'

What I find extraordinary is that Mollie protects Mrs Boyd from the truth. When Mrs Boyd asks her who is Marlene's father, Mollie smiles and tells her, 'I been going with two or three boys in town.' Everyone in the camp knows Mrs Boyd's son, Edward, is the culprit.

September 16th, 1968

I read 'Marlene' to Gwenda and Nora at morning tea, and then we had a chat about why we think Mollie decided to protect Edward.

Nora thinks it's because Mollie would be too scared to tell Mrs Boyd. 'Anyway, she likes her baby,' Nora said, 'and she doesn't need Edward. She's better off with her own people.'

Gwenda said that Mollie was probably raped, but she'd never say so. 'After all, what would be the point? Mollie knows Mrs Boyd wouldn't help her, nor would Edward.'

I wanted to talk more about Mollie, but our discussion was cut short because Maggot stuck his big fat head into our tearoom and told us to get back to work. One day...

September 17th, 1968

This arvo, Jill gave me Katharine's novel *Moon of Desire*.

'Katharine reckons it's just a yarn,' said Jill, 'Apparently, it's based on her holidays in Broome and Singapore.

'She wrote it because she thought Hollywood would be interested in turning it into a film. It has exotic settings, the pearling industry is dangerous and there's murder and intrigue galore – just the kind of stuff Hollywood likes,' laughed Jill, ruffling her copper hair. 'It's not your usual Katharine, Vicki,' she said, 'but I think you'll enjoy it anyway.'

'I reckon I will,' I said. I reckon I'll enjoy anything written by Katharine.

September 23rd, 1968

Just finished reading *Moon of Desire*; what a pot-boiler! I laughed a lot while I was reading this novel – I really liked it.

There's a strange post-script to *Moon of Desire* in which Katharine tells us that 'fragments' of the story came from a man called Charles Pryor, one of those English 'gentlemanly failures of the East who drift about, making a precarious living in all manner of small ways.' She claims she met him in a Rest House in Malaya, where she stayed for several days because of the monsoon.

Pryor tells Katharine about a beautiful pearl and the 'havoc it wrought in so many lives.' It eventually goes 'back to Loo-murn…the place of rest and peace the aborigines say lies somewhere over the sea, west of Broome.' Katharine says she received a letter from Pryor giving her permission to tell the story of the pearl, if she is 'still sufficiently interested.'

September 24th, 1968

I asked Jill this afternoon about the post-script to *Moon of Desire* and she just laughed. 'Vicki,' she said, 'except for the descriptions of the pearling industry up north, I don't believe any of it! It's a novel – it doesn't have to be true.'

I love the opening paragraph of *Moon of Desire*:

> 'Like a great pearl, the moon was rising over Roebuck
> Bay. Sky and sea lay dim and shining as the valves of an
> oyster shell forced apart by the wedge of dark land

running down to the bar.'

In the streets of Broome, 'poincianas' flare 'scarlet against blue skies'; old bungalows stand in the 'shade of tall palms and blossoming shrubs, oleanders, black-heart acacias, jacarandas and keopanger trees.'

Her image of Singapore is equally vivid. The streets are lined with 'tall old palms' and 'flame-of-the-forest trees in vermilion blossom.' Ramshackle buildings are 'pressed together along the side streets: shops on the pavement and living-rooms piled above. As much alike as peas in a pod, except that gaudy signs in Chinese characters proclaimed the wares within.'

I'd love to go to Broome! I'd love to go to Singapore! I'd love to go anywhere!

September 27th, 1968

Larry wasn't at book club tonight. I was looking forward to chatting about *Moon of Desire*. I left early; didn't feel like talking to anyone else and haven't read the club's book choice.

When I got home, I read Katharine's descriptions of Broome to Mum. I didn't say what book I was reading because she'd only make some nasty remark. But she's often told me she'd love to travel up north, so I thought she'd appreciate Katharine's writing about Broome. She said the descriptions definitely made her want to go to Broome and that she just might go up there one day – once I've left home and was happily married.

Predictable! I ignored those comments.

September 30th, 1968

On the bus this arvo, I decided the most interesting characters in *Moon of Desire* are the villains and there are loads of them! There are out-and-out thugs like Tony Sierra; there are murderers – Captain Godbewithyou and Matsumoto – and there's Fryer, the sneaky thief who causes trouble for everyone.

Captain Ebenezer Godbewithyou (what a name!) reminds me of Sam Geary in *Coonardoo*, of Brumby in *Brumby Innes*, of Dan Haxby in *Haxby's Circus*. Captain God, as he's called, is 'one of the wealthiest men in the nor-west.' He is 'vigorous, in the prime of life'; he has 'wicked sparkling eyes,' a 'buccaneering swagger' and 'coarse, ruddy-brown hair...threaded with grey' on a 'massive head.' He owns a fleet of pearl luggers, stations, and pubs; he's also an opium dealer and has no objections to dealing in stolen pearls.

Captain God pretends to help men like Fryer who come to Broome seeking quick and easy fortunes. He promises to show them 'the ropes,' then 'breaks them – and leaves them to rot on the beach.' He's a man you have to watch, claims Alec Mallane, 'most of all when he's friendly.'

Fryer's deal with Matsumoto begins the 'havoc.' Matsu is a brave and skilful deep-sea pearl diver, employed on an annual contract plus ten per cent of the shell he gathers, and 'a bonus on pearl.' He's 'risked his life often enough for the white masters who made a handsome profit on his labour' and that's why he believes the 'Moon of Desire' rightfully belongs to him although, legally, the pearl belongs to Alec Mallane, owner of the lugger. When Matsu whispers to Fryer that he'll go 'fifty-fifty' on the sale of the magnificent 'Moon of Desire' he seals his fate and pays with his life.

October 1st, 1968

Maggot was away today, so we had a nice long morning tea. I told Gwenda and Nora the story of *Moon of Desire* – Gwenda didn't think much of it, but Nora loved it. She likes stories about murderers, thieves, pirates, and drug dealers.

I told them Katharine didn't take the novel seriously, that she'd written it because she thought Hollywood would buy it and turn it into a film. Nora poured herself another cup of tea, and said, 'Wow, I hope one day someone will make a film of it someday. Sounds like an exciting story, and I love pearls.'

Gwenda and I laughed because Nora often wears a pink twinset and cheap pearls to work, and we always tease her because she looks like an old lady.

October 2nd, 1968

I didn't know a thing about the pearling industry until I read *Moon of Desire*. Katharine tells us who owns what, who does what, and describes the relationship between the owners of the luggers and their divers, shell openers and cleaners, what pearls are worth and how pearls are traded.

Katharine has an extraordinary way of investigating an industry – whether it's cattle, opals, the circus, timber, newspapers or pearling. Even in *Intimate Strangers,* a story mostly about a busted marriage, she tells us a lot about fish and fishing. I always learn so much about the world when I read her books.

October 4th, 1968

Mum and I had a fight last night. While we were clearing the table after dinner, I started telling her the story of *Moon of Desire*. 'It's by Katharine Susannah Prichard and a real pot-boiler,' I said. 'I read you her descriptions of Broome a few nights ago. You liked what she wrote, didn't you?'

She slammed the dishes into the sink, told me to wash them and stop raving on about a bloody old Commie cow, that I should be ashamed of myself for reading such rubbish. I instantly jumped to Katharine's defence. Told Mum how I love Katharine's books and that Katharine is changing the way I look at the world. 'I'll read whatever I want, whenever I want,' I said and poked out my tongue. She flicked a tea towel in my face. I called her a spiteful bitch and told her she could wash the dishes herself.

Later, she barged into my bedroom and said, 'Here's what's worth reading, Vicki,' and handed me a novel by Agatha Christie. 'I can't understand why you're choosing books written by such a radical woman,' she growled. 'You're lucky to live in a country like Australia. We have a stable government. John Gorton is a good prime minister. And we've got the Queen.'

I didn't say a word. She put her book on top of *Moon of Desire*, which was on my bedside table and left.

I've decided not to mention Katharine to Mum ever again.

October 8ᵗʰ, 1968

Jill told me tonight that Katharine didn't enjoy writing *Moon of Desire*. By the time it was finished, she was fed up with the novel and, in a letter to her friend Hilda Esson, said she wished she hadn't written it. 'It's just a yarn,' a 'concocted story' fit only for 'film production.' In her view, the novel is 'flat – and stiff and futile,' although she claimed it had 'some bits of the real K.S.'

As she had some free time, we browsed through the novel together, and Jill pointed out some of the 'bits of the real K.S.'

'One bit has to do with Dr Sung and the coming revolution in China,' said Jill. 'And there's her sympathy for the Aboriginal people in Broome. Katharine's view of them, I think, is summed up by Don Healy, who lives with an Aboriginal woman in a native camp. He is disgusted with white people's greed and unfairness and would rather live in a camp than in town with the whites.

'Then there's Ann Wade's opinion of the justice system, which sounds like Katharine. Justice is lop-sided; it is "blind to causes and their effects, penalizes weakness and failure, leaving the successful criminal unscathed."

'And early in the novel, Ann gives us a way to think about the pearling industry when she says that the life of Broome was based on the search for "a thing of such pure and lustrous beauty", but the town "reeked of the dark passion, rapacity and barbarism which had gone into possession of that rare precious beauty!"'

Jill has a way of summing things up that always makes me feel I need to further my education! But I did manage to put in my two bob's worth when I added, 'Oh, and there are constant references to how the desire to be rich leads to deceit, theft, betrayal, and murder.'

Jill looked a bit surprised, then said, 'Yep! And the only way to stop the chaos is to get rid of that fabulous pearl. Very Katharine!

'In the end,' Jill told me, 'Hollywood wasn't interested in *Moon of Desire* and Katharine was very disappointed. Although, I have heard that she believes her agents in the USA didn't even send it to a film producer. Shame,' said Jill, shaking her head.

'It is a shame,' I replied. 'I'd go to see *Moon of Desire* on film. I'd go to see any of Katharine's novels on film!' I said.

'So would I,' Jill laughed, tapping her pencil on the counter.

October 13th, 1968

It's a lovely springtime Sunday – I've been reading all day. Started in the deck chair in the backyard and ended up on my bed. Mum didn't say a word all morning and went to Mrs Cook's in the afternoon.

Just read 'Naninja and Janey' in *N'goola and Other Stories*, a tragic story about two old Aboriginal women.

'Old Naninja' is blind; her 'shadow' Janey has a stump for one arm – a prospector chopped off part of an arm after she'd been bitten by a snake when she was a child. He thought it was the right thing to do! These women live with their people among white prospectors digging for gold at Skull Creek, so-called because of the number of Aboriginal skulls found in the creek after a massacre. The latest prospectors have turned the Aboriginal people's water hole into a well and told them to go 'scavenging in the backyards and round the rubbish heaps' to find food because they won't be wasting their own food on the 'natives.'

Mary Moyle complains to her prospector husband, Jim, 'white people have broken up the natives' way of life…They managed to live well enough until we took their wells and scared off the wild animals. Now they're starving, have to rely on what we can give them to eat. And we haven't even been able to get government rations for them.' No one takes any notice of Mary Moyle.

Naninja is 'sick feller' and goes walkabout on the plains to die, taking Janey with her. After receiving a desperate letter from Mary, a reluctant Sergeant Gilligan and a black tracker take off on camels, well-stocked with food and water but 'none too pleased about turning out on this wild goose chase.' It takes them three days to find Naninja and Janey, and on their return to Skull Creek, Gilligan, with 'the air of a man satisfied to have done his duty,' tells Mary that he found the old women, 'but the dingoes had got there first.

I had the same sick feeling in my stomach when I finished this story as I did when I read how *Coonardoo* dies, her diseased bones breaking like those little black sticks in the fire.

October 14th, 1968

At morning tea, I brought up the story of Naninja and Janey dying out on the plains and the dingoes eating their bodies. But Gwenda and Nora were dunking their Arrowroots and didn't want to discuss it. 'Yuk,' said Gwenda.

'Give it a rest,' said Nora.

So I changed the subject to battles between white people and

Aboriginal people and told them about Skull Creek. 'I didn't know Aboriginal people fought against the whites,' said Nora. I told them that Katharine always researches her stories, and if she writes about massacres by white people, it would be true. Nora just shrugged. 'If you say so,' she said under her breath. It was obvious she didn't believe a word I said. 'Why do you read such awful stories?' Nora asked me, tossing her blond hair in disgust.

'Don't forget I have a project,' I reminded her. 'And I'll read anything I can get hold of written by or about Katharine, even if I don't like it or it upsets me.'

Gwenda nodded in sympathy. She understands what I'm doing. Nora doesn't.

October 19ᵗʰ, 1968

For some reason I feel really lonely tonight, so I've been playing 'Are You Lonesome Tonight' over and over. I suppose it was because Mum kept on and on at me at dinner – 'Why don't you go out dancing on Saturday nights? Why don't you join a club and meet a nice boy? Why don't you change your job if there aren't any nice boys where you work?' Why this? Why that?

She just wouldn't shut up. Felt like slapping her. Instead, I told her she's a horrible cook and slunk off to my bedroom.

It's not that I don't want a boyfriend. Maybe I should just wander up and down Hay Street one night and see what happens. Maybe I *should* go out more often and look for some nice bloke to marry.

October 21st, 1968

Sat in the library for an hour or more this arvo after work; didn't want to go home. Can't stand Mum at the moment.

I must've looked down in the dumps because Jill was really kind to me. She found an early novel by Katharine called *Windlestraws* and suggested I read it. 'It's light reading and not very good, but it's fun,' she said, 'and you should read it anyway for your project.' She smiled and touched my arm as she said 'your project' and I felt very grateful to her for making me feel I was doing something worthwhile with my life.

She also gave me a copy of a letter Miles Franklin wrote to Katharine in 1953 telling her that she'd attended some lectures at Sydney University and the lecturer dismissed *Windlestraws* as a 'lark.'

I have to read the book in the library. Jill says it's a rare book and can't be borrowed. That was music to my ears; now I have a good reason not to go home straight after work.

Apparently, Katharine wrote it before *The Pioneers*, but it wasn't published until 1916, after she was famous. Jill says it was serialized in *The Age* newspaper on Saturdays from March to June 1916.

I noticed that the publishers have misspelled her surname on the front cover. They spell it 'Pritchard'! I also noticed that on the inside, some lovely librarian has put a line through the 't' in Pritchard, added 'Mrs Throssell' and the publication date of 1916. All in pencil, of course. Maybe Jill did that. Tonight, she was too busy to ask.

October 25th, 1968

Larry wasn't at book club (again) tonight.

I haven't read their book and didn't want to listen to their discussion, so I left early.

Just started reading *Windlestraws*. It begins with a couple meeting on the London Embankment on New Year's Eve. They're both thinking about throwing themselves into the Thames.

Suicide as a theme certainly started early in Katharine's stories.

October 26th, 1968

Well, I think probably that lecturer was right! *Windlestraws* is a bit of a lark.

It's a lively romance about a young couple called Gene Day and Peter Varof, who is really a Russian Prince, no less! Gene calls herself and Peter 'windlestraws' because they are 'people who drift and whirl' but manage to cling together.

Gene Day is strong-minded, intelligent, hard-working, like many of Katharine's female characters. As for social conventions, Gene claims she's 'never had even a bowing acquaintance with them.' Peter is charming but fragile; his eyes are 'like the windows of an empty house' that tell of 'internal desolation.' He's been in debt, in jail, is a gambler; he's no good with money.' Gene claims to know Peter 'deep down' through his eyes. Gene's own eyes are referred to often in the novel: there's an 'elfish light in her eyes'; they have a 'mystical light' which reminds Peter of 'the legends of sirens who lived in pools – as green as her eyes were – and allured travellers…Only it was life and not death, he had found in her eyes.'

I'm trying to think of people I know who always look me in the eye when they're talking. Gwenda does; Nora doesn't; Larry does; Jill does when she's not busy and has time to chat; Maggot never does; Mum does when she's picking on me.

Gene and Peter steal a diamond ring from a toff named Sir John Britten and don't feel guilty about it. The theft, she tells Peter, is just a 'forced loan' and they will one day return what they stole. In the meantime, she easily convinces him to play Let's Pretend. 'I've got an idea,' she says, 'I can dance, you know…I could earn £100 per night…Let's pretend that we've got a fancy name…a Baronne de something or other.'

They end up calling themselves the Duc and Duchess de Windlestraws. Gene sets most of the rules in their relationship. He's not to fall in love with her. She promises not to fall in love with him; they are to be 'pardners' only and when they've finished their game, they're to go back to being themselves. He's to marry Nadia, his Belle Dame, and she's to do with her life what she wants. Of course, things don't work out that way. They fall in love, give their earnings of a thousand pounds to a beggar and decide to go wandering again.

October 30th, 1968

Nora was away again today. She's missed two days this week. Could be sick. Could have job interviews.

Gwenda told me at morning tea she's having another tiff with Andy.

'He can't make up his mind about going north and still carries on about going all the way with him.'

'Why don't you?' I asked her, and she looked at me in amazement. 'What!' she shrieked, slammed her cup into the sink and stalked off.

Well, I thought, it's been going on for so long, I'm quite surprised she hasn't given in. But then I thought, poor Gwenda, what if she gets pregnant? That's the real worry. Andy would probably marry her but she's not ready for kids. None of us are.

There's a bit of politics in *Windlestraws*, but nothing like what Katharine was later to write. Peter Varof decides that if Russia goes to war in the Balkans, he'll have to go home and fight. There will be no limit to his 'courage or his power of endurance…his self-respect had returned.' He has a brother who follows Tolstoy's ideas to 'live in simplicity' and dedicates his life to helping the peasants, much to their mother's disgust who detests this 'unsettling of the peasants'!

I've got mixed feelings about *Windlestraws*. I liked some of it but couldn't really get into it and I didn't like the ending. I wanted Gene and Peter, the windlestraws, to do something more interesting than play Let's Pretend. I like Katharine best when she's dead serious about what she's writing about.

November 1st, 1968

This arvo, Jill gave me a collection of short stories by Katharine called *Potch and Colour*. Jill told me to read the stories about life on the goldfields. 'They'll get you in the mood for her trilogy,' she said.

She also told me that Katharine considers her trilogy to be the best work she's ever done. 'Although, as usual,' Jill said with a frown, 'there are plenty of people who don't agree with her.'

Can't wait to read it!

November 2nd, 1968

Tonight, I started reading the Goldfields stories. They're really good fun!

I noticed Katharine dedicated *Potch and Colour* to her son, 'Ric Prichard Throssell.' I like the idea of giving a mother's surname as a middle name for her son. If I ever have kids, I think I'll do that too.

The first yarn I read was 'Mrs Grundy's Mission. Then I read 'The Gentleman on the Coals', 'Bad Debts', 'Luck' and 'Genieve.' They're all set in goldmining country around Coolgardie.

What I find really funny in these yarns is the way people speak.

Mexican Jack is a 'long slab of an American' and Corney is 'one of these broken-down aristocrat spielers.' Bill Langham was once a 'big husky kid but as silly as a meat-axe.' Jo Hegney is a 'dirty old blackguard', a 'hard nut to crack' but a 'great prospector' who's 'near done a perish for water on the track.' While the 'Rivirend Sprigg' is 'lyin' dead to the world', drunk on Corney's hop beer, Jack Mills and Blunt Pick have a 'set-to about something or other' and, 'before anybody knew what was happening, it was an all-in go.' Ted

Budge is an 'old wurt' with 'long ears.'

I had a good belly laugh while reading these stories. I bet Katharine enjoyed listening to these old codgers talk. Glad she recorded all their funny sayings. She has a great sense of humour and is a terrific listener and observer of people's behaviour.

November 7th, 1968

My favourite yarn in *Potch and Colour* is 'The Bride of Far-away'.

Mary's told by Speck O'Brien to stop working so hard because she's pregnant. She's surprised to hear it! She's so 'young and foolish' she doesn't even know she's having a baby.

And it's babies who are at the heart of this story, dead babies, that is. Mary's first is premature and dies after 'a few days in the blazing heat and drought of a late summer.' Mary and Mick never recover from the death of their first-born, but she has another child soon afterwards. This time, she goes to Coolgardie where she sees the only doctor in the town. He has the reputation of being 'better drunk than sober at his work.' The public hospital is made of hessian, water is scarce and typhoid is 'raging.' Their second child dies a few days after birth and Mary returns to Far-away.

For the birth of their third child, Mary decides not to go to Coolgardie; instead the doctor comes to her home. Patrick Michael lives for three months before dying of 'marasmus.' Two years later their fourth child also dies of marasmus – a condition that 'swept away nearly all the babies born on the early goldfields,' Katharine writes, 'and nobody knew how to cope with it.' I had to look up 'marasmus' in the dictionary; it means *undernourishment*.

It's all too much for Mary Ryan to bear; she goes to bed with a 'strange sickness' and Dr Flynn, who's paid £100 to come to Faraway, decides Mary has 'some septic germ' and won't live more than 'two or three days.'

The doctor orders a coffin for Mary and when 'a long box of golden pine' arrives on top of a wagon, Mary, now recovered, asks about this 'handsome piece of furniture' that has arrived all the way from Coolgardie. Mick comes out of the pub, sees Mary staring at the coffin with a silver plate bearing her name and yells to his mates, 'Take it away! Take it away and burn it!' Mary, 'thrifty by instinct' will not have such a 'useful box' destroyed. She tells the men to take it round the back; she'll use it for a 'wash trough' and it'll also 'be grand for scalding a pig in.'

I just love the ending of this story! Funny – but dark too. It got me thinking about death and dying and what I would do if I had a child who died within days of being born. I wonder if I'd ever get over it. Would I have another child afterwards or would I call it quits?

November 11ᵗʰ, 1968

I asked Gwenda and Nora at morning tea whether they wanted to be buried or cremated. Nora looked horrified; Gwenda laughed and said she doesn't care what happens to her body after she's dead.

So tonight, I asked Mum if she wants to be buried or cremated. Mum said she has thought about it and had often wanted to bring up the subject but didn't know how. 'Why do you want to know?' she asked. I broke my rule and told her I'd been reading some stories by Katharine, and death is in a lot of them. She stared at me and stuck out her chin. I could tell she was going to say something nasty about my project, but she changed her mind. 'Well, Vicki,' she said with a sigh. 'I think I'd like to be buried.'

November 29th, 1968

Whew! I am so relieved. I thought Larry had left our book group but he turned up tonight and we had a chat. He's been travelling around the Northern Territory.

We got on to Katharine very quickly because his first question was, 'How's the project going?' He's such a nice person; he's interesting because he's interested in everything.

I told him I'd been reading stories about the goldfields – how funny they are but how surprised I am to discover how hard life was. 'Lots of kids died of marasmus back then,' I said smugly, thinking he might not know the meaning of the word. He knew it, of course, and looked serious when he said there are thousands of kids all over the world right now dying of marasmus.

I felt a bit sick in the tummy as I ate the last of my lamington.

November 30th, 1968

I had planned to go to the pictures with Gwenda tonight but yesterday she told me she has decided to pick up again where she left off with that boyfriend of hers and they're going to the drive-in tonight. He must've bought or borrowed a car!

As she toddled off to her desk, smiling triumphantly, Nora sniffed, 'We all know what goes on at drive-ins, don't we?'

'Yep,' I replied. 'Lucky tart.'

December 9th, 1968

Just finished *The Roaring Nineties*, the first volume of Katharine's Goldfields trilogy. Couldn't put it down!

In her introduction Katharine writes that she wanted to tell 'something of the lives of several people', but the main story is about 'two people I have called Dinny Quin and Sally Gough', who, along with other characters, are based on real characters she met on the goldfields.

Stopped in to chat with Jill this arvo today and told her how much I like *The Roaring Nineties*.

Jill told me that Katharine hadn't been sure about the novel's title. 'She thought about calling it "Wasting Assets", then "Mirage", and finally settled on *The Roaring Nineties*. Excellent choice, as far as I'm concerned,' Jill laughed.

On the bus, I thought about 'Mirage' as a title. It could've worked, given that so many characters in *The Roaring Nineties* have the illusion that they'll make a fortune in gold.

Mirage is also one of Katharine's favourite words.

December 10th, 1968

Jill and I had a chat about Violet O'Brien in *The Roaring Nineties*.

'Her views on marriage are interesting,' Jill said. 'She doesn't want a man bossing her about and giving her children.' She was browsing through *The Roaring Nineties* as she was talking and found the passage she was looking for. 'Here, Vicki,' she said, stabbing the page with her finger. 'Violet says her father regularly gives her mother a black eye and a baby and takes off prospecting again. Violet calls her Mum a "god-damned slut" and reckons they're the "worst horde of filthy brats a man was ever cursed with."'

I've called other women quite a few things, but I'd never call anyone a slut!

'There must be millions of Violets in this world but I've never met anyone like her,' I said. 'We're told she has a beautiful voice. Shame she never gets the chance to go to Paris or New York, but at least she gets to study singing in Melbourne.'

'Only until her parents break up and they all end up back on the goldfields,' replied Jill. 'I felt very sorry for Violet, especially when she told Sally, "All I've got to do is pull beer and everybody's happy."'

Jill was turning the pages looking for something else, so I thought I'd better say something to keep the conversation going because I like Violet. 'Me too,' I said. 'I felt sorry for Violet.'

'Katharine sympathizes with women like Violet,' said Jill, running her finger along some lines. 'They're talented and ambitious but never seem to get the opportunity to succeed. On the other hand, she doesn't think much of Laura Brierley.'

'I reckon Laura is like Mollie in *Coonardoo*,' I piped up. 'Mollie's just a social climber who married for money and status but can't cope with life on Wytaliba – hates the heat, the dust, the flies, the Aboriginal people, spends months away in Perth, dressing up and hob-nobbing with the rich.'

Jill nodded. 'Yep, Laura's a lot like Mollie. It's also interesting that Laura is one of those women who can't live without a man. Remember how, after Alf's suicide, Laura gets drunk and flirts at the private parties upstairs in McSweeney's Western Star Hotel? She loves brushing against men and lets them kiss her and touch her breasts.'

'She's a bit of a hussy, alright,' I said to Jill.

'She is, but I sympathize with poor old Laura,' murmured Jill. 'She's fragile and needs a lot of love and attention, especially from men.'

'Too much attention, I reckon,' I replied. 'She was lucky McSweeney wanted to marry her and promised to treat her like a queen.'

'I like Sally's advice to Laura when she's sobbing over her memories of Alf,' said Jill, checking her watch against the time on the big overhead clock. 'She tells Laura that we all have to do the best we can with how things turn out. Now that is a very Katharine outlook on life!'

It was nearly closing time, but we managed a quick chat about how Laura snubs Mrs Molloy, one of those tough women Katharine admires. She has lots of kids, tons to do, but can always find time to help other women who need it.

'I laughed out loud when I read Theresa Molloy's joke that her husband reckons she'll get pregnant if he hangs his pants on the end of the bed,' I said to Jill.

'Yep, that's funny,' Jill laughed. 'But then Theresa asks, "So what can you do about it?" I think that Katharine is letting us know there's a deadly serious side to getting pregnant every year.'

I didn't know how to reply to Jill, and I worried about Gwenda all the way home on the bus. What if Andy finally gets her into bed and she gets pregnant? What then? I wish Gwenda would keep trying to get into university and forget about Andy.

December 11th, 1968

This morning Gwenda, Nora and I had a chat about getting drunk. I was telling them about Laura's drunken flirtations in *The Roaring Nineties*. Gwenda says that if she drinks a bit too much with her boyfriend, she always thinks about sex.

'I've never been drunk,' said Nora, 'but that doesn't mean I don't think about sex!'

'I'd love to get drunk one day,' I said, 'especially if I was with a nice bloke.'

We all had a good laugh and were just going to have another cuppa when our Maggot boss poked his big fat head in the door and said, 'Get back to work, you lot!'

He didn't see Gwenda stick out her tongue.

At lunchtime I wrote a sketch about a girl who goes to a party, gets drunk, passes out and doesn't go home for two days. I enjoyed writing about it, mostly because I thought about how much fun it would be if it happened to me!

December 12th, 1968

'Do you like Sally Gough?' I asked Jill.

'I do,' Jill replied firmly. 'She's one of those straight, hard-working women Katharine is so good at creating. Unfortunately, she's also one of those frustrated women who is so disappointed in her marriage that she dreams of running off with an exotic lover!'

On the bus coming home I thought about Sally and Morris Gough and Frisco. Yes, I know Frisco's a Casanova and Sally is a bit silly, but all the same, I wouldn't mind having a fling with someone like him! I wonder where I could go in Perth to meet a man like that.

December 13th, 1968

Having a bit of a re-think where Frisco's concerned – not sure if I would like to go out with a man like him after all.

Frisco Jo Murphy is another Jerome Hartog: dashing, cheeky, well-travelled, manipulative, knows 'all the tricks of the game.' He's a gambler, cheats at cards, is an outrageous flirt. The local women think he's the 'handsomest man in town' and, although a 'blackguard', he's a 'very fascinating one.' He seems to get away with everything! When Maritana, an Aboriginal girl Frisco has been seeing, turns up one day, naked and pregnant, Frisco lets everyone know he won't accept any responsibility for their child. The white men watching laugh 'uproariously' as Frisco belts Maritana until she drags herself off. No one blames Frisco, and no one seems to care about Maritana, not even Sally Gough, who has enormous sympathy for the local Aboriginal people.

Sally is both fascinated and repelled by Frisco. However, as time goes by, she becomes much more fascinated than repelled. Danny Quin warns Sally, 'You got to watch him.' While Morris is off prospecting, Frisco lends Sally money and visits her every night, bringing her little luxuries like grapes and oranges. He sings and strums his guitar and tells her about his adventures in Mexico and California. He carts water for her and gives her a three-legged chair with a bag seat that she loves. Sally feels grateful but uneasy when he's around. She suspects that the locals are wondering about their relationship. Still, gradually she starts to rely on him and take his advice.

At one point he tells Sally, 'Christ, I'm mad about you. I've loved you from the first moment I saw you...You know it too, you like me, though you won't admit it. Have fought against me...You've been afraid of me – afraid, all the time, of what there is between us.' Frisco knows she feels guilty about Morris: 'I love you more than Morrie ever could,' he argues. 'I'm a blackguard. Have never pretended to be anything else, but Morrie's worse.' He tries to convince Sally that he'd never treat her the way Morris once did, leaving her alone and sick on the track with only 'the blacks' to help her.

That's the first time, but not the last, that Sally lets Frisco kiss her.

I like how Katharine helps us see Sally and Frisco's relationship from different angles. When sixteen-year-old Paddy Cavan steals a pair of boots from a 'toff', for instance, Sally informs him it was the wrong thing to do. When he slyly criticizes her for accepting Frisco's gifts, she stops to think: 'What difference was there between letting a man give her more than she could repay and stealing a pair of boots?'

Marie Robillard, Sally's best friend, also gives us a clue to what many people must be thinking about Sally: that she's naïve and a 'sitting dove to a sharpshooter like Frisco.'

December 14th, 1968

I met Gwenda in town this morning and we went shopping. Well, she shopped. I window-shopped. I'm broke at the moment. Lots of people in town Christmas shopping, scurrying around like little quokkas.

Gwenda bought a fancy shirt for her boyfriend for Christmas. As we were saying goodbye, she gave me a sly wink and whispered, 'If he's lucky, he'll get me for Christmas as well!' My jaw dropped and I couldn't find any words to say, but as I left her, I started to laugh out loud. I must've looked mad, laughing away like that in the middle of London Court.

December 16th, 1968

At morning tea, I was telling Gwenda and Nora about Frisco. Nora tossed her blond curls and said she doesn't like men like that. To our surprise, Gwenda said Andy is a bit like Frisco! We immediately bombarded her with questions. How is he like Frisco? Is he gorgeous looking? Does he play the guitar? Has he travelled a lot? Does he mess around with other girls? Does he hurt you? Don't you trust him? Is that why you won't go all the way with him? Have you gone all the way with him?

Gwenda just dunked her Granita and frowned.

December 21st, 1968

Shopping in town was fun today. Somehow, I've managed to save a bit of money, and spent the lot! I bought a red bag, a white blouse and a black belt. Very swish!

Going in on the bus, I thought about my money, the money I earn at a job I don't like. I'm like Deb in *Working Bullocks,* I told myself. I work hard at a job I hate and give Mum most of my wages.

December 26th, 1968

Christmas Day was boring, and Mum was grumpy this morning because Mrs Cook didn't pop in as usual. 'She's probably drunk by now,' Mum said around ten o'clock, which is about the time Mrs Cook bangs on the front door. Mum was in a better mood after a couple of shandies and didn't complain when I played 'It's Now or Never' over and over at top volume.

Went to City Beach with Nora and Gwenda this arvo. Nora wore the bathers she got for Christmas – turquoise with white flowers. She looks gorgeous in them! Gwenda also has a new pair of bathers – dark blue – and looks terrific in them. She's been smiling a lot lately. Think she's up to something with her Andy. I have a new beach towel and a transistor Mum gave me for Christmas so we were all quite chirpy, lying on the sand chatting away, listening to the Top 40 and checking out the boys.

We didn't meet anyone on the beach, but Nora met a good looker at the milk bar. They talked for a while and Nora flirted like mad, but he didn't ask her out.

I'm looking forward to book club on Friday night and talking to Larry about *The Roaring Nineties*. I hope he comes. He may decide not to because we have our Christmas/New Year's party on December 31st and he might only want to go to that.

December 27th, 1968

Hurray! Larry turned up tonight! Apparently, he promised to help Miss plan our party, so he's staying after book group.

We had a good chat about *The Roaring Nineties*. I asked him about the alluvial diggers and their grievances against the government and the mining companies. 'I don't understand what the diggers were on about,' I told him. He chuckled.

'Well, before the mining companies moved in,' Larry explained, 'these old diggers were looking for alluvial gold. Reef gold, found in quartz, is much deeper and only mining companies would've been able to afford the machinery needed to get it.

'To mine alluvial gold, prospectors had to have a Miner's Right, a licence permitting them to search for gold. In 1898, the WA government ruled that alluvial gold miners could dig for gold only to a maximum depth of 10 feet. Under the new ten-foot-rule, diggers could search for gold up to ten feet or go "cap in hand" to the mining companies and ask to be allowed to work deeper "on tribute". The miners were furious – they rioted, held mass meetings, threatened violence, refused to obey the law. Some miners were sent to the local lock-up for contempt of court, some were sent to jail in Fremantle.

'There was talk of Eureka, but nothing would've suited the mine owners better than to give the cops an excuse for making arrests, so they kept the fight clean.

'These new laws caused a huge problem for the Western Australian government. By then, Australia was talking Federation,' Larry continued, speaking slowly as he always does when he's serious. 'But John Forrest wasn't interested in Federation. There was chaos on the goldfields where most people supported Federation and threatened to create their own state called Auralia and join the Federation.'

He started laughing, so I took a big breath and said 'Whew!' I realized I had been listening for dear life, like a schoolgirl preparing for an exam. 'As Prichard writes in *The Roaring Nineties*,' said Larry, 'for Forrest it was lose the goldfields or federate, so he caved in. And that's how we Sand Gropers joined the rest of Australia!'

He chuckled, so I giggled, pretending I'd understood everything he'd told me. 'Next time I'll give you some notes about the period, seeing as you're interested,' he said. He touched my shoulder and gave me a wink. I wasn't sure if I should wink back, touch his shoulder or what, so I gave him a huge, clumsy grin. He laughed.

Mum's always slinging off at the eastern states. I suppose if she'd lived during the 1890s, she would've voted against Federation. I'm pretty sure she'd vote 'Yes' if we had a vote on secession right now.

Anyway, I'm so glad Larry has cleared up that bit in *The Roaring Nineties*, even though it was a bit too much to take in at the time. But now I understand what was going on back then with the diggers, and I would've been on their side.

December 29th, 1968

In *The Roaring Nineties*, one Monday morning, Sally Gough and her friends go to a bank to look at samples of the famous Londonderry gold. They meet a 'demented throng, exclaiming wild-eyed and with strange oaths as this new display of secret wealth which had been torn from the surrounding country.'

As they walk home, they're both a little depressed; they've come to realize 'the dread and sinister influence of gold: the madness it put over men like an evil spell.' Sally asks Laura, 'Why should it be so important – gold?'

'You funny little thing,' Laura replies. 'Gold means wealth, power. That's why men are so crazy about it. They can get all the things they want, if they've got gold – enough of it.'

Sally says she knows that but points out that the value of gold is just a superstition; copper and iron are more useful. A shocked Laura tells her not to let anybody hear her say that. 'Gold's the god they worship up here.'

I was eating my toast this morning and Mum was listening to the ABC news as usual. Towards the end there was something about gold prices.

'Why are they talking about gold, Mum?'

'I don't know. I suppose rich people are interested in gold. I know I'm not.'

I'm not either. I reckon most of us couldn't care less about the price of gold.

December 30ᵗʰ, 1968

Kept looking at Gwenda at morning tea to see if anything looks different about her. 'Did you give your boyfriend his shirt?' I asked innocently. She shrugged and said she gave it to him on Christmas morning and he loved it.

She left to go back to her desk and I whispered to Nora, 'Has Gwenda said anything to her about finally giving in to Andy?' Nora tossed her hair and told me not to be so nosy, but then she paused and said, 'Why? Has she said anything to you?' I told her about London Court and she jumped up to make herself another cup of tea. 'Tell me all about it!' she said, sipping her tea and settling back for a good gossip. Just then, Maggot rapped on the window and gave us the signal to get to work. We dawdled back to our desks.

December 31st, 1968

This arvo, we were allowed to leave work early! Maggot stuck his fat head into the tearoom and said, 'You lot can leave at twelve. Top management decision. Not mine.'

'How nice,' replied Gwenda with a sly little smile.

'It's killing him,' sniggered Nora.

I didn't want to go home so I went to the library and hung around waiting for Jill. I scribbled a couple of sketches about people I'd seen Christmas shopping in town but wasn't in the mood. I tried to find a communist magazine, but I don't think the library has any, so I ended up flipping through the latest issue of the *Bulletin*.

When Jill arrived, we had a chat about gold rushes. Jill told me that Katharine and her husband followed a rush in Larkinville in 1930 and that's when she first started research for her trilogy. 'She made notes, yarned with miners and prospectors, even chatted with prostitutes,' Jill said. 'Oh, and she knows how to use a shaker, the basic gold mining tool the early prospectors used.'

'Gee, she's clever, isn't she? And adventurous,' I added.

'Yep, she is those things and more,' Jill grinned.

Jill found me a copy of an article Katharine wrote for *The Daily News*. It starts with a funny little poem written by an old prospector she met:

'Here's to the dry blower!

When he dies to Heaven he flies

With dust in his eyes fit to blind him.

What a rattle he'll make as he goes

through the gate.

Dragging his old shaker behind him.'

'Katharine's funny,' I said to Jill.

'She's mischievous, isn't she!' Jill chuckled.

We had a long discussion about Katharine's ability to describe technical details. In *The Roaring Nineties* we read about gold mining tools I've never heard of. There are dollies, pots, pans and shakers; tins, dishes, trays, pegs, picks and shovels, cradles, top hampers, dry-blowers, batteries, stamps, poppet legs, pumps and scales.

To kill time, I read the passage about how Sally works a shaker, moving its arm gently looking for slugs among the pebbles and rubble that are 'dancing and jumping on the tray.' She understands the 'movement of the lighter stones and the way gold, being heavier, hung back or fell to lower trays, where the blower fanned off grit and dust.'

Reminded me of Sophie's polishing skills in *Black Opal*.

The library's big clock finally ticked over to six pm so I wandered over to Jill's desk and said as casually as I could, 'I'm off to my book club's party, Jill. Happy New Year!'

'And to you too, my friend,' Jill laughed.

I left the library feeling on top of the world.

So here it is, the end of 1968. I've managed to complete two years' worth of scribblings in my diary of discovery. Haven't been counting but I must've finished at least a hundred lunchtime sketches. I know two educated, lovely people who call me 'friend'. I'm still dead keen on finding out more about Katharine's work and ideas.

Lucky me.

At our party, we had Christmas cake, bon bons, balloons, streamers, sherry, beer and Sparkling Burgundy! But before the party got cracking, as promised, Larry gave me some notes. 'Look at some of the historical people Prichard mentions in *The Roaring Nineties*, he said. 'They were all involved in various ways with the early days on the goldfields. She's top notch when it comes to research.'

While he was off chatting with Miss and a band was playing Peter, Paul and Mary, I sat down and had a squiz at his notes. Alongside the names he's jotted down a few comments to give me an idea of who they were. I recognized Bayley and Ford, Paddy Hannan, C.Y. O'Connor and John Forrest, but I've never heard of all the others. The most interesting person on Larry's list is Father D.P. Long, a Catholic priest, who was tricked into believing an enormous gold nugget had been found in Kanowna. He told local prospectors who trusted him, of course, being a Catholic priest, and they immediately started a rush. It was a hoax! Amazing what greed will do to people.

At the bottom of the list Larry has scribbled: 'The locations Prichard mentions are real; all the mines existed; she uses the real names of some of the men who took part in the alluvial rights movement; there *was* a short-lived movement to separate the goldfields from the rest of Western Australia.'

How clever is Katharine to have real people interact with her fictional characters! She did the same thing in *Subtle Flame*, but there are even more in *The Roaring Nineties*. Can't remember reading any other novel with so many real people in it, except perhaps *The Timeless Land*, but I'm pretty sure there aren't as many in that book as there are in *The Roaring Nineties*. And Katharine's figures are much more interesting than all those governors, squatters and la-di-da ladies who come and go in Eleanor Dark's story.

The party was fun. I had three glasses of Sparkling Burgundy. Larry had quite a few glasses of sherry. As he was heading off for more, he squeezed my shoulder and asked me if I'd like another glass of wine. Feeling confident, I touched his elbow, leant towards him like the film stars do when they're flirting, and said, 'I'd love one.'

We all sang 'Auld Lang Syne' at the tops of our voices well before midnight 'because of the neighbours.' Can't remember the exact time we packed it in, but it was before twelve o'clock.

Felt tipsy on the bus going home. Mum was up when I came in. 'Well, Vicki, how was the party?' she asked me. 'Any nice young lads there?' She doesn't know there's only one male in our club, and that's Larry.

'Wouldn't you like to know!' I replied.

January 1st, 1969

Started a new notebook this morning! I loved turning the cover and staring at the blank page for a while. Then I got stuck into the gold rushes.

There are so many: Southern Cross, Hannans Reward, Kanowna, Mount Charlotte, Mount Catherine, Lake Darlot.

It makes my head spin trying to remember them all.

Some of the rushes are a disaster. Katharine tells us about 1,000 prospectors on the Darlot field who overnight packed up and headed for a rush at Mount Black. When they found out there was no gold, some headed off to another site, some went 'on the tramp back to the Darlot.' In a 'wild stampede' they chucked out everything they'd been carrying, but, without food or water, many men died. 'This gold fever gets hold of a man: makes him do things he'd never dream of normally. We're a bit mad, all of us up here,' Morris tells Sally.

I couldn't help thinking, 'That's what greed will do to you.'

I hate the way those early prospectors tried to hide their finds during a rush. Goldfield law demanded that they reveal any gold they discover so others can share the wealth. Still, there are lots of examples in *The Roaring Nineties* that show us how mean many of the prospectors were about sharing their finds. 'When we report these slugs, there won't be any stopping a rush,' Morris tells his mate, Con, during one of their prospecting expeditions. Con replies they won't report it right away because 'a man'd be a mug not to hold back a bit of alluvial when it suits him.' Then there's Jack Mills and his mates, who refuse to disclose how much gold they've found when applying for a mining lease and manage to hide what they've been up to for seven weeks.

All greedy buggers, if you ask me.

How interesting is Dinny Quin's opinion that the government didn't like the gold rushes because they interfered with land settlement? 'The early settlers were land hungry,' he says. 'What they were after was land, and more land for cattle and sheep, wheat growin'. They were scared the discovery of gold would rob them of labourers, send workers scourin' the country for wealth that would make 'em their own bosses.'

Is that true, I wonder?

Can't believe what these people put up with in their search for gold. They live in tents made of bags or shelters made of hessian and rusty kerosene tins. Their diet is tinned meat and damper with the occasional vegetable. There's hardly any water and what there is costs money. Hot red dust fills their eyes, ears, noses and mouths; there are flies and filth and dysentery. They suffer festering sores called barcoo rot; sandy blight bungs up their eyes and typhoid rages.

Every day there are funerals and the cemetery is in a 'terrible condition: the stench overpowering, and graves falling in over the hurriedly-interred dead.'

The outskirts of the towns reek with the 'ordures of men and beasts' and flies spread infection and pollute the food and water. On hot, still nights, 'a stench hung in the air…Even the dry musky fragrance of mulga burning on the camp fires did not prevail against it.' Around water wells are manure heaps 'reeking with filth' – which most blame on the Afghans and their camels that are 'bad with mange.'

Why do they put up with these disgusting conditions?

'Gold! Gold! Gold!' Katharine writes. The lust for gold is 'unabated.' All over the goldfields there is a 'reckless spirit of defiance' that keeps men 'fighting for the fortune' they're convinced is waiting for them out there in the 'grey limitless scrub, under the red sunblasted earth.' Remaining 'cheery and dauntless' becomes a source of pride; to 'groan and growl' means a man has 'poor spirit.' Nobody talks of anything else; nobody thinks of anything else but gold. Only the crows 'kaa-ed a warning,' and the men who understand their warning hate them.

January 2nd, 1969

At morning tea, I was telling Gwenda and Nora about the gold rushes in *The Roaring Nineties* and asked them if they had any gold jewellery. Nora says she has a little gold cross on a chain she wears sometimes when she dresses up. Gwenda doesn't have any gold jewellery.

'If I ever get married, I want to wear a silver wedding ring or none at all,' I said. Nora and I looked at Gwenda, hoping she'd say something about Andy. She sipped her tea and dunked her Granita.

January 5th, 1969

Hot day. Should hop on the bus and go to the beach but can't be bothered. Mum has gone to Mrs Cook's so it's nice and quiet and I'm browsing *The Roaring Nineties*.

There are lots of storms in Katharine's work and I love her descriptions of them. There's a storm in *Working Bullocks*, in *Coonardoo*, *The Pioneers*, *Intimate Strangers*, *Haxby's Circus*, and in many of her short stories. Storms bring chaos, but afterwards, peace and hope. The cyclonic storm in *The Roaring Nineties* restores Morris Gough 'to normality' after his breakdown and greatly relieves Sally. Her marriage may not be happy, but she realizes it's workable, and that's something.

But storms and rain are rare on the goldfields and the desperate need for water is everywhere in *The Roaring Nineties*. On the first page Katharine tells us how many white men die because 'neither their wits nor their magic taught them to find food and water in a dry season.' What a sly way of telling us about the stupid things white people do, and I always kept that in mind as I was reading *The Roaring Nineties*.

There are tales of men who drink their urine; there's the story of a man who kills his horse and drinks its blood. In her boarding house, Sally uses drips of water from her cool-safe to scrub floors and re-uses that same water on her tomatoes 'growing in the shade of bag screens.' Alcohol on the goldfields is much cheaper than water. There's a lot of beer, whiskey and champagne in *The Roaring Nineties*! Sally gets tipsy on champagne – twice!

I've never had champagne. I think I'd like it.

January 6th, 1969

Thinking about Larry and our New Year's Eve party. I feel a bit embarrassed at my attempt to flirt with him. I wonder what he thought of it. He did squeeze my shoulder, after all, but he might've done it as a teacher might lightly touch a student. I've also been thinking about Frisco's New Year's Eve party in *The Roaring Nineties*.

Sally is sitting on the steps in the moonlight, wondering why Frisco hasn't asked her to dance. She's wearing her yellow satin dress and has a Spanish comb in her hair, but he hasn't noticed. She thinks she's lost her charm now that she's in her twenties and has three kids.

Eventually Frisco rolls up, tells her he's still mad about her and begs her to run away with him. Sally is so relieved to discover he's still after her she starts to cry. He puts his arm around her and, suddenly, the 'passion that flowed between them was too strong to be denied.' Their pash is disturbed by a guffaw from below, and Sally looks down to see a bunch of 'moon-white faces of men in the yard' looking up at them. How embarrassing!

Frisco takes off, telling her to wait for him. 'You can't leave me now, my love,' he says, and she sits quietly, 'dazed and oblivious of everything except the fury and exhilaration of the passion for Frisco which possessed her.' Not until her baby cries that she realizes she's being ridiculous. She storms off, 'appalled' by what nearly happened. 'With a baby by one man still on the breast, how could she let another man be her lover? It would have been shameful. Never again could she have held up her head: had any respect for herself.' Then she admits that it was only because of that guffaw that she'd stopped herself from giving in to Frisco, 'not any strength of mind.'

'This weakness must be exorcised,' she tells herself; she has to 'root it out of her system.' Sally can never explain her lust for Frisco: 'was ashamed of it. Never intended to let it run away with her, or interfere with her devotion to Morris. But there it was, something she would always have to fight and be on her guard against.'

January 7th, 1969

I asked the girls if they've ever stolen anything. I was thinking about the miners in *The Roaring Nineties* who steal small amounts of gold and how they get away with it.

Gwenda piped up immediately and said she'd stolen some money at primary school when they were doing the banking. 'I knocked a sixpence off the table and slipped it into my pocket,' she said. Nora asked her if she felt guilty about it, and Gwenda said, 'Nah'.

'You must feel a bit guilty,' Nora insisted, 'or you wouldn't remember it.'

Gwenda sniggered and went cross-eyed: her favourite question is, 'What's the crime of robbing a bank compared to the crime of founding one?' Sometimes she asks it out of the blue, just for fun.

'I stole some chewing gum once from the little shop across the road from school,' I said. 'On the way home, I rubbed the packet on the ground to make it look like it had been dropped and trodden on. Told Mum I'd found it. I don't feel guilty about stealing it or lying to Mum. Don't know why, I just don't,' I said. Nora tossed her hair, pursed her lips and said nothing.

'Well?' asked Gwenda. 'What's your story, Nora? Come on.'

So Nora told us when she was seven, she 'found' a charm bracelet. It fell off the wrist of a girl at school lunchtime and she picked it up and was going to give it back, but one of the charms was a silver sea horse. 'I've always loved sea horses', said Nora. 'I thought I'd keep the bracelet for a while until I had time to have a really good look at the sea horse, then I'd return it.'

Nora never did return that bracelet. She kept it and, every night for months, would take it out of her drawer in her bedroom, turn on the light and gaze at the sea horse. 'I still feel guilty about it, especially because the little girl who owned the bracelet was my best friend.'

'Naughty Nora!' Gwenda said, rather nastily, I thought. 'And you're a Catholic who's supposed to believe in the Ten Commandments.'

I finished two sketches during my lunch hour: one based on Gwenda's sixpenny story and the other on Nora's sea horse. I like the one about Gwenda best; it's daring and sneaky!

Going home, I thought about the stolen gold in *The Roaring Nineties* and other stolen symbols of wealth and power Katharine has written about: black opal, the Moon of Desire, the diamond ring in *Windlestraws*.

I like Katharine's point that the gold mining companies have 'raked millions out of the mines, swindled shareholders with impunity and were strangling the town now to demonstrate their power. The wealthy men behind the mines saw no connection between their crimes and the crimes committed against them. The miners and the alluvial diggers did...there was something of a grim joke for them in exploits which relieved the mining companies of some of the wealth they owed the people.'

That attitude reminds me of Gene Day in *Windlestraws,* who talks about how the rich con millions of people, whereas her thieving was done for a lark and hurt only one wealthy man. I was always on Gene's side when I was reading *Windlestraws* – couldn't have cared less about the fat, rich bugger she robbed.

January 8th, 1969

This morning we talked about how, when we were sixteen, we thought we would be doing all kinds of exciting things by the time we turned twenty but there doesn't seem to be much hope of that. Here we are, nearly twenty years old, typing documents for an insurance company in St Georges Terrace with a slavedriver of a boss who needs a bloody good telling-off but none of us has the guts to give it to him!

I'm so glad I have my project! That's something, I told myself as I sauntered back to my desk. Yes, at least I have Katharine.

January 10th, 1969

Met Gwenda and Nora earlier tonight and we walked along Hay Street and had a spearmint milkshake. Nothing exciting was happening; never is in town.

Gwenda suggested going up to King's Park to look down at the city lights, but Nora and I are a bit scared to go up there at night. Gwenda's meeting her boyfriend just before midnight; apparently, he's going to a party first. We asked her why she wasn't going with him, and she just shrugged.

'Are you dead serious about Andy?' Nora asked Gwenda.

'What do you mean?' Gwenda looked surprised.

'Well, would you marry him, for instance?' Nora replied.

Gwenda shrugged again.

'Hmm.' I thought. 'That's two shrugs in a row. Something's up.'

Then Gwenda said, 'I'm a bit mad with him at the moment, but yes, Nora. I think I would marry him. If he asked me.'

'What about university?' I asked her.

'Well, why would Andy stop me?' she replied.

'Andy might not, but a kid would,' I warned.

She nodded in agreement.

January 11th, 1969

I've been thinking about Sally and Morris Gough's difficult marriage. For a start, Morris is a lot older than Sally. She was only eighteen when they eloped; she's twenty-two when *The Roaring Nineties* opens. In the early days of their marriage, 'Morris had been like a god' in his lovemaking, filling her with delight. 'Her whole being had thrilled to his touch.' However, by the time we meet Sally, her feelings for her husband have changed into 'prosaic affection.'

Not only is Sally much younger than Morris, but their backgrounds are very different. Morris Fitz-Morris Gough comes from a wealthy conservative English family and can never 'quite forget that he was an Englishman'. Sally, according to Morris, is just a 'colonial.' Morris has a 'secret allegiance to traditions' Sally doesn't respect and he can't accept the 'democratic tendencies in the colonies.' Sally has a 'queer plebeian streak in her' that perplexes and 'irks' him.

Apart from being a snob, Morris is hopeless with money. After eloping with Sally, he buys a station with a family allowance, sells it, and buys a house and a gold mine in Southern Cross, hoping to make a quick and easy fortune. His father is furious, stops his allowance and from then on, Morris borrows and is constantly in debt. He makes 'rash' financial decisions; he won't pay his bills; he won't pay back money he's borrowed; he says he can't give Sally housekeeping money yet goes off to play cards and loses most nights.

All this drives Sally up the wall. She hates being unable to pay bills; she hates borrowing money; she hates being under 'any kind of financial obligation to others.' Sally has always been afraid that Morris would never 'have the luck which came to many other men so easily. It would be a hard and weary road they would have to tread,' she thinks, but she expects him to share the burden. Deep down she's not convinced he will. Deep down, Sally doesn't trust her husband to do the right thing by her.

Sally's never ashamed to work, turning their home in Southern Cross into a boarding house against Morris's wishes. He despises the boarders and tells her it's 'almost more than I can bear to see you fetching and carrying for these hobbledehoys.' He irritates Sally when he speaks to people in his 'distant, lordly way.' She has 'no intention of allowing him to drift and forget his obligation' to her...Her life was going to be a partnership in which her clear brain and energy should have a chance. She would not fail in her duty to him; but he must also realize her right to a policy in their affairs.' She will not forgive him for losing money at cards, for making bad decisions, for not paying what he owes. She can't forgive him for not coming home from prospecting to help her with her first pregnancy and birth. Morris, she decides, has 'forfeited his right to the child...Dick was hers as if Morris had disowned him, and she must be responsible for having brought him into the world.'

Over the years, Sally notices Morris stops talking about finding a fortune and fulfilling their dreams. She's puzzled and disappointed with his decision to become a bogger in the mines, then, after a heart attack, to become the local undertaker. Deciding there's nothing for it but to 'hold fast to each other and make the best of their lives together' doesn't stop her from feeling heartbroken when she watches Morris walk down the main street beside a hearse in his 'shabby frock coat and tall hat with black weepers round the crown.' Has he 'abandoned hope and decided to settle down to a humdrum existence?' Sally asks herself.

Sally begins to see herself 'as if in a dream, plodding along…beside Morris, through all the ups and downs, rushes and slumps, dust storms and mirages of their life on the fields.' Whenever she pictures a 'life with love and happiness' with Frisco, she tells herself 'contemptuously' that it's all a 'mirage.' 'You're a respectable married woman, Mrs Gough,' she says to herself. 'Ought to be ashamed of yourself behaving like this.'

There are many mirages in Katharine's work.

Sally's marriage reminds me of Elodie Blackwood's in *Intimate Strangers*. Like Elodie, Sally is raped by her husband. Well, Morris doesn't exactly rape Sally, but when, in their tent on the Hannans rush, a starkers Morris insists on sex then instantly falls asleep, Sally feels like she's been raped. She listens to the men outside, only a 'few yards' away joking about 'Morrey turning-in early', and she's 'incensed' and humiliated because Morris has now 'exposed her to the lewd gossip of the camp.' This 'crude, vicious copulation' has meant nothing to her. 'Never again,' Sally tells herself, will she 'allow Morris to abuse their relationship in this way.'

There are, however, many nights afterwards when Morris takes her 'with a rough passion quite unlike the tender love-making of their first years together', and her resentment against Morris builds slowly over the years.

No wonder Sally is attracted to Frisco – I bet he does things in bed that women like!

January 14th, 1969

Had a chat with Jill today about Frisco's opinion that he and Sally are the same kind of people because they both have 'the spirit and guts to keep on being alive.'

'That idea is very Katharine,' said Jill. 'Think of Billy Rocca's advice to Gina in *Haxby's Circus* – to act hard, steer straight and stand up to things. Think of Sam, the shingle splitter, in *Wild Oats of Han* who tells Han to shake her fist at life.' Jill raised her fist in the air and shook it, and we had a laugh together. Then she told me to wait a minute and came back with a folder marked 'Katharine Susannah Prichard: Letters.'

'Here's what she once wrote to her son,' she said. 'We have to stand up to things and go on with our job. It's the test of real quality in a man or woman.'

Very Katharine. Very Sally Gough, too, I thought, on the bus coming home.

Although they both have 'spirit and guts,' I don't think Frisco and Sally are the same kind of people. Sally is honest, responsible, loyal and trustworthy, and she can shake her fist at life. She cares about people; Frisco doesn't. His film star looks, arrogance, cheekiness and his stories, make him exactly what Marie Robillard calls him: a sharpshooter. That 'look in his eyes' when he talks about Sally Gough, or when someone mentions her name, doesn't fool Marie Robillard! Even Sally questions whether or not they are the same sort of people because she hates many of the things he does and believes in.

Sally and Elodie, and even Louise in *Bid Me to Love,* have all got me thinking hard about getting married. I'm starting to worry – is marriage really such a good thing? What if I ended up with a husband like Greg Reed, Greg Blackwood or Morris Fitz-Morris Gough? What would I do? Put up with it? Dump him? What if we had kids?

January 15th, 1969

The way *The Roaring Nineties* begins is gripping.

It is dawn; there is a 'puff of dust' in the distance. The Aboriginal people fear this dust, knowing it means white men and their beasts are coming to grab their hunting grounds. They've already learned that their spears are no match for the white man's 'fire-sticks' that spit death, that white men will force them to find water, or trick them into finding it by feeding them salt meat and bacon until, 'maddened by thirst', the natives will lead them to the nearest soak.

At night, the whites hear the blacks 'making corroborees for rain and wailing about the desolation that had come on them.' But they also laugh and make up songs about the white man's 'madness for the stuff called gold which no one could eat or drink, and the way the white men burrowed in the earth like boudie rats, searching for it.'

Among this group of Aboriginal people is Kalgoorla, a young woman who has been stolen from her tribe, raped by white men and given birth to a daughter called Meeri, whom we know as Maritana. Kalgoorla comes and goes throughout *The Roaring Nineties* – sometimes mysteriously, sometimes for a particular reason. Even though she's always there to help Sally Gough with child minding and housework, 'all her life Kalgoorla clung to the ways of her own people' and never loses her 'fear and hatred of white men.'

Sally gratefully accepts Kalgoorla's help with the children and never forgets that Kalgoorla saved her life when she came down with typhoid on the track. When Morris growls to Sally that he doesn't know 'how on earth you can stand having her about,' Sally tells him wearily that she's always 'glad enough to have her to do the washing and the cleaning.'

I had a bit of a snigger over that, who wouldn't want someone else around to do the washing and the cleaning and mind the kids! I know I would if I were in Sally's shoes.

Morris calls Kalgoorla a 'dirty old swab' and tells Sally, 'That's one thing you'll never have against me...Dirty, stinking creatures, these aboriginal women...Beats me how a decent man can have anything to do with them.' Sally ignores him: she likes and trusts Kalgoorla and always defends her. She is also fond of Maritana, who has 'beautiful brown eyes' and hangs around Sally 'like a little wild animal out of the bush.'

By the end of *The Roaring Nineties* white men have drained the Aboriginal peoples' soaks and water holes and destroyed their hunting grounds. The 'natives' have learned they can get food, wine and tobacco from the whites and 'congregated round the camp like flies, living on any garbage the storekeepers threw out: butcher's offal and the dregs in tins and bottles.' They wear 'odds and ends of cast-off clothing'; the men barter their women for food and tobacco.

I've never been taught about, and have never understood, what happened to Aboriginal people. After reading Katharine I'm beginning to get the picture, and it's a bloody awful picture!

January 16th, 1969

I brought up the Aboriginal people at morning tea, and Nora sighed, folded her arms and closed her eyes. But Gwenda's very interested in Aboriginal people. She has a friend up north who has told her a lot about how Aboriginal people are treated. 'I'd believe anything Katharine has to say about the ways white people destroy the Aboriginal way of life,' said Gwenda, noisily washing her cup.

Nora opened her eyes, coughed loudly, then muttered something about how few Aboriginal people there are anyway and that they couldn't expect to live their way forever.

Gwenda glared at her.

'You sound like my mother,' I told Nora.

Nora shrugged.

January 31ˢᵗ, 1969

At book club tonight, Larry asked me if I'd like to go for a walk and have afternoon tea in King's Park on Sunday. 'We can talk about Prichard,' he said with a grin. 'You know, *The Roaring Nineties* has been translated into nearly a dozen different languages – it was a big success for her,' he said.

'Oh, I'm glad,' I said. Didn't know what else to say, so I gave him a big smile instead. I was so relieved he didn't mention our New Year's party.

I'm a bit nervous about meeting him – I'm always scared about being uneducated and boring. Haven't told Mum I'm meeting him; she'd go on and on about how I should find someone my own age to go out with instead of a retired schoolteacher. And then she'd ask a million questions about him before running him down.

February 2ⁿᵈ, 1969

After our walk, Larry bought me a spearmint milkshake at the tearooms in King's Park. While I was happily slurping away, he summed up a few things for me. '*The Roaring Nineties* is all about the 1890s; *Golden Miles* deals with 1914-1927 and covers the First World War. *Winged Seeds,* volume three of the trilogy, begins in 1936 and ends shortly after the Second World War. Sally Gough and Dinny are there from start to finish,' said Larry, piling sugar into his tea. 'Prichard's damned good at research, I reckon her trilogy is a very valuable historical record of WA's goldfields as well as a good read.'

I asked Larry if he likes Sally Gough and he said, 'Yes, of course I do.'

'Do you like Frisco?' I asked, hoping he didn't.

'Oh, he's interesting enough, but, no, I can't say I liked him as a character. He carried on like a teenager over Sally. Mind you, so did Sally over him! That annoyed me, and I couldn't understand why she fell for him. She was too smart to be conned by someone like that. Didn't think much of Morris either. I tell you who I really liked,' said Larry with a grin. 'Marie Robillard.'

'Me too,' I said.

'And I reckon someone like Lili, the prostitute, would've been fun to have around. I enjoyed the section where she dances in her corsets and high-heels while Sally gets tipsy on champagne!'

He looked a bit pervy when he was talking about Lili, and I was embarrassed, so I stirred my milkshake. 'You know,' he said with a sly grin, 'when she was doing her research, Prichard used to go to the Ladies' Room at the pub and have a few drinks with friends, including prostitutes. They had a great old time gossiping and joking around.'

I didn't know how to reply, so I just jiggled my straw.

February 15th, 1969

I've just finished *Golden Miles*, the second volume of Katharine's Goldfields trilogy, and I really like it. There's a lot of satisfaction reading about settings and characters you already know.

I love Sally's relationships with her sons. Sally has four sons: Dick, Tom, Lal and Den. I like Den most because he loves mucking about with horses and yarning with drovers and refuses to volunteer to go to war. Lucky Den finds a feisty country wife and will inherit Sally's family's farm. I like Tom too, but he's hard going sometimes.

Kalgoorla's daughter, Maritana, opens the novel. She's sitting in the front seat of 'an old rattletrap, drawn by a pair of rough-haired horses' heading towards Sally's boarding house. Once a 'wild, shy aboriginal girl,' Maritana has become a 'tall, scraggy woman, with skin like dirty brown paper, sagging on her high cheek bones.' Her brown eyes have a 'shrewd glint,' her wide mouth has become 'thin and hard', and a 'sour expression lingered about it as though Maritana had tasted something vile and could not recover from the effect.'

Maritana is married to Fred Cairns. They have a 'swarm of youngsters, a herd of goats and a few hens', and she's a 'gatherer and go-between for a gang' called the Big Four who deal in stolen gold. Nobody knows who the Big Four are, and Sally certainly doesn't want to know. All Sally knows for sure is that Paddy Cavan, one of her boarders, gives Maritana a 'cut' on the sugar bags of 'snide gold' she takes home to Fred, who then passes it on. Sally's fed up and wants Paddy to leave. He can't understand why she's carrying on about it – after all, he argues, he doesn't steal gold directly. 'You know well enough nobody blames a man workin' underground for takin' a bit of his, now and then.'

One day, Paddy Cavan refuses to give Maritana her 'cut' and her 'Aboriginal blood boiled.' She threatens to tell everyone what a crook Paddy Cavan is, so he arranges things to ensure her mouth is permanently 'shut.'

Of all the crooks in *Golden Miles* – and there are plenty of them – Paddy is the worst. He's a swindler who becomes an internationally successful businessman, eventually being rewarded with a knighthood.

February 16th, 1969

What a racket all this gold stuff is! I can barely follow the national and international twists and turns in the gold trade. Must've taken Katharine absolutely ages to research!

Towards the end of *Golden Miles*, Dinny sums up what he thinks the gold industry is really all about: 'there was a struggle for wealth and power in which the mining proprietary companies had demonstrated the most unscrupulous efficiency, not only by extracting profits from production and share mongering, but by sacrificing hundreds of lives to their greed for profits.'

Sally's optimistic, though. While she doesn't believe the mining industry functions in the interests of miners, she believes in the power of the miners whose spirit is as 'strong to-day as when Dinny and his mates had defended their alluvial rights and when the miners put up their fight for union principles.' She agrees with her son, Tom, who argues that the main goal has to be to 'make the mining industry serve the interests of the people.'

Just as Sally ponders workers' rights and 'the cruel exploitation of working men and women' she sees a 'horde of natives...drifting in a swirl of dust' along the road. They look like a 'group of scarecrows.' A trooper is yelling at them to clear off. Sally recognizes Kalgoorla and tells the trooper she'll take her home and look after her. The trooper refuses. 'I've got me instructions,' he says. 'Reg'lations just issued lays it down abos is not to be permitted to approach within five miles of the city of Kalgoorlie without a permit.'

Fancy someone who speaks English like that having the right to order Aboriginal people around!

I like Sally's response: 'Good lord,' she exclaims. 'What haven't we thieved from them?...We've taken everything they had. Expect them to live half-starved in the back country when we've ruined their waterholes and hunting grounds...What do we do for them now? Give them a miserable ration at some government centre: a bit of flour, sugar and tea, sometimes a scrap of meat – not enough to feed a dog.'

Kalgoorla is standing by a dump on the roadside and starts 'pouring forth a torrent of native abuse.' She swings the stick she's carrying as if trying to 'thrust back all the forces of evil which had overwhelmed her people...Fierce and mournful Kalgoorla's screeching ended on a high winding note of derision and defiance. Koo! Koo! Koo! Like the cry of a bird it circled and flew in the twilight. A stark, wild figure, as if she were a dead tree, Kalgoorla stood against the sunset.'

What a magnificent protest! While I was reading *Coonardoo*, I always hoped Coonardo would do or say something to fight back, but she never did. I like Polly in *Brumby Innes*, for all her faults, because she stands up to May and has the guts to tell Brumby he's a liar! But out of these three Aboriginal women, all fascinating characters, I like Kalgoorla best. Like Sally Gough, Kalgoorla's alive; for me she's real.

February 17th, 1969

Along with Kalgoorla and Maritana, Sally has changed physically. In *Golden Miles*, she's in her fifties and often looks 'bedraggled' in her 'down-at-heel slippers and dirty apron.' She wears her hair in a 'heavy plait round her head, and although a few silver threads showed, it still broke in a loose dark wave round her face.' By the end of the novel Sally's hair is grey. But, as we find out when she goes to Cottesloe Beach, she's still slim and looks good in a bathing suit and Frisco's still after her.

As I was getting ready for bed, I thought about what Mum looks like in bathers. She's in her fifties, like Sally, but she's pretty fat. She often goes for a paddle at City Beach on Christmas Day, so not looking good doesn't seem to bother her.

February 18th, 1969

I've been thinking about Sally Gough's friendships. Her two most valued female friends are Laura and Marie.

Sally met Laura in *The Roaring Nineties*, and they certainly had their differences. At one point, Sally thinks Laura, while charming and friendly, is 'stupid and a little patronizing in her manner sometimes.' By the time we see Laura in *Golden Miles* she's fat and 'tightly corseted,' and although still 'handsome,' her 'faded eyes' look out from a 'flabby, unhappy face.' After McSweeney's death, she discovers he's left most of his money to Catholic organisations, an annuity and a bungalow for her, but nothing at all for her daughter, Amy, despite McSweeney's promise to look after her.

Not long afterwards, poor ol' Laura is knocked down by a car in the main street of Kalgoorlie, dies on the way to the hospital, and that's the end of that friendship.

Laura had been, on and off, a good friend to Sally, but her best female friend is Marie Robillard. Marie is kind, intelligent and fun. In *The Roaring Nineties*, we're told that she understood when people were anxious or unhappy without them having to say a word. Over the years, Marie has spent many afternoons and evenings with Sally, shopping, gossiping, sewing. After the shops on a Saturday afternoon, they'd pop into the Ladies Room at the pub for a beer and a chat.

Throughout *Golden Miles*, when things go wrong for Sally, Marie is always there to help. She does housework, looks after the kids, cooks for the boarders, and fusses around Sally after the birth of her sons. After Sally's firstborn son, Dick, dies, Marie watches over Sally for hours, her 'dark eyes sharing her anguish.' When the suspicion of suicide comes up, Marie immediately insists that Dick's death was an accident: 'Dick wouldn't 've done a thing like that. He wouldn't willingly have hurt you so much,' she assures Sally.

Marie is the only person Sally could ever tell she regrets not being Frisco's lover: 'He's a devil and I hate him,' she says one day. 'But I wish we had been lovers, years ago, Marie.'

Wow!

I wonder – if or when I ever get married and then happen to meet a man like Frisco, would I just go for it?

February 19th, 1969

At morning tea, we chatted about friends and how long friendships last. Nora has a friend she's known since primary school and sees him now and then. She sometimes runs into him in town, and they trot off for coffee and a catch up. 'He's had the same girlfriend for two years and I can't understand why they don't get married. I'd want to marry a chap I've been going out with for two years,' she said with a sideways glance at Gwenda.

Gwenda says she's lost contact with all her friends from school. 'But I do have a friend who lives up the street. I've known her since I was six. She comes over some Saturdays and we listen to the Top 40.' Gwenda's lucky – her parents put up with loud music. Mum always yells at me: 'Turn that bloody music down, Vicki! Who wants to listen to Elvis Presley's whining?'

I had a best friend called Barbara at school, but it didn't last. One day I told her, 'You never want to do anything I want to do!' She replied, 'That's because the things you want to do are boring.' I haven't spoken to her since. I heard she got pregnant two years ago and went up north to have the baby. She would've had to put up with a lot of gossip when she got back. Serves her right.

At lunchtime, I wrote a scathing sketch about Barbara. It was like taking revenge and felt good to write.

February 21st, 1969

I'm still trying to understand how and why Sally gets mixed up with Frisco again.

In *Golden Miles*, she first sees Frisco when he arrives at the Gough's house one morning, 'debonair and well-groomed, in English tweeds.' He's come to see Paddy Cavan, so he's obviously up to no good. Sally has been picking up wet clothes blown onto the red dust by a gust of wind and is startled to see him. She stiffens to a 'protective dignity', and her eyes meet Frisco's with a 'challenging smile.' She knows right away that Frisco hasn't forgotten her, and he knows she's still interested!

I laughed out loud while reading the scene in the pub when Frisco comes in drunk, looking 'very dashing and gallant in his new uniform.' He orders whiskey and tells Sally and Marie the latest news about the war. As he gets stuck into the gossip and the whiskey, he and Marie start speaking French. Finally Frisco tells Marie in English, 'You know I adore Sally, Mme. Robillard. Always have I adored her! Not for the world would I do anything to hurt her feelings.' Sally stares at him, 'transfixed.' Marie, ever loyal to Sally, is terrified to hear Frisco talking like that. She watches Sally looking at Frisco as if she 'were almost as demented as he.'

'I can't get you out of my mind, Sally. No matter what I do', Frisco tells Sally. 'Aren't we ever going to be together? Aren't we ever going to be lovers before we die?' When Marie tells him to 'shut up' because 'everybody is listening,' he shouts, 'What do I care?...The whole world can know as far as I'm concerned.' Sally comes to her senses, picks up her shopping bags and, as 'if the spell he had put over her were broken,' gets ready to leave. When he demands an answer to his question, Sally's 'eyes blazed' and she tells him, 'It's the same as it's always been.'

What that means is a bit of a mystery – to her and to him, I think.

This cat-and-mouse game goes on for ages!

At Dick's wedding, Frisco slyly whispers to Sally, 'I'm a blackguard. You were right, Sally.' His 'derisive familiarity' infuriates Sally, who says she doesn't want to speak to him. Frisco tells her he only came to the wedding to let her know that the Australian Expeditionary Forces have received their 'marching orders.' She hasn't forgiven Frisco for the things he's done and said, but even so, 'her heart quailed at the thought that he was going into the midst of the war and its dangers.' When she asks if he knows if her son, Lal, will be going too, he tells her, 'You're such a damned maternal little creature, Sally. But still the most fascinating woman in the world to me.' Sally's answer is oddly flirtatious: she simply asks: 'Damned maternal! Is that what I am?'

He confides in her that his 'beautiful bitch of a wife refuses to have children.'

Sally reminds him he has a son by Maritana whom he's 'never acknowledged'. She furiously spits out that Maritana had 'more guts than any of the white men who knew more than she did' about dealing in stolen gold; for that she was murdered. When Sally accuses him of being as 'responsible as anyone', Frisco puts his head in his hands and mutters, 'Don't say it, Sally! For God's sake, don't say that.'

Boo hoo! I didn't feel sorry for him; he's just trying to squirm his way out of what he's done to Maritana. As for his declarations to Sally, this man just doesn't give up. Frisco's a real ratbag – but Sally can't stay away from him.

February 24ᵗʰ, 1969

This morning I asked Gwenda and Nora if they thought a woman has the right to refuse to have children, even though her husband wants them. Gwenda says a woman has the right, but Nora believes that if the man wants children, the woman should have them.

'The problem is,' Gwenda said with a frown, 'the woman ends up caring for the kids and the man gets to go to work. Or, even if the woman wants to work, she'll probably have to find night work or part-time work somewhere so she can fit in with her husband's and her kids' routines! It's not fair and –'

'My mum worked three nights a week for two years as a receptionist in a hotel when I was about six or seven,' Nora interrupted. 'I always hated the idea of her working late at night, and I used to lie awake waiting for her to come home. I was always tired the next day at school and got into a lot of trouble with the teacher. That was Mum's fault. She shouldn't have gone to work.'

February 26ᵗʰ, 1969

I love the section of the novel where Sally goes to Cottesloe Beach with her sons and Dick's girlfriend, Amy. It's a 'glorious afternoon, hot, with scarcely a breath of wind to ruffle the crest of the surf.' Sally watches the waves and dreams about how she used to 'dive naked' into the sea. A heat haze lifts 'now and then to a light breeze' and everything seems so peaceful, Sally finds it hard to believe the world was at war.

Sally has borrowed Amy's bathers, much to Dick's surprise. 'I'd no idea you had such a good figure, Sal-o-my!' he teases his mother. Sally replies, 'Don't be absurd…I don't run to fat, that's all.' After a swim, she grabs a towel and drops down on the sand to sunbake. Suddenly, who should turn up but Frisco! 'Well, I'm blest,' he says. 'A real goldfields party!' He sprawls beside Sally, telling her, 'God, Sally, you strip well.' Her eyes sparkle with anger. 'Why do you talk like that?' she asks him. 'It's the only way of getting behind your defences, I suppose, Mrs Gough,' he smirks. She's furious but can't help checking out his 'lean brown figure' and his eyes, with 'their demand and derision'. Yet again she feels like Frisco has cast a spell on her. As she snaps out of it, Frisco warns her, 'You can't get away from me, now – or ever, Sally.'

Marie Robillard is right: Sally's a sitting duck – or did she say dove? Can't remember. Either way, she's a dead duck where Frisco's concerned.

February 27th, 1969

'Listen to this,' I said to the girls over morning tea. 'How would you like a man to say this to you: "Christ, I'm mad about you." And this: "I can't get you out of my mind." And what about this one: "You're the most fascinating woman in the world to me."'

'I'm a bit shocked with the first one,' said Nora.

'Why?' Gwenda asked.

'Because I'm a Catholic – not a good one, I'll admit, but still, I don't like blasphemy.'

'What about the rest, then, Nora?' I asked with a grin.

'Yes, they're romantic. I had a bloke tell me once that I was the most beautiful girl in the world,' replied Nora, tossing her blond curls.

'What about you, Gwenda?' I asked. I wasn't going to let her off the hook.

'Well, Andy tells me he dreams about me a lot. And sometimes he tells me he loves me, but in the next breath he says I drive him bloody crazy.'

'Why?' Nora asked innocently.

We both knew what her answer would be.

February 28th, 1969

Larry wasn't at book club tonight. I was disappointed. I'd been looking forward to talking about *Golden Miles* and asking him about the First World War.

I hardly listened to any of the discussion – haven't read their book anyway. As I was leaving one of the members called out, 'How's the "Red Witch", Vicki?' I turned to answer her, but she was smirking. I couldn't be bothered replying and left without saying goodbye to anyone.

On the bus going home I thought I might have to quit the book club. I haven't read any of their books for ages, and the only person I have long talks with is Larry. They may be getting fed up with me.

March 2nd, 1969

Frisco's 'strapping figure' is the last thing Sally sees as the troopship steams out of Fremantle harbour bound for war. She realises that not only her son, Lal, but Frisco too, may be 'going out of her life for ever.' When she goes back home to the goldfields, she admits to a 'guilty awareness that her love for Frisco was not as dead as she had hoped it might be.'

Sally will never betray Morris, though. We've known that from *The Roaring Nineties,* and she doesn't waver in *Golden Miles*. She always remembers the day she married Morris in an old church in Fremantle; she recalls how 'handsome and debonair' her young husband had once been. At one point, Sally looks at her husband and thinks, 'My poor Morris...he hasn't had much luck.' In turn, Morris watches Sally knitting and thinks, 'My poor Sally, she's had a tough spin with me.'

When he's framed for stolen gold and sent to jail, prison nearly finishes Morris. When he comes home, he has no energy, isn't interested in anything, he looks like 'an old man, ill and broken...His eyes were dull behind their smudgy glasses.' Lal's letters from Egypt and Gallipoli are the only things that rouse him. Morris is all for conscription and reckons 'shirkers and slackers' should be made to fight.

After Lal dies in the war, the doctor tells Sally that Morris's heart is bad, and Sally isn't surprised to find that one afternoon she can't wake him. She kneels beside his 'heavy quiet figure, weeping not only for him, but that so much disappointment and sorrow had shadowed their life together.'

March 3rd, 1969

It's interesting that Katharine writes almost nothing about Sally's grieving for her dead husband. After Morris dies, the next few chapters of *Golden Miles* are about returned soldiers, unemployment, riots and fights between local workers and foreigners, the rise of unions, strikes, and Dick's death, which Sally mourns for months.

The story takes off in a different direction when Dinny tells Sally that Frisco has returned from the war, blind and broke and 'livin' in a shack on Misery Flat.' Dinny's off to rescue him: after all, says Dinny, Frisco has 'his good points...When he had plenty of cash...he was always generous and ready to help an old mate down on his luck.'

To Dinny's surprise, Sally immediately offers to go with him. As they walk towards Boulder, Dinny is amazed to see Sally 'stepping out briskly and talking with more animation than she had shown for many a day.' She asks all kinds of questions about Frisco – how long has he been blind? How long has he lived with the 'unemployed and dead-beats' on Misery Flat? 'I've been living in a bad dream, Dinny,' she says. 'To-day I seem awake for the first time since – since Dick's death.'

As I was reading this, I kept thinking about the kind of power Frisco has over Sally.

They find Frisco lying in a shack 'made of rusty kerosene tins flattened out, with the rain pouring through.' Dinny wants to take him to the hospital, but Sally insists on bringing him home. Frisco's immediate response to seeing Sally is fury. 'God damn and blast you, Dinny...Take her away! Clear out, both of you. I'm done for. What's the game, anyhow? What the hell's the game? Come to gloat over a man when he's down?'

When Sally convinces Frisco to come home with her, she becomes a 'new woman, with a glow and wilful energy about her.' Dinny has heard an old rumour about a love affair between them but has never believed it. He's not so sure now: 'How could Missus Sally look at that pitiful wreck of a man with such concern and be so determined to nurse him herself if there were not something between them?' he asks himself. He 'frets and fumes', scared of what people will say, especially Sally's son, Tom, who has never liked Frisco.

Frisco recovers in Tom's old bedroom, and Sally nurses and tends to him until he's well enough to be 'stalking about again', although the black shade over one eye is a reminder that he will never again be the 'good-looking rake he had once been.' Frisco shows no sign of moving on: he settles in at the Gough house 'as if he were the star boarder.' Dinny resents Frisco; he is 'grumpy and miserable' and 'jealous of all the attention Missus Sally lavished on Frisco.'

If Sally's best female friends are Laura and Marie, there's no doubt that her best male friend is, and has always been, good ol' Dinny. For years they've shared an 'indefinable affection', and they've never had a quarrel. But Dinny hates the tittle-tattle about Frisco and Sally; he can't stand how they walk around town or sit in the park 'as if they were young lovers.' When Dinny tells Sally people are gossiping and offers to move out, Sally replies: 'This place has always been your home, and always will be, I hope. But it's my home, too; and I'll do as I please in it.' Dinny groans that living under the same roof as Frisco is 'not goin' to be easy.' Sally pleads for Frisco: he's 'different now,' she says. 'I'm happier than I've been for years. I can say this to you, Dinny, because we're old friends.'

Poor Dinny becomes 'fidgety and irritable' around Frisco. He spends a lot more time with Tom and his wife, Eily, and goes to bed early.

March 4th, 1969

Dropped by the library to ask Jill what she thinks of Sally's obsession with Frisco. She was in a bit of a mood. 'I reckon Sally's a twit for carrying on like she does with Frisco,' she growled, slamming a book on the counter. 'At her age, and after all she's been through, you'd think she'd be fed up with men.'

I didn't say anything because I have mixed feelings about Sally's affair with Frisco. It's very interesting that Sally decides she and Frisco can be lovers now that he's blind. After all, it's always been through their eyes that they have sparred with each other. In a way, now that he's blind, I suppose Sally has beaten Frisco, so she can relax.

As I left the library, I waved to Jill, but she was sorting books and didn't look up. She seemed pretty grumpy; maybe she's having trouble with her man.

March 5th, 1969

This morning, I asked Gwenda if Andy tries to boss her around, especially when it comes to having sex. She laughed and said, 'Of course he tries to boss me around! But when it comes to sex, I'm the boss in that department!'

I'd love to ask Mum when she and Dad stopped having sex, but I wouldn't dare! We've never discussed sex and Mum would be too embarrassed to talk about her relationship with Dad. I'm thinking that Sally is in her fifties by the end of *Golden Miles*, and my mum is in her fifties now. Sally's obviously still interested in sex. But Dad's been dead for years, so unless Mum has a secret lover, I'd say her sex life is dead and buried.

March 6th, 1969

Sally enjoys being involved in a '*scandale.*' 'You should see the winks and grins go round when Frisco and I walk along the street or into a pub,' she tells Marie. 'Surely, now we're grey-headed, we ought to be able to live together without people making a fuss about it?'

But where Tom Gough's concerned, it's much more than simply 'making a fuss.' He doesn't trust Frisco and he doesn't like him. When he asks her how she can 'suffer that man,' she replies 'I don't suffer him...I like him to be with me...I've done what I ought to for a long time. Now I'm going to do things because I want to do them.' Tom responds that she can have it her way, and she replies, 'I intend to.' But Sally notices he doesn't come to see her as often as he used to.

By the end of *Golden Miles*, Sally accepts she has 'betrayed Tom's and Dinny's confidence in her by giving Frisco a place in her home and her heart.' Even Sally doesn't entirely 'approve of her passion for Frisco.' But, she thinks, 'there it was, something imperious and irrational, putting a glory round her like the sunset. She was quite impenitent about it, and satisfied that she and Frisco could go on living together in their old age.'

I wonder if that's how things work out between them in the third volume of the trilogy, *Winged Seeds*? Dying to know the end of their story.

March 7th, 1969

We had a long morning tea today – Maggot's sick. Ha, ha!

I suppose we should care, but we don't. We talked about inheritances. I told Gwenda and Nora about how Den is Sally's youngest son, yet he will inherit the family property, Warrinup, and how happy Sally is about that. 'I think it's a bit odd. It's her childhood home, and she has a brother and four sisters. You'd think they'd all get something in the will, yet everything is going to Den,' I said. 'I hope my mother's will divides things equally between me and Peter. Not that there's much to inherit, but still.'

'I'm not sure my parents have a will,' frowned Gwenda. 'They've never said anything, but I hope they leave me plenty!'

Nora says she's been told she'll inherit her fair share of the family home, but she comes from a big family, so she probably won't end up with much.

We got onto the topic of big families. Nora says she loves having brothers and sisters and misses her brother who's joined the Navy and the other who's moved out of home. 'I love kids. I want at least four of my own,' said Nora.

Gwenda and I have no idea how many kids we'd like, if any. 'I don't want kids for ages,' said Gwenda. 'Perhaps never. I want to do more than just being a mum.'

'I do too,' I said.

I wrote a sketch about a girl who finds out she's pregnant, fails an exam because she can't concentrate, tells her boyfriend she's pregnant, and he dumps her. I was thinking of Gwenda the whole time I was writing.

March 9th, 1969

Lal was Morris's favourite son; Dick was Sally's. Dick was 'such a joy to her when he was born. Coming of the other babies, she had taken more as a matter of course, sometimes even with bad grace.'

Dick calls his mother 'darling', 'darl' and 'Sal-o-my.' Sometimes he calls her 'Sally.'

My mum would have kittens if I called her anything but 'Mum.'

Dick is slim, good-looking, dark-haired; girls are 'crazy about him.' He's also 'the brains of the family.' Sally has always wanted him to have a top job. She and Tom finance his education and he goes to a boarding school in Adelaide called Prince Alfred's. Later, he studies for a degree at the University of Sydney. Although he passes his first exams 'with honours,' he doesn't finish his degree.

In Sydney on business, Frisco contacts Dick, persuades him to give up his course and gives him a job. But when Dick realizes Frisco is making 'extravagant claims' about the quality of the WA mines, he fights with Frisco and goes home to the goldfields.

Sally is pleased to see he has 'manners and confidence' but also sees 'disappointment and disillusionment' in Dick's eyes and knows he's ashamed of giving up his studies and taking the job with Frisco.

March 10th, 1969

Dropped in to see Jill tonight on my way home from work. We had a chat about Dick Gough, and she told me Prince Alfred's is a posh boarding school that Hugo Throssell and his brother, Ric, attended. 'They were taught what the school called "heroic values,"' Jill explained. 'You know, things like loyalty, duty, patriotism.' Jill told me that when Hugo returned home to Australia after being awarded the Victoria Cross, he visited Prince Alfred's, and they gave him a hero's welcome. 'He slept the night in his old dorm, had breakfast with the boys the next morning then attended the school assembly.'

'Did he like boarding school?' I asked Jill.

'I've read that he did,' she replied. 'Although he wasn't what you'd call bookish. He preferred football, boxing and athletics. He won the school medal for sprints, hurdles and gym, and was captain of the school's football team in his final year.'

I've never met anyone who went to a boarding school, but I've met a few boys who attended all-boys schools. I reckon it's better to go to schools where boys and girls mix. They learn how to get along.

March 11th, 1969

Just reading the part in *Golden Miles* about how the Government sends out cards asking every man of military age whether or not he intends to enlist, and if not, why not? Dick, unlike his brother Lal, decides not to volunteer.

Dick receives a white feather in the mail. Sally is horrified, 'realising that what she dreaded was happening: the war was reaching out after Dick.' She tells Dick that only 'crazy Janes' send those feathers and that he should ignore his.

I remember reading a novel called *The Four Feathers* a few years ago. It was about a young man called Harry Feversham who refused to go to war. He didn't want his three best mates to go, so he burned the telegram containing the Army's orders for them to report for duty. His three mates later sent him three white feathers in a little box. They'd found out what he'd done and wanted to make sure he understood they thought he was a coward. Harry wasn't surprised. What surprises him and me too is that his fiancée rips a white feather from her fan and adds it to the other three! I couldn't believe it when I read it. She knew it was the cruellest way to break off their engagement, but she did it anyway!

I was on Harry's side all the way as I was reading that novel. And I was on Dick's side, too, for refusing to go to war and ignoring his white feather.

I sat down at lunchtime to write a dialogue between a young woman who hands her boyfriend a white feather, telling him, 'You're a bloody coward.' But I found it so hard to imagine I stopped writing after only half a page. Instead, I wrote a dialogue between a young man, who's been conscripted, and his father, a war veteran.

When he informs his father he will register as a conscientious objector, his father replies, 'I'm proud of you, son. I'll support you no matter what.' I felt much better after writing that dialogue.

March 12th, 1969

At first, I liked Dick's relationship with Amy, but, in the end, their marriage is a disaster and Amy's to blame.

Amy's 'vivacious', 'seductive', 'tempestuous'.

She likes men and they like her. Paddy Cavan has always had a 'passion' for Amy, and she's the main reason he's determined to become rich and powerful. He knows Amy is fickle enough to walk away from her marriage to Dick if she's offered something better.

Dick and Amy start out okay – young, full of life, happy, in love. They even have sex before marriage, although Dick is initially reluctant. Amy tells Dick not to be silly. 'We're engaged, aren't we?' Afterwards, when Dick tells her, 'We should have waited,' Amy tells him she 'wanted it – just couldn't bear waiting any longer. Why should we, after all?'

Soon after, Amy's mother, Laura, hints to Sally that something 'might happen' unless Dick and Amy aren't married 'quite soon.' Sally puts two and two together, then decides that, being 'well-brought up young people, they should have waited...until they were married, for the satisfaction of those instincts,' but, she reasons, 'boys and girls matured early in the hot, dry climate' and she understands that their 'first thrills of sexual experience' happen 'naturally and carelessly.' Now and then she's heard of a girl being 'in trouble,' but who cares, thinks Sally, so long as the young couple concerned were prepared to do the 'right thing by each other.'

I've been thinking about how Sally believes that marrying Amy will 'bring out all Dick's finest qualities.' Well, how wrong she was.

After their son Bill is born, Dick loses his job. He knows what's 'expected of him' – he joins the Army and tells Amy she'll get a pension for life if he dies in the war. Amy has a little weep then trots off to Perth, telling everyone she's going to stay there until Dick comes home. She gets involved in 'the hectic whirl of the summer in Perth,' which includes fancy dinner parties at Paddy Cavan's place. Paddy is now 'one of the wealthiest men in the Commonwealth' through his 'various deals in the Eastern States,' and Amy likes what she sees. When Sally cautions Amy, she just laughs: 'I can't just sit at home and mope until Dick comes home, can I?'

When Dick finally comes home from the war, Sally notes that nothing is left of his good looks; he drags his feet, stoops 'as if his shoulders had become set to crawling through dug-outs.' His voice is 'harsh and brittle.' He can't stand 'the crowd Amy's getting round with...They seem to be sorry the war's over. Can't talk about anything but the good times they've had,' he tells Sally. Things go from bad to worse, and Sally is 'horrified' when Dick comes to visit her and tells her, 'Oh, the gilt's off the gingerbread, I'm afraid, mother. Amy's never been the same to me since I came home.'

Katharine uses that gingerbread phrase to describe the Blackwoods' marriage in *Intimate Strangers*, and she also uses it in *Bid Me to Love*. I wonder if she ever felt this way about her own marriage.

Soon after, Amy runs off with Paddy Cavan, leaving little Billy behind. Dick has a fatal accident while working underground on Boulder Reef. On that 'black morning', in his pockets full of Dick's 'small belongings,' Sally finds a letter from Amy telling him that Lady Cavan is dead and Amy wants a divorce.

Is Dick's death really an accident? There are so many suicides in Katharine's work we're left wondering. But Dick's brother, Tom, insists that, while Dick had been 'troubled' and the letter might've been on his mind, he just got careless.

March 15ᵗʰ, 1969

Mum was on the warpath again this morning. 'Why don't you go out tonight, Vicki?' 'Why do you spend so much time in your room reading, Vicki?' 'You'd better watch it, Vicki, or you'll end up an old maid.' I wanted to scream, 'Shut up, Mum. Just shut your mouth for once!' but instead told her I was going window shopping with Nora. When I came home Mum was vacuuming the hallway. I managed to sneak into my room and shut the door quietly. Didn't want to listen to her whining about how it's high time I find a hubby.

I scribbled a couple of sketches about people I'd seen in town but they weren't any good, so I re-read the passage in *Golden Miles* where Sally watches Lal on horseback in the parade before he goes to war.

Sally hears an old Colonel declare that these soldiers are 'the sort of men we ought to breed from.'

'How many of them will come back to breed?' Sally asks the Colonel.

The Colonel replies, 'We pay a great price for our Empire, ma'am.'

I like Sally's answer: 'Nothing anybody pays is comparable to what those boys are going to pay. An empire isn't worth it.'

Made me think – why in the world *do* young men volunteer to fight in a war? It can't be to save a bloody empire! Maybe they should read Hugo's Northam speech and think about it before they trot off to war.

Sally keeps telling herself that Lal is going to fight 'for a good cause: that there would be no peace on earth until Germany was defeated' but Marie Robillard warns Sally that the war isn't being fought for the reasons Great Britain, France and Russia have given. Sally doesn't know what to think but Marie's words stay with her.

It's fascinating how Sally's mind leaps from images of battlefields to musing on how war stirs 'the sex instinct.' How men 'going to wrestle with death' become 'greedy of every joy' and 'both men and girls' respond to a 'fundamental urge' to 'defy the threat of extinction forced upon them.'

As I was reading this, I thought of Mum's stories about the fun she'd had during the war. She giggled and tossed her head like a teenager as she was telling me about the soldiers she went out with. I wonder what she got up to. Quite a lot, I bet, although she'll never give me the whole story.

March 16th, 1969

In her introduction to *Golden Miles*, Katharine tells us that Lal's letters are the 'authentic letters of a young soldier who took part in the Gallipoli campaign.' At first Lal's letters are 'light-hearted and amusing' but his later letters are full of gruesome descriptions of the battlefields.

There are plenty of gory details of battles in *Golden Miles*, and I must admit I skipped through a few pages – horrifying what went on; I felt sick reading it. I'd hate to be a man and have to fight in a war.

Lal is killed in action and Sally's mind whirls 'crazily in her rage and grief' as she asks herself, 'How did women come to tolerate this insane business of war? How was it possible to let young men be taken in their strength and beauty, and smashed to bloody pulp?...Why do women bear sons if this is to be the end of them?'

She remembers what Marie had said and starts reading banned books and papers, searching for the reasons for the war. 'Women like herself felt the lives of their sons and husbands were at stake,' Sally thinks. 'It was outrageous that any government should tell grown men and women they must not read criticism of the way the war was being conducted, or hear what anybody had to say about the causes of war.'

March 17th, 1969

After work, I popped in to see Jill and asked her straight out what she thinks are the causes of war. Jill laughed and said, 'Ah, Vicki, I'm not as good at explaining the causes of war as Katharine is. Wait a tick,' and off she went to the shelves and brought back an article by Katharine called 'Peace and War.'

'Have a read of this,' said Jill. 'She wrote it in 1939, but you can bet she hasn't changed her mind about a single thing.'

I read it.

Here are the bits that made my jaw tight:

We learn that Katharine's brother was only one of more than ten million men killed in the war. Millions were maimed, blinded, and disabled. Katharine began to ask herself: 'What are the causes of war?' 'Who benefits by war?' 'How can the causes of war be eliminated?' 'How can we make organisation for peace and international arbitration the supreme objective of peoples and government?'

She argues that the causes of war 'are to be found in the struggle for sources of wealth, spheres of influence and markets.' Katharine believes that 'the power of the people is the only power which can curb the rabid lust for wealth and autocracy in its interests which threaten to submerge them.'

Before I went to bed, I wrote a sketch about a mother who receives a telegram informing her that her son has been killed in a war. It was no good. Writing it made me feel even more miserable.

March 22nd, 1969

This morning, I ran into Larry in Forrest Place! He gave me the biggest smile and asked me to have a cup of tea with him. He said he's been in London and that's why he hasn't been to book club for a while.

I told him I'd been reading about Dick's white feather, and he nodded, then said some women sent feathers to young, fit men during the First World War to encourage them to fight. 'Here's a little ditty about conscription that was popular back then,' he laughed:

'Your king is Calling, your Country's Calling,

Your women are Calling, too –

We Want a Hundred Thousand Men

And the First We Want, is YOU!'

'And here's a popular anti-conscription song that was banned, but audiences took no notice. They sang it at all the peace meetings in Melbourne, Sydney and Brisbane.'

'I didn't raise my boy to be a soldier

I brought him up to be my pride and joy

Who dares to put a musket on his shoulder

To kill some other mother's darling boy?

The nations ought to arbitrate their quarrels

It's time to put the sword and gun away

There'd be no war today

If mothers all would say

I didn't raise my boy to be a soldier.'

He looked at me for a little while without saying anything until I realized it was my turn to talk. So I told him I thought Katharine would agree with the second song. Then I told him I've been reading about how Lal writes to Sally from the front: 'Tell dad I'll put on the gloves and give him a go round the yard if he votes for conscription.'

Larry asked me if I remembered the descriptions in *Child of the Hurricane* of the arguments the Prichard family had about conscription. How Katharine had at first voted for conscription, then later changed her mind. How she wrote a newspaper article in favour of a 'No' vote, and the editor, who was for conscription, told her that his son had written from the front, 'I'll put on the gloves, Dad, and give you a go when I come home if you vote for conscription.' I nodded like mad, pretending I remembered everything, but will have to re-read those bits when I get home.

When he got up to leave, he said he'd give me a list of all the real people Katharine mentions in *Golden Miles*.

Going home, I suddenly remembered that Rob, in *Subtle Flame*, writes to his sister from the warfront. 'Beginning to think you were right, Myff...Tell dad, I'll put on the gloves and have a go with him when I get home for not giving me the oil.'

When I got home, I read Sally's answer to Morris when he asks her to help him hand out pro-conscription pamphlets. Sally says, 'No. I don't any longer believe conscription is in the best interests of the Australian people. Reinforcements have been kept up, and I wouldn't trust this government any further than I can see it.'

Now there's a political Sally we haven't seen before! But I can imagine a world war would make anyone change their views and get involved in politics.

Before I went to bed, I asked Mum if she's seen any war films or read books about war.

'No, I haven't, Vicki,' she sniffed. 'And I hope you're not reading books about war. Love stories are much more interesting. Especially when they have a happy ending. Like a wedding.'

March 23rd, 1969

Just been making notes about Tom.

Sally Gough often compares Tom with Dick: Tom is a 'quiet, plodding little chap, with a pudgy, rather plain face and blue-grey eyes. He is 'inclined to be sulky,' but he is a 'good boy…so staunch and reliable.'

Tom's a really good brother, especially to Dick. He and Dick stick together when there's trouble at school and Tom knows immediately if something's up with Dick. Dick trusts Tom and tells him things he would never discuss with anyone: how he slept in a park in Sydney when he was 'stony, motherless broke.' How Paddy Cavan had tried to get him involved in the stolen gold trade. How he wishes he'd had a lot of money before he married Amy.

I wish I'd been close to Pete when we were growing up, but he usually ignored me. Once I punched him because he told me to shut up when I was singing along to an Elvis song. He didn't hit me back, which surprised me! We hardly ever hear from him these days. In fact, I'm not sure I know where he is – somewhere up north, I think, working in the mines. Or in Queensland. We get a letter from him now and then. I tell Mum that's another good reason to get a phone – so she can talk to Peter.

March 28ᵗʰ, 1969

Tonight at book club, Larry asked me if I'd noticed Katharine dedicated *Golden Miles* to Doon? I replied I did notice, but I don't know who Doon is. 'Doon is a good friend of Prichard,' he told me. 'Her real name is Winifred Stone and Prichard stayed with her in Kalgoorlie while she was researching the trilogy. Apparently, she thinks Prichard is the ant's pants!'

'That's good,' I laughed. 'I think Katharine's the ant's pants too!'

I asked him what he thinks of Tom. 'Ah, yes, Tom,' he said. 'He's a familiar character, isn't he – a lot like Michael Brady and Mark Smith.

'I thought you might like my list of the most important historical figures in *Golden Miles*, Larry said, shoving some papers in my hand. 'I've made a few comments as well,' he said with a grin.

'Gee, thanks, Larry,' I said. 'I love the way Katharine includes real people in her work.' I popped his notes into my bag and said, 'I feel like a student!'

'Well, Vicki,' he replied. 'I'm beginning to feel like a teacher again! And I thought I was retired!' He gave me such a big smile, I knew he was feeling good about not being retired after all.

March 29ᵗʰ, 1969

Just finished browsing Larry's list. I like Montague 'Monty' Miller best. He was a union organiser and a socialist against conscription and was sent to jail twice for his political activities. He died in 1920. Hugo and Katharine attended his funeral at Karrakatta. In *Golden*

Miles, Sally and Dinny both know and like Monty Miller, who often sits on the verandah 'expounding his views on socialism and industrial unionism, and reciting whole essays from Emerson and speeches from Shakespeare's plays.'

I'd love to know a man like that!

March 31ˢᵗ, 1969

Tom has one goal, 'To get into the mines and be earning a man's wages, as soon as possible.' He starts work in the mines when he's seventeen and gives his pay to Sally, who gives him back a few shillings. He spends most of his spare money on books and saves the rest. Tom's savings help pay for Dick's school fees. Years later, he admits to Sally that his savings had mostly come from bringing up a few 'weights now and again.' She tells him she understands why he did it. It becomes clear that Sally has always known where the money Dick needed for an education had come from, but she has never mentioned it. As Tom confesses to Sally that he had stolen gold, Sally sees the 'surge of blood to Tom's quiet face', yet neither admits that she had also been 'a guilty partner in that affair.'

Dinny is the one person in *Golden Miles* who understands Tom and accepts him for what he is. He has a 'great affection for the boy; loved the latent strength in his grave quiet face and grey eyes...Tom would discover the right way to go.' He thinks Tom is much like himself: 'born with a query in his brains.' Tom has read all of Dinny's books: 'Bellamy's *Looking Backward*, Kropotkin's *Fields, Factories and Workshops*, Tom Paine's *Rights of Man*.' Tom also reads books that Dinny admits are 'too tough' for him: Haeckel's

Riddle of the Universe, Darwin's *Origin of Species*, Carlyle's *French Revolution*, Dietzgen's *Positive Outcome of Philosophy*, as well as books by 'Emerson, Huxley...Edward Carpenter and Frederick Engels.' Also on Tom's bookshelves are 'mining reports, paper-covered booklets and pamphlets on every subject under the sun.'

I've never heard of any books Tom's read, except Darwin's *Origin of Species*! I am going to give Jill the list of Tom's books and ask her about them.

April 2nd, 1969

Jill had a good laugh when I gave her the list of Tom's books! She said she was sure that all the books listed are books Katharine herself has read, and most are political. 'I've read only *The Rights of Man, Origin of Species*, and *The Condition of the Working Class in England* by Frederick Engels, which I loved,' she said. 'All the rest are pretty specialized texts and Tom is certainly a very special character!'

I asked her if she likes Tom, and she said yes, but she likes Dick best of all Sally's boys. 'Do you think he committed suicide?' I asked her, and she said, 'No. It was an accident. Gold mining can be really dangerous. Hundreds of men have died in mines; they still do. From diseases as well as poor safety.'

Going home on the bus, I thought about Tom's bookshelves: they're made of 'red karri shingles used for fruit cases.' They're similar to Michael Brady's bookcases in *Black Opal*: his shelves are made from wooden boxes and old fruit cases. The books and pamphlets Michael collects are similar to Tom's, and, like Tom,

Michael Brady reads 'tracts, leaflets and small books on almost every subject under the sun.'

I would love to have a bookshelf made of red karri. My bookshelf is made of plywood and, even though I painted it bright red, it still looks awful.

April 3rd, 1969

Flipping through all the descriptions in *Golden Miles* of working conditions the men have to put up with on the goldfields. Horrible jobs these underground miners do.

There are many pages about how hard and dangerous goldmining is, but I felt angriest and saddest when I read this passage:

> 'Old men and young had the same, tense, driven look on their faces. In their dark, shabby working clothes, every man carrying his black rib bag, they seemed to be...an army of men, condemned to hard labour for life...Dull and apathetic, coughing and spitting, holding themselves together with a sort of desperate jocularity, they allowed themselves to be transported to the hell of their daily work in the mines, always with the secret fear that they might not come out of it alive, certain that at best they were going to swallow dust and fumes which would eat out their lungs and destroy them before their time, knowing that the wages they received were a paltry fraction of what they earned for the boss: no more than enough to pay the rent, buy

food and clothing, and a few pots of beer to keep a man from worrying about being a man and a miner.'

Gradually, Tom accepts that, 'ignorance and apathy dogged every attempt' he made to force the miners to realize their rights and power.' Yet Tom has a 'stubborn loyalty to the men he worked with…He could not separate himself from them, and from the struggle of the working class for a better way of life. Always on the horizon of his consciousness, like a mirage, glimmered that vision of a better way of life.'

I suspect that's how Katharine feels, especially when I think of how often she uses that word – 'mirage' – in her work.

April 5ᵗʰ, 1969

Nadya Owen in *Golden Miles* is an interesting character.

She has 'brilliant hazel eyes,' a 'husky' voice, and there is a 'queer magnetism' about her. When she argues with the men about politics, her face becomes 'beautiful with the intensity of a spiritual fire burning within her.'

For some reason, Nadya reminds me of an old neighbour who used to sit on her front verandah for hours, staring at the street. I was fascinated by her, especially when Mum told me she was a 'White Russian' and had been involved in all kinds of things during the war, so it would be best not to talk to her. But this neighbour always looked like she would've loved to have talked to anyone passing by, and I was often tempted to run up to her verandah and say hello. I wish I'd had the guts to do it. Would've loved listening to her story.

Tom meets Nadya at Marie Robillard's where people gather on Sunday nights to discuss politics with Marie's father-in-law, an 'old communard.' Tom and Nadya exchange books and ideas and walk home together, much to Tom's delight.

Sally's not happy about Tom's increasing infatuation: 'How could an older woman with a husband and children ever bring Tom happiness?' Sally asks herself.

Sally is also sceptical about Nadya's view that the 'land and anything in it or on it, belongs to the people.' She tells Sally that workers have to be organised to 'claim what belongs to them, and build a new economic system, based on their ownership...few men cannot hold property and wealth, and use everybody else to serve their interests.'

I've read enough to know by now that this would be Katharine's view, but it's not Sally's! Sally Gough isn't convinced by Nadya's belief in a workers' revolution. Nadya, Sally thinks, is 'obsessed by a wild, hopeless dream' and Nadya senses Sally's 'pity and vague hostility' towards her.

Not only is Sally scornful of Nadya's beliefs, she is anxious to find out what's really going on between Nadya and her son. At one point Sally asks Nadya outright: 'Mrs Owen...What is there between you and Tom?' Nadya admits she doesn't understand what's going on between them, but reassures her, 'If Tom thinks he loves me, it will pass. I am not young, or beautiful – and doomed.'

Nadya is seriously ill with 'phthisis of the throat' and dies in Wooroloo Sanatorium but not before asking Sally if Eily O'Reilly can visit Sally. 'We have worked a lot together and I hope that so good a young comrade and Tom will find happiness with each other, some day.'

After Nadya's death, Sally wishes she'd got to know her better as she'd 'caught a glimpse of the fire and purity of the woman's character, her intellectual brilliance and infinite sympathy.' Sally finally understands why Tom had been in love with her but is relieved to think that Tom just might be happy with Eily O'Reilly instead.

I'd love to meet women like Nadya and Eily. Wonder how I could meet them? Probably Katharine knows women like them, but where could someone like me go?

April 6th, 1969

Nora and I had Easter breakfast in King's Park and a good yarn about Gwenda. We know she hasn't been going to night classes lately. She's been spending an awful lot of time with Andy.

'Do you reckon she'll marry Andy and forget about uni?' Nora asked.

'She might,' I replied. 'She's pretty keen on him. It's a shame. I've always thought Gwenda would go to university. She used to be so determined. Since she's met Andy, though, she's changed, don't you think?'

Nora nodded and took a bite of her toast. 'That's what happens when you fall in love,' she said matter-of-factly.

'Well, I'd like her to fall out of love immediately,' I chuckled.

'Nothing we can do about it,' Nora said, pushing her chair back. 'Let's go for a bush walk.'

April 9th, 1969

Eily O'Reilly has shy blue eyes, a 'tumble of dark hair' and is the daughter of Charley O'Reilly, a member of Industrial Workers of the World. Eily has read 'every book her father's got...and can give him points in an argument.' Her views are the same as Tom's when it comes to socialism.

She hero-worships Tom, and Sally's reaction is interesting. She's 'taken aback' and 'amused.' She's never thought a girl could ever feel like that about her 'dear, good, stolid Tom', whereas she's always understood why the girls loved Dick. Nevertheless, she's 'grateful to Eily for loving Tom with such youthful ardour: making no attempt to keep it out of her eyes.'

Eily knows Tom doesn't feel the same way about her. One day she confides in Sally that 'the working-class movement is all he cares about, really. I love him for that as much as anything.' Sally isn't impressed; 'It's beyond me', she says. 'I've never had time to do anything but run a boarding-house and look after my husband and children. Maybe, some day, I'll be able to study politics and economics, like you and Mrs Owen.'

Sally gradually accepts that Tom and Eily are 'prepared to sacrifice everything, including their love for each other, to their crazy notion of serving the working class.'

I don't know if I could hero-worship a man simply because of his ideas. I'd like to be able to talk about big ideas with my man, of course. But I'd also like to go to the beach, stroll through town, have dinners at nice restaurants and talk about books, go to the pub and play darts, meet up with friends. It would be boring listening to a man who only wants to sit around talking politics.

April 10th, 1969

After hearing about the Russian Revolution, Tom and Eily walk along a dusty road in a 'gash of gold, from the setting sun.' Both feel as if some 'unbelievably miraculous thing had happened; something they had dreamed of, yet scarcely believed could be anything more than a dream.'

Their dream-like walk reminds me of Katharine's description in *Child of the Hurricane* about how enthralled she was when she walked across the Prince's Bridge in Melbourne and saw posters about the Russian Revolution. I wonder if Katharine was trying to recapture that moment when she wrote about Tom and Eily?

Tom and Eily celebrate the revolution by marrying 'quietly at the registrar's office, with Dinny and Sally as witnesses.' They seem to have a pretty ordinary love life but are good mates and deeply committed to socialism and the union movement. Eily loyally supports Tom in every campaign he gets involved in, including the violent battles between foreign workers and returned soldiers. They end up having three children, two boys and a girl, and they take in little Billy, Dick and Amy's abandoned son.

Sally and Eily get along famously. Eily and the kids visit Sally every week but Tom, who can't stand Frisco, visits his mother 'rarely.'

April 11th, 1969

I love little Billy. He comes to see Sally after school to eat her rock buns. One day Amy, now Lady Cavan, arrives from London.

Wearing a 'smart black hat', her hair curled into 'little golden sausages,' she visits Sally to announce she's in town to re-claim Billy. All Sally can think is: 'Go away, I don't want to see you! I don't want to speak to you.' Amy, Sally believes, is as determined to 'regain possession of her son as she had been to marry Dick and to grasp everything in life she had desired.'

Sally thinks Amy's declarations of 'heartache and unhappiness' are no more than a 'symptom of the overwhelming egotism.' Sally's conscious of a 'dumb rage and distrust of the motives behind Amy's babble' and decides she will do nothing to help Amy 'recapture' Billy. By now, Billy is almost thirteen and Sally tells Amy he's old enough to decide what he'd like to do.

Billy's face goes white and stiff when he sees his mother again. 'I don't know you. I don't want to know you,' he tells her and dashes to his bedroom, where Eily finds him 'lying face down on his bed, full of rage.' He tells Eily his friends call Amy 'Paddy Cavan's whore' and he hates his mother.

Billy doesn't fall for Amy's promises of a good school, trips to France, Italy and Spain. Nor does he believe his mother when she tells him that 'Sir Patrick' is prepared to be his father. 'The rotten old swine…I let her have it then, gran,' he tells Sally. 'Forgot my manners and everything. Told her what I thought of Paddy Cavan and his sort, and that some day they'll be treated like the criminals they are.'

Sally is proud of Billy; she knew he would never give in and go back to his mother. She's even more proud when Bill confides that he and Tom have worked things out for the future. When the 'workers own and control the mines,' he tells Sally, 'profits will be devoted to big schemes for irrigation and new industries…Uncle Tom says Lenin reckons some day gold'll be used for making lavatories. Gee, how'd you like a gold lavatory, gran?'

Doesn't sound like any thirteen-year-old kid I've ever met, but then I haven't met many. However, I had a good laugh thinking about that gold lavatory!

April 12th, 1969

Katharine has a great sense of humour – there are lots of things in her work that make me laugh. In *Golden Miles*, there are many funny little incidents that make me giggle.

For instance, a character called Bill Dally has been a boarder at the Goughs for a long time and Sally knows him well. 'Drunk or sober, he would hold forth on the beauties of socialism: liberty, equality and fraternity for all men.' Tom doesn't think much of him, telling Dally, 'All you care about is boozing.'

Sally has several rows with Bill Dally about his drinking, but the one I like best is the afternoon he comes into the kitchen, drunk, and asks Sally to have a beer with him. She's busy cooking sausages for the evening meal and can't be bothered with Dally when he's drunk. He jokes about Mrs Baldy Mack, the wife of a mate. She is a 'tartar' and a 'tiger,' or better still, a 'hip-hippo-potamus. God, if she fell on a man', he chuckles, 'it'd be the end of him.' Sally can't help but smile, but she's had enough. She grabs his bottle of beer and marches him across the yard to his room.

There's a serious side to this story, though. As Dally says, 'a skinful of booze helped a man to forget the drudgery of his work underground.' The mine managers see to it that there's always plenty of beer. Beer is the dope 'the bosses sold to keep a man from worrying about being a miner, and a wage-slave…What could you do about it, when a man was too dog weary and thick in the head to care what happened, so long as he could put new life into himself swigging beer, glorious beer?'

I remember Dad liked beer. He drank a lot of it during footy season and gallons of it at Christmas. At first, he was always full of jokes and yarns and then got aggressive. Mum hated it when he drank and never laughed at his jokes. She just wanted him to shut up and go to bed. Come to think of it, I never got his jokes either, but I enjoyed seeing him blotto. When he started to get nasty, I took off outside or went to bed.

April 13th, 1969

Mum was out all afternoon, so I had a lovely quiet time in the lounge room browsing *Golden Miles*. Mum doesn't like it if I spend a lot of time in the lounge room; it's more her room because of the television. She likes me to go to my bedroom or out in the backyard if I'm going to read.

Another funny scene I liked in *Golden Miles* takes place in the Ladies' Room where Sally and Marie are having a beer. A 'tall gaunt woman' sitting alone yells out, 'God save us, if it's not Mrs Gough!' It's Mrs Gallagher, 'a sturdy old whaler' known as 'God-Save-Us-Sarah' because she uses 'God save us' at the beginning of almost every sentence. During their chat, the old whaler advises Sally, 'Never you go to bed with a strange man and let him get hold of y'r money,' she says.

'I won't,' Sally replies.

I immediately thought of Frisco. He may not be a stranger, but he certainly sponges off Sally.

When Mrs Plush comes into the Ladies Room, the conversation gets even more amusing. 'I've always kept meself respectable,' says Mrs Plush. 'What's respectable?...Well, it's workin' hard, bloody hard, like I've done, and payin' your way, and never carin' what anybody says about who y'r drinkin' or sleepin' with. That's what I call respectable.'

I reckon Katharine would agree.

April 14th, 1969

Gwenda told us this morning she had an argument with Andy over the weekend.

'What did you fight about?' asked Nora.

'He wants me to go on the pill, but I don't want to take the pill. I've told him over and over that even if I wanted to, I couldn't get it. He doesn't believe me.'

'Tell him there's not a doctor in Perth who would prescribe the pill for you!' Nora exclaimed.

'Or tell him to go to the chemist and buy some French Letters,' I scoffed. 'Why should you be in charge of birth control?'

'He hates Frenchies,' Gwenda replied.

'Oh, so you've gone all the way with him then, have you?' Nora asked.

Gwenda glared at Nora and gritted her teeth.

'Leave her alone,' I growled and squeezed Gwenda's hand.

She gulped her tea and left.

Nora smiled triumphantly and said, 'Well, well, well!'

'Well, what?' I snapped. 'Gwenda's got enough on her plate. She doesn't need us hounding her about Andy. She'll work things out.'

'Yep,' said Nora thoughtfully sipping her tea. 'She'll have to.'

April 15th, 1969

I like Katharine's descriptions of Kalgoorlie and Boulder. The earth everywhere is red. In the distance lies a 'sea of scrub, spindly snap and rattle, pale blue cotton bush and saltbush.' In these towns, people see only a 'fragment of starry sky' and the 'dark heave of the ridge' that runs down towards the 'great pyramid of the Horseshoe dump.' A 'feathery, white vapour' drifts across the stars and poisons the air. The 'rattle and crash of batteries' are reminders of the 'ceaseless toil...grinding so many lives to dust.'

It's a bleak environment, yet Sally finally understands what Morris told her years ago: 'This country will get you.' It had finally 'got her,' she admits. 'Her roots were embedded in its soil, as much as roots of the silvery grey mulga, which had weathered so many droughts, and could still cover itself with golden bloom.'

One day, I'd like to go to the goldfields and compare Katharine's description with what's there now. Probably hasn't changed much.

April 16th, 1969

Jill told me this arvo that there had been a big fuss about Tom Gough among the critics of *Golden Miles*. 'There was an argument about whether or not Tom was a "vital revolutionary figure",' said Jill. 'Katharine had always hoped that readers would consider Tom a good communist, but almost no one thought so, including Soviet critics.' Jill laughed and shook her head. 'They thought she should have used Tom to explore the role the Communist Party had in supporting and organizing the goldminers,' said Jill. 'But Katharine put them in their place quick smart. She told them the Communist Party didn't exist in WA during the period covered in *Golden Miles*, so it couldn't have had any part whatsoever in organizing the miners.'

Jill showed me a couple of pretty harsh reviews. One critic thought *Golden Miles* was just a bundle of words; another didn't think much of the writing or the ideas, but at least the characters were full of life.

Yep, I thought when I read that: I feel as if I know most of the people in *Golden Miles* – especially Sally Gough.

Jill also told me about a reviewer in the *West Australian* who didn't believe the dialogue between the gold miners. 'But Katharine claims that five miners wrote a letter to the newspaper telling the reviewer that is *exactly* the way miners talk. Their letter was never published. She doesn't have much luck where the *West Australian* is concerned,' Jill shrugged.

As she was sorting out some stationery, Jill told me that Katharine was disappointed with the sales of *Golden Miles*. 'She had expected to make some money out of it, but when that didn't happen, she lost confidence and started to wonder if it was worth going ahead with the final volume of the trilogy,' Jill said. She frowned, then said, 'I've heard she nearly lost her house in Greenmount because she couldn't pay the mortgage. But she's generous to a fault and gives money to all kinds of people. She donated her royalties from *The Roaring Nineties* to the people of European villages destroyed by the war to help in reconstruction.'

'That sounds very Katharine,' I said to Jill.

'Yep,' she nodded, sharpening a bunch of pencils. 'She's a generous lady, that one.'

Borrowed *Winged Seeds*, the third volume. Can't wait to read it.

April 25ᵗʰ, 1969

Sally Gough's birthday! I've almost come to believe she's a real person! And it's ANZAC Day. Something to celebrate, something to mourn.

Mum was out when I got up this morning. She likes the ANZAC Day parade, so she has probably gone to see it. I felt like doing something, so I went into town and walked around Forrest Place. I must admit that I was hoping I'd run into Larry.

There were too many people in town, and I don't like the parade, so I hopped on the bus to go home. After three stops, a big, fat, sweaty slob who stank of beer got on and sat next to me. Why I do not know! There were plenty of other seats on the bus. Anyway, he kept pushing his knee against me. When I shifted even closer to the window, he pushed harder. I got up and climbed over him to change seats. He laughed at me, and I glared at him and stomped on his big, fat foot. He grabbed my arm but I broke free and rang the bell. Got off at the next stop.

I hate ANZAC Day.

At least I've got material for a sketch!

May 10th, 1969

Finished *Winged Seeds*! Loved it. Mostly because I really like Sally Gough and Dinny. The story is good too; lots of stuff happens.

May 12th, 1969

Popped into the library on my way home. Jill told me she liked *Winged Seeds* more than *Golden Miles*. 'My favourite, though, is still *The Roaring Nineties*,' she said.

'I think it's mine too,' I replied.

Jill told me Katharine wanted to call the final volume 'Wasting Assets.' She must've liked that title because she wanted to use it for the first volume. 'However, she changed her mind after a little adventure,' said Jill. 'One day Katharine went for a walk and picked up a wild pear seed. She brought it home and it split in the heat. She found a shower of thistledown on her notebook. "Winged Seeds", she said to herself, and that was that. I thought she'd borrowed the title from Shelley's "Ode to the West Wind",' Jill said, 'but I was wrong.'

I was pleased to hear that story because I wondered if the final scene in *Winged Seeds*, where Sally yells out to Dinny to look at the kalgoorluh that cracks open and begins to shed its seeds, was based on a real incident. It's such a vivid image it seems to be a memory. Sally picks up a handful of the seeds and murmurs, 'Seeded wings...winged seeds...they'll find a corner where they can grow, even in this hard ground.' She tells Dinny that the seeds they've sown together will 'grow like wild pears, no matter how hard and stony the ground where they fall.' Dinny chuckles and replies: 'And it's up to us not to let anybody forget it.'

Jill also told me that Katharine's old friend, Miles Franklin, loved the title 'Winged Seeds.' She wrote to tell Katharine that she was 'inspired by the title...because it is an inspired phrase – a poet's inspiration.'

I'm glad Katharine ditched 'Wasting Assets'!

June 2nd, 1969

No one I know, except Gwenda, ever discusses Aboriginal people. I remember she once flounced into the tearoom and announced that white people have always systematically and deliberately tried to get rid of the Aboriginal people. 'They deserve compensation for all the terrible things white people have done to them,' said Gwenda, sticking out her chin. Nora snorted into her tea and I stared at my Ginger Nut. Gwenda waited for us to say something. I couldn't think of anything to say. Nora sighed and got up to make another cuppa.

But, having read Katharine, I'm now beginning to understand

what Gwenda meant by that remark. I agree with Dinny in *Winged Seeds* when he says, 'If natives are put under the dog act...something ought to be done for them by way of compensation.'

At the end of the novel, Katharine sums up the fate of the local Aboriginal people in the scene where Sally and Dinny are burying Kalgoorla's body. Bardoc agrees to bury her 'white feller way' because there are 'no more black feller round about.' The two old men, one white, one black, work all night digging a deep grave for Kalgoorla so her bones won't be scattered. Sally sits nearby, watching the men and thinking about how precious Kalgoorla's friendship has always been. How Kalgoorla had looked after her during her bout of typhoid fever; how Kalgoorla had worked hard for her in the bush dining-room; had looked after her children when they were little. Sally 'reproached herself for not having done more for Kalgoorla.' After all, she had been witness to, and partly responsible for, Kalgoorla's 'grief and despair' over the loss of her 'tribal life' by the white men's 'insatiable lust for wealth and power.'

June 20th, 1969

Jill told me Katharine was depressed and often ill while writing *Winged Seeds*. 'She has a weak heart, high blood pressure, and gets migraines,' said Jill.

'I don't believe Katharine wrote what she felt because she didn't think anyone would publish it. She knows how hard it is to get published in Australia when you have radical views!

'But she's such a bloody hard worker,' Jill chuckled. 'She finishes *Winged Seeds* then off she trots to write *Subtle Flame*. She organizes collections of her short stories and then publishes *Child of the Hurricane* in 1963. She was eighty-one years old by then! Talk about determination!'

'Talk about energy!' I said. I can't imagine being that energetic, ever.

June 27th, 1969

Tonight at book group Larry came up to me, laughing, and said, 'I come armed to the hilt with something I know you will want.' He was eating a sausage roll and some of the pastry was stuck in the sides of his mouth. I didn't know where to look or what to say, so I just grinned.

He handed me his list of the most important real people Katharine mentions in *Winged Seeds*. 'They were all against fascism,' he said. 'And Prichard knew some of them personally.' He wiped his mouth with a serviette and I was so relieved I giggled. He glanced at me then shrugged.

'Well, Vicki?' he asked. I had no idea what he wanted me to say, so I blurted out that I'd skipped over quite a few pages in *Winged Seeds* about fascism, about Spain, about international agreements, about Germany and Italy and the British. 'I think I need a history lesson,' I gulped, trying to make a joke of my ignorance.

'Have another look at Chapter Three in *Winged Seeds*,' he said. 'That's when Bill speaks at the meeting of the League for Peace and Democracy. The meeting's a fizzer; only a handful of people come, and I think someone says the locals would turn up for a fight or free beer but not to listen to a speech against fascism. The League itself was a true organization, and Prichard explains the problems in Europe before the Second World War pretty clearly. You'll get your history lesson from her, that's for sure!'

He told me that, even in Australia, there were fascists roaming around before the Second World War. 'Some of them had guns,' he said.

'Who in the world were they going to kill?' I asked him. I was amazed by this story!

'Socialists, communists, anyone opposed to fascism. You had to be very careful if you were a socialist or a communist back then,' he said. 'Actually, that's true even now, as your Katharine would know. People in high places in Australia are always anti-communist. Victoria once even had a Deputy Premier who was a fascist.' Then he gave me a sly grin. 'I wouldn't worry about the fascists now, Vicki,' he chuckled.

'That's a relief,' I replied. For a moment, I was scared he was going to tell me there were still maniacs like that roaming the streets.

Mum caught me reading Larry's list as I came in the front door.

'What's that you've got your nose in, Vicki?' she called from the lounge room.

'Nothing, Mum,' I yelled and walked past her as quickly as I could.

Gosh, there are a lot of them this time! Larry has written at the bottom of his list: 'Prichard would've given much thought to how she could link these people to her fictional characters. She did a good job.'

Of all the people on Larry's list, I like Aileen Palmer and John Cornford best.

Aileen is the daughter of Nettie Palmer, one of Katharine's good friends. A student of modern languages and a political activist, Aileen went to Spain during their civil war to work for the International Brigades as an interpreter. John Cornford was a friend of Aileen. He was a poet and a member of the Communist Party of Great Britain and encouraged Aileen to believe that art can be a tool of revolution. He died in the Spanish Civil War, poor bugger.

Larry didn't list Egon Kisch, probably because we've talked about him before, and he trusts I'd remember. In *Winged Seeds*, Bill gives a speech about the 'dragon breathing fire and brimstone over Europe, and menacing even far away places like Australia.' He tells his audience how Egon Kisch came to Australia as a delegate for the World Peace Congress and was refused permission to land. But, he told them, when Count Felix von Luckner, a Nazi who wanted Australia to side with Germany in the Second World War, arrived in Australia, he was welcomed by the Prime Minister and 'made a great fuss of in Sydney.'

It is difficult to understand why Kisch was treated like an outlaw, but a fascist sympathizer can hobnob with the powers that be. I suppose lots of people agreed with those 'huckstering industrial magnates and conservative statesmen' who, in *Winged Seeds*, howl, 'Better fascism than communism.'

June 30th, 1969

After work today, I popped into the library and asked Jill about Francis Adams, who's an Australian poet mentioned in *Winged Seeds*. She told me she didn't think much of his poetry, but she gave me a copy of his *Songs of the Armies of the Night* and I found the one that Bill quotes during his speech. It's about the 'Power of Powers.'

Sally recalls how proud she was of Bill on that 'wild stormy night.' She thought Bill was like a 'young Prometheus' who defied 'Power which seems omnipotent' to champion the cause of the workers. 'That was it,' Sally tells herself. 'The spirit of mankind struggling through the centuries against injustice and oppression was the Power of Powers.'

Good old Prometheus! He's been with Katharine all her life. I thought about that on the bus all the way home.

When I got home, Mum told me she'd left my dinner in the oven. I told her I wasn't hungry, and she asked if I was sick. Out of my mouth popped, 'It's because of Prometheus!' She glared at me, shook her head, and told me I should go straight to bed. Which I did, gladly.

July 1st, 1969

Tonight, I've been thinking about how in *Winged Seeds*, the dust storms are linked to the 'gritty particles of news flung about by frenzied speculators and corrupt politicians.' People everywhere are 'struggling against a blinding dust being thrown in their eyes.' They are 'suffocating in an atmosphere of vicious intrigues designed to dupe and betray...The air was thick with rumours of war, fears and prognostications of what the next few months might bring.'

Sally hates the present and dreads the future. She mopes around the house and garden. Why should she bother, she thinks, whether her roses bloomed when the 'lives of men and women were being blasted...What did it matter that her wild hibiscus was a bouquet of diaphanous mauve petals, or the bird of paradise bushes gay with yellow wings and vermilion tails...when death and destruction were ravaging helpless people.'

It takes Sally Gough a long time to get involved in politics, although she sympathizes with the miners and speaks out against war.

It's the Japanese who finally stir Sally into action.

She is 'so enraged and alarmed by the record of Japanese crimes in China, and the threat which Japanese imperialism held over Australia' that she joins Bill and Eily in their campaign to boycott Japanese goods on the goldfields. She distributes leaflets with Eily and helps put up posters that say: 'Don't buy Japanese goods, they're bloodstained.' She and Dinny barge into shops and harasses the shop assistants: 'Selling Jap stuff?...The workers won't stand for it. Didn't you know there was a boycott on? Better tell the boss.'

One day, Frisco comes to warn Dinny about the 'new regulation' that is 'going to hit the coms pretty hard,' telling him to get Eily to 'clear out every scrap of paper or book she's got connected with the Communist Party, or any organizations affiliated with it'. If she doesn't, she'll go to jail. This also stirs Sally into action: she and Dinny go straight to Eily's home and help her burn newspapers and pamphlets. Dinny takes Eily's and Bill's books to a safe place he knows in the bush. Sally takes care of Bill's papers, declaring, 'Over my dead body they'll get them.'

Sounds a lot like what happened to Katharine herself when she was raided!

July 3rd, 1969

Gwenda stormed into the tearoom this morning, sat down, folded her arms, then started to cry.

'I'm just so furious!' she choked. 'Andy's in the birthday ballot. If he's picked, he could be sent off to Vietnam. We're both scared. He could be killed!'

'Or he might have to kill someone else,' Nora said.

'Makes me sick,' said Gwenda. 'He can't legally drink, but he can be forced to go to war!'

'It's not bloody fair, Gwenda,' I said.

We didn't talk anymore; just sipped our tea and quietly returned to our desks.

I wrote three portraits and one dialogue during lunch and felt much better afterwards. Writing always makes me feel better. Things seem much clearer when they're organized into sentences and paragraphs.

July 6ᵗʰ, 1969

Katharine has a good sense of humour. She often makes me laugh out loud.

The funniest bit in *Winged Seeds* is when Eily takes little Nadya to a school concert and, at the end, the children are asked to go up on stage and sing 'Ave Maria.' They all march up and kneel to sing, their backs to the audience. But little Maria Rossini's dress gets caught up, and her bare bum is exposed to the audience. It is 'the most innocent, lovely little bottom,' but the nuns are shocked and close their eyes. Maria's mum tells them, 'with great dignity,' that her daughter does have a 'pair of drawers, but they're in the wash this week.' As Eily tells Sally the story, she laughs like she hasn't laughed 'in a long time' and is still smiling when she says, 'It was such an indictment of poverty on the goldfields, that little bare bottom!'

We are probably not meant to laugh at Mrs Rooney, Frisco's mistress, but I did. One afternoon, Sally sits in the public gardens, thinking about how Frisco never has time these days to go with her to this oasis and how much he's been drinking lately. She trots off his office to talk with him but Nora, Frisco's secretary, tells her he's out. She shuffles her papers and pretends to be busy and irritated with Sally. She puts paper in her typewriter and starts 'clacking' the keys frantically, trying to drown out the 'smothered laughter' between Frisco and Mrs Rooney, who are having it off in Mrs Rooney's flat, which is right next to Frisco's office. The rooms in the building are partitioned, the walls are 'thin, paper-covered hessian on a framework of light timber', and you can hear everything that goes on. When Sally recognizes Frisco's laugh, Nora jumps up gasping 'Mrs Gough!' while Mrs Gough raps on Mrs Rooney's door to find out what's what.

What happens next is like a silly comedy, and I couldn't help sniggering as I read it. Sally threatens to break the door down, then hurls herself against it and the 'lock parted from the rotten woodwork.' She sees a 'fat naked woman disappearing behind a bead curtain' and Frisco on the couch, 'pulling on his trousers.' When Mrs Rooney comes back, she's dressed in a kimono and smirks at Sally 'coyly and with brash satisfaction,' telling her that she can't 'expect to be the only pebble on the beach.' Frisco tells her to shut up. 'I love you, Sally…This woman doesn't mean a damn thing to me,' he says. Mrs Rooney is offended: 'Not an hour ago I was your "little honey pot" and "the best cuddle on the G.M.",' she says to Frisco. Her 'swivel eye' squints 'maliciously' at Sally, and her 'soiled kimono' falls away to show her 'huge floppy bosom.'

Sally bolts out of the room in a fit but finally decides there should be 'no pain in knowing Frisco had destroyed her faith in him for that stupid, slovenly woman.' After all, she tells herself, she's always known 'the sort of man he was', and she had taken him in, knowing it.

When Nora comes to collect Frisco's belongings, Sally hands her his 'handkerchiefs, two clean shirts, and two or three pairs of socks' and tells Nora she'll send the rest of his clothes to the office the next day. Just like Elodie in *Intimate Strangers,* Sally Gough is determined to have 'everything in order.' She will wash and iron Frisco's clothes and his suits will be 'meticulously pressed as usual.'

As much as I like Sally, I couldn't understand her in this episode. I wanted her to punch Frisco in the face and chuck his clothes into the street! But then I remembered she'd once told herself, 'There was so much in Frisco's past she had had to ignore in order to be happy with him,' and I felt sorry for her.

July 7th, 1969

I was telling Gwenda and Nora about Frisco and Mrs Rooney this morning, but Gwenda didn't seem interested. She interrupted me to say that Andy has been seeing another girl. After his confession, they had a big fight. 'He sent me a letter saying how sorry he was and told me he loves me,' Gwenda said, spitting out her Granita. 'I'm still thinking about whether or not I'll answer it.'

'But I do miss him,' Gwenda wailed. 'What if he gets called up and sent to Vietnam, and I never answered his letter! I'd feel terrible.'

Nora, as usual, was pouting into her mirror. She tossed her hair and said, 'Just dump him, Gwenda! Find someone else.'

Gwenda and I both stared at her. Then Gwenda's bottom lip started to tremble, and she said, 'I know Andy can be a real bugger sometimes, but I love him. I can't see myself with anyone else. And that's that.'

July 8th, 1969

I dropped into the library on my way home and Jill and I had a chat about the funny bits in *Winged Seeds*. 'Katharine does have a good sense of humour,' agreed Jill, 'but she doesn't use it often enough.' As Jill spoke, she was rummaging around in the catalogue then said, 'Just a tick,' and took off to the shelves. She came back with an article and pointed to a paragraph. 'Read what Katharine has written here, Vicki.'

'Perhaps I have not made readers dream and laugh enough. The wit and gaiety I admire so much in other writers, I have lacked. But, in all the varieties of expression, my conclusion stands that the "noble candid speech in which all things worth saying may be said", is the best means of communication and fulfilling the sublime mission of art in literature.'

'Oh,' I said, 'well, it might be true that she doesn't make me laugh often, but she certainly makes me think!'

July 9th, 1969

Been thinking about some of the characters in *Winged Seeds* – who I like, who I don't.

For instance, I can't stand Paddy Cavan; he deserves everything he gets. Also hate Ted Doherty, Daphne's boss – I was so glad when Nell McIntyre, the union girl, barges into the pub to inspect the wages and hours book, and Daphne ends up £50 better off.

Pity we don't have a union to inspect our company's wages book. We work long hours for pathetic wages, and Maggot is a nasty pig. Lately he's started prowling around our tearoom, threatening to cut back our break time. He reckons we should work back fifteen minutes every arvo because we deliberately dawdle back to our desks after morning tea.

Don't like Tom and Eily's son, Dick. Sally doesn't like him either. She believes Dick has always been jealous of his cousin, Bill, and has no patience with Dick's attempts to 'dissociate himself from his father and all he represented.'

When Tom dies, Dick puts the boot in. He refers to himself as Mr Richard Fitz-Maurice, signs a document pledging loyalty to his employer, and marries the boss's daughter, a 'stodgy', unpopular and plain girl called Myrtle Langridge, who is several years older than Dick. Sally thinks Myrtle is 'as predatory as a female spider,'

After Tom's funeral, Dick argues all night with Bill about the value of spending time and energy supporting the cause of the workers. 'I'm not going to waste my life for a mob who'd rather swill beer and bust up their pay at the two-up, than try to better themselves and live as well as they could,' he tells Tom. 'I don't believe they ought to have the power to run the state. I don't believe they care a bloody damn for what you call their democratic rights...I hate the workers, Bill. I hate the stupid, cowardly crawlers. "Feed 'em and make 'em work for you", that's what old Langridge says. And I reckon he's about right.'

Dick stops visiting his mother. Eily finally goes to see him after hearing that men have been sacked from the Gold Star mine and accuses him of being involved. At first, he denies it but looks 'so shifty and self-conscious' that Eily knows her son is guilty. He claims later that the men were 'possible trouble-makers' and that he would do 'the same again' to 'safeguard the interests of the company.'

At one point, Dick passes Eily in the street and greets her with a casual 'Hullo, mother.' He wears a soldier's uniform and speaks at patriotic meetings, urging 'drastic action' be taken 'against any reds on the goldfields' who are 'disrupting the war effort by circulating illegal literature' – something his own mother has been doing for months.

Gee, I don't get along very well with Mum at the best of times, but I'd never pass her in the street and not have a chat.

Actually, that's a nice thought: living away from home, running into Mum, and stopping to have a gossip. Maybe one day...

July 12th, 1969

Well, I've had a very happy Saturday! Went shopping in the morning and bought a red blouse to go with my black skirt. And ran into Larry, who was also shopping in town. He showed me the shirt he'd bought – light blue, very nice – and invited me to lunch. We tried to get a table at a couple of places but in the end, we went into the food hall at Boans and bought ham, cheese and tomato rolls to take away. We were going to catch a bus up to King's Park and have a picnic, but we waited ages for the bus and were so hungry we ended up eating on the steps of the Post Office. We had a long chat about lots of things, including, of course, *Winged Seeds*.

I can't quite remember all the details, but he went on a bit about the Second World War and the Americans. I stopped listening when he got into why Dinny was optimistic about Czechoslovakia and China. Instead, I watched some pigeons eating crumbs on the footpath. When he stopped talking, I looked at him. He was staring at me in a funny way, so I apologized and said I definitely need some history lessons. I thought he'd laugh at me, but he just smiled with his kind brown eyes.

July 14ᵗʰ, 1969

Dropped into the library on my way home from work and asked Jill her opinion about Bill and Pat's relationship. I've been puzzling over the idea that Bill and Pat claim to reject the 'romantic illusion' called 'loove' despite fancying each other. I read out loud the passage that strikes me as being very interesting:

> 'It was not the urge and affinity part of what was called love they rejected, but the illusions, bargains and fantastic conception that two people could mean more to each other than anything else in the world, for ever and ever, amen...Love which was supposed to transmute life to a paradisaical existence was a myth.'

'Do you think this could be what Katharine believes about happy-ever-after love?' I asked Jill.

'Vicki, my friend,' she replied. 'I think you're on to something there.'

I walked out of the library feeling very proud of myself. Jill called me 'my friend' again!

July 15ᵗʰ, 1969

I like Bill more than any other character in the trilogy – except for Sally Gough, Marie Robillard, and Dinny, who are my favourites.

I like the way Bill jokes with Sally. When he comes to see her after work she loves to see 'his eyes light up and smile at their understanding, the secret joke they seemed always to be sharing.' One day, Sally laughingly tells Bill, 'The gossips say I'm a miserable sinner...But what does that matter? I don't mind, and I hope you never will.' Bill knows she's referring to her affair with Frisco, apparently still a scandal 'busy-bodies in the town discussed a good deal.' Like Tom, Bill doesn't like Frisco but loves seeing his grandmother 'looking so handsome and full of the joy of life' and tells her affectionately, 'Oh, you...You could get away with murder, darl, and nobody'd blame you!' For her part, she calls Bill 'My beloved sonny-bun.'

I like Bill's views on gold, 'What's the good of gold in the world to-day?' he asks Sally. 'Millions are spent digging it out of the earth and it goes back into vaults in America. We've got to find a better use for gold – if it is any use.'

I like Bill's reply to Frisco when he says with amusement: 'You're a bit of a com, y'rself, Bill, they tell me.' Bill whoops: 'I've been more than a bit of a com, a long time, haven't I, gran?' He loyally defends Tom when Sally criticizes him for dragging Bill 'into his committees and things,' telling his grandmother, 'Tom didn't drag me into anything...I've got enough common sense to work things out for myself.'

I like Bill when he battles it out in the thick of the nine-week strike over penalty rates and how he whistles and sings for days after the workers win.

I like Bill when, at night, he reads 'ravenously all the papers and books he could get on the military strength of the powers, the economic and political factors dominating national policy.' He is convinced now is the right time to 'expose fascist tendencies' everywhere.

I like the way Bill puts up with the 'chiacking" from Dinny, Blunt Pick and the other old miners who want him to 'buy himself a new suit, and go off to Melbourne and marry Pat.' Bill agrees with Sally: this 'wild-fire armour between himself and Pat would fizzle out,' and he laughs at these sentimental old men and leaves them with a 'jaunty so long!'

I like Bill because he was worried sick about his sister's pregnancy and trusted his grandmother enough to seek her advice. When she tells him, 'We'll find a way to look after Daph, and beat the gossips,' he is mightily relieved and has no criticism with what she says next: 'Though mind you, Bill, I'm no prude. I've never believed a woman should bear a child if she doesn't want to. We've learnt to control other natural forces. Why not this one? But there's so much prejudice – and danger – attached to these illegal operations, I wouldn't – couldn't let Daphne take any risks like that now.'

I like Bill when he stands up, terrified, in front of the audience at the Boulder Town Hall but then, finally, in a clear and steady voice, 'the fire of his faith and purpose' rising within him, he tries to convince the few who've turned up that 'powerful monopolies have seized the wealth of Australia, and use the labour of the people to maintain their own interests...They control the press on which we depend for information about national and international affairs...they bring pressure to bear on parliaments, on legislation, on our educational system, on the judiciary, on public opinion, and on our relations with other countries.' While his audience mutters and fidgets restlessly, Bill tries to convince them that they are all supporting a 'system of barbarous terrorism.'

I like Bill because, as Sally says, he's like a 'young Prometheus' who never gives up.

I was disappointed that Katharine decided to kill Bill in the war – I could've done with a lot more of Bill.

I wonder where I could go to meet someone like him – a man who reads a lot, cares deeply about fairness and people's rights, is a bit shy, is funny too.

July 16th, 1969

At morning tea, I told Gwenda and Nora about Sally's reaction to Daphne's pregnancy and asked them what their mums would say if they got pregnant. Nora shook her head, rolled her eyes, and said she's sick of hearing about Katharine Susannah Prichard's stories. I rolled my eyes back at her.

'Would you keep the baby?' I asked Gwenda.

'I think Mum might accept that I was in trouble and let me stay home, but my father would be beside himself,' said Gwenda. 'He'd send me up north to have the baby and then...'

'I meant would you have an abortion,' I said.

'I might,' she replied.

'What's the latest with Andy?' Nora asked Gwenda.

'I haven't answered his letter yet,' Gwenda replied. 'I'm still mad at him.'

July 19th, 1969

Went into town early this morning and hung around Forrest Place for a while, hoping to run into Larry.

He goes to the Post Office sometimes. I think he might have a post box because he usually has letters in his hand when I see him there.

Anyway, I waited until just after ten, went and had a cup of tea, and walked back to Forrest Place. No Larry, so I caught the bus home.

On the bus, there was a boy I went to the Ambassadors with a few months ago. He said, 'Hello', and smiled. I said 'Hello, Mike', and moved to the back of the bus. I didn't want a conversation. When I agreed to go out with him, I thought he'd be fun. He put his arm around me during the film, which I liked. Afterwards, we walked around town but discovered we had nothing to say to each other! I mentioned I was working on a diary of discovery about a local writer known as the "Red Witch." He wasn't interested. I asked him if he liked to read, and he replied, 'Read? Nah.' Most of the boys I've been out with don't read. That night, Mike didn't offer to take me home, but he waited with me at the bus stop, which was a relief. Since that man chased me, I've always been wary at bus stops. Just as the bus arrived, he asked if he could see me again. I pretended I didn't hear him as I waved goodbye.

July 25th, 1969

Larry wasn't at book club tonight. I asked a few of the members where he was but they didn't know. One woman gave me a sly look and asked why I was interested. Then she said, 'Vicki, isn't it? We've noticed you haven't been reading our choices for quite a while.'

'But I listen to the discussions,' I lied.

'Well, Vicki, the idea behind book groups is to read the books they choose,' she growled. 'Not carry on side conversations with someone about what you and only you are reading.'

I had nothing to say, so I left. On the bus coming home, I thought it's probably a good time to leave the book club.

July 26th, 1969

Nora, Gwenda and I bought shoes in Betts and Betts and then went up to King's Park for a spearmint milkshake and a gossip. Gwenda has decided to answer Andy's letter: she's going to suggest they break up for a while and wants to go back to night classes. Nora was in a bad mood and told us she'd been looking for a better job for months but hasn't found one yet.

Mum seemed very relaxed when I got home. We had a bit of a gossip over a cuppa about the neighbours two doors down, whom we never speak to, and about how the husband drinks too much.

July 27th, 1969

I've been browsing the trilogy and thinking about Dinny's friendship with Sally.

In nearly all the major turning points in Sally Gough's life, Dinny is right beside her – loyal, sympathetic, clear-eyed. He finances the building Sally turns into a boarding house, making sure he gets a room at the end of the verandah which he calls a place 'of me own, a home to come back to.' He mortgages the house to buy the undertaker business for Morris to run so Morris won't have to go back to work in the mines, knowing Sally will be relieved.

By the time of Den's wedding in Warrinup, Dinny has become part of the Gough family. Den introduces Dinny to his guests as 'my godfather...an old mate of my father's and a pioneer prospector of the Coolgardie goldfields.' I chuckled when I read that because Dinny is really Sally's 'old mate,' not Morris's.

After kicking out Frisco over his affair with Mrs Rooney, Sally admits to Dinny she wouldn't have minded if Frisco had had an affair with Nora, but 'to destroy all there was between us for that sloppy, cross-eyed female – I can't get over it.' Dinny murmurs, 'Oh, well...Mrs Rooney isn't the sort gives a man the ghost of a chance if she's after him.'

Interesting that he doesn't run down Frisco and blames Mrs Rooney! After all, Frisco's hardly the type to get trapped by a woman and Dinny can't stand Frisco anyway. This is the one time he isn't on Sally's side. I wanted him to blame Frisco!

Sally values Dinny as much as he does her. During the night Dinny and Bardoc dig Kalgoorla's grave. Sally sits nearby watching and realizes that her life 'would be unbearably bleak without Dinny. Their companionship had become very dear to her: the peaceful, pleasant reliance of old friends on each other.' Towards morning his 'old pumper' starts 'playin' up a bit,' and Sally wails: 'Don't you crock up – and leave me.' He laughs and tells her: 'When the Warden of the Universe comes lookin' for me, you'll still have Eily, Daphne and the children.'

'It's not the same thing,' Sally replies. 'You've been with me through so much. I've depended on you. I don't know how I'd have pulled through without you, sometimes, Dinny.'

On the drive back home, Sally looks at the landscape and comments 'bitterly' that she had always hoped 'it would show signs of a better way of life for workers on the Golden Mile...Living on the goldfields is as hard now as it ever was.' Dinny disagrees: 'There's been some improvements in the way the mines are run...We've got ventilation, workers' inspection and a shorter working day...None of that's been a hand-out from the bosses. It's been won by the organization and struggle of the workers themselves...I reckon we had something to do with sowin' the seed for a better system, too, when we put up a fight for our rights in the old alluvial struggle.'

While reading the trilogy, I kept pushing myself into believing that Sally represented the optimistic side of Katharine. Now, when I think about it, it's Bill and Dinny who come out on top for me in that department.

August 4th, 1969

Gwenda is thrilled to bits! Andy went to her house and told her he'd read her letter. He hasn't been called up by the Army, they've made up, and they're going to the Ambassadors tonight.

When Gwenda left the tearoom with a big smile on her dial, Nora said, 'Lucky tart,' and I said, 'Yeah.' But I'm not so sure. In a way, I'd rather hear Gwenda say she's finally dumped Andy and is back on track to try for uni.

August 6ᵗʰ, 1969

Gwenda can't stop talking about her boyfriend: it's 'Andy this and Andy that' and blah, blah, blah.

I had been going to ask her if she'd like to go out at lunchtime and window shop, but she probably would've kept on about Andy. Instead, I wrote one dialogue and two descriptions and added them to my file, which has been getting thicker by the week. I reckon I've written over two hundred short pieces by now!

August 11ᵗʰ, 1969

I asked Jill a couple of weeks ago if she could find some general information about *Winged Seeds*. I went into the library this arvo and she gave me a lovely red folder full of items on the novel. I cradled it on my lap all the way home.

Just as I was coming in the front door, Mum was going out.

'What's that you've got there, Vicki?' she asked suspiciously.

'Oh nothing, just something from the library.'

'What's the point of wasting time at the library? When are you going to find a nice boy to go out with? That's what I want to know.'

'Soon, Mum.'

I didn't ask where she was going; I don't care. I raced off to my bedroom and opened Jill's folder.

There are some notes about how hard Katharine worked on *Winged Seeds* in her Greenmount studio during Christmas and New Year; how it was boiling hot; how the novel gave her no rest, 'always wiggling and niggling in and out' of her brain; how she was 'more anxious about this book than the others because it must not flag, but carry interest and spiritual zest to the last gasp.'

There's a copy of a letter from Katharine to Nettie Palmer where she tells her friend: 'I've still been tinkering with my last chapters…What's worrying me, I think, is whether Sally stands out as she should, monolithic, a tragic yet human figure, intrepid and undefeated…Goodness knows whether *Winged Seeds* will have any wings, or be the worst flop I've ever conceived!…I can only say to myself, as usual: "Do your damndest, and what anybody else thinks doesn't matter!"'

There's also a copy of a letter from Katharine to Miles Franklin, dated 6th October 1949, in which Katharine writes that she has finished *Winged Seeds* and has posted it to Jonathan Cape. 'Wouldn't be surprised if he turns it down – in view of the rampage going on everywhere against my political outlook,' she writes. However, Katharine believes that her 'best work has gone into the story' and although 'the press will swat it…who cares, so long as one is able to say the thing as it ought to be said – or write it as it ought to be wrote!'

Jill's note reads: '*Winged Seeds* was published in London in 1950 and was immediately attacked, mostly because of its politics. Katharine expected negative reviews from "all the mugwumps". She certainly got them!'

My heart sank when I read that note. Well, there's something wrong with me, I thought. I loved *Winged Seeds*!

Katharine must have been disappointed and possibly angry with some of the reviews Jill has included in the folder. Turns out they mostly hate her politics rather than the story.

One *West Australian* newspaper reviewer called *Winged Seeds* propaganda and ridiculed the description in the novel where Bill goes to the School of Mines ball where he tells himself that he 'had no right to forget even for an instant the bitterness of the class struggle: the suffering of the Spanish people: the menace of fascism and war looming on the not very distant horizon.' Personally I can't see why worrying about people's suffering and fear of fascism and war should be called propaganda.

Another reviewer in the *West Australian* believes that, in writing her trilogy, Katharine paid far too much attention to historical details and politics and should have spent more time developing her characters and the plot. On top of that, Bill Gough is called a 'downright bore.'

What? I thought when I read that! Bill Gough is certainly *not* a 'downright bore'! He's one of my favourite characters, hands down.

There's a review by G.A. Wilkes from Sydney University, who believes Katharine obviously worked hard on her trilogy, but he thinks it's embarrassingly awful. He concludes that, while it could be considered 'reportage', it is not literature. After reading that review, I felt very angry, I disagree with everything this bloke has to say!

I like the letter Jill's included in the folder from Miles Franklin to Katharine. It's dated 28th December 1950, and she tells 'dearest Katharine' that critics 'don't matter a hoot' and that 'writers of any pungent tonnage must draw fire from pygmies'!

Yes, I thought as I was reading this letter, a writer of tonnage like Katharine should just ignore pygmies.

Jill also included a quote by Katharine in response to some reactions to her work:

> 'I know, very well, that some criticism of my writing is justified, but not sweeping condemnation of its essential value...There's the need to...insulate against hostile criticism – which is just hostile for the sake of being hostile. Honest helpful criticism one can think over and accept. But sometimes, the hostility acts as a blight, if we don't just make up our minds not to let it – and do our damndest in our own way.'

Scribbled at the bottom, Jill writes, 'Katharine herself points out that millions of people all over the world read her novels, so clearly her work can't be worthless.'

The positive reviews in the folder include one from The *Newcastle Morning Herald and Miners' Advocate*, 9th December 1950. This reviewer admires Sally Gough as a character and applauds her abilities to confront and solve problems. He also thinks Katharine's descriptions of the goldfields are realistic and historically accurate.

On 18th January 1951, a *Tribune* reviewer thought that *Winged Seeds* sometimes moved too slowly but praised its realism and described Katharine's portrait of Bill as 'fine and strong and real.'

A review by Jack Lindsay is full of praise for her imaginative writing in *Winged Seeds*. He also believes it's a very valuable historical record of gold mining in WA.

The last page in the folder is a copy of a passage from Henrietta Drake-Brockman's monograph on Katharine. In general, Drake-Brockman admired Katharine's trilogy because it is realistic, life-like and colourful and sensitively explores all kinds of different relationships between the multitude of characters who come and go throughout the three novels.

At the bottom of the page, Jill has scribbled: 'Katharine and Henrietta were not great friends, but Katharine trusted Henrietta and told her a great deal about her life and work. In the end, Katharine was pleased with the monograph, which was published in 1967, although she suspected that Henrietta Drake-Brockman "probably will join the chorus of disapproval when she reads *Subtle Flame*", published in the same year.

Katharine was upset when Henrietta died in 1968. She probably never read *Subtle Flame*.

August 25th, 1969

Gwenda and Nora were both away today! I haven't heard what's wrong with them. When Maggot stuck his boofy head into the tearoom this morning, I asked him if they had the flu. He shrugged and walked off. So I sipped my tea and thought about how annoyed Katharine must've felt after reading negative reviews of *Winged Seeds*.

But they didn't stop her from moving on – she got stuck into other stuff right away. She wrote *Child of the Hurricane* and *Subtle Flame* after the trilogy and organized two collections of her short stories.

Yep, she's a writer of 'tonnage' alright!

September 1st, 1969

Nora is back at work, but Gwenda is still away. We're both wondering what's up.

We asked Maggot at morning tea, but he said as far as he knows, Gwenda is still sick.

September 15th, 1969

Gwenda has disappeared off the face of this earth! None of us knows where she's gone. Maggot doesn't know; Nora doesn't know; I don't know. We don't know Andy's last name or where he lives – but we all reckon that wherever he is, she's with him!

I'm devasted Gwenda didn't say anything to us before she left. She could've at least told us *something* about her plans. I hope she's not pregnant. I hope if she is, Andy will be good to her. I wish she'd stuck to her goal to go to uni. I hope she doesn't end up being just a housewife with a couple of kids. I hope she writes to me to tell me what she's up to.

October 4th, 1969

Katharine is dead! Mum told me she read in this morning's *West Australian* that Katharine died on October 2nd and was cremated today at Karrakatta! I can't believe it!

Her doctor was with her, and he told Ric Throssell that his mother had died just an hour or so before Ric arrived from

Canberra. Katharine had been waiting for him for hours, preparing the house for his arrival as she always did when he came to visit her.

Went for a walk in King's Park this arvo to let the news sink in. What will I do without Katharine? How often I've thought of her, living up there alone in Greenmount, writing for hours in her little cottage, pouring out words that are so powerful and so very important. How I've dreamed that one day I might have the guts to go up there, knock on her door, and tell her how much I admire her work. I've imagined asking her to sign the books she wrote that I own. I might even dare tell her about my project and how much I've learned since reading her work.

I felt miserable and sick on the bus going home. I thought I could read some of her work tonight, but I'm too upset to try. I look at her name on the covers and remember how mad she must've been when her name was misspelt. My heart is a cold rock and I know I won't sleep.

October 25th, 1969

It's taken me a while to get over Katharine's death. Hard to believe she'll never write again!

Katharine has changed my view of the world forever. She's taught me to question what I've been told to believe and has made me determined to change my life.

October 27th, 1969

Jill told me this morning that Katharine had been having problems with her heart for years before she died. She started sorting out and burning her papers long before her death.

She also told me that Katharine had wanted a communist funeral and she got it. Her coffin was draped in the Red Flag. A bunch of leschenaultia was placed near the flag – wildflowers Katharine adored.

Jill showed me a poem called 'Leschenaultia' by T. Inglis Moore, dedicated to Katharine. I love the lines, 'You and the leschenaultia glow/As a blue flame of hope, a fire/Smiting the darkness with double sign/Of skyward beauty and eager desire.'

Jill said that Katharine once wrote, 'Good to think of becoming part of the earth, and perhaps nourishing a wild flower.'

'She wasn't sentimental, Vicki,' said Jill kindly. 'And she wasn't afraid of death. Her ashes were scattered in the hills around Greenmount, nourishing the wildflowers, just as she had wanted.'

Somehow, knowing that makes me feel better.

November 17th, 1969

Nora told me she's finally found a job that suits her! She's leaving in two weeks to work at a bloody bank, of all places. Gwenda would groan at that news. I can't think of a worse place to work.

Maggot gave Nora a big bunch of flowers and a 'thank you' card, so she decided not to give him the nasty little speech she'd prepared and rehearsed. So Maggot got away with it in the end. Typical!

Not a word from Gwenda.

I'm looking for another job with better pay. I'll start saving for a trip as soon as I get one. I might go to Emerald to check out that cottage that once belonged to Katharine.

November 25th, 1969

I've just enrolled in a night course on journalism and travel writing. I'm a bit nervous about it but I've been writing sketches and my diary for a while now, so I reckon I could manage a proper course in writing. I hope the instructor is lively and gives us lots of tips. It's a workshop, so I'll get to read other people's work and they'll read mine. That will be terrific. I'm going to enjoy talking about writing almost as much as I enjoy writing.

One day, I want to wander around different places with a notebook, poking my nose into other people's workplaces, describing what I see, checking up on bosses and writing about it – just like Katharine used to do. Only I could never do it so well.

November 28th, 1969

Went to book club tonight and got kicked out. Larry wasn't there, so I had to put up with a couple of old tarts carrying on about how I haven't read a book chosen by the club for a long time and I never will, which is probably true. If Larry had been there, he would've stuck up for me, but the old bags told me it was a 'unanimous decision' and I was asked to leave immediately. I did manage to tell Miss how much I hate her Chinese vase before I walked out.

Anyway, good riddance – although I will miss the club. It was somewhere to go on the last Friday night of the month – got me out of the house and away from Mum for a few hours. And I always enjoyed talking to Larry. I learned a lot from him.

At least I'll have my night course. I plan to spend a lot of time working on whatever they want me to do. And I've already started saving to buy a portable typewriter.

December 26th, 1969

What can I say about Christmas this year?

Mrs Cook came over on Christmas morning, vomited all over Mum's new front door mat and passed out on the couch.

Mum had a fit because I wouldn't eat her trifle.

We stopped speaking around four o'clock.

It's now midnight and I'm wide awake, thinking about stuff. I'm excited about my writing course. I wonder if I'll meet a nice bloke in the class. It would be fun to go out with someone who wants to be a writer. I still can't believe Katharine is dead. I hope Gwenda's okay. I hope Nora likes her new job. I wonder if she'll keep in touch. I hope we get a telephone next year so we can ring Pete and ask him to come home for Christmas. I wonder if I'll *ever* manage to save enough money to get out of this dreary city and travel the world?

December 27th, 1969

Ran into Larry in Forrest Place this morning! He's off to London next week. His brown eyes were all twinkly and he looked very excited. We talked about Katharine's death. 'She may be dead, but there's her work, Vicki, don't forget that. Her books are there for you to read whenever you feel like it.'

I nearly said, 'I know that Larry, but you won't be here to talk about her with me anymore.' Instead, I told him I've been kicked out of the book club. He frowned. 'Do you want me to sort that out when I get back?' he asked. I shook my head and said, 'No thanks, I've got better things to do these days.' He looked interested so I told him about the journalism course I've enrolled in. 'I start it in February,' I said. He gave me a big grin, patted my shoulder and said, 'Good on you, Vicki. So, you've found another project.' He didn't offer to help me or tell me when he was coming back.

Felt a bit forlorn going home on the bus, thinking about how Larry won't be around for a while. Even when he does come home, how will I know? We've never exchanged addresses, I have no phone, I don't know if he has one, and I'm not going back to that bloody book club to see him!

January 5th, 1970

I went to the library this arvo to wish Jill a happy New Year and tell her I've enrolled in a night class. She was really pleased with my news. 'Come into the library whenever you can, Vicki,' she smiled. 'I'm happy to help you anytime with your assignments or the course material.'

She's put on a bit of weight. Bet she's pregnant!

She told me to wait a tick and came back with an article. 'This is a copy of Dorothy Hewett's eulogy for Katharine,' she said, running her fingers through her hair. 'Read it and tell me what you think.

I sat down in a corner of the library, took a deep breath, read it, and sat for a few minutes thinking about it before I went to speak to Jill.

'It has some good bits but I think it's pretty nasty, don't you?' I asked Jill. She nodded.

'I snorted at that bit where Dorothy Hewett tells us a Catholic friend of hers claimed that Katharine "kept her faith till the end. She never changed her beliefs.",' Jill said, spinning her pencil on the counter. 'I'll bet that Catholic friend has never changed their beliefs either! Why should Katharine have changed her beliefs? She told everyone communism was like a religion to her.'

Jill and I discussed Dorothy Hewett's opinion that Katharine has always been either criticized or praised for her writing abilities and for her lifelong support for communism. We agreed that Hewett's view neatly sums up most of the criticism of Katharine's work.

But Jill reckons Dorothy Hewett was wrong when she said that Katharine lived in an isolated 'dream world' and rarely had visitors, most of them literary or political figures who were just passing through.

'Katharine was very social and welcomed dozens of people – locals and overseas visitors – into her home, even when she was old and frail,' said Jill, shaking her head. 'Her work has been translated into nineteen languages and she was famous all over the world. Katharine would've been choosy about who popped in to see her.

Otherwise, she would have had to have spent most of her days talking to an endless stream of visitors and entertaining them. It would've exhausted her.'

As I was leaving, Jill said firmly, 'I reckon one day Dorothy Hewett might regret that eulogy, Vicki.'

When I got home, Mum asked me if I was going out tonight. 'There are so many nice young blokes about these days, Vicki,' she grumbled. 'Why don't you go out dancing and find one!'

I slammed my bedroom door and looked at the books I own by a writer of pungent tonnage who may be dead but, in my mind, her mighty works, ideas and hopes for a better and fairer world are alive and kicking.

Acknowledgements

I acknowledge the Gadigal peoples of the Eora nation, traditional custodians of the land on which I wrote this book.

Thank you to Karen Throssell, Katharine Susannah Prichard's granddaughter, for permission to quote from Katharine's work, and for meeting with me to discuss this project. Karen's own book about her father, Ric Throssell, gave me the final push to finish this book.

Thanks to Nathan Hobby whose blog and Your KS # helped keep me motivated, inspired and enthusiastic. His recently published biography of KSP, *The Red Witch*, unfortunately came too late for me to refer to while writing this book, but I've since read it and it's a cracker!

Thank you to Lisa Wolstenholme at Dragonfly for publishing this book and for designing the beautiful cover. We know that windflowers had a special meaning for Katharine.

Thanks to my conscientious editor, Rebekah Sheedy, for all her hard work. At times she sat at her desk well into the early hours of the morning working on my manuscript and her suggestions were greatly appreciated.

Thank you to James Domingo for photographing the book covers and for putting up with my chatter about KSP without a yawn.

Thanks to Jo for the King's Park photos. They triggered many memories.

Thanks to the KSP Writers' Centre aka 'Katharine's Place' for access to KSP's tin trunk and the Lazy H1T plaque.

Thanks to the State Library of NSW for access to *Windlestraws, Fay's Circus, Moon of Desire,* the Australian Pocket Library edition of *Haxby's Circus,* Miles Franklin's Waratah Cup and her Visitors' Book.

Thanks to the State Library of Victoria for access to the Whitman Cabinet.

Thanks to members of Writing NSW's manuscript development workshop whose valuable feedback and encouragement early in the piece gave me the confidence to keep writing.

Apart from Katharine's novels, short stories, plays, autobiography and articles, I read numerous books, articles, theses and Internet items about her, or that mention her, but the main books I most frequently consulted, and without which I could not have written this story, are, in alphabetical order: Jack Beasley: *A Gallop of Fire*; Carole Ferrier: ed., *As Good as a Yarn With You*; John Hamilton: *The Price of Valour*; and Ric Throssell's *Wild Weeds and Windflowers*; *My Father's Son* and (as editor) *Straight Left*.

About the Author

Denise Faithfull was born and grew up in Western Australia. She left to travel in Europe and worked in London before moving to live in California with her photographer husband.

After eight years in publishing and journalism, Denise returned to Australia and settled in Sydney. She worked in journalism and as free-lance book editor before joining TAFE where she taught Film and Media Studies, Communication and HSC English and began research for a PhD.

Denise's PhD thesis, completed at the University of Sydney, explores the process of adapting literature to film and is the basis for *Adaptations: A Guide to Adapting Literature to Film,* published by Currency Press.

She has published numerous short articles on film and literature including 'On Literary Pilgrimages' which appears in *Kaleidoscope: The Colours of Katharine,* a commemorative anthology honouring Katharine Susannah Prichard published by Wild Weeds Press.

One of Denise's favourite activities is to go on a literary pilgrimage. She has followed the footsteps of many of the writers she most admires, including Katharine Susannah Prichard, James Joyce and Virginia Woolf and is thinking about her next pilgrimage.

Katharine Susannah Prichard

4 December 1883 – 2 October 1969

Photo c.1927 taken by May Moore. Image courtesy of State Library of New South Wales

Author, wife, mother, communist.

Katharine's Works

In the order in which Vicki read them:

Cover	Interior Title	Title, Edition & Publisher
		*Coonardoo* (1956 edition, Angus and Robertson)
	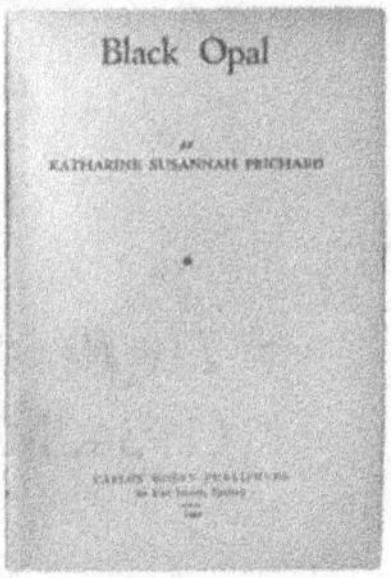	*Black Opal* (1946 edition, Caslon House)
		*Child of the Hurricane* (1964 edition, Angus and Robertson)
		*Haxby's Circus* (1945 Pocket Library edition, Angus and Robertson)

Cover	Interior Title	Title, Edition & Publisher
		Fay's Circus (1931 edition, Angus and Robertson)
		Why I am a Communist (c. 1956, Current Book Distributors)
		The Real Russia (1934, Modern Publishers)
		The Pioneers (1926 edition, Hodder and Stoughton)
		The Wild Oats of Han (1928 edition, Angus and Robertson)

Cover	Interior Title	Title, Edition & Publisher
		Brumby Innes (1927 edition)
		Kiss on the Lips and Other Stories (1932 edition, Jonathan Cape)
		Working Bullocks (1956 edition, Angus and Robertson)
		N'Goola and other Stories (1959 edition, Australasian Book Society)

Cover	Interior Title	Title, Edition & Publisher
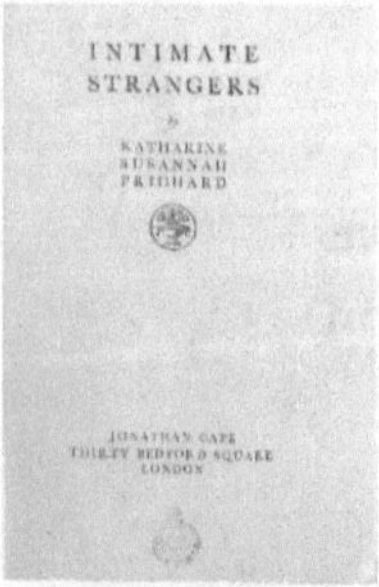		*Intimate Strangers* (1937 edition, Jonathan Cape)
		*Subtle Flame* (1967 edition, Australasian Book Society)
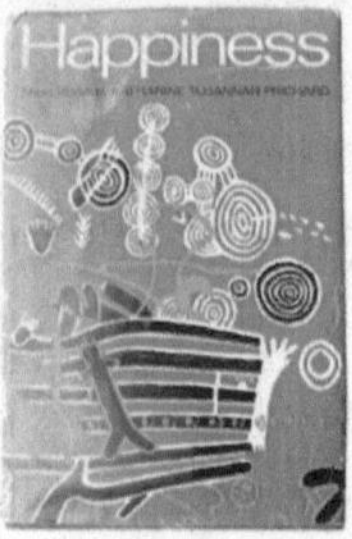		*Happiness - Selected Short Stories* (1967 edition, Angus and Robertson)
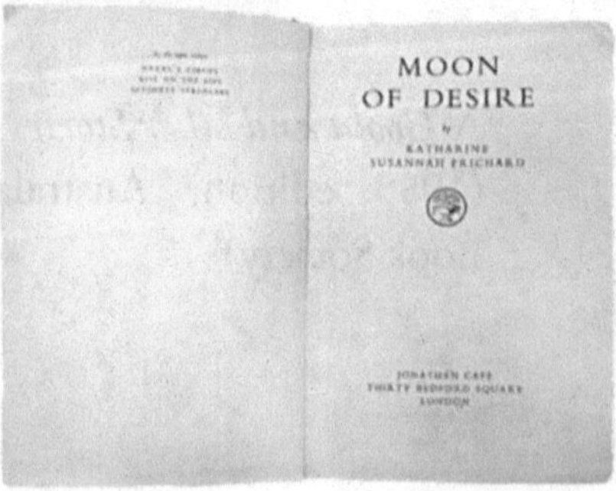		*Moon of Desire* (1941 edition, Jonathan Cape)

Cover	Interior Title	Title, Edition & Publisher
		Windlestraws (1916 edition, Holden and Hardingham)
		Potch and Colour (1944 edition, Angus and Robertson
		The Roaring Nineties (1946 edition, Jonathan Cape)
		Golden Miles (1948 edition, Jonathan Cape)

Cover	Interior Title	Title, Edition & Publisher
Winged Seeds / Katharine Susannah Prichard	WINGED SEEDS / KATHARINE SUSANNAH PRICHARD / Australasian Publishing Company	*Winged Seeds* (1950 edition, Australasian Publishing in association with Jonathan Cape)

Note – the photos/images are either from the author's personal collection or accessed and used with permission from the State Library of New South Wales.

Need to talk?

If you are affected by any of the issues raised in *Discovering Katharine*, know that help is within reach:

Lifeline

www.lifeline.org.au

13 11 14

Providing 24-hour crisis counselling and suicide prevention services.

Beyond Blue

www.beyondblue.org.au

1300 22 4636

Offering telephone and online counselling for individuals grappling with anxiety, depression, or suicidal ideation.

Suicide Call Back Service

www.suicidecallbackservice.org.au

1300 659 467

Providing around-the-clock telephone and online counselling to address and support individuals dealing with suicidal thoughts.

The National Sexual Assault, Family & Domestic Violence
Counselling Line

www.1800respect.org.au

1800 737 732

A counselling line for those who have experienced, or are at risk of,
family and domestic violence and/or sexual assault.

Full Stop Australia

www.fullstop.org.au

1800 385 578

Providing counselling to people whose lives have been impacted by
violence and abuse.

Head to Health

www.headtohealth.gov.au

1800 595 212

Connecting people with the help and support needed to maintain
mental well-being.